Manifest

BY

ADAM PHILLIPS

First Montag Press E-Book and Paperback Original Edition January 2021

Copyright © 2021 by Adam Phillips

Montag Press ISBN: 978-1-940233-85-7
Design © 2020 Amit Dey

Montag Press Team:

Editor: Kathryn Sargeant
Managing Director: Charlie Franco
Cover Design: Sam Mills

A Montag Press Book
www.montagpress.com
Montag Press
777 Morton Street, Unit B
San Francisco CA 94129 USA

Montag Press, the burning book with the hatchet cover, the skewed word mark and the portrayal of the long-suffering fireman mascot are trademarks of Montag Press.

Printed & Digitally Originated in the United States of America
10 9 8 7 6 5 4 3 2 1

Killer lineups and all the cultural cache one could ask for in an ambitious novel set in the Pacific Northwest. *Manifest* is a sprawling portrait of the American dream differed. Clever, insightful, and poetic, Adam Phillips strikes so deeply at the heart of what makes baseball timeless it's hard to not want to devour the book then quickly dig out your worn old glove, a scuffed-up ball and head out to shag flyballs with an old friend. Like dispatches from a forgotten time, *Manifest* reminds readers why we loved taking the field in the first place – the clean lines, the situation bunting, and the monsters that inhabit the field, lurk in the bleachers, and often cling to our own spirits. This novel is everything a fan of the sport could ask for, but what I could not have imagined, and what will endear all readers, are the unexpected manners in which Phillips examines the unstable, fleeting nature of America's national pastime, weighing it against the social mores and difficult introspections that faced our country's past, and still echo today. Exploring cultural inequality, incarceration, family trauma and the heartache of unfulfilled promise, *Manifest* brings home a riveting plot, flawed and captivating characters, and a love of humanity and the game of baseball.

—Christian Winn,
author of *Naked Me* and
What's Wrong With You is What's Wrong With Me

With Manifest, Adam Phillips gives us a compelling novel populated by a rich collection of vivid, sometimes nearly mythic characters who actually seem to breathe on the page – characters on the edge of hopelessness whose sole chance for salvation lies in the redemptive power of baseball.

—Joe Schuster,
author of *The Might Have Been*

Adam Phillips writes with verve and bravado, and stories within stories pour out of his pen, each more incredible and entertaining than the last. *Manifest* is a great ride, fast, funny, and right on the outside corner.

—Kevin Baker,
author of *Sometimes You See It Coming.*

Manifest, the incomparable novel by Adam Phillips, captures two American institutions in their infancy—baseball and the U.S. prison system—and grows them under the harsh western sun. The eclectic cast of inmates plays every game *because* their lives depend on it. Warning: Phillips paints the sport so vividly that your own baseball memories might be replaced by scenes from this book. Which is to say, you'll never see the diamond the same way again. Even mother nature gets an at-bat.

—Simeon Mills,
author of *The Obsoletes*

One of the most singular baseball novels ever written. Adam Phillips possesses a narrative voice that takes hold on page one and never falters.

—Steve Kluger,
author of *Last Days of Summer*

The Natural meets *The Dream Songs*. A book where life itself is a metaphor for baseball. Deep in sense of place, purpose and gravity. This is an excellent contribution to the canon. We can, as Phillips says, be better things.

—Zachary Amendt,
author of *Stay*

DEDICATION

*T*his book is dedicated to Priest River Little League, my dad, Dave Niehaus, Cormac McCarthy, Stephanie & Ezra & Harlan, the Pacific Ocean and the entire town of Rockaway Beach, Oregon.

BIOGRAPHY

*A*dam Phillips lives close enough to the site of the imaginary death row prison that he could hit it with a baseball, if it existed. He has a very good arm. This is his second novel. His first, *Something Like My Name*, is available from Propertius Press.

PROLOGUE

$\mathcal{P}$erhaps if someone could still remember, things would go differently.

For days, as the sharks gorged on the corpse of the leviathan, Cuscular clung to a remnant of the dugout crushed by the monstrous beast's tail. As the seagulls ate the flesh of his lips and the tip of his nose. As the sun cooked his flesh to blisters and the glare scorched his eyes until he could no longer tell if they were open or shut.

Then he was drifting, no longer amongst the sharks.

It began to rain, and he opened his mouth.

Two boys, digging clams in a cove, spotted what they mistook for an effigy of burnt seaweed lashed to a plank banging amongst the rocks and they waded out to retrieve it. As they stumbled closer the pitted black face of the effigy grew two large, pale blue eyes and the boys, recovering from their momentary horror, realized it was Cuscular, the missing blue-eyed hunter, sent back home from some hellish section of the afterlife.

After a week of lying on the beach wrapped in healing seaweed, with a request to Return This Warrior's Soul Home written on his face in seal's blood, Cuscular sat up and summoned the entire village to surround him. Once his neighbors had arrived, he delivered a speech that was so articulate it seemed as if some spirit power must be using his desiccated near-corpse as a conduit. "Our current method of hunting the creatures," he explained in a rhythmic monotone, the crinkled sphincter of his mouth unmoving, "is hopeless. First of all, they are far larger with thicker skin than we had surmised from the carcass that washed up last winter, so that any hunter near enough to throw a spear is also at imminent risk of being crushed, drowned, catapulted. And their blood is thick, flowing slowly, allowing them to run and roll for a long time before succumbing."

"Even if the spirits are so benevolent as to grant us a kill," he said, waggling a bony black finger at his audience, "it would take every canoe in the world a month to drag the creature ashore. We would be lucky to arrive with the meat of a salmon head, after the sharks and crabs and seagulls pick it over."

"But most importantly (at this point his audience began to squirm, shooting sideways glances; how many layers of impossibility would Cuscular deem sufficient to excuse his failure?) *even if* every one of these potentially deadly and impossible problems could be removed, *even if* somehow, in some magical future, a man could simply walk to the waterline, fire an arrow, and wait for a dead beast to come rolling ashore…"

"If we know what's good for us, we'll leave those giant fish the fuck alone." His chin sunk to his chest, pale blue eyes swimming with final frantic movement before sealing over in a glaze, trapping whatever thoughts squirmed behind those eyes deep within his brain forever.

But despite the ominousness of Cuscular's admonition, by the following spring the Clatsop had figured out how to kill the leviathans. One harpooner, wielding a long barbed spear tied to hundreds of feet of coiled hemp cord, sets out upon the

hectic misty ocean poised over the prow of a huge dugout propelled by eight burly oarsmen. Sighting a beast at repose, the
harpooner unleashes his missile, piercing the thick hide as the
oarsmen heave aft, whereupon the monster, infuriated and terrified at this sudden bolt of pain, begins to run. The huntsmen
then unwind the rope until, as slack expires with a wrenching jolt
the boat commences flying with the beast, the warriors hoisting
in the oars, leaping into a heap in the bottom of the craft, grabbing onto loops of rope embedded in the boards as handholds.
After an eternity the creature succumbs to inertia, seeking just a
moment's respite from the searing, digging pain in its ribs or the
side of its head, pausing to coast, sides heaving, eyes hooded as
the craft creeps closer and the harpooner, carefully now, cuts the
leather strops holding the scrimshaw lance along the side of the
boat and hoists aloft this otherworldly weapon, longer than four
men. Taking careful aim, he plunges it deep into the beast, twisting and cranking as if stirring some hearty stew until he strikes
the heart and gouts of black blood spatter from the blowhole
as if oil has been struck. The warriors, bathed in gore, cut the
hemp cord and paddle off a distance to watch and wait for the
culmination of the death throes.

When finally the beast lapses, rolling, floating like an island
of flesh, the hunters move in, adhering hooks carved of oak
and scrimshaw to tow the monster home. A flotilla of dugouts
drag the carcass. And if any of these hunters ever feel a sudden
burst of cold wind like a long dead hand drug along the back
of his neck, or notice an oddly-shaped black cloud pacing their
progress…the uneasiness quickly dissolves in anticipation of the
heroes' welcome awaiting them at home.

And so it went. Prosperous years ensued. As soon as the meat
of one beast had been consumed, the oil sweating from its bones

lit afire and the bones themselves sharpened into weapons and tools, another fish would be harvested. Though the whaling crews frequently came back missing a man who had been pulverized by a swinging tail, caught up in ropes and drug under, skewered in the jumble of men and weapons rolling around the bottom of the boat, the village proliferated. A new generation came of age more robust than the last, spreading down the beach. The bones of men and whales slid along the bottom of the sea, tumbling in the surf, clattering into a tangled heap on shore.

One day Cuscular, who the children called "Old Clatsop" not as a term of deference and respect but due to the word's original meaning of "dried salmon," rose under his own power for the first time in years, limping from his dank hut onto the beach.

With the waves frothing over his hornlike toenails, he raised a tremulous finger at the horizon. "There," he said, "right there. Just like I goddamn told you." He spit on the sand, pale blue eyes blazing beneath their cataracts. That evening as the sun settled bloodily into the ocean the towering ships materialized spitting barbed fire, chasing the Clatsop forever back up into the forests.

Cuscular remained longest, sitting in the smoky shadow of the hut like a gargoyle returned to its perch as the pale ghosts flocked across the beach. The old man blew a puff of air at the alabaster shade ducking through the entrance with a pistol in its hand.

On and on relentlessly for years they came, breathlessly chasing some ignis fatuus trembling over the sea. Chasing the evanescent shape of a woman's body or a part of a woman's body or a heap of coins, chasing the titanic nebular outline of a hand outstretched, the ghostly impression of a mother or father.

They came in waves and the shaman called them Destroyer. Purge and redeem It, said the spooky old man.

Back and forth like this. The relatives of the slain whites came upon a village of Clatsop women and children and burnt it to ash and charred bones. The Clatsop deer hunters, returning to their decimated village, raced their horses through vale and valley, along the spine of a mountain, finally coming upon if not those same murderers then at least men who resembled those murderers, torching their habitations and spilling their brains steaming upon the chilly ground. In turn, the kin of those killed set forth from England, California, Spain, grimly describing revenge throughout months, years of travel that oscillated between difficult and impossible. Many sojourning seekers of vengeance paused permanently in Mackinac or Tijuana or El Paso to drink and sleep with prostitutes. Many terminated their quests in Arikara villages to sleep with girls. Many died of venereal diseases. Many drowned in rivers. Many starved to death at the bottoms of canyons after weeks of drinking piss and eating moccasins. Many ate poisonous berries, or clams infected with a toxin that caused amnesia, inspiring them to wander off to freeze, drown, fall off cliffs. Some were murdered by their fellow travelers to be eaten. Many froze to death on mountains. Some travelling by sea exhausted their rations and drew lots amongst themselves to determine who would be eaten, and who would go mad with guilt and horror after murdering and eating their crewmates. Some didn't die but probably should have because instead they became wild reeking monsters in the forest, abominations with sick embers for eyes, eating and raping the corpses of forest beasts. The beach accumulated bones and the trees bore the scars of bullets and arrows, the scorched coronas of explosions, the ligature scars of victims bound and struggling.

Into this haze of smoke and blood The Astoria Company, backed by millions of dollars and Thomas Jefferson and its own navy, built a trading post and the Clatskanie burnt it down. The Astorians rebuilt, driving back the Indians, but within a couple of months the men tired of living in the mud with no women and abandoned the post, sneaking away either to die in the forest, sometimes practically on top of the bones of the same Indians they'd rebuked and killed, or die at sea. The Army constructed a fort and the Nehalem blew it up. The nascent state of Oregon built a prison at Rockaway Beach and the King Tide swallowed it, dragging men out to die like insects. Every so often a store, or bar, or hotel sprung up along the beach like a mushroom, only to be discovered scant months later by some lost traveler as, at best, a charred husk in a clearing, or even less, just the tops of fractured posts jutting up through the sand.

America had come prodding, groping drunkenly in the dark, and the darkness had coalesced and twisted Her fingers back. And every so often, even with no one around to see, the ocean ate some of the land and spit some bones back up onto the sand as a warning.

Tread lightly. Lighter. Be a better thing. Justify yourselves.

CHAPTER ONE

*A*ndrew Best was born in a valley between mountains in Northern Idaho to parents living under assumed names because, unlike Andy the deathrow inmate, his father *was* a murderer.

Lynn Butler, Andy's eventual father, orphaned at the age of nine, had gone to live on his rich uncle's tobacco plantation in Owsley County, Kentucky. Upon the boy's arrival, which represented something of a miracle, young Lynn traipsing three hundred miles living off nothing but his wits and the natural bounty of the land, locating this uncle who had existed in the Butler household as nothing but a dark innuendo, the equivalent of Satan, He-Who-Shall-Not-Be-Fucking-Named, by intuitively following a *drop of water* through the forest, a trickle of rain as it meandered through the black muddy hills, following it from the top of a mountain to the river behind his uncle's plantation, somehow innately knowing that it was calling to lead him and should be followed, Uncle Conrad had ordered the coonhounds' kennel partitioned and a cot rolled in for the boy.

The following morning, while still road-weary and harrowed and half-starved, little Lynnie was put out to work digging irrigation trenches in the ninety-five degree heat, hatless, gloveless, shoeless. From that day on, Lynn worked like an animal, dining on the slop unfit for the hogs. The creek served as his canteen, bath, latrine and washbasin. He slept with neither blanket nor pillow and, unpaid, clad in rags, performed the tasks the hired hands wouldn't, and then as he grew older and stronger, the ones they couldn't.

All of this, as the boy would eventually come to surmise, stemmed from the fraternal hatred harbored by his uncle based on the perceived theft of the tall lithe Southern beauty who had become Lynn's mother. Since the moment the girl had chosen Lynn's father, Conrad Butler had done little for himself that could not be traced back to his desire to harm his brother and sister-in-law. Arguably his entire vast fortune came as a byproduct of actions intended, first and foremost, to wreck the couple. After both succumbed to tuberculosis, a direct result of the utter penury imposed by his relentless interference, Conrad had begun suffering a not-insignificant twinge of melancholic nostalgia. *What am I supposed to do now?* he asked himself lying awake late at night. *My life's work is done...*

Then suddenly, as if dropped into his arms from heaven, came the boy.

A catalogue of childhood illnesses, another direct result of Conrad's tireless machinations against the family, left the boy with a limp, stooping shoulders, sagging facial muscles. Owing to his deficient stature and cretinous physiognomy, everyone on the plantation treated Lynn as if he were obliviously stupid, helpless, subhuman. There were, however, several pieces of information they did not possess that might have led them to reconsider their actions.

Such as how the boy, sick of subsisting on the table scraps of a perpetually paltry larder, had at the age of six obtained employment stacking kindling behind the schoolhouse in the evenings and on weekends, an occupation that he had kept hidden entirely from his parents until their death. How, never having attended said schoolhouse, he had taught himself to read and write utilizing nothing but self-determination and a stack of purloined penny dreadfuls from the rack at the drugstore. How, as the youngest of seven brothers, he had weathered the abuses of his elders only until the precise day when he felt physically strong enough to smash his eldest brother Harvey's teeth with a hammer as the teenager slept, thus serving definitive notice to the others that the indignities had ceased, effective immediately. And finally, in what would prove to be the most shocking and consequential development of all, how Lynn had fallen deeply in love with his cousin, Savannah.

The moment that Lynn himself had become aware of his contraband feelings, he commenced to do two things. First of all, lying in the kennel, watching the low golden moon through the slats in the ceiling, listening to the soft noises of the sleeping beasts with whom he shared his home, he began wracking his brain, suddenly rendered hot and spasmodically bright as a Fourth of July sky, for ways in which, at his significant disadvantage, he might court her. The second thing was that he began to shoot. He didn't know why. It made him feel better.

Perhaps it took his mind off things.

Perhaps it didn't.

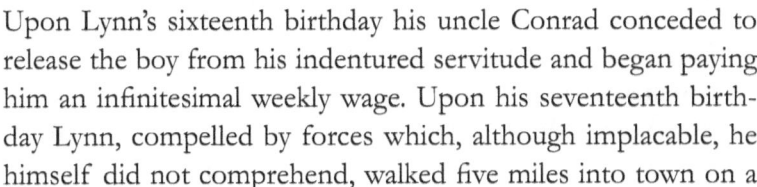

Upon Lynn's sixteenth birthday his uncle Conrad conceded to release the boy from his indentured servitude and began paying him an infinitesimal weekly wage. Upon his seventeenth birthday Lynn, compelled by forces which, although implacable, he himself did not comprehend, walked five miles into town on a

Sunday bearing the sum total of his year's wages to purchase a used Colt forty-five and a box of one hundred shells.

That evening Lynn took a lap of the acreage collecting rusted cans and dirt-encrusted pop bottles. He took his armload of garbage and his gun out to the furthest reaches of the plantation, a disused corner of weedy land abutting the forest, where he balanced the cans and bottles upon the mossy tops of crooked fence posts, loaded the gun, walked fifty paces, turned, and began to shoot.

Drawn by the sound of gunfire, the hands came out to take a look. Soon a small crowd gathered, the men smoking cigarettes and passing flasks as Lynn sent one hundred slugs clattering into the woods without so much as wobbling a can. Throughout the fusillade of errant shots, the men jeered sarcastically.

"Looks like a goddamn monkey trying to stick his pecker into a cracked coconut!"

The next Sunday Lynn returned to town, wages in hand, for another box of shells.

An hour later, three cans lay pinched and torn in the dust. The following Sunday, staid and silent, Lynn took his fifty paces, turned, and executed the entire lineup of beverage containers with sixteen shells to spare. The next week he tore ten cans and detonated twenty bottles left to right, without a single miss. The next week he switched to twigs wedged into cracks in the fenceposts. By spring, the clown show had become a shooting exhibition, with the hands and their invited guests setting bundled match sticks on the posts for Lynn to ignite and flipping coins for him to knock whizzing into the forest.

"Man alive! Goddamn monkey riding a unicycle on stilts!"

And so it came to be that Uncle Conrad, kept from his usual Sunday of tippling and fornication in Lexington by a painful bout of gout, retiring to the front porch for a lungful of air, should hear the clattering artillery and inquire, "What the hell…"

Archie, the factotum, smirking with his big dim face like a medicine ball, the silver tray in his hands with its snifter of bourbon and dishes of crushed mint and sugar rattling with mirth, said, "All that ruckus out there? That's Lynnie."

"That's Lynn shooting, or getting shot at?"

"Out there playing Annie Oakley. Amusing the mudsill. Shanti said the dumb son of a bitch's been doing it every Sunday since fall. Spends half his day off gathering garbage and the other half shooting it off of fenceposts."

Conrad raised an eyebrow, cocking and shaking his head.

He literally did not think of the boy again until months later, the final day of October, when his nephew materialized in the estate's open doorway. Lynn looked odd, with his hair gleaming and plastered to his head, in an ill-fitting beige suit undoubtedly culled from the church's charity bin most likely worn once as its former owner had left Eddyville and once more at the viewing of his body.

Lynn stood shuffling his feet, wringing the beige hat in his enormous callused brown hands. Conrad had long ago lost interest in tormenting his nephew, and Lynn's continued existence came as a mild and inconsequential surprise. Looking the boy over, Conrad did not conceal his amusement. Lynn's attempt at presentability only accentuated the dolt's congenital foolishness; a monkey with a greased hairdo wearing clothes.

The old man, regal in his purple smoking jacket and coiffed white hair, smiling with cold eyes and a crease down the center of his brow, said, "Lynn."

"Uncle Conrad…" the boy shifted, twisting his hat. "I know you're…Can we sit?" He gestured toward the red velvet chairs in the front sitting room.

"I can't imagine that whatever is on your mind is going to warrant a lengthy conversation, Lynn. And you have, of course, caught me during a very brief interlude between the things I must attend to—"

Lynn met the old man's eyes and his nervous hands fell perfectly still.

"You're going to want to listen to me for a moment."

It had all started, Lynn supposed, (though in truth it seemed like a thing that had always existed, an element he'd known long before naming it) the day that he, an invisible specter pulling weeds at the periphery of the fine ladies consuming their cakes and tea on the back veranda, had noticed how Savannah, though incredibly beautiful and the youngest amongst the group by half a decade, looked old compared to the other women. Old and worn out. Practically a ghost.

For two years after that Lynn watched her sitting in the gardens, stiff and pale in her garish dresses. He watched her climbing into the coach to be transported by one of the plantation hands to see a play or vaudeville show. He watched her shadow moving through the blinds, and he sucked up hints of her perfume drifting on the breeze.

Lynn was spreading horseshit into the flowerbeds when his cousin leaned from her window and asked, in a languid tone he'd never heard before, "Lynn, where did you come here from?"

He squinted up into the dark spot of her face against the sun. "Bullitt County."

"What was it like, there?"

Lynn looked around. "Not much like this. Less flat and forested and more mountains, with caves in the mountains. Canyons. Hotter and not wet like this."

She shook her head, laughed through her teeth. She looks nothing like her surroundings, thought Lynn.

"Sadly, Bullitt County sounds like Paris, to me. I've never been further than the Nickelodeon in downtown Lexington."

"Why don't you go somewhere?"

She sighed, and spoke to him as if they had known one another for a very long time. "And how exactly would I get there, Lynn?" Her eyes wandered and her tone grew darker. "And who would hide me when they came looking?"

She's odd, Lynn thought, squinting up at her eyes. He could tell by the way those eyes sat unsteadily in her beautiful thin face, as if they belonged to another face that had simply been covered over, that she did not experience the world as he imagined other people did. He'd never spoken to her before; the possibility of her being strange had never crossed his mind. In his fantasies, he'd always been rescuing her, transporting her to safety as she swooned, her misty eyes rolling. But now he realized the stupidity of this. *No, no. Those eyes will not be a-rolling for anybody.* As the schoolboy element of Lynn's unrequited love suddenly died, he realized with a thrill that he'd now have to rethink everything.

"When who comes looking?"

Savannah shook her head, waving away the question with a pale languid hand. "I'll get married the day I turn eighteen." She rubbed her face. "I'll have children and host parties for various charities. That's my story."

"It's a nice life," Lynn whispered. *Holy shit; something's happening.*

She watched him very closely, seeming to choose each word as carefully as if he were a riddle-giving sphinx. "It *is* a nice life... And I would do nearly anything to make another."

"I sorely hope I'm not out of line, here, but...you can't mean that. You'd do nearly anything? Wouldn't you miss...all this?"

She rubbed her lips, tilted her head. "You're not out of line, Lynn...and in fact you're absolutely correct in saying that I've misspoken. It isn't true that I would do nearly anything to change my lot."

She leaned forward into a slightly darker part of the universe.

"I would do *absolutely* anything."

They looked at one another, her from above, him from below.

Lynn nodded, swallowing, struggling to maintain his balance as the world spun and hitched beneath his feet.

As the boy, less esteemed than the dogs he slept with, informed Conrad that the two of them needed to talk, the old man's stoneface twitched, a ghost of movement, a sub-liminally brief glimpse of roiling insects beneath the skin of the fruit.

"You have the full brunt of my attention, Lynn."

"I...I'm going to pay you the respect of just coming right out and saying it, sir. Savannah and I don't think it's right, you keeping her locked away like this, like some porcelain doll. If you wanted to keep her like that, then you shouldn't have raised her up to be so smart. You ought to be proud that she isn't con-tented with this type of sheltered life. You really have no right to keep her locked up like this." Lynn's voice trembled, his face flushed and his hands shook. This was not at all the speech he had planned, and he felt the situation getting away from him. Perhaps he'd made an irrevocable mistake.

The old man, his huge white smile broadening as if to consume the boy, asked warmly, "And you, Lynn...May I assume that you intend to accompany her, in this leaving?"

"That is my intention."

"And does she know you're speaking to me about this?"

"She does not."

"And will she be joining in on this conversation?"

"I hope to convince her to do so, sir. As soon as you'd be willing to have that conversation."

The old man looked at his nephew, motionless, silent. Then his face spilt like an infected organ bursting and the smile crept up, skin bunching around its irresistible crawl like a wrinkled carpet. "Well...It's not what I would have recommended, Lynn, but I do have to admit that what you all are saying is making a lot of sense. You have my blessing. In fact, let me go get you a little something to help you get set up...wherever the two of you decide to go."

"You don't need to do that."

"Oh no, I insist. What's the point of any of this," he motioned expansively at the opulent surroundings, "if you can't look after the people you care about?"

Conrad turned from the boy, ascending the stairs to his bedroom, retrieving a long-barreled Colt Paterson from the bureau. He played it quickly in his mind; unfortunately, with Savannah returning from her Saturday show at any moment, there would be no time to lure the boy away somewhere remote, less messy...But it couldn't be helped. As soon as Conrad shot the boy, he'd have Archie wrap the body in a tarpaulin and carry it out to the back forty. A couple of discrete, non-English-speaking hands could be enlisted to bury it in the woods behind the house.

While Conrad would sooner rouse the maid Rosa in the middle of the night than lift a hand to clean the ring left by his water glass on the bedside table, this type of work he did not particularly mind. He ran through the progression again and confirmed that yes, all of this would play just fine. Since Lynn was an adult and a transient, there could be no reason for reporting his exodus, and it was utterly inconceivable that anybody would come asking after his whereabouts. With a thrill and sense of purpose such as the old man had not experienced since last he had withheld the boy's meals or ordered him thrown naked out into the snow as punishment for some invented offense, Conrad tucked the pistol beneath his robe, and descended the staircase.

Coming to the final step, turning to face the ornate foyer, in what was unequivocally the most shocking moment of his life the old man found himself staring down the bore of Lynn's pistol. Lynn the gimp. The dipshit. As the flint clicked, the bore flashing luciferous as the shadow of the slug came rocketing through the fire, Conrad screamed not for his impending death but from shame at the stupidity of failing to see this coming. His left eye caught a brief glimpse of the gore from the disintegrating right half of his head and he jerked back onto the floor and died.

The door beneath the stairs banged open and Archie came racing out, unarmed, committing the exact same gadarene blunder as his recently deceased employer. Lynn extended an arm and blew the top of his head off in a sanguinary mist.

Leaving the bodies where they lay, Lynn trotted from the house, across the sprawling rolling lawn into the woods. A storm had been steadily accelerating, knocking the slender willows against one another, tearing away leaves and pushing them along the ground, so that the world slashed and clattered, swallowing the sound of the gunshots before they could echo beyond the house. Lynn turned his eyes to the churning sky, nodding in gratitude.

Coming to the cottage deep in the woods, he found the accountant Jacobsen alone with a book and a glass of wine at the edge of a hissing fire. The tall wiry bookkeeper looked at Lynn, removing the spectacles from the tip of his nose. Lynn extended the pistol. "Get up and come with me." Jacobsen blinked, frowning lightly. Lynn fired and the wine glass exploded, driving shards of thick leaded glass deep into the meat and bone of Jacobsen's thin hand so that the accountant shrieked, eyes bulging, ogling the hand at arm's distance—

"Now. Get up and come with me now," Lynn said, pressing the bore of the gun to the man's thin quivering suddenly bloodless cheek. They marched through the driving rain, Jacobsen babbling questions and Lynn proceeding in silence. Jacobsen stopped at the door to the mansion, saying he didn't want to ruin the carpet with blood from his shredded hand, hesitating in the threshold until Lynn shoved him inside and the sight of the half-decapitated bodies on the floor knocked him into a state resembling calm. Without being instructed to do so he climbed the stairs to Conrad's room, opened the safe hidden between the bed and the wall, and handed Lynn the burlap sack taken from within.

Gathering himself, drawing his trembling voice down to a calmer tone Jacobsen said "I swear I won't tell anybody any of this. After whatever head start you want, I'm on the first train to Ithaca. I've got family there. I'll stay there. No one will ever know. Don't shoot me. I'll never tell anybody anything…"

"I'm not going to kill you to keep you from saying my name."

Jacobsen's wire-taut frame loosened, sagging with relief.

"Not that it's apt to be much of a mystery, who did all this killing. I think people are going to figure this out just fine, with or without your help."

Jacobsen blinked, uncertain.

"No, sir. I'm going to kill you for helping the old man pull the deed from my mother and father's house. For helping him squeeze them out of the inheritance. For killing them."

Jacobsen managed a single inarticulate noise as his head bucked and spattered in spots and shards against the wall. With the bag and his gun, speckled in blood, Lynn went outside to simmering lightning and the dull rolling crack of thunder. He saw Shanti's team and coach racing from the end of the road, undoubtedly intent to beat the storm, and he ran, low and gripping the shadows, to slam the gate fast and throw the lock. He ducked into the bushes, watching as the good-looking cowboy jumped down, shielding his dark eyes against the first wave of rain, cursing as he confirmed that the gate was, indeed, locked. "Well," Shanti shouted into the coach, "let's wait here a minute. They must be working on something up at the house and don't want us getting in their way. We can head over to my place if it ends up taking awhile."

Lynn slipped from the bushes, coming towards them up the driveway to the gate.

Shanti dropped down from the coach, slamming the door, face sour beneath the dripping brim of his hat. "What the hell they sending *you* out here for, Lynnie?"

"The back field flooded from a busted irrigation gate. We're pumping the water out now, and it's all hands on deck. Savannah's supposed to just sit tight until Archie comes out for your rig. Conrad said we've got an unmanned pump and a pile of sandbags with your name on them."

"God*dammit*! I don't guess the old man's out there pumping in the fucking rain?"

Lynn shrugged.

"And now Archie's fat wet ass is coming out to ruin my upholstery? Well *fuck* that." Shanti exhaled. He shrugged, shook his head resignedly. "Alright, then. I'll tell her." He leaned back into the coach cussing softly, shaking his head. Shanti said something to the girl, then turned walking past and ahead of Lynn as if he weren't there.

They moved along the path through the woods to the field, Shanti walking fast, just wanting to get the damn thing done with and get out of the rain. Lightning burst right as Lynn shot him in the back of the head. Shanti's hat landed next to his pulped head, a large hole smoking in the black velvet. Eyes following the smoke, Lynn saw that across the field lightning had cleaved a tree in half and it too lay smashed and smoking. He nodded to the split tree.

Lynn raced like a creature through the driving rain and darkness, back to his kennel where he let fall the blood-spattered shirt in favor of a new one. He used his wash basin, one final time, to wipe away the blood. Running low he returned to Savannah.

Lynn quietly stuffed the heavy canvas bag taken from the safe into the jockey box before climbing into the coach. "There's... bad news," he said, without looking at his cousin.

"What is it?" she asked softly.

"The flood...that was a lie. I just sent Shanti in to get the real story from Conrad. The truth is..." Lynn ran a big hand over his face and sighed.

"What is it?"

"I, and I hope to God I didn't overstep, but I just couldn't see you keep suffering like that. I...The reason the gate was locked is that Conrad and I were having an argument. I told your father he had no right to keep you living locked in there like a prisoner."

Savannah covered her mouth. "Oh, God."

Lynn nodded. "He...He told me I've got an hour to get myself off the property." Lynn placed his hand on the gun in his pocket. "He gave me twenty dollars, and Shanti's rig, my inheritance, he said, and told me if I ever get within range of this plantation again, the hands have orders to shoot." Lynn looked at her in the stormswept darkness. "I think I may have gotten you in a bit of trouble as well. I'm so sorry."

"What did he say, Lynn." Her voice was flat.

"He was angry. Angry at me. He didn't mean any of it. I'll go back in and tell him I was lying, that you're happy here, and I was just jealous and trying to cause problems..." Lynn pushed up from the seat as if to exit the coach, but Savannah grabbed him gently by the biceps, nodded for him to continue.

"He said maybe it would be best if you...if you left, for awhile. If you left to give yourself a little perspective on this life here on the plantation that you're finding so disagreeable...But he was bluffing. Trying to scare me into thinking I'd made an even bigger mistake. I'll go back in there and tell him the whole thing was coming from me..."

Savannah turned full to face him, looking hard into his face. Some shadow, some ripple, seemed to shift beneath the surface of her skin. "No," she said, nodding, nodding faster, gaining conviction. "He's right. He said I ought to go see what else is out there...Well, this is my chance. I can come back whenever I want."

"Are you sure?"

"I think I am. I'm always talking about it…"

"Unless you have other plans, I'm happy to take you wherever you might want to go. Bring you back whenever…"

She leaned closer, her face suddenly revealed in the lightning. "One concern I have, Lynn…Has my father sent any money, to keep me safe while I'm off learning my lesson? Or should I head on up to the house and ask about that?"

Lynn spoke softly, watching her. "There is some money. Yes."

"A little? Or a decent amount. I'd hate to feel like I needed to come back before I was entirely ready."

"I think you can go wherever you want to go, for as long as you want to stay."

She nodded one final definitive time, her eyes trailing down…

Lynn followed her gaze to his large callused hand. He saw the spray of blood on the back of it, like flame, an instant before Savannah covered it with her own.

Though Lynn, having renamed himself Hal Best, would stake a claim deep in the wilderness of Northern Idaho, slashing back with his own two bleeding hands and a slingblade the ancient shadow of the forest, fending off Indians and claim jumpers, hacking out a profitable logging operation single-handedly, providing a life sufficient to keep his beautiful wife happy while siring a tribe of world-beaters, he would perpetually remain in the eyes of his neighbors a stooge. Hal the limping dipshit. The open-mouthed gimp.

As he aged, the discrepancy between what he looked like, and what he actually was, only grew more pronounced. With the progression of the years, Hal's spectacles thickened, his nose grew and his hair thinned. The sheath of fat widened around his waist and dangled beneath his weak chin, drawing attention away from the bundles of cable that occupied his forearms, the rigid bulk of his chest and the massive hands capable of compressing the skulls of recalcitrant bulls and tearing faulty logging cables in two.

When he and his wife Georgia attended church socials, holiday parties, chamber of commerce dinners, Hal attracted a crowd because he seemed forever poised at the precipice of doing something outrageously shameful; farting or spilling a drink or reaching to stretch and accidentally squeezing a passing breast. The men who purchased his lumber or sold him equipment would shake their heads ceaselessly, smirking at whatever brand of unlikely, dumbass luck had kept the family alive out there in the brush for this long.

"That whole arrangement? Now *that* will forever be a real turd in the woodpile, boys. I tell you what, though...If that wife a his survives whatever shithead mistake kills the rest of em...There will always be a place in my stable for that little filly."

This false face of fecklessness did not come without its benefits, however. Several times the impression of clownishness, of lesser-than, served as Lynn's alibi. When a rumor trickled down through the woods that federal marshals were asking after a stranger with a Kentucky accent and a beautiful wife arriving unexpectedly ten, twenty years ago, a quadruple murderer who had somehow overpowered an entire estate full of armed men, seducing the beautiful maiden...

Clearly they weren't looking for Hal Fucking Best. Maybe if the crime in question was shoving his pecker into someone's prize pumpkin or farting on the advent candle and burning down the church.

And so when Andy, the second eldest son, became a precocious force of athletic acumen, everybody looked at clumsy stumbling Hal and said that the last thing in the *world* they would have expected him to sire was a professional ballplayer. Later on, after the boy's true essential nature had been gruesomely revealed, they would look at sweet bumbling Hal and say that the last thing in the *world* they would have expected him to sire was a death row murderer.

But ironically, if they'd have seen beyond the shell, the mirage, and understood the man, these might have been *precisely* the two things they'd have expected most.

"Come on," Andy said to Henry Hester, who he'd found on that frost-caked mid-April Saturday morning setting beer bottles on fence posts and shattering them with rocks. "They've got a baseball game going in town. I read a flyer at the store."

Both boys were thirteen and with the exception of one another, friendless. In Henry's case, the solitude was imposed. Most people found his appearance displeasing, with his huge head capped with furry red hair and strangely long limp pale hands. Henry's personality consisted of an extreme reticence that sometimes, at moments of excitement or agitation, erupted into high-pitched laughter, hand-flapping, red-faced, so that people frequently thought he was retarded. Henry had nothing to offer that drew people to him.

Andy, on the other hand...His large, muscular stature, the body of a man ten years his elder, automatically garnered respect and trust. He emanated physical capability and calmness.

Nothing could go too wrong, it seemed, in his presence; and if it did, he'd take care of it. He had full lips, a perfectly shaped head with close-cropped blond hair, dusky skin and icy grayish blue eyes like an animal. He too had oddly large hands, but whereas Henry's seemed designed to do God-knows-what in the clammy darkness, some pallid fungus growing at the ends of his freckled arms, Andy's hands were made to take a firm grip upon the world and handle it. Whereas he, too, was quiet, instead of projecting stupidity like his redheaded friend, he exuded precocious wisdom and competence.

To their schoolmates, both boys were irremediably alien. One below, the other above, beyond, but equally unrelatable.

Henry looked at Andy with his mouth slightly open. Andy couldn't tell if Henry knew what baseball was, or not. Andy wasn't sure exactly why he himself knew; all he could locate was a vague memory of watching soldiers play as a little boy sitting at the edge of a field someplace that wasn't his home, soldiers shirtless or in undershirts, looking like statues or figments of his imagination, behemoths crashing and howling against the fiery red sun as it dropped into crooked black cornstalks.

They walked the dirt road through the woods and over the Longbridge in silence. Cresting the muddy hill overlooking the fairgrounds Andy said "Hold up," stopping Henry with a forearm. Some semblance of a baseball diamond had been imposed upon the vacant acreage, unused outside the occasional itinerant circus or Baptist revival. A painted sign leaning against the fence demanded a dime a head to get in. "How much money do you have?"

Henry turned out his pockets. "This nickel."

Andy frowned at him. "Hell. You always have plenty of money."

"I know I do. In my other pants at home. You didn't tell me we needed any."

Andy nodded, conceding the point. He scanned the interlocking segments of six-foot-tall metal fence protecting the action on all sides. Posted at the front entrance was a loud-looking fat woman with frizzy blond hair spilling from beneath a straw hat adorned with flowers in a huge red dress selling tickets. A quadrant of men patrolled the perimeter, one to each side. Andy sighed, thinking, his quick gray eyes searching the sky.

"Shitface," said Henry.

Andy looked at him. "Come again."

"Oh, just Shitface Watkins." Henry pointed to a tall thin boy in dirty ragged clothes with a prominent dark birthmark covering the left side of his face. Shitface came carefully from the woods squinting at the people and objects that had mysteriously materialized inside the fairgrounds.

Suddenly Andy straightened up, galvanized. "Here. Let me have that nickel." He took the coin and started down the hill. Speaking to the tall tattered boy, he shook hands passing the coin. Coming back up the hill to Henry, Andy said "Get ready," and Henry, without a word, tensed his body, pricking his ears and spreading his eyes. He'd never in his life questioned anything that Andy had told him to do. They watched as Shitface, squinting at the ground, squatting as he walked, stuffed his pockets with stones.

Approaching one of the men tending the perimeter, Shitface began throwing rocks. After a few grazing shots, the man shouting and batting the projectiles out of the air, Shitface struck him square in the eye. Staggering, bleeding through his fingers, the sentinel chased the tall slatternly boy into the forest. "Come on," Andy hissed, racing down the hill, Henry at his heels.

Reaching the wall, Andy leapt, catching the top in both hands, disappearing over the top, and Henry followed. They were in. Beneath the bemused looks and teasing admonishments of the people nearby drinking beer, smiling, a sunny day, the boys rose from the dirt dusting themselves off, smoothing their clothing, making their way to the bleachers.

The players came trotting onto the field, a team of West Indians from the mission at St. Pious in bright white uniforms opposing a squad of college boys from Washington State University in pinstriped black and red. The bat cracked against the ball and the ball cracked from glove to glove and the men slid and spun…

Andy leaned forward. Suddenly the circuit carved by the ball was the only thing that existed in the entire world.

"Hold on," he whispered, big fingers gripping white beneath his seat, as rapt and vertiginous as Doctor Thomson first spying the raw hot building blocks of life. "Hold on just a goddamn minute." From the first pitch to the last he stared deep into the game like a boy who had glimpsed a corner of the blueprint of the universe, straining to see more.

Here, he recognized something he'd known long, long before he'd been born.

One day not long after, Andy arrived to collect the big-headed red-headed boy, bearing a pared down lacquered fence post with a hard clay knob at one end and a milking bucket over-flowing with baseballs stitched from wadded rags and braided corn silk.

"Here Henry, throw me some of these so I can hit."

Henry looked at him blankly.

"Hit them with this bat. Like that baseball game we went to."

The big boy took a step back, hands extended, pale face blanching further so that his pimples burned black. "No, I...I don't know how to do it—"

"Oh hell," Andy pressed one of the homemade baseballs into Henry's hand, "it doesn't matter if you know how or not. Just..." he backed off a distance, sticking out the makeshift bat, "toss it right *here*."

Grimacing, Henry sadly lobbed the ball with old womanish delicacy. Andy, frowning at it, stepped and brought the bat to it, sending the ball flaring like a meteor. Henry flinched as the whitish streak passed above him, warping, unraveling, plopping to the ground like a dead dove. Henry lobbed another and Andy battered it out of existence. And again. Again. After they had exhausted the supply, a hundred balls, Andy stopped, pointing the bat at his big friend. Henry panted, sweat running in streaks down his puffy cheeks. "Alright now, Henry. I've got three actual baseballs here," Andy dug in his pocket, removing his hand with the balls wedged between his massive fingers for Henry to behold. "Throw it in here harder." Andy looked dubiously behind him to the creek in the near distance. "But don't get carried away. I don't want to go swimming. Just throw like you been throwing." He tossed a ball out to Henry, who weighed it in his huge ham-colored hand. Andy looked at him, thinking. "Step into it, now. Throw your body forward...." he turned his hips, "like *this*." Henry, with bright cornered eyes, grinding his teeth, stepped and threw, coming forward with the pitch, blinking in the path of the ball as it came in straight and true. Andy slapped it back. They stood looking at one another. "That wasn't bad, Henry. That was pretty good. Now throw that ball hard. Throw it as hard as you can." Andy hunkered down, dug in.

And then came the pitch that would change all of history.

It was as if Henry's entire life his joints had been rusted, his body full of cumbersome weights sliding back and forth, pulling him one direction and jerking him the other, burdens rolling painfully inside of him crushing his guts, his balls, the tender parts of his brain.

But suddenly as he threw, left foot planting, huge body riding light as a feather up over the pivot, the fulcrum, his skeleton fired off a series of cracks as parts congenitally misaligned snapped into place for the first time, smooth and perfectly balanced. The ball, coming off his hand like a miracle, a dream, banged off the side of Andy's head with a pop like a cow's hoof through the frozen crust of the earth.

The ivory sphere arced back up into the air, sailing past Henry as he surged forward screaming, sobbing, reaching for the corpse of his only friend. Andy lay flat on his back arms akimbo and legs spread like a drunken sailor in a comic strip, unresponsive as Henry garbled out his name "Andy! Andy can you hear me! Can you—"

Andy's eyelids fluttered and he grimaced, taking hold of Henry's shoulders, pulling himself up.

"Goddamn," he said, limping towards the bat that had dropped from his murdered hand. "Goddamn now we're talking. Do that. Do it like *that* again. Except for right here..." he held the bat at waist level. "Hard as you can, right there."

Henry, miserable and weeping, moped away a distance, turned and lobbed in a pitch that Andy caught in his bare hand.

"Now *throw* it, Henry. Just like you did. Harder than that, even. You won't get me again. You couldn't if you tried. I'm paying attention now. I know what's coming. I've seen it now. I promise."

<hr/>

Though the Hesters lived scarcely a mile down the road from the Bests, the families occupied entirely separate spheres of reality. Whereas the Bests were noise and dust, cooking smoke, crying baby, Georgia and eldest daughter Myrna a little drunk on homemade wine, playing phonographs and laughing at Hal and the boys when they came home covered in sawdust and oil, the house growing incrementally rowdier...

The Hesters were ordered dusted silence.

Charlene Hester and only child Henry sat quietly on separate floors of the huge house with no sign of the patriarch for weeks. Harold Hester ran a shipping interest, an enterprise that provided his family, as he was quick to remind his wife whenever his vaguely justified extended absences came up, a far more than adequate living. Henry's mother spent most of her time sitting at the huge front window of their beautiful home, drinking vodka, looking presumably out into the forest. Whenever service staff entered her purview, she would conscript them, whether maid, gardener, cook or handyman, to sit and visit and have a glass. From time to time word of this would somehow reach Harold, whereupon he would tell her to stop, to which she would blowzily counter that things could be a hell of a lot worse considering that he was never home. At which point Harold would let it go.

Neither father nor son recalled ever speaking a dozen words to one another.

When Andy came around to collect Henry, he would usually find the boy simply sitting in his room, apparently oblivious to sunlight or darkness, either waiting for something or perhaps utterly thoughtless, his huge head like a large thick block. "Come on, Henry," Andy would say and together they'd walk to the Bests' to fish in the nearby creek or ride the horses, Henry staying for dinner, often falling asleep as they sat listening to Hal read, waking in the morning with a flare of disappointment, remembering that this was not in fact his family, his home, his life.

That evening pitching to Andy, every molecule of Henry, body and soul, fell into sync, and for the first time in his life he became a part of the world, no longer sequestered fungal in the dark of his room. With radiant light shining from his ears and the cracks between his teeth, deaf and dizzy within the miracle of this sudden transformation, Henry heaved the ball like a bolt of lightning, smashing through the barn in an explosion of fluttering splinters. Andy smiled and nodded and drug over a hundred-pound bag of chicken feed to block the hole.

As Henry threw harder, and harder, blowing the ball past him, slicing it in to bloody Andy's knuckles or hooking it away to skip weakly off the tip of the bat, Andy dug his feet deeper into the loose soil, gritting his straight white teeth, ripping the ball off the defunct tractor in the weeds of deepest left-center or jarring dust from the chicken coop a mile away in right.

The sky went orange, pink, black, the soft warmth of the soil giving way to cold but Henry gave no notice. He would have pitched until he collapsed had not Andy, after sending a screaming line drive back up the box into the thickening dark, the raised thread of which stamped a chain of Xs along Henry's cheek, dropped the bat into the dirt. Tugging the ball from Henry's hand, he said they could play again at dawn.

Henry, walking the white strip of dirt road under the bright moon and glittering dust of the stars and the overarching black skeletons of the trees, raised his pocked moonface to the pocked silver moon, watching tendrils of cottony cloud drifting across its face. He realized that though he had existed beneath this same moon, this same beautiful black starry night every night, last night, tomorrow night, he had never seen it before now. Henry brought his hands, long and freckled and white, a source of lifelong shame, from his pockets.

He looked at his beautiful long white hands, turning them over in the moonlight, marveling at the miraculous things they were capable of.

Clutching the mitt he'd sewn from a leather swatch cut off the seat of his father's old tractor, formed cinched in twine with a ball in the pocket stuffed under the mattress he and two of his brothers slept upon, beat every morning and evening with neatsfoot oil, stretched and worked beneath the hooves of the family's half-dozen cattle until it flapped soft and pliant as a bird, Andy stopped, watching from a distance.

The men clambered through the dust, bleary and slow, smashing into one another, absorbing the ball with their barrel chests, throwing high and tight, swinging the bat as if they hoped to kill or destroy something. Although they toiled, grunting and sweating in the bare dirt field behind the Methodists, still the game played true. Andy recognized the rudimentary power, the same elemental force he'd seen surging through the natives and the college kids that day at the fairgrounds.

There were things, the boy had noticed, that *fit* as perfectly within the overall shape of the world as star-shaped candies set into the shape of a star on a star-shaped cake in a star-shaped box. He recognized it when he saw it: the motion of the stream behind their house twitching and sparking in the dawn, the clear steady blue eyes of the cougar roaming the perimeter of the farm…and now this.

He slipped the glove onto his left hand and came closer.

The man playing third base, red faced and pale eyed, belching after a drink of the whiskey bottle he slipped from his back pocket, took notice of the homemade mitt and, pointing, called, "How come you bring your mama's purse into town to watch the game, hillbilly?"

Andy shrugged.

The left fielder called in, "What's that long look on your face, Jethro? You sent out looking for your mama and your sister and just realized they're one and the same?"

The catcher, a perpetually grimy silver miner, his pallid visage peering out through the soot like the face of a skeleton, spat and took a step forward. "You got a picture of your mama in that little old handbag, shepherd boy?"

"I came to play." Andy's eyes passed over the eyes of each man on the diamond.

The men didn't care for the directness of either the statement or his gaze. Several stepped forward with bad intentions until the man on the pitcher's mound, face obscured in a big red beard, working the white ball in his bright red hams of hands, decreed in a deep warm voice, "You'll sit and hope for your turn, boy. Perhaps something will happen." His gaze lingered for a moment.

For the rest of the day Andy stood stiff and alert just outside the first base foul line, working the mitt in his hands, watching the men throw their big bodies back and forth across the diamond, sliding in dirt and blood. The sun got hot, then soft, then began to fade. The players packed their gear, brushing past Andy as if he were a post driven into the dirt.

The next Saturday morning, as the space began to accumulate men, groggy and stiff, tamping down the fumes of yesterday's whiskey with fresh whiskey, there stood the boy. The mitt dangling from his hand looked even darker, more flexible. This time, despite his yokelish appearance, several of the men noticed his long arms like clustered cable and his large hands. His gray eyes.

At high noon, sun silver and brash, the ballplayers blinking sweat from their eyes, a particularly whiskey-laden athlete, sprinting across the outfield, leaning for a ball kicking down the line, lost his balance, throwing back his arms to catch that balance, glancing up just in time to take the iron pole marking the property line between the Methodists and the Diamond Match Company square between his eyes. Down he went with the ringing of the vibrating pole like a somber church bell, a melancholy dirge, rolling slowly to his back, spread eagle, coins and screws and a jackknife falling from his pockets. The men watched for a moment. As the first momentous snore flapped from his lips they turned in unison, a dozen scarred homely faces, the one with the red beard pointing to Andy, motioning with his thumb to some general area out behind him. "You're in, boy."

Finding a pocket of space amongst the established men Andy flexed his knees, arching his back, raising his eyes to the batter. The bearded man, who the others called Ovid, looked at the boy for a moment, then wound and pitched.

Andy knew the ball would find him. As if by fate's design it came kicking off the bat, a horsehide crucible, bearing down upon Andy as the boy surged smoothly forward in his crouch, watching the ball settle into his glove, reaching in with his bare hand...

But miraculously, the ball was nowhere to be found. He turned, watching it bound into left field. Everyone stood straight up. The winning runs raced home, pumping their fists. The silver miner with soot on his teeth and in the creases around his eyes flipped away the catcher's mask, rushing to seize Andy by the collar, raising his right fist into the air, allowing it to pause as he explained, "That's a steak dinner and a bottle of whiskey you just cost us, you miserable snot-nosed son of a bitch!"

As the callused dirty fist began its descent, a soft voice, deep and dark, intoned "That's to be the last thing you'll recall doing today, Owen, if you strike the boy."

And the miner Owen, younger than he'd initially appeared but ugly, a red-eyed yellow-toothed chimpanzee, stopped, fist and lips quivering.

"I've a feeling that's not how it's apt to go the next time," said Ovid. "This day is theirs. There will be others."

And with that, Andy had been inducted.

Like a plant contorting to reach the sun, achieving the only shape it could possibly have enacted in order to survive, once included in the weekly games Andy's body grew to the precise dimensions optimal for his newly discovered vocation. Even off the field, he retained the slow ambling gait and perpetual squint of the seasoned ballplayer, one hand habitually tilting his cap back by the bill while the other hand slid over his cowlicks. Even out in the woods, even running the length of a log with the spikes of his cork boots digging into the slick wood, pitching poles onto the pile, hacking limbs with the Pulaski, he looked like a ballplayer.

Every Friday night he would slip unnoticed out to the barn to arrange his glove and cap and bat. Like a fakir with his smoke and bones Andy would gaze upon these phylacteries in the hissing quivering light of a lantern and feel that to master this, would mean to master life. This game, with its dirt and sweat and sun, with its patterns like a diagram of the universe or God's face or something, could eventually propel him dissolving into the fabric of existence. With great relief he realized that this would be the purpose of every breath for the rest of his life.

On Friday night, he prepared. Donning the gear on Saturday morning he became a spectacle. A rainbow tangled in a tornado. Passersby who didn't even know the name of the game, didn't understand the purpose of this organization of grown men in dingy pajamas chasing one another with a lacquered stick and a lumpen sphere, would immediately home in on only him. "Watch that one..." somebody would say, pointing out the big teenager with muscular forearms and scars from the woods, sensing that somehow this stranger's movements explained everything, rendering the ostensibly pointless utterly profound. Even as a boy, he looked like a photograph of a famous man. Quickly it came to be that Andy's presence rendered the Saturday games moot, guaranteeing victory to whichever team won him in the coin flip with such consistency that the contests began to deteriorate, those players relegated to the preemptively doomed squad faking injuries or suddenly recalling previous obligations right after the coin had landed. After several consecutive weeks without fielding a game, Ovid suggested, "Perhaps there are nine down the road who would like to buy our meals..."

And so the newly christened Priest River Loggers began heading to neighboring towns, to army forts and Indian villages in search of opponents. During these contests Andy settled into his natural position at catcher, from whence he threw the ball as if it had been fired from a Gatling gun, and he acquired the nickname The Kid.

By the time the snow fell, driving baseball weather away until spring, the Loggers had fought hard in every contest, winning more than they had lost, and each man met the winter with an extra roll of dollars in his pocket. While his teammates headed west to Spokane to drink until the snow melted and logging season resumed, Andy rose into the bleak metallic predawn, plumes of breath drifting from his mouth and those of his sleeping brothers as he dressed in the dark, moving quietly through the silent house and across the world, alien beneath its drifting miasma of frost and grainy shadow trod upon by he and he alone.

And every morning he wondered sleepily if any other soul had ever seen and felt this. In the barn he lit and stoked the furnace until it thrummed and throbbed bright red. He hoisted a yard-long chunk of tractor axle, swinging it like a bat, listening to his muscles creak beneath the skin. Hundreds of swings, until one or another sleepy brother appeared in the doorway, dragging a milking pail full of baseballs and a bat with the shuffling head-hanging mien of a boy preparing to slog through his morning chores.

This brother, Matt or Ben or Pruner, all budding sandlot legends in their own regards, would hit one-hoppers from a distance of ten feet while Andy slid side to side absorbing the ball in the muscles of his bare abdomen, pulling it up out of the scattered hay to fire it into bags of feed propped against the wall. The bags responded with a grunt and a puff of dust.

After wearing out one brother, Andy would send him inside for another, taking up the bat himself. He would hit and hit, driving the ball from one uppermost corner of the barn to the other and back, then step across the home plate he'd cut into the floorboards with a pocketknife to perform the same feat of hitting left-handed, then back to the right, back left, until this replacement brother shook his head, florid and flushed, pitching arm dangling like meat. At which point they would quit with a pledge to reconvene for the same program in the afternoon, and again in the evening. Out there sweating and bleeding in the barn Andy knew that the goal was unattainable. He would never be finished. And for this he was inexpressibly grateful.

This relentless pursuit did not come without its share of collateral damage. Boards splintered under the unremitting onslaught of baseballs, farm equipment slumped into fractured heaps of dinged tin. Andy battered his brothers so that chores went undone, and in one particularly notorious and regrettable instance, he killed a horse with a one-in-a-million ricochet leaving the barn through a high shattered window.

Lynn permitted this destruction to his estate, watching from a distance. In the boy's exertions he recognized his own emergence as a man of destiny. Lynn watched the blood running from the boy's palms and the supernatural crackle in his eyes as if looking into some other world that did not yet exist but contained the only true space in the entire universe. In the figure of the son, grinding his teeth within the throbbing glow thrown by the furnace, Lynn observed his own trek through the forest, the gunshots in the rain, the blood.

But if he could have seen where all of this was leading his boy, wouldn't he would have interceded to stop it?

Perhaps.
Or perhaps not.

By anyone's best estimate Big John Score was nearly thirty. He lived off in the brush with his idiot grandparents, who, year after year, kept sending him to school. Either out of benevolence, since unspeakable behaviors obviously marked life in the Score household, or reluctance to confront the enormous man, once John set off for school, no one ever turned him back around towards home. Walking to school with John was like walking with a vicious animal. He drug the littler kids off into the woods to fondle them and be fondled, attacked them and ate their lunches, keeping everyone silent to these indignities under credible threat of death to their families.

On the first day of the school year, John Score was like a monster too long deprived, bent to take out an entire summer's worth of his tragic life on his classmates during a single thirty-minute walk. He shoved a little boy down into the gravel, grabbed another and tore his jacket asunder, took a third boy's hat and put it upon his own head.

All of this Henry watched from a distance, careful not to make eye contact with anybody. If he felt the odd shifting inside himself, a restive sort of itch or aching, he merely wrote it off as discomfort in the face of another's suffering. And so when Big John grabbed the thin deaf girl by the scruff of her neck and began to pull her into the woods, Henry was as surprised as anyone when he himself stepped forward to seize the beast, ordering it to desist.

His eyes fell incredulously upon his own long pale hand gripping the sleeve of John Score's torn dirty jacket. His own voice echoed in his ears, "Leave her alone, plug-ugly," as if the phrase were some distant explosion echoing up from the iron center of the earth portending the apocalypse. Henry's heart and bowels sunk like cannonballs, and his back and soul bent, realizing he'd called on the attention of Death, as John Score let the girl fall from his arms, and turned.

Henry would undoubtedly have taken it back, apologizing and running home, if it weren't for those summer nights pitching to Andy, the changes they had enacted inside of his body and soul. Buoyed by the flaming wings that had blossomed that fateful irrevocable first night throwing the baseball, Henry took a step forward, and that same hand that had discovered its destiny in throwing clenched and leapt up, and the blood exploded from John Score's nose, and Henry came on, throwing the other hand, again and again, until Big John went down. Henry crouched above him, continuing to throw the hands, the blood running in roots over the frosty gravel, and here Good Lord was yet another unknown thing his newly discovered body could do quite well, until the ogre screamed "Stop stop stop—"

As Henry stood, leaving the big body crumpled and covering up in the dirt he delivered the point of it, decrying, "If you ever touch these kids again I'll hear of it and this" —he pointed at the big man's ruptured lumpen face— "will look like a kiss from your shit-eating grandmother compared with what I'll do to you!" Henry's throat vibrated with the sudden dark power of a brand-new voice as he looked at his hands.

His world-crafting hands.

Thus the demon was vanquished, pissing itself in the dust, shrieking in anger and shame. The children ganged Henry all the way to school like a messiah. The die was cast, his neck leaning ever closer to the noose.

Once that beast, the jaw-breaking blood-scenting one, was unleashed, the other beast, the ball-throwing one, grew fiercer a thousand times over. Out at Andy Best's, Henry thrust the ball back behind his ear and hammered it forward like thunder. He would toy with hitter after hitter, men down from the mountains or schoolmates recruited from town, benevolently allowing them to foul a few into the high weeds before disposing of them with a fastball that shook the foundation of the barn.

Until Andy's turn. Everyone would fall silent as the prodigy dug into the box, low in his crouch, light eyes locked in, mouth slightly open. Henry's big red brow would furrow like an oxen brute, a caveman, and the eschatological battle would begin. The squid and the whale. Rain of fire and deep blue sea. Pitch after pitch they would fight, bats shattering and balls battered to hemorrhaging cubes.

As the years passed, and Andy made a reputation for himself, so did Henry. In Seattle Andy drove a ball clean through a water-logged centerfield fence, leaving a perfectly ball-shaped hole, creating a famous original conundrum that ended with the home plate umpire shrugging and twirling his finger for a homerun. Henry supposedly bit off a man's middle and index fingers in a fight over a spilled beer at a horserace. Andy thrice threw out Billy Hamilton in an exhibition game in Missoula on the same day that Henry, lured beneath the Long Bridge by a girl and jumped by a trio of her co-conspirators, filled his practically lethal fists with a pair of literally lethal pistols, backing off the attackers, bringing an entirely different context of danger to his legendary name. As the Priest River Loggers approached a baseball diamond, a crowd gathered, shaking Andy's hand, requesting his autograph. As Henry slouched against the side of a building smoking, the caricature of a lurid pulp periodical cover, young men across the street inconspicuously raised fingers from their hips, pointing him out to one another. Some of them wanted to pledge their undying fealty, and others wanted to kill him.

But no matter how divergent their paths might become, once or twice a week Henry would show up at the Bests', dragging a bucket of baseballs out to the worn scarred pitching rubber, bringing Andy from the house, working the handle of a bat in his huge palms. "Top one, nobody on, oh oh..."

Each year, the Loggers expanded their schedule, slashing and burning victoriously through San Francisco and Portland, Los Angeles, Tijuana, British Columbia...

And during this time the famous Philadelphia Phillies scout Boar Johnson began to hear a story, a story about a barn in darkest Northern Idaho, in a ravine or at the top of a mountain, a fantastical barn surging and bleeding light like an immense fiery heart, from which in the dead of winter, in the dead of night, echoing for miles across the wilderness came the thumping, splintering, rhythmic beating as of a violent brittle heart. This sound, portentous yet somehow comforting, beat night and day all winter, millions of beats, until on the final day of the dead season the heart opened spilling forth a man-sized boy brandishing a bat.

Phillies who'd played winter ball down in Tijuana came into Boar's office to tell him the Mexicans couldn't stop talking about some barnstorming hillbilly kid out of Idaho. Second coming of Deacon White, the Mexers said, except this kid runs like a panther and hits homeruns like he's goddamn David flinging the ball out of a sling.

Although the dubious story kept coming back with the mindless repetition of a boomerang, Boar had been scouting far too long to go beating through the brush after every school-boy doing things on the diamond that "nobody had ever seen before," and besides, the whole thing sounded like nothing but silly bullshit. He'd nearly written it off as nothing but an oddly persistent legend when he received a visit from his mentor and surrogate father, the venerable scout Joe Heller.

Thirty years earlier, Heller had transformed Boar from a kid selling newspapers and cigarettes out in front of the Copper Coliseum into the most successful scout in the history of the game. One afternoon, buying his pregame smokes, Heller had asked the kid whether he ever went in to watch. "I only spend my nickel to watch them win. Today they're gonna lose, mister. I'll take another look tomorrow."

Heller had smirked, lighting up a cigarette. "How come they're gonna lose?"

The boy had pointed to a gap between boards in the right field fence. "I watch the warmups. Cloninger's out of gas. Every-body's been saying," the boy had shaken a newspaper for empha-sis, "this first month's been unlike him, that he's in a slump. But that's not it. This first month has been *exactly* like him. From now on, I mean. He's finished."

"Why do you think that?"

The paperboy had blown a puff of air through his clenched teeth, pointing again at the fence. "Watch his warmups. It's written all over. The ball looks okay, but everything else…

sheesh. He'll get clobbered early. Today and every day for the rest of his life."

Heller had chuckled, shaking his head as he left the presumptuous urchin. Settling into the press box, he'd watched the pitcher's warmups closely. Cloninger looked fine. Good arm speed, strong kick, ball coming off quick and live. And yet, by the end of the third inning, Cloninger had been relegated to the showers after surrendering five home runs, the first misstep among several that would lead, by the end of the month, to his exile back to hog farming in Iowa.

The next time he'd seen the paperboy, Heller had asked "That day you predicted Cloninger was going to get lit up; I thought he looked fine. What were you looking at?"

Young Boar had shaken his head, shrugging. "I guess I can't really point it out. It's just a thing."

"Did you watch warmups today?"

"I watch warmups everyday."

"What's gonna happen?"

"Same thing that's about to happen for the next ten, twenty years. Pat Foote is what's gonna happen. Unless those ignoramuses, no offense if you're one of them, send him back out to the farm before he gets a chance to get settled in. Otherwise, if nobody sabotages that …there's your answer to the question. Pat Foote."

*Pat Foote…Who the hell…*After a moment, Joe had retrieved the image of a short, skinny kid, big Adam's apple, pimple-faced, arms like corn stalks, filling in at second base while Garret Dickerson got his vertigo under control. Heller had snorted. "Pat Foote. That's nobody."

The kid had looked him up and down. "Do you help set the lineups?"

"I'm a scout."

"Too bad for you. Pat Foote. You're looking over him because he's weak and he's ugly. But he's plenty strong enough to turn around a baseball, and he's fast, and he's the best glove you've got."

"Everything you just said about that kid is wrong."

Little Boar had shrugged, turning back to selling papers.

Two months later, with Foote batting .387 and Dickerson traded away, Heller had invited the kid to tag along on a trip upstate to scout a tournament of factory teams.

Thirty years later, Boar tapped on the bar for a fresh pitcher and another glass. Heller poured himself a beer, drained it, and poured another. "Well…I've got a tip for you, Bobby."

"Yeah?"

"Yeah. And Bobby, this…this here is the one. This is the one, and there ain't nobody else been looking."

"So why don't you go get him, Joe?"

"Two reasons. First of all, you know those bastards in the front office wouldn't sign Jack Glasscock if it was me suggesting it. Secondly, I went out and saw him play this spring, and that's the last trip I've got. I head back into those Idaho woods, that's it, I ain't coming out."

"Kid's name, he's a catcher, Andy Best. You go find him up twenty miles northeast of a little logging town called Priest River. I got a map."

Boar sighed, resigned, shaking his head. "All right. Off the reel. Tomorrow morning first thing," he said, addressing himself to the relentless pestering universe as much as to the old man across from him.

Boar caught the Loggers in Steilacoom, Washington. Settling into the grandstand with his frosty mug of beer and German sausage, Boar craned his neck looking for "The Kid." *And just once*, he thought, *can't I check out a prospect who isn't called The Kid?* "Where is he?" Boar whispered out loud, leaning forward, twisting the lineup card in his hands, examining the thirty-odd men in nearly identical gray uniforms milling around the periphery. Then an umpire appeared shouting for Priest River to take the field, and Boar made out which one was supposed to be The Kid, number 1.

Wincing, he crumpled the lineup, spilling half his beer. "*Goddamn* fool..." he accused himself, shaking his head, gritting his teeth. He should have known. He *had* known. Had one of these trips ever paid off? He was too fucking old to be pulling shit like this. Speaking of old, looking at Best's wide shoulders and big hands, Boar laughed sardonically. He put The Kid at about thirty-five, thirty-six. Meaning that even if this guy was everything the legend claimed and more, by the time The Kid weathered the inevitable transition period to the big leagues, made the adjustments, learned the ropes and adapted to the schedule, he'd be good for one, maybe two seasons tops. It wasn't worth the effort, when the organization had any number of young guys they could bring up a year early or vets they could keep under contract with about the same result. Boar resolved to finish his beer and see about getting back to Seattle in time to catch a train east. He drank, slid his notebook back into the leather case, and took half a glance up as the umpire bellowed "Play ball!"

Andy dug into the batter's box...

For the rest of Boar's life he would tell the story of how the instant the bat came to rest on The Kid's shoulder, all the sound, all the air, surrounding the field suddenly sucked up into the ether, leaving a frozen scene of two-dimensional paper dolls against a brightly colored background. As Best's cold eyes took control of the pitcher, Boar experienced the fantastic sensation that somehow Andy was channeling an ancient essence or inventing something the world hadn't ever seen. That's why The Kid had seemed so old. Now, as the bat came off The Kid's shoulder, easing the ball majestically up and over the right-field fence, he seemed ageless. As he trotted the bases, head down, The Kid was seeing into another world. The past. The future.

Throughout the rest of the game Andy slid back and forth behind the plate blocking pitches, and Boar would have liked to see him throw more, but after he pegged their fastest runner trying to steal second by fifteen feet, so that the rabbit just stopped, shaking his head, the rest of his mates refused to hazard a try. Andy's second trip to the plate he laced a single, stole second, stole third, and induced the pitcher into rifling an errant pick-off throw out into the river, at which point he walked home. On his third trip he beat out a bunt, then concluded the day with another homerun, this time (inducing Boar to rub his eyes, joggle his head, triple-check his notes) from the right side of the plate.

As the umpire called for Steilacoom's last ups, Boar gathered his notes and slipped away into the gloaming. It was his policy never, under any circumstances, to speak to a prospect directly after a game. Give it a few days. He'd catch the team back in Priest River. Even Sherry Magee, even Togie Pittinger, he'd let marinate for a few days.

But this, said a voice in his head, causing him to turn around, linger at the gate, *is no Togie Pittninger.*

This, continued the sibilant whisper, *is the best thing you have ever seen. And you haven't seen but the corner of it.* Boar took a step back towards the field.

The scout turned and walked up Main Street whistling.

CHAPTER TWO

They bumped into one another on Main Street, Andy in his grease-and-sawdust-coated coveralls, Henry bloated and pale in some weird getup.

Andy looked him up and down. "Why the hell are you dressed like that?"

Henry pulled the dark glasses to the end of his nose, tipping the bill of his fedora, popping up the wool collar of his trenchcoat. "Disguise. I got all this shit out of that rich widow up Indian Creek's house last night. All this stupid *shit,*" he raised his arms, let them drop again, "and not a goddamn cent. And not a fucking drop of booze. Waste a goddamn time. So here I am poor as Job's turkey. Now I guess I'm at least gonna use the clothes to help me get the booze...Where you headed?"

"Leonard Paul's."

"We're going to the same place. What's your business?"

"Saw oil. Let me go in first. Wait until I come out."

Henry gave him a look. "Alright. Hurry up, though. I ain't standing out here forever."

Andy made his way through the cluttered store, past the hanging Persian rugs, the barrels of pickles and stacked flour sacks, antacids and daffodils, the shovels and waders and boots and knives, to the fumy displays against the back wall of Sterno and formaldehyde, oils and gas and bottles of bourbon.

"You need saw oil, sweetheart?"

Marge Leonard, ageless totem of the town, had come from New Brunswick by wagon eighty years before, leaving along the trail a dead husband and several dead children. Still a teenage beauty despite the hardships and horror, Marge had married the local Clatsop chief, Sha-al, then eventually the Army captain who killed Sha-al, Shawn Paul, with whom she'd opened the store, running it herself after he'd died of liver failure thirty years earlier.

"Yes ma'am."

"Here, sweetheart, I've got a fresh crate in the back. I thought maybe I could get away without restocking today. That's what I get for thinking. Give me just a minute." She came out from behind the counter, wizened and grisly in a beaded buckskin smock, one eye curdled with cataracts turned to the ceiling but striding like a woman half her age. As she rummaged in the back room Andy pulled a Pulaski from a stand fashioned from an elephant's hoof and began swinging, visualizing a low looping curveball, fastball high and tight, slider biting into the dust…

The front doors eased apart and Henry came in, clownish in his disguise, slouching and looking every direction at once. He came back to Andy in a pucker. "Where is she?"

Matching Henry's harsh whisper, "In the back, getting saw oil. Pull foot, now. Give me thirty goddamn seconds to buy this, and I'll clear out, and you can do whatever the hell nonsense you came here for. Which I'm guessing is probably something you ought not to be doing, anyhow." Andy sneered. "You smell like a goddamn mash barrel."

"Fuck you. You been in here for a fucking hour. I can't have everybody in town spotting me standing out there in this stupid goddamn costume…And why the fuck am I arguing about this? This is none of your goddamn business anyway. *Jesus."* Henry's famous fists clenched as he stepped towards Andy, reaching to hoist a pair of gallon whiskey jugs, spinning for the door right as Marge emerged from the hall holding a dun aluminum oil can.

Henry panicked, breaking for the door, tripping over his own feet, the jugs exploding as he hit the floor. Marge, screeching "Plank up!" dug her fingernails into the back of his neck, hoisting him up off the floor. Henry tried to speak, but Marge's hand lashed out to slap his face and he shoved her, knocking the old woman over, her historic skull striking the concrete floor with the crack of a fallen bough.

As Henry stood over her, gaping at the black halo of blood creeping ineluctably, irrevocably outward from her thin hair and crone's face, a face that in that particular moment struck him as a face of ancient power, his fingers settled quaking upon the thick shards of glass jutting shockingly from his own midsection. He'd fallen upon the shattered jugs. Touching the glass, feeling it move inside of him he vomited blood. He took a step for the door and slipped in blood and smacked his head on the floor and passed out.

Andy hoisted Henry up, staggered purposelessly around Marge for a moment, then left the store carrying his friend. Henry's breathing seemed to issue from a torn sack. Andy carried the big boy for a block, heading towards Doctor Falter's. A group of men intercepted him, wincing and whistling at Henry's condition. They took him out of Andy's hands. Andy sent some of the men back to the store for Marge. Suddenly alone in the middle of a dusty, silent Main Street, Andy set out walking back into the woods.

If I had only taken Henry into town with me that day to play ball behind the Methodists, he'd be on the team too, and none of this would ever have happened, he thought. But he quickly corrected himself. There were some things, like death, that each man must do alone.

Hal awoke in the dark, groping beneath his bed for the rifle, drawn up out of sleep by some instinct long dormant but never diminished.

They'd come. Finally they had come.

Savannah looked at him and he nodded. She slid out of bed, crawling towards the hall, towards the baby's room. Lynn stepped to the window, parting the curtains. Already too close, too spread out and too many. By the time two or three lay dead the others would be shooting indiscriminately into the house. The baby, the children...he looked at Savannah, fighting down a nearly irresistible urge to cross the room, touch her one last time. "Thank you," he mouthed. "It's been..."

She nodded, and they both smiled. Lynn eased the rifle onto the floor and stepped out the side door, palms spread, raised to his ears.

"Okay," he said, moving out into the iron dawn. "You got me."

"We're here for the kid," said the man in front, shaking his rifle for emphasis.

This made no sense, and Lynn simply stood staring. He realized these were not in fact the federal agents or bounty hunters he'd been expecting for the past twenty years, but merely a handful of local assholes: the sheriff and his deputies and some of their friends.

Lynn shook his head. "What the hell are you carrying on about, Jared?"

Into this confusion, Savannah came from the house, carrying the baby, leading Matty by the hand, moving quickly into the frozen mist, away from the guns. As the sheriff turned towards them, his gun coming up, Lynn stepped forward, punching him in the jaw, knocking him unconscious, picking up the rifle and drawing a bead between the eyes of the second-in-command before anyone else had moved.

He spoke evenly and calmly, the only still figure amongst the group with quivering guns and quivering legs. "Put down those barkers and get away from here, now. Somebody's about to get hurt. Jared already got a little hurt," he nodded down at the man lying unconscious bleeding from the lower half of his face which had shattered like a vase in a sack, "but somebody's going to get hurt badly." All of them started shouting at once, panicking, and Lynn had just decided that these men couldn't be trusted to keep it together, and that he'd need to begin shooting, when Andy came walking purposefully out of the house, holding up his hands.

"Hold up," he said, speaking only to his father. "It's Henry. They need me to tell them about Henry. I won't be long."

Back in Priest River two days later, Boar was pleased to discover that the feeling of destiny had not abated. He dressed leisurely, had lunch and a couple of drinks at the hotel's restaurant before setting out on a long walk around the town, during which he indulged in peart fantasies regarding Andy Best's imminent superluminal ascension to stardom, and the part he himself would play in it. If he had not made this trip, it was doubtful that anyone would ever have come this far, and Best would have been stuck playing for steaks, working in the woods until he caught his hand in a saw or dropped a round on his foot. Boar had ventured West, into the dark mouth of the beast, as it were, and inadvertently discovered his opus. And in the process, redeemed another life, as well.

The scout bought a pint of top shelf whiskey and, drinking it at a picnic table on the riverfront, rewrote the standard rookie contract in his briefcase, adding additional years and more money. Although technically such a move was strictly forbidden, the moment the organization had gotten a look at Best they'd do nothing but thank him.

As evening fell pink over the black treetops, glinting off the river, Boar set off whistling towards the diamond. He was glad he'd waited to grab Best on his home turf; he'd make a spectacle of presenting the contract, let The Kid bask in his shock and glory in front of the hayseeds. Who knows, maybe some of these rubes would make a trip back east to watch a local boy made good…might as well sell a couple of tickets for the home team, while he was at it.

Boar cruised up River Street through the gates of the park. Players from both teams were milling around the diamond, confabulating, but he didn't see Best. He approached a group in Priest River uniforms, several ragged looking customers and a big oratorical-looking man in a beard.

Boar stepped forward, smiling beneficently. "I've come for Andy Best."

There was a flash of movement and a cracking sound inside his head and the lights went out.

When he came to, propped against a foul pole, legs splayed out before him, he found himself looking up into a constellation of rough, solicitous faces.

"The...the paper..."

"The contract."

The men looked at one another. "The contract fell out of your briefcase, and we read it...Ovid read it..."

"I'm sorry, mister, about...I ain't exactly no Philadelphia lawyer, and I just thought—"

Boar worked his aching jaw, accepting the proffered hand and rising unsteadily to his feet. "I don't have time for whatever backwater, hillbilly bullshit..." Looking from face to face his pinched expression fell. "Where's The Kid?"

"Kid's gone. Bogus fucking murder charge."

"You're too late, mister. I seen you at Stellacoon. What the hell you waiting for? You shoulda..."

A tall player with jug-handle ears spit into the dirt. "Of all the goddamn people to be arresting for god knows what. With all the assholes in the world, it's Best those dumb sons of bitches are running around worrying about."

Boar kneaded his brow between his thumb and index finger, eyes closed, looking sick. It wasn't the first miracle he'd lost to prison, grave, or asylum. "Pile on the agony..."

"Shit mister," the ugliest amongst them shifted back and forth like a schoolboy, "I sure hope this, me hitting ya, won't count against him...I mean if, you know. If it don't stick, and he comes back."

Boar got his legs beneath him and stood, exhaling deeply. "Quite the opposite."

⌒〜〜⌒

Up on the stand, Henry described grabbing the bottles and running, he remembered falling, at which point he'd sustained the near-fatal injuries to his abdomen, and as he lay there bleeding to death, darkness creeping in, the light beckoning him to follow, he remembered Marge standing over him, appearing to reach for a pistol. Then he remembered seeing Andy, Andy his lifelong friend and protector, Andy who had always looked after Henry looming up behind the woman, her head whipping back as Andy grabbed her...

"And then...I guess I blacked out from the loss of blood from my punctured guts, because I don't remember nothing else. But whatever might have happened," he sobbed, breaking down, gripping his giant head with those long pasty hands, "whatever part Andy might, or might not have played in the old woman's death," pleaded the fat-headed boy, "he shouldn't be judged too harshly, since it wasn't nobody's fault but mine."

The jury was quite moved, watching the big ugly red-headed bezonian breaking down like that. Though Andy had a surprisingly expensive lawyer, provided by his father, and the weight of the full truth on his side, in this case the truth came rather dispassionately into the world, Andy taking no relish in reliving the murder nor condemning his friend. And perhaps even more damning, wasn't there something about those calm, cold gray eyes? Like the hillbilly bastard thinks he knows something the rest of us don't...

After forty minutes' deliberation, the jury declared that while they couldn't confidently say one of the boys had killed that old lady and not the other, both boys had definitely been inside that store, doing something, and both had come out with blood on their hands...

Both were found guilty and sentenced to death.

After a ten-hour train trip along the spines of mountains and through tunnels bored into mountains, then an hour-long truck ride through the desert to the state penitentiary outside Boise, the boys were briskly loaded back into the truck, driven back to the train.

The Idaho Pen, the boys would eventually learn, had been stuffed to the gills after a silver mining dispute had escalated into a machine gun fight, producing all kinds of brand-new murderers. There literally was not room for another killer. So a message had been dispatched, replied to in the affirmative. They were being taken to Rockaway Beach, on the Northern Oregon coast of the Pacific Ocean.

CHAPTER THREE

*N*at Hamelin began working in the railroad yard on the out-skirts of New York City at the age of six, choking on tar fumes, digging the slivers from his hands with tweezers whittled to razor-sharp points, bent and aching, hacking up black phlegm. He would bathe in turpentine to strip away the tar, deaf from the clanging of hammers on spikes, hands warty with blood blisters and scars. Despite the father who would not look at him nor utter his name, despite the vaguest memory of a mother, the boy sensed that somewhere in the world, goodness existed. He knew, however, that it was not here. It was not within the shadow of the shack, where his father sat, haloed in the metallic poison of the smelting plant, drinking homemade wine with his good hand and muttering at the other that had been fused into a purple knob.

But it existed somewhere. Somewhere else.

Every day, from the moment he awoke on the vermin-infested hay-stuffed pad in the filthy shack, one thought persevered:

I have to get out.

———

The railyard sat at the top of a sere hill rolling down to a lush green field where, during his infrequent breaks, Nat would watch the boys from the private high school running to and fro in a codified pattern, tossing a gleaming white ball, periodically striking it with a plank. And what a plank! Shimmering and smooth, so unlike the biting poisonous lumber he handled all day. To hold something like that, to slide it through your palm...

One day an older co-worker, coming upon Nat staring down at the ballplayers, told the boy that a place in that game at the bottom of the hill, along with the accompanying iced tea and lawn chairs and spotless cotton uniforms, was a boy's reward for exceptionally hard work in the railyard.

That's for me, thought young Nat, wiping the mucous and blood from his grimy face, staggering away from another sixteen-hour day with the crackling silver lights tumbling across his brain and the wiry muscles in his small arms cramping his fingers into claws. The next morning Nat attacked the ties like a dervish, stumbling across the yard with the oiled lumber slung over his shoulder, ignoring the pain and blood as the last shred of skin tugged from his palms, powering through cramps so severe his heels swung up to his buttocks, throwing him to the ground, locking him up like a rigor mortised corpse.

At the end of the day, beholding the incredible stack he had produced, more than any pair of the older boys, Nat raced to the yard supervisor with every cell in his body screaming like a church choir *Thank God. I've just saved my own life.*

Finding the boss, a turtle-faced boy with puffy eyes and a pitted nose, sitting at an overturned cable spool in a dirty turtle-necked sweater playing cards with a pair of slatternly men from the docks, Nat drug him by the sleeve to the stack of ties, face beaming brightly through the sweat and tar.

"Right there," chirped Nat, pointing, "that's me, all me, I done that just today. I'm ready. I'm ready to go down the hill. Just send me, just gimme—"

The supervisor's thin, dirty, freckled hand lashed Nat's mouth, sending him rolling into the dirt.

"What in the hell are you talking about, wasting my time, costing me that last hand, you dumb son of a bitch..."

Nat pushed himself up and walked to the edge of the hill.

The air above the boys in their white uniforms glowed.

Many nights Nat put himself to sleep on his wooden cot in the tar paper shack amongst the ticks and rats by imagining that he had somehow joined the lithe long-limbed ballplayers. On other nights he imagined himself rolling down the hill like Death atop a plague of vermin to rip those long arms from the sockets and tear their faces into flapping strips of flesh. And though he had been dis-avowed of the misconception that a boy could stack a hundred ties and be sent triumphantly down the hill, he did not abandon his belief in the truth of that analogy. Up here, within the railyard; this was nothing. Debris. A life the size of a garbage-strewn city block.

But down there, well...down there was everything. The world. Love and abundance. Down there, warm hands squeezed your shoulders and passed you cold beverages between innings. It wouldn't happen in a day, and it wouldn't be so direct as a simple stroll down the hill...

But I will get there.

One way or another, he would escape the railyard, slough the greasy coveralls, don those immaculate garments, sip his tea, and take his rightful turn at bat.

When Nat was ten, he overheard two of the older boys in the railyard talking about heading West to become Indian Killers.

"Two dollars a goddamn scalp."

"And what I'm going to do, you get far enough West, none of them dumb 'skins ever even seen a gun, or a white man. You just walk right up to em like you wanna shake hands, and...Bang!"

"As far as those dumb motherfuckers know, you're a goddamn ghost with a magic wand."

"Magic wand that makes their heads explode."

"Sitting ducks."

"Chief Sitting Duck."

"Fish in a barrel."

"Where'd you all sign up?"

The neophyte killers looked at the long-limbed big-nosed kid, his head shaved to avoid lice and his eye black from fighting. Any other ten-year-old they would have asked *Who the hell wants to know*, smacked him around, told him to go ask his mommy for directions...but something about the gangly homeliness of the kid and the bluntness of his question made them answer him straight.

"Down at the end of wharf sixteen."

"But you better move your ass. They didn't look to be settin up there very long."

"Grubby little fiste like you, got to convince em you're seventeen."

"An got your own gun."

When his shift ended at dusk, Nat headed off in the opposite direction from that beautiful green field and the boys in their alabaster uniforms, through the tar paper shacks, down to the splintered posts and sewage fumes of the wharf, past drunk sailors and crazy old men twisted like crushed spiders and tattooed monstrosities with slivers of bone through their noses and whirling designs of puffy scar tissue burned into their faces. He hated the ocean, which he knew only from the times his father had sent him out looking for his mother along the docks. He hated the smell of sludge and dead birds and garbage and dead fish slopping around beneath the pier. All his life, the horizon in three directions had consisted of nothing but coruscating gray ocean, waves like thorns or razor-sharp stalagmites, leaving only one possible direction for his escape. West.

Pushing aside the stiff animal hide hanging over the doorway of the shack at the end of wharf sixteen, Nat noticed that the nautical tack, the buoys and ropes, had not been removed but simply pushed to the side. In the center of the dusty space stood a desk with the shape of a man.

Nat stepped forward, tipping his chin. "My name is Nat Hamelin, I'm seventeen last month with my own gun and I'm here to make a fist of hunting redskins—"

A tremulous hand, sallow and chapped, scuttled over the desk like a crab presenting a crinkled sheet of yellow paper. Nat's eyes adjusted to the dust and the darkness, and he looked at the man closely.

His cheeks were crusted red and yellow with pimples, sweat running through the valleys between sores to darken his collar, and his eyes were as vitreous and hot as the bubbles of tar upon which Nat routinely burned his hands.

"Sign," the man croaked. "You're the last one."

Recognizing the look and jerky movements of the unpredictable men and women he had encountered slouched in sewage ditches and garbage amongst the shacks, Nat resolved to expedite his exodus however possible.

He leaned over the paper, carefully accepting the proffered pen, and signed his full name.

Each morning before dawn, as the children headed to work, nuns would canvass the closely packed shacks berating the parents and snatching at the children, dragging the easiest targets away to a makeshift schoolhouse for an hour of instruction before releasing them back into the railyard or textile factory or brick oven. While the other boys ran or fought to get away, Nat would allow himself to be drug inside the schoolhouse at St. Michael's, installed behind a desk with a Bible and a lesson book. During that daily hour he had practiced sedulously, learning to write, to read, to work with numbers. And while Nat couldn't exactly imagine when these academic skills might apply, he felt with the certainty of a premonition that all of this learning, somewhere, sometime, would play to his advantage.

Whereas he could see that each of the contracts splayed across the desk had been marked with a dense thick "X," he signed in a tall, florid script "Nathaniel Tyrus Hamelin." He waited. The man looked at him like a sick toad. "Train leaves at six sharp. Don't..." Waving a scabrous hand, the ghoulish recruiter fell into a coughing fit, stringers of dark blood flipping onto his chin. Nat left.

That night, crouched in the shadows between shacks, Nat waited until the he heard his father snoring, and then an hour more. He crept into the shack, sliding his body along the floor, snaking an arm beneath his father's bed until his fingers fell upon the gun. Sliding back across the floor with the pistol, he crossed the night, down to the tracks to sit waiting for the train.

Right at sunrise, he blew a kiss back towards the baseball diamond. "I'll be back," he whispered.

For two years Nat passed time at an army outpost in the desert of the New Mexico Territory. He learned to shoot the gun he'd stolen, and he learned to ride a horse. One night he got drunk with some other boys and learned he didn't like to drink, and one night after the camp bully, a thick-witted giant from Oklahoma with cauliflower ears and hair like patted tar, had refused to relinquish Nat's bunk, Nat had drug him out by his oily hair and beat the shit out of him, garnering a reputation.

One afternoon, as Nat sat inside the sweltering tent playing cribbage with the two boys who had accidentally recruited him in the railyard a world and a lifetime ago, the order finally came in the form of the sweating red-faced red-haired nephew of their lieutenant shoving his head through the flap shouting, "Get your shit together! The flint is fixed! We're going! We're moving out!" As Nat emerged squinting, boys threw supplies up onto horses and shouted running back and forth. The horses knocked boys over full chisel and reared and the officers shot their guns into the air, a gesture intended to still the chaos which only stoked the sudden panic into a headless flailing frenzy. Nat ducked back into the tent to grab his pistol. He wrenched his way into a uniform, rumpled and oversized, the only one not yet seized in the pandemonium. Back outside, he stumbled into the dust as shapes thundered and spun by him and he somehow seized the bridle of a horse and hoisted himself aloft. The horse fell in with a pack of horses, many of the riders in civvies or partially clad, men and equines looking equally wild-eyed and uncertain. Like a bundle of snakes they thumped and rolled out into the desert, raising dust. For awhile the horses ran with the devil at their heels, frothing, hissing, the men burying their heels and fingernails into the flesh of the beasts and shutting their eyes. By nightfall, the horses had begun to walk.

A boy to one side of Nat said "We must be going out to defend some frontier city, some fort or trading post..." Fear and glory burned hot, white and gold flame, in his eyes.

"We ain't defending nothing. Acknowledge the corn, you dumb shit," said a fatter, uglier boy with a smear of dark freckles. "We been settin around with nothing to justify our existences for the last year, eatin on the army's nickel, so now we're goin out lookin for scalps. Make the guvermint some money, at least." He sighed. "The less we know about what we're getting into, the better. Ain't none of my funeral." Nat watched an officer working a flask as if it contained the last handful of air in a coalmine. Up ahead, another in a turquoise coat, replete with stripes and medals, spiked a brown glass jug exploding against a rock. The officers were drunk. Nat mulled this over. Before he had decided what, if anything, he wanted to do about it, the entire regiment had stopped at the edge of a deep but gently sloping canyon.

"We're going down," came the order. "There's the village." They looked down upon a smattering of stone huts and ponds, bluish and silver in the moonlight. The boy who had been contemplating Wild West heroism was nothing but wide eyeballs and shiny Adam's apple. Without prelude, suddenly into the midst of this tense silence one of the officers raised his sword and shouted and they went thundering down the hill, each horse chasing the previous, their hooves hammering blue sparks off the rocky decline. Drawing amongst the rudimentary buildings the riders leapt off their horses and Nat heard gunfire and saw great puffs of arcing sparks thrown through the darkness. He saw a woman, her wrap torn from her, hoisted to an officer's shoulder and rushed into a hut. He saw an old man trampled beneath the horse of the heroic wide-eyed boy and the boy leaping down, firing his rifle into the old man's head which disappeared into mist spackling the rocks. He saw a shrieking child struck from behind by a sword.

It took a moment for Nat, still seated upon the idling horse, to recognize the complete absence of men. The young men were gone. All of the warriors were gone, hunting or fighting. The soldiers swaggered stiffly through the shrieking crowd of women and children and elderly men like golems, like automatons, hacking with their swords, crushing with the butts of their guns, coupling with the dying and groaning like animals. Nat could see in the fading light of their terrified eyes that the boys had surrendered their spirits, set fire to their futures, the moment they'd jumped into the pillaging slaughter. His eyes grew wide and he scooted back in the saddle and spit into the dirt. No sir. Not me. He had not clawed his way out of that god-forsaken railyard and traversed the country just to squander his soul by spilling some poor old lady's brains onto the corpse of some defenseless child. He could have done that back home and finished the fucking thing years ago.

Nat wrenched the reins and his horse stood up, punching the air. He turned the beast sprinting off across the plateau towards a horizon he had never seen. For hours he ran the horse, crossing lots through high bush and thorny hell though no one seemed to be pursuing him. Around noon, in the fire-swept desert, the horse took a wobbly step and dropped dead, pitching Nat into the hot sand. He shed the army's shirt and hat, becoming any boy in a white undershirt and wool pants.

Far up ahead, within the shadow of the scrubby hint of an impending forest, he thought he glimpsed the ghost of a dirt road.

Nat staggered into town filthy, half-starved, with blistered lips and sunburnt eyelids, covered in gallinippers turgid and purple with his thin blood, with the foremost priority at the front of his mind to keep his head down, avoid notice and allow some time to pass. After a couple of nights sleeping along the river he followed his indigent neighbors to work, falling in with a crew of men who looked no better than he, laying railroad tracks.

Months later, after pounding home the final spike, the crew went to a bar in a nearby town. Nat sat drinking Cokes while the rest of them shot whiskey like all wrath. He listened to the conversation flashing and spiking and booming all around him, soaking up the essence and energy of it and thoroughly enjoying himself until a face, vaguely familiar, pale beneath a foppish mop of red hair, floated towards him through the shadow and smoky haze. Nat felt himself seized by the collar and wrenched up out of his seat like a man caught struggling in a dream...

"*You-*" said the face, flushing and contorted. The lieutenant's nephew. "You *yellow*, cut and run, chickenshit, stool pigeon-"

This apoplectic nephew went for his gun but got caught up in the holster, and Nat lunged forward, tipping the table, swinging his Coke bottle. The boy went down in a geyser of carbonated blood. Nat stood over him. The boy's eyes rolled, tongue bitten in half, dangling by a thread. His legs jittered and he tensed, head turning to reveal the fractured dent, pinkish gray meat swelling through the fissure.

Nat flinched at the hand on his shoulder, but as he turned the deeply wrinkled face looming there with its sunburn and moustache bespoke only weary kindness. "Boy," said the bartender, shaking his head sadly, pointing first to the dead man's military uniform, then the gun still snug in its holster, "you're going to need to get yourself on out of here."

⌐⌐⌐

By the time Nat left the singing, staggering, shouting town, his thoughts had already cleared, leaving the fractured skull and leaking brains of the dead boy behind. He trotted along a dirt road until it became a trail in the forest, then a rut, then nothing. Running down a steep, densely wooded hill, tugging at branches to keep his balance, Nat suddenly felt the earth disappear beneath his feet and pitched facefirst into a fetid, soupy swamp. He came up gasping, crawling back to the incline, grabbing at the gnarled roots of a tree like a troll's hand to pull himself up. He found himself at the bottom of a basin filled with rainwater. The air was thick and cold with the smell of rotting vegetation, a heavy moonless night. The swamp was full of flowers, and on a whim he ripped one off its fleshy stalk, stuffing it into his pocket to examine later. Wet, stinking, he picked his way around the swamp, climbing the opposite slope.

The night passed without further incident. A walk in the woods. As the sun came up, setting the birds to hopping and singing, unearthing the smells of millions of years of rotting and wet pale life pushing from the soil, Nat pictured the railyard that had weaned him, the endless groggy Sunday afternoon of the army camp, the massacre, and he realized that his current circumstances really weren't that bad. Ripping a low branch from a tree he pantomimed a swing, produced a cracking noise in his cheek, and trotted through the brush, cheering for himself.

All through the day Nat walked, and though the muscles in his legs tightened, and his stomach contracted, and his tongue swelled, he sucked in air and felt strong, as if he could continue forever. Right as the sun went down, the dusty lemon beams of light shrinking, wavering, disappearing to shadow, Nat began again to descend a steep muddy decline, and he smiled, congratulating himself because this time, instead of floundering heedlessly down into whatever might lie at the bottom, he stopped, carefully extending a foot.

Just as he might have expected. Another swamp. Nat laughed aloud in triumph. I'm learning, he said to himself. A real woodsman. Just as before, minus of course the clownish fall, Nat began to pick his way around the circumference of the swamp.

Beholding the boot prints pressed into the mud, Nat froze. All the sound sucked out of the universe. He eased his foot reluctantly forward. A perfect fit. By the last shadow of twilight, he saw that the flowers gawking from this putrid swamp were red, and he pulled last night's red flower from his pocket. Somehow he had spent the entire day circling back to the fucking swamp. He thought about this. He'd try not to do it again. He followed his own footsteps up out of the basin.

Back in the forest, each time Nat thought he recognized something, he altered his course, turning away from what he'd done the first, and apparently second, times. As day gave way to darkness, his eye twitched with the first faint tickings of an internal clock, signaling that perhaps things were winding down quicker than he had thought. He resolved, though exhausted, to walk through the night. At daybreak he licked the dew off the leaves until his tongue began to burn and blister. He walked through utterly unimagined terrain, past trees like wavering serpents, an equine jawbone half pushed into the dirt, clusters of hairy insects roiling in the canopy big as boulders.

At nightfall, he returned to the swamp. Ineluctably. As if it had already been written.

As the sun went down, Nat found himself once again toeing the lip of the basin, watching the wiggling reflection of the moon. He swayed beneath the same fate-struck helplessness of the fourth generation within a single family dying of the same cancer. The same sense of preordained dread as the man who overcomes a phobia only to be killed by the previously-feared anathema.

I knew it. My entire life, I've heard it coming for me. And there wasn't a goddamn thing to be done.

He tottered forward, slipping on the muddy slope, rolling, smacking the back of his head against a rock, squiggling silver tracers exploding across his brain, his limbs flopping loosely against rocks and roots. With an arm and a leg in the sulfurous, soupy water of the swamp, he dreamt of water, fresh crystalline spattering water, dropping in wobbling globules from a clear blue sky, exploding coldly over his shoulders, bursting at his feet, rinsing the filth from his mouth…

Until the water changed.

A brownish tint, darkening. Struck by the sun, drops full of tiny organisms, writhing bundles of centipedes and twisting spiders. The drops turned black with the multiplying insects and their filth, their blood as they began to cannibalize one another. Nat felt the blood and the shit and the poison caking his mouth and he dug at it, scratching at his cheeks and his tongue, cramming his fingers down his throat, vomiting into the swamp. A swarm of spinning iridescent coronas consumed the sky and the trees began to run and melt, signaling the onset of some ethereal event. Nat watched this empyrean spectacle, tears running down his bunched visage. The lights dimmed, blackness, leaving a single thread of sparkling light, white and green, leading up out of the basin. Nat pushed himself up, head and arms dangling, and began to climb the strip of light hand over hand like a rope. Pulling himself up over the lip of the basin like a man struggling from a tumultuous ocean onto a chunk of bobbing debris, he staggered, toe to heel, following the trail of light into the brush.

Like a prophet in the desert. Prophet in the forest. Come to bring me home. I will bring you home.

⌇

Days later, when he finally emerged into the clearing of men, men with beards and stocking caps sitting on logs eating, he could no longer recognize them as men, nor did he understand the concept of men, nor could he remember why coming upon a group of men would be of any significance to his current state of affairs.

He stopped, wavering, at the center of their circle.

"Thundering Christ, boy. Take a look at *you...*"

⌇

After a week of lying on a cot in a cabin next to a burning stove, re-caulking his guts with oatmeal and biscuits, Nat emerged to accompany the men into the woods in the pre-dawn dark. Within a few days he had established himself as the crew's limber, working his long-armed wiry body up through the tangled branches to the tops of the two-hundred-foot-tall pines to hack enormous limbs crashing through the forest canopy like heavenly corpses. Nat thoroughly enjoyed the work. Each limb thundering and splintering to ground felt like an event, like the culmination of a righteous battle. Though he once again found himself returning home to a shack after a grueling day with splinters in his hands and aching bones, Nat felt like he had finally found the beginning of a life.

At the tips of the tallest trees he would pause, looking miles off to the vast expanse of the Pacific Ocean, bottomless gray, an impenetrable solid dusted with glittering flecks. Up there in the damp pine-scented sky, it was easy to forget where he'd come from.

He hadn't been murdered by the red-headed soldier, nor had he starved within the interminable black forest. He hadn't died of heatstroke in the desert, nor been shot in the army. He hadn't died in the railyard. He hadn't been killed in the shantytown.

Because all the while he'd been headed here.

Nat might have become a contented old man amongst the sawdust and trees, declaring these woods his personal version of the genteel ballgame at the bottom of the hill, his journey complete, if it hadn't been for the federal marshals storming their camp one morning at dawn.

Galloping black shapes came tearing through the mist, casting Nat and the other veterans back to their respective battlefields. The loggers seized whatever lethal implements lay at hand, axes and saws and pikes, so that the clearing might very easily have turned to war if not for the lawmen dismounting, hands held high, presenting badges. But before the marshal in charge could even state their purpose, a logger named Jake Jacobsen came forward announcing it was him they were looking for. And so it was. The previous winter, during a time of scarcity, Jake had ridden into Portland to rob a bank.

As the grum marshals put him under arrest the other loggers began advancing, saying Jake had only committed the robbery in order to keep them all from starving to death, and that every man had partaken of the supplies he'd brought back, and that the marshals were either going to have to try and take all of them, or leave without any, or some third option they'd rather not mention. The lawmen put their hands upon their guns, and again it looked as if the men might start killing one another, until Jake called them off.

"Go ahead get back. I'll head into town with these fucking nincompoops and get things sorted out. I'll be back by dinner tomorrow." The men knew Jake as a man who did exactly as he promised (such as robbing the bank), and they backed off.

While the outfit immediately returned to business as usual, the incident left Nat with an apprehension he could not shake. He had, of course, assumed they'd come for him. And that day, hacking limbs, leaping from tree to tree like a squirrel, replaying every move he'd made since leaving the railyard, he came to understand the flaw in his thinking. Both with the railroad crew and now here in the woods, he had been seeking sanctuary amongst the anonymous and derelict, populations that, he saw now, tended to draw violence and policemen. Murdering an enlisted man, the nephew of a lieutenant, was no small matter. If he kept bumping into the law, it could only be a matter of time before Nat himself wore the shackles and handcuffs. That very moment Nat resolved, looking to the vitreous alien landscape of the ocean from the top of a tree, to seek out entirely different company, to embark upon a radically new life.

A plan materialized in young Nat's head and he slid down through the branches and set down his saw, striking out through the forest to bring that plan to life.

Nat took a deep breath of the damp Portland air. He would hide in plain sight. He would disappear not sequestered in the wild with the other law-breakers but by immersing himself in respectable people. And not just any people…

By his reckoning, the surest way to avoid incarceration was to walk into a prison by his own volition each morning. It was the last place the authorities would expect to find a fugitive taking refuge. He applied for, and obtained, work as a corrections officer at the brand-new Oregon State Prison.

As the weeks passed, Nat carried out his duties quietly and efficiently. He grew a moustache. He stayed out of trouble. Each evening he went straight from work to his room in a large boarding house on the waterfront. Months passed. He grew out his hair. As waves of co-workers and inmates came and went, Nat stayed. There were no promotions, no scandals or grand romances. Years passed with the predictability of a drizzling Tuesday afternoon. And every single night, thousands of nights, just after sunset Nat would stand on the boardwalk, watching the whorling glittering water and waiting patiently, watching the raucous parties on the Mississippi-style riverboats and the Indians sliding by silently in birch bark canoes. And through it all, never for a single instant did he consider hanging up the fiddle. Because something was going to happen. He just wasn't sure what. He knew only that he had walked all the way across the country to precisely this spot, and that something was going to happen.

And then it did.

CHAPTER FOUR

*P*ortland's brand-new, million-dollar prison had a problem. In order to maintain a humane ease of motion and the illusion of ample space (two keystones of the governor's prison reform agenda), the facility had been built with one wing, containing the cells and exercise yard, on the north side of A Street, and the other, which housed the mess hall and infirmary, on the south side. Six times a day, back and forth to breakfast, lunch, and dinner, four hundred prisoners were herded across the street. The warden had employed every conceivable logistical configuration: crossing in a mob, a single-file line, shoulder to shoulder, single-file walking backwards, a V, hands in the air, blind-folded, hands in pockets, holding hands, in groups of fifty, ten, five, individually at five second intervals, sprinting, shuffling, crawling...

And no matter how they travelled, by the time the inmates arrived at the opposite side of the street, women had been groped and purses snatched. Pockets overspilled with Arkansas toothpicks and pistols, anti-fogmatic, laudanum, and opium. Prisoners ran for the hills. After a particularly chaotic weekend, during which Senator Burt Walker's elderly parents, out for a Saturday evening stroll, had been mugged and thrown into the mud by a boodle of prisoners, and three double-murderers had run off into the sunset after Sunday dinner, the warden visited Mayor Castor with an urgent plea.

"You've got to close down that goddamn street. There's going to be a serious problem."

"And the problem will be yours. I realize it's not your idiot design, nor your inane reform agenda. But the place belongs to you, now, Samuel. Solve these problems, or I'll find another man who can."

The following day, a guard recently arrived from San Quentin, not yet properly briefed, fired down from his tower at an arsonist who had catapulted the fence using a severed length of the prison's steel rain gutters. This guard, excited by an opportunity to prove himself at his new job, pulled the bullet to the right, missing the arsonist but punching a perfectly spherical hole through the outstretched palm of Mandarin Beatty, grand old dame of Yamhill Street, widow of former Governor Waldorf Beatty, president of the Temperance, Women for Timber, and Southern Preservation Societies, as she waved to a friend across the street.

That evening, the warden was again summoned to the mayor's office.

"So all right then," said Castor, pinched and uncomfortable in the dark silk suit he appeared to have outgrown, "no more bullets for the guards while you're crossing the street. But we also cannot have Billy the goddamn Kid running through the Saturday market. We need to get this solved *now*. This whole thing could have been a hell of a lot worse. So here's the plan the governor signed off on. Any of those sons of bitch tysts who you'd feel compelled to be shooting should they choose to run, deliver them to the waterfront tomorrow morning by seven. We'll have a boat waiting. Tomorrow's your chance. After that, anybody you don't put on that boat who pulls any shit from here on out…that's your ass."

The warden frowned. "A boat to where?"

The mayor waved a hand vaguely, frowning with impatience, as if that part of the plan was utterly inconsequential. "Oh they'll go up the Indian prison on Neahkanie Mountain. Until we can find a more permanent solution somewhere else."

The official order, signed by the mayor, head of corrections, and the governor, decreed that a new prison would be established exclusively for the state's death row inmates. This document described the construction of an institution in such a remote location that, even if the prison doors were left unlocked, a prospective escapee would have nowhere to go. The edict included a map with fifteen potential sites, spanning Oregon's four corners and the densely forested peaks of its interior. For months, the heads of state government made the creation of this prison their top, and in fact only, priority, contacting dozens of construction companies throughout the country.

Ultimately, they failed to find anyone willing to lay a single brick.

No outfit of even the most tenuous reputation was willing to lug timber into the unmapped Indian-and-bear-infested back country. The triumvirate powers-that-be were stymied. They'd exhausted their lists of both potential locations and prospective builders. They had no more lists, nor the means to create others.

Meanwhile, the situation up on Neahkanie Mountain was steadily deteriorating, with the Indians and the whites, after tiring of attacking one another, banding against the guards in an insurrection that had the overcrowded prison splashed bloodily all across the national news. And so it came to be that the mayor, governor, and head of corrections decided to find themselves a scapegoat.

This chosen one would serve not only as warden of the unbuilt prison, but also project supervisor, responsible for the determination of location, the hiring of labor, and the day-to-day activities of construction. This sacrificial lamb would also, they were utterly confident, never get anywhere near erecting the imaginary correctional facility he was supposed to preside over.

Then, after the new "warden" inevitably failed…

Well, none of the men knew what they hoped would happen after that. They knew only that the current situation was impossible, and that their careers depended upon someone else taking the blame for it. As for the scapegoat, they needed a man ostensibly competent enough to justify the hiring, yet utterly devoid of potential. They didn't want to inadvertently sacrifice someone who might be put to more legitimate use down the road. After an exhaustive search and three sleepless nights of contentious over-caffeinated debate, they narrowed their list to one name:

Nat Hamelin.

Concluding his description of Nat's promotion the governor rose, brushing his hands against one another as if clearing a layer of grime. "As part of your duties overseeing this project, you will have discretion over a hundred thousand dollars of taxpayer funds. On December twenty-fourth, regardless of what you have, or have not, accomplished, ninety-three prisoners will be released into your charge." He cleared his throat and leaned over the desk, narrowing his eyes in a withering stare. "I suggest that somewhere, somehow, you get yourself a prison built between now and then."

The dark stares of the identikit men in their suits with their burgundy faces and dyed black hair brought a cold shadow into the room, and no expression of panic on their victim's face, realizing the colossal responsibility and the weight of retribution for failure just heaped upon him, would have surprised them.

But then Nat Hamelin did the one thing capable of shocking them, and it shocked them.

With easy steel resolve he nodded and arose to take his leave as if the men, otiose to the essential purpose just assigned to him, had suddenly ceased to exist. "It'll be done, gentlemen. Now if you'll excuse me."

Leaving the governor's office with a leather-bound checkbook bearing the seal of the State of Oregon, the men watching his back quizzically, blinking in his wake, wondering in what way they had misjudged this man and whether it would play to their advantage or detriment, Nat thought back over every single night invested in waiting.

And now, of course, it was time to settle the hash. He'd finally been admitted to the ballgame.

The next day he used the first of those checks to purchase a fully outfitted horse, and rode west.

Froth undulating along the spines of the crashing waves like the steaming crests of serpents. Wispy pale clouds between the dark sky and the sea like smoke preceding the entrance or return of the demon. And strewn along the beach, a menagerie of bones. Whale bones. Ribs like sylphic lean-tos. Spines like strings of skulls. Phalanges like the hands of men. And buried beneath the sand, the bones of men. Indian bones. Priestly bones. Sailors' bones. Bones borne from islands with forgotten names. Bones heaped, burned, cracked, scored.

The ocean took the bones away, out into the unfathomable dark, letting them move for awhile, letting them dance and fight, before returning them. The wind ran and the bones trembled. A pocked tin sign reading Rockaway Oregon slid back and forth in the surf. A statue of an angel leaned from a jagged clump of stone rising from the sand, feet embedded as if she had risen up out of the earth with the thrust of magma, blind and all-seeing.

After three days of riding past farms and through the mountains, he broke through tall brush onto the beach, waves crashing white. This, he thought, could only be the very beach, the reverberation of the same sparkling waves he'd glimpsed from the tops of the trees during that former life as a fugitive and a logger.

"Here. By God," he said to himself. "This is the spot."

If either the statue or the witch doctor's blue-eyed ghost had any commentary regarding this proclamation, both kept it to themselves.

CHAPTER FIVE

By the time the leaves had begun to change, Nat had contracted a shipbuilder from Garibaldi to build the prison. The wright had never built a terrestrial structure before, but he had the tools and multiple tons of oiled timber and a crew of able hands standing dormant since the whaling industry had begun to wane. When the dairy farmers from Tillamook hired to level the building site walked off the job due to the abundance of burial sites they were uprooting, skulls and knobs of bone poking through the scooped earth like polished stones, Nat doubled their pay and work resumed within an hour.

On the first day of December, Nat returned to the Oregon Department of Corrections administrative offices in Portland to report that they now had a prison and a gallows, and if the governor wanted to expedite the transfer from Neahkanie, that would be fine.

The head of corrections, a man with a thick burgundy acne-scarred face who dyed his hair with shoe polish, sat stunned. This was never supposed to happen. Who's the certified architect? he asked.

"No sir," Nat answered. "That isn't how we did it, in that amount of time, with that budget. I did the plan. Myself and the builder from Garibaldi."

"Safety and code inspector?"

"None." Nat shook his head, and the bureaucrat, shiny and florid to Nat's weathered tan, caught in a perpetual dyspeptic belch, his eyes the blue of a drowning pool while Nat's were the blue of a chemical fire, ceased his questioning.

~

A caravan came creaking and staggering out of the forest onto the beach. It might have been the army marching to defend the coastline, judging by the quantity of men and their profusion of arms.

Trailing the cavalry high on their horses, the local volunteer militia with their long rifles and machetes, were the prisoners, shackled and cuffed, shuffling in a line, gaunt and scarred from their tenure up on Neahkanie. Standing alongside the path that cut through the weedy dunes, Nat looked into their eyes, which either dropped or grabbed ahold of his and lunged.

That night, after the last man had been installed within his rough wooden cell, the last packet of intake paperwork sealed within the last labelled file, Nat strolled out through the gates, down the beach, to where the water lapped up over the toes of his hard leather shoes. Behind him, the weak light of lanterns swayed within the prison's few small windows. Every so often a noise, a clatter of metal or a shout, cut through the baritone rumbling of the surf. Other than that, the entire universe was silent. Nat looked out over the black endless ocean, then back to the prison.

And this belongs to me alone.

~

That night Nat's deputy warden, Melvin Bronson, a tall pale very thin young man with a large head covered in wispy blond hair, arrived, struggling with a huge leather suitcase, apologizing for the bureaucratic miscommunications that had delayed his arrival by a week. Within minutes of meeting his assistant, Nat was intrigued.

Whereas all the men Nat had worked with in the past had come from rough circumstances, so that even those presenting as feckless or physically weak would eventually expose some capability for dominance, Melvin seemed like a different type of man. Up in Nat's office, amongst the scents of lacquered pine and ocean mildew, he related the circumstances of his arrival. He'd come west with the intention of writing a book cataloguing his adventures. With his Columbia University education, he'd quickly obtained work in the Portland mayor's office as a factotum, a job that certainly hadn't yielded any book-worthy escapades. At the same time he'd discovered, through a series of terrifying albeit brief experiences, that the more adventurous Western settings, such that may have given him something to write about, were utterly beyond his skill set. He'd been stymied, close to conceding and returning home with nothing, when this opportunity came along. A prison, hewn of raw wood, tucked between the black forest and the thrashing deadly sea, stuffed with society's worst miscreants, furthest banished, most unfit for society…now that sounded like a book.

"Not, of course sir, that there's any chance I'd let that hobby in any way interfere with my discharging the duties I've been hired to perform. That's the thing, first and foremost. The job sounded like an interesting opportunity." He nervously gauged the warden's reaction.

Nat smiled, shaking his head. He loved the idea of being featured in a book. "By all means, I fully endorse the idea of a book. I hope you've come to the right place for it."

The young man took his leave, retiring to his quarters, a small cabin at the base of the mountain, half a mile up the main dirt road from the prison. Unpacking, he considered the parts of himself that he'd intentionally withheld during his brief interview with the warden. How, amongst the many facilities maintained by the state, he'd been quietly, softly but persistently, angling for a job at a prison. A death row prison. A death row prison as far outside the purview of its overseers as possible.

And then this place had popped into existence like yet another fish thrown down from God.

He hadn't come west to write a book. He'd come west to kill a man. Men. He'd been thinking about this his entire life. And here were a hundred of them, just waiting for him to do exactly that.

As Nat began to research the area, requesting materials from the Portland Library, talking with elderly homesteaders and Clatsop fishermen, an intriguing enigma developed surrounding the statue of the angel in the dunes overlooking the beach.

An article referenced in *The Oregonian,* originally appearing in *The New Hampshire Gazette,* on August 24th, 1782, related an elderly sailor's tale of a shipwreck on the far coast precipitated by the sighting of an overwhelmingly beautiful white woman bound to a stake and screaming. After tearing the ship's hull in a minefield of submerged rock, the survivors trudged heroically ashore, cutlasses and blunderbusses drawn, to find not a woman but there amongst the weedy dunes a marble statue of an angel, hands thrown back beside her hips with palms spread, large sad eyes with no pupils, large bare breasts with no nipples, sword in a scabbard on her hip, long hair flowing behind her, long rippling skirt, feet in sandals at the ends of long muscular legs, feathered wings fanned half-open. Between her feet, the brass plaque reading *animus summissu*s.

Clatsop legend described the Salt-Chuck Klootsh' variously weeping blood and spewing bile the first time the white man's ships approached shore, or possibly serving as a beacon to guide him. Several sources claimed her presence predated the tribe's existence. The predominant theory, repeated by whites and Clatsop alike, held that she had been brought by Spanish missionaries to stand sentry over a mission, but that the Spaniards had starved or been murdered by Indians or lost their minds before building anything.

There did not seem to be, however, as far as Nat could tell, any evidence to this theory beyond the fact that it made the most sense.

Every night Nat walked down through the dunes to the ocean. Standing there amidst the mist, the lapping swirling water, with the earth changing beneath his feet Nat looked at the rugged arches of the Twin Rocks and he took stock of his life.

During those years in Portland, after he'd finally caught his breath, had ceased hearing the thundering hooves of the military police or bounty hunters in every gust of wind, after he'd stopped jerking up out of sleep with a sense of the red-headed corpse lurking crooked in the corner of his small room, when he'd quit tasting tar and turpentine, Nat had finally begun, for the first time in his life, to enjoy the luxury of regretting something. And the thing he'd regretted was this:

Whenever Nat arrived to his ultimate destiny, he would almost certainly be arriving alone. There would be no one with whom to share his truth. No one, whispered the voice deep in the darker part of his mind, through which to perpetuate this truth…no next of kin. No possible way to square the ledger for his own cold loveless upbringing. No one to love.

On those dreary Sunday mornings in Portland he would walk from the boardinghouse on the waterfront to the row of small houses along Third Street, crossing downtown like a fugitive, sticking to the shadows, checking over his shoulders for co-workers. Nat wasn't ashamed to be visiting a prostitute; he simply didn't want to be forced into a conversation about visiting prostitutes. Outside these conjugal visits, Nat had no contact with women. There were no female prison guards, none lodging at the waterfront boardinghouse, and the only ladies he had ever spoken to while strolling the boardwalk were thieves, unincorporated prostitutes, or lunatics. Even if, inexplicably, an eligible young woman should somehow wander into town, she certainly would never venture anywhere near the trajectory of Nat's daily life for fear of Shanghai tunnels, tongs, and roving bands of drunken hooligans.

Despite the hopelessness of this situation, or perhaps because of it, Nat often fantasized about love. Or at least his conception of it. As a boy in the railyard, he'd often heard the other boys talking about fucking, how they'd done it standing in an alley with a girl from the textile factory or on a straw mattress in a shack with one of the young toothless bruised prostitutes who slunk amongst the workers' shacks like rats. And he'd seen it, pairs and trios and groups rutting in the secluded spaces of the shantytown. Nat had, at that young age, found it interesting though a bit unsettling, not unlike watching a fight. As he'd gotten older his understanding had broadened, and he'd been able to at least imagine the tenderness of it, the way this act might relate to the state of being with somebody in a more substantial way. He'd felt brief flickerings of these feelings, when one of the girls on Third Street had softly taken his hand, pulling him down onto the bed, or lain looking at him, for just an instant, afterwards.

Nat knew that he wasn't terribly handsome. That he looked, unfortunately, a good deal like where he'd come from, with his large-nosed thick-lipped long face, wearing his black hair longish with a thin moustache and goatee. At six feet two inches tall, with arms too long for his body and big hands, every part of him bespoke primitive criminal.

I look like a cagey ape who tasted blood and likes it.

But in truth, he hadn't liked it. He'd been weaned on blood and crime, born amongst it, and his soul had turned away nauseously. Instead of seeking more blood, he had scratched and fought for three thousand miles chasing the loftiest aspirations of his heart.

Nat took a deep breath of the ocean air, a man standing alone at the edge of the world.

Owning the edge of the world, but standing alone upon it.

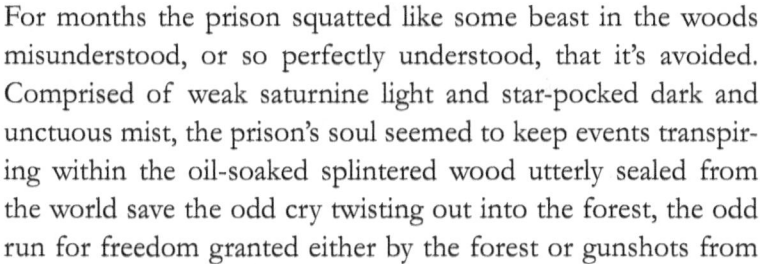

For months the prison squatted like some beast in the woods misunderstood, or so perfectly understood, that it's avoided. Comprised of weak saturnine light and star-pocked dark and unctuous mist, the prison's soul seemed to keep events transpiring within the oil-soaked splintered wood utterly sealed from the world save the odd cry twisting out into the forest, the odd run for freedom granted either by the forest or gunshots from behind. Then came a fat man on a donkey accompanied by a couple of lumberjacks. The jacks cleared away a stand of trees, built a couple of shacks, and left with their pay.

The man, Woody Love, tall and fat with a black beard in a bright red flannel shirt and green wool trousers, with a voice like a sea lion, nailed a sign to one of the shacks reading "GOODS" and the prison guards came flocking, supplementing their meager contracted fare with plugs of dried venison and smoked salmon, bags of sugar and coffee and hand-rolled cigarettes to wash down their rations of stale tobacco which had been heavily stepped on with hay and desiccated leaves. A fat red-cheeked woman and four fat children joined Woody. The lumberjacks returned to clear more forest. A huge log cabin replete with stone chimneys and wooden pillars appeared, surrounded by a half-dozen buildings labelled "BAR," "TACK AND STABLE," "FARMACY," "DOCTOR," "THEATRE," and "SCHOOL." Women and children arrived. Men dug outhouses and a distance up the mountain they dug wells. Every so often they dug up the remnants of some previous attempt at a similar settlement, fractured chunks of timber and faded signs, sometimes a bone, but if anyone acknowledged the implications, he did so silently.

Soon, men who were neither inmate nor guard nor proprietor arrived looking for work. A trio of sisters, the virginal daughters of a preacher from Mississippi, arrived and within a week were sleeping with men for money, leading to speculation that they had either undergone a sea change in response to their new scenery or had misrepresented their provenance. Either way, the nascent society had acquired a brothel.

A soldier came staggering out of the forest, presumably having deserted in Mexico, wandering the dirt streets shouting at the sky, scratching the flesh of his arms. One morning at dawn he grabbed a young woman on her way up the mountain to fill a bucket at a well whereupon the girl's brother, who had been splitting wood at the base of the path, cleaved the skull of the soldier. This incident inspired the populace, after quietly throwing the body into the ocean, to enlist the services of Kendric Sampson, a tough-looking old man who had putatively served as a sheriff in Arizona before coming to the coast to sell his homemade pine bough wine. Each citizen in the vicinity was required to drop a dime into the kitty every month to pay the lawman.

And so it went. Every so often people came out of the forest, either intentionally or as the conclusion to getting lost or run off somewhere else, while others left or died or disappeared. Ships and wagons and riders on horseback arrived with supplies for the various businesses and the prison. Babies were born. A chamber of commerce formed to organize the cutting of a road and laying of tracks skirting the coast, south, to Tillamook.

Nat took his coffee up to the ramparts of the prison and looking back towards the suddenly sparsely forested mountain realized that the prison had begat a town.

He had begat the prison, and the prison had begat a town.

From the moment his prisoners had filed past him on the dunes, Nat had recognized that the eyes of these men were not glass marbles, nor bubbles of tar. Those orbs held pain and anger, love, history, humanity. Regardless of the nature of their crimes, each of these prisoners was a man, a man who regretted his choices or didn't, who probably loved somebody, who entertained impossible dreams extending far beyond these tarred splintered walls. A man who laughed and experienced nostalgia. A man who was terribly afraid to die.

In Portland, Nat had developed the habit, during his slow graveyard shifts, of reading the prisoners' files, the stories of their lives, all concluding ineluctably with a crime. At first the reading had been cursory, simply educating himself about his clients, so to speak, but as time went on he'd delved deeper. Reading about a stevedore who late one night crept up on his boss as the old man sat poring over the books in an otherwise deserted office, slashing his throat with a knife, fleeing with the box of petty cash, seemingly insignificant details lodged and turned in Nat's mind like a kaleidoscope, generating the colorful life of a story. The murderer had come West four years earlier from Maine. Children ages three, two, and one. Wife Angelica age nineteen. The murder weapon had been lifted from a bar two blocks away.

Suddenly Nat was inside that tiny shitty apartment, wallpaper stained in brown rings with greasy cook smoke, three babies crying and the wife, the beauty he'd wooed with his muscular physique and bold dreams of a West Coast life, beginning to break down, to slump beneath the strain of their poverty, the absence of light on the horizon. He had to do something. He started small, sliding a chocolate orange into his pocket after breaking open the crate, a silk scarf, a tube of lipstick, baubles to bring home and make her smile. But he recognized these smiles as bittersweet, the girl half pleased with the gift, half acknowledging the discrepancy between the life she'd been promised and this. So he decided to deliver what he'd promised. It was shockingly easy, sliding a crate of rum from the loading dock every month or so to sell from the back of the bars downtown. Within a few years, he'd be able to get them out of that apartment. Or perhaps sooner would be better, he thought, each night coming home to the decaying countenance of his beautiful wife, his filthy children...

By the time he realized that it had gotten away from him, it was too late. The night of the shipping dock's annual inventory rolled around, the old man sedulously tracking down every spool of ribbon and stick of gum, and here he'd been knocking off a case of booze practically every day for the past month. So he sat in the White Eagle, drinking, waiting. Not only was he about to go to prison for the purloined rum, but in doing so would abandon his family, ironically, to the utter nadir of the very fate he'd been trying to resist. Within weeks, their former existence eating rice and sharing one mattress within the shitty apartment would sound like the life of Riley, compared to the brand of poverty awaiting his wife and children. She'd be forced into the houses up Third Street and the children would be dumped into the Catholic orphanage. Such was the picture flickering, looping in his head, when out of nowhere his one shot at redemption came to him like a flash in the darkness.

Reading the court-ordered attorney's declaration of "crime of passion" Nat shook his head. No, sir. Precisely the opposite. This man had calculated the odds, and had decided that the life of one miserable old man was an acceptable price to pay for even a forlorn hope of saving his doomed family. He'd simply gambled, not unreasonably, and lost.

Immersed in the files, Nat inhabited the decades of simmering resentment and loneliness that led the fratricide to murder the more talented younger brother. He killed his cheating wife and her lover, knowing full well that he was terminating his own life in the process, but willingly choosing this fate over a lifetime of shameful cuckolded torture. Hungry, sick, confused at why things had gone so poorly for him when so many others, who hadn't tried nearly as hard, nor behaved half as morally, owned more than they could possibly use, he crept across the dark street, pressing the bore of the pistol against the well-heeled gentleman's spine...

Sitting in the prison's administrative offices late at night, Nat would read these files immersed within the deeply human sound of four hundred sleeping men breathing peacefully. Each of these men, Nat understood, had been seeking his own ballgame at the bottom of his own hill, and not one of those dreams had ever involved ending up in a cage at the water's misty edge awaiting the hangman. Rethrow a single die, and any one of their stories could just as easily have been his own. Thus he strove to make their final days as edifying as possible. Nat ordered the boiler room converted into a library, purchasing damaged discards from the Portland Public Library. He ordered a large flat area on the sandy mesa overlooking the beach fenced off as a recreation yard, stocked with boxing gloves, equipment for racket sports, and weights.

Behind Nat's back the guards teased him, calling him Big Ugly Mama, and The Babysitter. A couple of the guards, after observing Nat coaxing a gorilla-sized uxoricide to read a children's book, began calling him Jesus. And perhaps that wasn't too far off. But that was not the only Bible story young Nat had internalized, hunched over his desk beneath the watchful glares of the nuns of Saint Michael's. He'd also memorized the flood, and the Angel of Death.

He'd also reread, again and again, the parts about the lions.

One night, strolling the silent halls, Nat happened upon a severely beaten prisoner in a locked cell.

He gathered the guards in the mess hall. "However things may have been carried out in your previous facility, that isn't what we're doing here. As far as your job is concerned, you might as well be working in a hospital—" He paused to wilt a dozen smirks. "No different at all. It's none of your business why a man's in here, or for how long, or in what state he's going to leave. While he's here, you take him to his meals, to his showers and his exercise, and you keep him safe. Not a goddamn whit more or less. Do you understand?" Each head nodded. As they filed past Nat made mental note of the half-dozen men with split scabbed knuckles.

Nat continued taking his walks. He knew what he knew. The window for self-delusion had passed. One night he inadvertently surprised a pack of guards in the mail room divvying up the valuables and throwing away the drawings, the mementos, the professions of love and devotion, of abandonment, of deaths and births and reality. "Get out," Nat said softly, drawing their attention. As they attempted to leave the mail room, he blocked the doorway. "And do not misunderstand me. Leave your pistols and your uniforms with Arthur at the intake lockers. You will not be returning. You can stay in the barracks tonight, but I'll expect that tomorrow morning when I come through, I won't see you." The guards looked amongst themselves, then to Nat's hand resting white-knuckled on the butt of the pistol in his belt.

Three days later, an older guard who'd followed Nat from Portland came to tell him, "Those six boys you ran out of here the other night? They're coming back to get you, supposed to be tomorrow night. Normally I'd think it was just so much wind working its way out of those assholes, but Woody says they've been into his store six seven trips buying whiskey and ammo, talking to anybody who'll listen and a good deal of people who won't about what all they intend to do to get back at you."

Nat thought about this. "Where are they?"

"Just north of Lake Liddle, right at the base of the hill." The old man crossed his arms, pursing his lips disdainfully. "There's a camp out there."

"Just them?"

"Other people *live* there, but as far as coming in here to get you…yes, I think just those six."

"Who else lives out there?"

"Dross. Men who came out here looking for industry and didn't find it. Women who can't get taken up by the brothel."

After a moment, his eyes briefly travelling elsewhere, Nat stood. "Okay, then."

Nat dropped from the horse, waving at the three guards who'd accompanied him to stay back amongst the trees as he himself went into the clearing. From the saddle, he unstrapped a shotgun and a metal can of kerosene.

He wrinkled his nose at the stench of it, dodging garbage and piles of shit between the plywood lean-tos and makeshift tents. A woman ducking out from a rudimentary shack, young but toothless, face like a topographic map, clad in just a torn skirt, dirt and ash smeared across her face and her large hanging breasts, saw him first. Nat put his finger to his lips and she nodded calmly. He pointed towards the trees, and she disappeared from the clearing. Despite the cacophony of slurred shouting, crying children, barking dogs, he clearly heard the voices of the former guards. Crossing the wretched encampment, he found them seated around a fire. Each wore a pistol on his belt, and a pair of long Enfield rifles leaned against a tree. Their conversation, drunk and rollicking, stopped as Nat stepped amongst them. In their rheumy, bloodshot eyes Nat saw contempt and impulsiveness. *Damn shame,* he thought.

"You boys didn't get far enough away. I'm still hearing about you. And now, I'm still compelled to spend part of my day looking after you. We're going to have you gather up your things, and get out of here, now, for good." Everyone remained motionless.

"Now."

The men stood. Nat saw the bad decision taking shape behind the slippery eyes. "Don't do it Gail. Don't—"

Gail Bradford, a mountain of a man with an underbite that rendered his speech snuffling and nearly unintelligible, reached for the pistol in his belt. Out of all of them, Gail was the least likely to successfully execute such a maneuver, with his huge hands and big slow body, and Nat fired the shotgun from his hip, ripping Gail's shin into bone fragments and blood, so that the big man pitched into the dust caterwauling while his boot remained standing.

One of the others threw up, and a dead calm descended upon the scene. Nat, as if addressing a squad of athletes slow coming out of a water break, raised his brows and said, "You better get that thigh tied off, and start working out a way to get him into Tillamook, or he's not going to make it."

Turning his back on the men, Nat uncapped the can of kerosene. Walking slowly back through the encampment, he splashed the clear liquid over the filthy cloth and stained wood of the makeshift dwellings, crouching to check the rancid tents for stragglers. He struck and flipped a large wooden match, casting the clearing into streaking blue flame.

The newly displaced, gathered near the horses, watched him coming forth, a dark figure against the flame, throwing the metal can behind him. When a young man in a filthy white shirt, sturdy but sad-eyed, called plaintively, "That's all we had," Nat stopped, looking him up and down.

"Well, I'm guessing now you'll do better."

❦

A week after Nat turned the indigent encampment into scorched earth, he was scheduled to preside over his first execution. He could still taste the kerosene. It reminded him of turpentine.

While Nat had not exerted any discretion over who would die first, simply going down the list of those who'd occupied death row the longest while exhausting their appeals, he secretly felt as if he couldn't have asked for a more perfect situation.

Li Jun appeared to be about sixty, though he himself had lost track years ago, small and stoop-shouldered, with a broad liver-spotted face and dark eyes sunk deep into pockets of crinkled flesh. He never wore the prison garb, opting instead for a rust-colored cotton t-shirt and baggy denim jeans, a violation of the rules that Nat had never seen any reason to address.

Nat's interest in Li Jun had developed for a number of reasons. The old man had been the first patron for Nat's boiler room library, selecting *Moby Dick* and *Little Women,* Augustine's *Confessions,* Freud's *The Interpretation of Dreams.* He'd quickly established himself as the prison yard table tennis champion, working his way through all comers first right-handed, then left. Nat had never once seen the small man sitting idly, as he always seemed to be praying or writing in his cell, jogging laps around the yard, performing calisthenics.

After fleeing poverty and conscription in China, Li Jun had worked as a gardener and a house painter in Portland, until he'd discovered his far more lucrative calling as a crimp, crouching in the subterranean dark of the Shanghai tunnels beneath the city, waiting for the deadfall above him to bang open dropping some unsuspecting body tumbling down onto the brick at his feet. Li Jun, compact and powerful, would leap upon the stunned victim, lash their hands and feet, and knock them unconscious with a sap, dragging the body through reticular miles of tunnel from basement to basement to the waterfront, where the men were sold to the departing whaling ships and the women were sold to the Southern-bound white slavers.

And it was not even these ruined lives, hundreds if not thousands by Li Jun's own estimation, for which he was being punished, but the one that he had taken in the commission of a botched robbery aboveground. The dead man, a developer from Boston brought west to carve a respectable neighborhood into the lush hills overlooking downtown, had been out wandering. After a few beers in Hobo's, he'd been walking back to the Hotel Portland when Li Jun, just up from the tunnels after a frustrating and demoralizing night lurking amongst the smell of piss and rat shit without a single customer, on something of a whim, perhaps nostalgically recalling the habits of his fiery youth, crossed the street to the staggering, well-heeled, obviously misplaced man, sliding the Hudiedao from beneath his yellow silk jacket, saying, rather politely, "Give me that watch, and your shoes, and all the money in your wallet." Hardly had the request left Li Jun's mouth than his head rocked back, blinded by the pain of a broken nose.

I have grossly misjudged, he thought, pinned by the nattily dressed man to a brick wall, one large hand squeezing his throat while a fist battered his head. Falling quickly into unconsciousness, Li Jun had been left with no choice but to flick the butterfly sword. The stranger's throat popped in a burst of blood, pattering to the ground, and he fell back. Li Jun staggered three steps before joining him, sinking into the blackness, where he would remain until the police happened by to collect him later in the evening.

Therefore Li Jun represented, in Nat's estimation, the absolutely ideal candidate for execution because not only had he been taking full advantage of the prison's self-improvement program, he also unequivocally deserved to die.

After several increasingly pleasant conversations regarding literature, Nat broached the topic of Li Jun's impending execution. Sitting on a picnic table in the yard smoking, Li Jun, enjoying the shadow of a smirk, said, "In my opinion, I've been wrongfully imprisoned. This is not justice."

"Are you joking? What you've done, this is the absolute *definition* of unlawful murder. This is a lesson in why we have laws and consequences. If there's ever been, anywhere, any such thing as justice, this is *exactly* it."

"How so?"

"That man, a father of four, a productive member of his community, had done nothing to deserve his death. This wasn't even a particularly rough neighborhood, where we might have accused him of stupidity. He was simply living. You fell upon him with ill intentions, which, let us admit, you were in no way compelled to exert. You're not a starving child. There were other options available to you that did not involve crossing that street."

Li Jun thought about this. "True," he said. "Possibly true, but even so…what about the circumstances that had led me into this?"

"And what do you mean by that?"

"Starvation. Slavery. Forcible conscription into the Emperor's army." Li Jun looked at him very directly. "I am under the impression that you understand the permanent effect of such things in a man's youth."

Nat pursed his lips, holding up a finger, struggling to reestablish his moral footing as the solidity of his position suddenly shifted. Would he, in order to escape the railyard, have slashed that Boston developer's throat? The answer came quickly. Every day. With a rusty blade. Every day a different innocent man for the rest of his life. But thinking further, the comparison was not so apt as it had initially seemed, and he said, "But you didn't have to kill that man to avoid starving. If he'd been somehow blocking your ability to get on that boat forty years ago, that would be one thing. But this is different. Nothing irresistibly compelled you to cross the street *that* night."

Li Jun tilted his mouth, nodding, considering. "But perhaps I've been disposed to behave certain ways by my past. Whereas another man...I certainly never asked to be born into such circumstances."

Nat smiled. "I think you've had sufficient time to adjust."

Li Jun shrugged, brows raised. He seemed to have enjoyed their conversation. And so Nat brought it up again a few days later, visiting the condemned man in his cell. Li Jun, after brewing a tin can full of green tea on a small propane burner he had somehow acquired, proposed that even if one conceded that the punishment was warranted, it ultimately served no function. "The man will not be resurrected. No father will suddenly be returned to his children, no husband to his wife."

"True, but now notice has been served to the next thief, who might think twice. A life could be saved specifically through your example."

Li Jun huffed dismissively, waving a hand. "Nobody even knows I'm gone."

"I don't know about that. People talk." The men sat in silence. After awhile, Nat said "Here's the answer, I would think.

There's a system of laws. Neither you nor I designed them, but they exist, they're there. You were aware it was illegal to cut somebody's throat, yes?"

He spread his palms in acknowledgement.

"So then, you knowingly acted in a way that doesn't work within our system. At the end of the day, it doesn't matter whether or not we as individuals agree with the rules. No man gets to decide what's there, dictating his life. No man gets to entirely write out his own fate. He can tinker, but not entirely control it. What if that policeman had bumped into a friend a quarter mile down the road, and never wandered onto the scene? What if you had drowned in the Pacific Ocean forty years ago? All of us operate within systems that were formed without our input. The best you can do is recognize that, and work within it."

Li Jun thought deeply, the muscles in his flat face pulling at one another. He liked this. He smiled. "Due to my particular circumstances, I can't agree this is a good thing. But I think your description is accurate. I think perhaps you're right."

Through the small slot in the wall they watched the burning orb of the sun hit the water, exploding into a diffuse wash of light. They drank their tea. As the ocean and sky bled into one another, three objects stood black against the monochromatic flatness; the loops of the Twin Rocks, the winged angel jutting crooked from the cluster of igneous stone, and the child's block of the Tall House. Nat looked at the simplistic structure where, within the month, this man, with whom he was sitting, talking, and laughing, would die. In designing the building within which to house the gallows, Nat had been seeking the most generic, nondescript shape imaginable. There was nothing ominous or intimidating about the drab rectangle he'd constructed, a pair of shipping containers purchased from a defunct whaling outfit in

Garibaldi, turned on end and bolted together. No natural association with gallows or death. The prisoners were fated to die there; they didn't need some specter of death looming every time they stepped outside or looked through the window. But now, looking at the anonymous rectangle, Nat wondered if perhaps he'd made a mistake...

Maybe this was worse. Worse than an open gallows. Worse than some squatting ghoul of jagged steel and angular dark wood. In his attempt to avoid creating a symbol of death, he'd created a blank slate for each man to project his own version of the horrible and haunting fate that awaited. The imagination ran wild...

Which would I rather pass on a deserted street; a man snarling, or a man whose features have been wiped away in a smooth sweep of flesh?

If the gallows had been clearly, openly, admittedly gallows, declaring loudly "I am gallows. I am here to break your neck," the inmates might have become acclimated. They would have been constantly aware, at least, where their impending deaths awaited. But as it was, Nat had created an ominously unpleasant stranger, forever reappearing a step behind, making the men wonder for a split second "What is..." before recalling with a dark chill.

He cleared his throat. "Have you thought about your last words?"

"Last words...A man's final statement. Final definition of the man on this earth."

"I'm hard pressed to think of anything with greater gravity and dignity."

"A few things come to mind. I'll put some thought into it."

That evening, after they had finished their tea, Nat left the cell infused with an overwhelming sense of righteousness. In

Li Jun, here was a man who had improved himself greatly during his final months, whose execution would inarguably serve justice, and who appeared to have come to some type of philosophical peace with his impending death. This was exactly what Nat had come here, been sent here, to do.

He was to be executed an hour before dawn, while the rest of the prison slept.

Nat dressed, supplementing his usual workday attire of dark-toned suit and tie with a matching derby. It wasn't every day that one played steward to a soul's exodus from this world. Walking through the quiet halls, Nat absorbed the hissing lanterns, steady shushing of the ocean, the prisoners snoring, muttering, no doubt dreaming dreams exactly the same as those on the outside. Soft sounds, seeming to indicate that even here, in this place, ultimately things were going to be okay.

Lost in the rhythm of his steady stride he ruminated upon Li Jun's choice of last meal; green tea, brown rice, seaweed and a perch culled from the very sea beyond his window. It was imperative, Li Jun had written in his request, that the fish be fresh caught, from the beach he looked upon every day. Nat had honored this request, outfitting a trio of guards with rods, paying them an overtime shift to fish. Nat was certain that he would remember the condemned man's menu forever. The simplicity and earnestness of it. A final taste of the world's raw materials.

Nat turned the corner to the back hall, reserved for the calmest, usually oldest, prisoners, to guttural shouting, clattering metal, so obscenely out of place in the peaceful shadow. He quickened his pace. Already prisoners up and down the hall were pressing their faces against the metal bars, joining in the

cacophony. Coming to Li Jun's cell, he found his frequent inter-
locutor mysteriously naked, restrained by a pair of guards. The
old man was gnawing a washrag, grunting and huffing like an
animal, eyes rolling, tears streaking his cheeks. His metal dining
tray lay upended on the floor, the meal he had requested spattered across the oiled wood.

Upon seeing Nat he amplified his thrashing efforts, screaming a muffled appeal to the warden, kicking his feet, sobbing. He
began to gag on the washrag. His cheeks swelled with vomit, and
he began to urinate, his desiccated penis spurting streaks across
the floor.

"Get him dressed and bring him out to the Tall House," Nat
said, turning from the cell.

Li Jun crossed the yard supported by the guards, toes dragging
through the sand, glassy-eyed, face bruised and swollen.

Nat was aware of the other prisoners, awoken by the com-
motion, observing this degrading spectacle from their small
glassless windows. As Li Jun entered the Tall House, facing the
noose dangling from a former ship's mast, he exerted one final
surge, thrashing and spitting, biting through his tongue. A guard
took a fistful of the old man's hair, yanking his face down to
keep the blood from going airborne. Another elbowed him in
the side of the head, stilling his thrashing. They led Li Jun, docile
and stumbling, up the thirteen steps to the platform.

The wright had done a masterful job constructing the gallows. Sometimes in the course of his evening strolls Nat had
come to look upon it introspectively like a statue or a garden.
Now, however, seeing the thing in use, Nat's lips drew back from
his teeth and he stifled an urge to call out *Wait, now, hold on...* The

dark blue hood passed over Li Jun's head, cinched with a black cord. One guard positioned him in the center of the platform and, without further ceremony, another pulled the lever releasing the trapdoor. He was light enough his neck did not break. For several minutes kicking, hissing like a cat, his eyes bulged against the tight hood as circles of dark blood appeared over his nostrils and mouth. His customary cotton trousers darkened with urine, and his bowels let go loudly. An erection rose stiffly against the loose denim trousers, blood spreading at the tip.

As Li Jun was finally forced into his everlasting peace, Nat turned stiffly, exiting the Tall House, walking down to the ocean. *So this, despite everything, is the man Li Jun, the most eligible of condemned men, chose to present to the world as he left.*

Looking over the water, gray and flat against the dawn, Nat realized he'd forgotten to inquire after any last words.

Nat returned to his room and slept. When he awoke to the sky above the sea already shot with stars, the image of Li Jun's (*his friend* Li Jun's? Very nearly…) last moment of corporeal existence refused to leave his mind.

Nor would it fade in the days to come. Nat found himself searching the eyes of every man he passed, prisoner and guard alike, for accusation; *how do they feel about what I have done, what I will continue to do?* Watching the men studying sedulously in the library or exercising in the yard, Nat could not help but envision those same minds fallen permanently into mush, all that freshly acquired knowledge wiped out, the body rendered a helpless, useless bag leaking refuse for the rest of endless eternity.

Ultimately, each of these stories could only end one way.

This, Nat suddenly realized, involuntarily picturing all the corpses he would produce here at the beach, *couldn't possibly be the purpose of my journey.*

Not that he had misheard the call. This impossibility would never cross his mind.

This simply wasn't the final destination.

CHAPTER SIX

*L*ord, thought Debra Elkin, smoothing the distaste from her face as she strode unannounced into Nat's office, *that is a generally good-looking man looking very, very bad.* She cleared her throat, laying her elegant hands upon his desk. "Nathanial, honey, we're gonna need you over in Tillamook Saturday morning after next."

Nat, peaked and sleepless, nodded his acquiescence without asking why.

<hr/>

While in any other part of the country, Ms. Elkin may have been accused of obtaining her post as first female mayor west of Kansas via "unconventional means," nobody around Tillamook thought of it that way.

Having come west as a teenage runaway, one of a contingent of prostitutes imported from Oklahoma to serve the gold rush, Debra Elkin, far from accepting her mediocre lot, had inadvertently discovered the key to the universe, establishing herself as a force of nature and a leader of men.

It had all begun on a drizzling Tuesday morning when her first client of the day, a short plump banker named Robert, entering in his customary attitude of deferential, bashful excitement, had suddenly lost his composure gawking.

"What happened to your face?" he asked.

It took her a moment to realize what he was talking about. "Oh," she said, raising fingers to the swelling beneath her eye. "Do you know Hank Blalock?"

Robert nodded.

"He came up in a pissy mood about something last night. I don't even remember what I said...but it must have been the wrong thing." She laughed.

Robert cleared his throat. "I..." He scratched his face, bit his lip. "I just remembered something. I'm so sorry, I'll..." He laid twenty dollars on the night stand. "...I'll come by later."

Debra shrugged. "Okay, hon."

Several hours later Debra was heading downstairs for a shower and some dinner when a coworker asked if she'd heard about Hank Blalock.

"No. What?"

"Well, he must finally of pissed off the wrong person. Couple hours ago he steps out behind Shorty's to take a piss, and when Shorty goes out back to grab another case of whiskey, there's old Hank, laying there in the mud with fifty stab holes in his chest." The girl smiled, poking her tongue through the space between her front teeth. "Looks like you got a regular space in your schedule to fill."

Debra chuffed through her nose. "Looks like it." In the shower, she thought about this. Hank Blalock had been a crew boss for Diamond Logging, and before that, some type of officer in the army. It was absolutely inconceivable that Robert could have overpowered him in the alley.

The next day when Robert arrived, entering even more tentatively than usual, she simply asked him straightaway "Robert, sweetie, did you kill that poor old Hank Blalock?"

He shook his head vigorously, cheeks jiggling. "No, no. I heard about what happened, but, as far as me…No, certainly…"

"Robert, honey, but did y'all have something to do with it?"

"No no, of course I, I…" The pudgy face fell into his hands. His voice came tortured, issuing from the bottom of a well. "Nobody can be allowed to treat you that way. I paid… somebody…I have people…" He raised his miserable sagging wet eyes to her. "I'll go to the police if you want me to."

She laughed. "Oh…no, sweetie, no."

Jesus Christ, she thought.

Debra immediately began testing the limits of her newfound power. If, lying in a post-coital embrace, she expressed a sudden craving for a steak dinner and a horn of whiskey, a new summer dress, tickets and coach fare to a show…somehow the imagined items would appear, regardless of whether the restaurants had already closed, the summer stock been shipped back, the ticket office sold out.

But Debra Elkin had not survived her brutal childhood, the harrowing trip out West, and five years in a brothel just to watch musicals and eat free steak. She was still considering how best to utilize her magical conjuring power, undecided, when the girl who kept the books ran away with a Haitian sailor. Debra approached the Madame. "I can do the books."

"No offense, sweetheart, but Charlotte had been serving in that capacity for fifteen years. I think I'm going to take the work out of house, now."

"I'll do it for free."

"Why?"

Debra thought about this. "I'm not sure." She wasn't being coy. She genuinely didn't know why she wanted to do it. But she had a feeling.

After watching her a moment, the Madame shrugged, pointing to a stack of ornate black leather folders with gold gilt lettering in a metal crate on the floor. "We can try it. You should know up front, though, hon, you won't be handling any of the actual money, just the receipts. Even Charlotte never had a dollar passing through her hands. And if you're asking for the job hoping to redirect some of the profits, now's your chance to shut your mouth and turn around...but I'm sure you know that things would go very hard for you, if you ever stole from me, right?"

"Oh, I know that."

"Okay, honey."

That very same evening, looking over the ledger by candlelight, Debra realized exactly what she intended to do.

⌒⌒

Dennis Rathdrum looked at her with his mouth open as if examining some mysterious creature found dead in the forest. "By the horn spoon, Missy, I'm going to do you the incomparable favor of pretending these last ten seconds never happened. And I strongly suggest you do the same." He rattled the ice cubes in his glass of whiskey.

Debra smiled. "Honey, I want to feel like you're listening to me very carefully, because I'd hate for you to make a decision you're going to regret."

He laughed with his large, friendly face, shook his big head. "Listen, Deb, I understand...you're just a kid, you don't know how the world works, and maybe you read about blackmail in one of your detective magazines...But this? What you've got, here? This isn't shit. You think the voting public of Tillamook is going to give two shits about the mayor dropping a couple of dollars in a whorehouse? That just shows I'm a man of the people. Or what? You think my wife is going to throw me out of the house? I *built* that fucking house. She'd be living out in the goddamn street if it wasn't for the money I bring home. And besides that, she's not exactly a jealous woman when it comes to yours truly." He laughed. "She's *grateful* I stop off here on my way home, instead of pestering her. *Jesus.*" He shook his head. "Missed it by a goddamn mile."

Debra smiled, patting his leg. "You are definitely on the right track, hon, as far as the voting public, and you dropping a couple of dollars. But that's not quite how I'm seeing this." Debra narrowed her eyes thoughtfully, leaning closer. "I'm sure you're right that people don't care a bit what you're doing on your time, with your money. But there's the rub. It's not your money, Dennis. It can't be. The numbers don't add up. You'd have to be the mayor of every city on the West Coast to earn the cash you spend in here."

"So now I guess the question becomes, do I think the voting public is going to give two shits about you dropping a couple fifty thousand of *their* dollars in a whorehouse? Do I think the dairy farmer whose kids are walking to school hungry and barefoot, the logger who cut off his hand felling trees to pay the rent, are going to care? Care that they're buying your whiskey and your girls while their own families are skinny and sick? What do *you* think? Because I think, of course I could be wrong, I guess we'll find out, but I think that depending on how the information is presented, that the answer is going to be yes. Big yes. Tar and feather, burn your house down yes."

A look crossed through the mayor's face, red and tight as a fallen tomato, turgid and about to split in the hot black dirt. He rose. "I'm going to walk down this hallway into Heidi's office, and she's going to throw you out of here. And I must say I wish you hadn't have fucked this up. I'm truly going to miss you."

Debra smiled sweetly. "Somebody will take me in, sweetheart. I'm very popular. And that ledger book I was talking about? It's waiting for me safely somewhere. So really, hon, you make a good point. I don't need..." she looked around her, "this place for anything I'm intending from here on out."

He set down his glass, opened his mouth, but nothing came. Leaning over the desk, Debra set the long lacquered red nail of an index finger on his lips. "Hold on, now. Just one more thing, hon. I just want to go ahead and get every little last bit of the air cleared while we're still sitting here, before whatever's going to happen starts to happen..."

"Let's say maybe you're thinking about sending somebody around to come and *see* me. Now sweetheart, if we want to get into a battle of loyalty with the men in this town, what is it that you can provide?"

Dennis Rathdrum blinked at her as if he'd been hit on the head with a hammer, all the charisma draining from his broad face and lodging in his throat.

"That isn't a rhetorical question, hon. If tonight you sent somebody over here to scare me, beat me up, make me give them that ledger book, why would they be doing that? What could you offer them?"

"Money..." He answered hesitantly, an oft-rebuked pupil.

"Okay now. Because here's the thing with money; I've got a lot of it. You *know* how much you leave on that dresser every evening. Well now there are a lot of hours in a day, a lot of days in a week, weeks in a year. I've been here for five years, and I've got nothing to spend it on. Anything you could send a man over with, Dennis, I'm pretty sure I could send him out of here with that much, plus some more. And I think we'll both agree, with everything else being equal, I'm capable of being a hell of a lot more persuasive to a man than you are…"

The tenseness snapped from Dennis Rathdrum's face like a popping balloon, and he smiled.

Before becoming mayor of Tillamook City he'd canvassed Texas making rain with aerial dynamite and before that he'd managed pugilists in Mexico City. He had not attained his position in life by grasping to the untenable, by fighting wars already lost or won. He knew when to get the fuck out of there. He was beat. He shrugged his concession. "Well then," he said, "I suppose it's up to you, what happens next."

She smiled, put her hand on his knee. "Good for you, hon. You're definitely making the right decision, stepping down as mayor to spend more time with your family. And it isn't like you're losing much, here. You can be my minister of shipping. Practically the same salary."

"You realize everybody's going to know you honey-fuggled your way into this."

"And what exactly are you thinking they're going to get out of knowing that, hon? At the end of the day, what's that going to keep you, or me, from doing?"

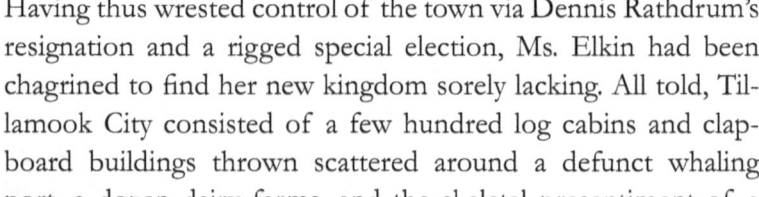

Having thus wrested control of the town via Dennis Rathdrum's resignation and a rigged special election, Ms. Elkin had been chagrined to find her new kingdom sorely lacking. All told, Tillamook City consisted of a few hundred log cabins and clapboard buildings thrown scattered around a defunct whaling port, a dozen dairy farms, and the skeletal presentiment of a downtown. It was a persimmon far beneath the huckleberries dotting the northern coast. "This will not do," she said to herself and to others.

She set to work. She taxed the whorehouse and the Madame threatened to kill her. She taxed maritime imports and the ship owners commissioned a militia to lay siege to town hall, at which point she disseminated an edict stating that any man arriving to defend the city would receive ten dollars, whereupon a multitudinous mob materialized from every direction, clearing the premises and littering the ground with torn clothing, shattered spectacles, dislodged false teeth, and a pair of dead bodies. She taxed the sales of alcohol and cattle, and with the full force of the city's suddenly overflowing coffers she commissioned the construction of a state-of-the-art pasteurization facility, so that the dairy farmers' somewhat hardscrabble existence suddenly exploded into sprawling expanses of grazing land hacked out of the forest, supporting estates so ornate they became tourist attractions. She constructed a boardwalk with telescopes, several large gazebos on the cliffs overlooking the ocean, an outdoor amphitheater for plays and concerts, the largest public school in the state of Oregon outside Portland, and still she ran a surplus.

Despite Debra's tireless efforts, Tillamook City's renaissance remained the coast's best kept secret. If the average person had heard of Tillamook at all, it was only in reference to the valley's periodic floods, during which hundreds of bovine corpses came rolling down from the foothills like grotesque terrestrial clouds, or the seemingly annual occurrence of some farmer going nuts in the winter and murdering his family with a field implement. So whenever an opportunity for positive press presented itself, Mayor Elkin dove in with both feet. As she went on to explain to Nat that he would complete the roster of The Tillamook

Community Leaders in their exhibition baseball game opposing The Mordecai Goldman Traveling Hebrew All-Stars, he turned from the window, abandoning his increasingly dark contemplation of the ocean, and smiled broadly.

The ballgame at the bottom of the hill.

Involuntarily, Nat coughed as if coughing tar and flexed his hands as if working splinters out of the bones. "I would love to participate," he said.

It had always looked easy enough.

During his vespertine walks along Portland's waterfront, Nat often stopped to buy a hotdog from the steam-emitting vending carts near the young men playing on the grass. You threw the ball, you hit the ball, you caught the ball. Though he did not possess a terribly firm grasp of the game's objective or how that objective might be realized, he felt that he, a man who had been technically unqualified for any of the many impressive things he had accomplished during his life, could cope. He'd always been physically precocious. The first tree he'd ever climbed was nearly three hundred feet tall. His first fight had been with two boys three years his elder and he'd knocked both unconscious with a railroad spike. Playing ball was not a daunting prospect.

During the days leading up to the game, in the moments right before dropping off to sleep and the moments right after waking Nat saw the white ball like a great ostrich egg floating in, and knew exactly how to hit it, and would hit it, sending the ball cutting off across the hot blue sky, not the pastel Rockaway sky but a searing East Coast blue. He saw, as the ball continued its ethereal trajectory, the opposing squad spiking their caps to the ground and his teammates hoisting him to their shoulders. Nat dreamed of this and his soul, which had been slowly leaking air since the execution, swelled up to resemble itself again.

Then came the morning of the game.

Nat disembarked, smoothing his custom-tailored pinstriped red on gray uniform, breathing the lemon-hued sun and tangy ocean mist. Today was the day. This diversion, he thought, wringing the creases from his new cap, could not have come at a better time. He'd been floundering, having lost the thread of his path, daunted at the prospect of backtracking to find it. To make matters worse, instead of charging in, he'd uncharacteristically frozen, holed up in his office, waiting for some further directive he knew might never arrive. Then this game came along like a geyser of icy sea water in the face. Tomorrow, he could resume figuring his future. But as for today...

Shit. Today he had a ballgame.

The Tillamook train station stood at the end of a dirt road a quarter mile from the diamond Debra had ordered cut into a fallow watermelon field, surrounded by bleachers made of timber from the former schoolhouse. Coming off the train Nat surveyed the crowd, and a thrill corkscrewed into his stomach. There had to be four hundred people sitting in the bleachers or picnicking in the grass. Seeing that The Community Leaders were already taking their warmups, Nat slid his hand into the cool leather of the brand-new mitt and trotted up the dirt road to join them. *Here we go.* A perfect day for baseball. As Nat drew close enough to survey the attire of his teammates, he stopped short. Some were clad in the accoutrements of their respective professions, such as Eldon Trole in his sawdust-peppered green wool pants and cork boots, or the barber Ed Hale in his puffy candy-striped sleeves and leather vest. Some men simply looked ragged, draped in torn layers and ratty items culled from the rag bin, while others dressed duncishly, like fat Woody Love squeezed into his college baseball uniform from a distant past, or Hammond Griffin digging his iron spikes into the dirt at third base, playing the ball off his chest and neck like a bulldog but exhibiting such hard-nosed fearlessness wrapped in his wife's Sunday flowered dress and wide-brimmed hat. Examining the custom-tailored freshly pressed uniform of which he'd been so proud, Nat suddenly felt as if he'd volunteered for some certain death military detail and been assigned instead to a regiment of clowns performing for the actual soldiers.

"Nat!" shouted Debra Elkin, waving from beneath a parasol, sitting on a bear skin rug in a private wooden box, attended by a pair of dusky, muscular young men who watched everyone but her suspiciously. "Get on out there!"

Feeling as if the pit of his stomach were a drain and his head were beginning to spin slowly, Nat smiled queasily and jogged out to the center of the diamond. He'd been studying. According to his reading, the best men in the business were Babe Ruth, Ty Cobb, and Bobby Veach; therefore he, like them, would naturally find his place in the outfield.

Young Eldon Trole, precocious crew boss of Coastal Aqua Logging, approached Nat, smiling quizzically. "So now it's pitching for you, Nat?"

"I will take centerfield."

Eldon laughed. "Okay...But that's the pitcher's mark there buddy, beneath your feet. Centerfield's out there."

Nat turned his flushing face, mumbling, "Yes, of course..." and jogged in the direction of the boy's pointing finger.

Infield warmups began, with Eldon, who Nat seemed
to recall from a conversation at the Fourth of July social had
played semi-pro ball in Texas, hitting grounders with a long slim
bat. From far out on the grass, Nat watched his teammates stab
clumsily for the ball, throwing it meaninglessly into the dirt. This
was not how it was supposed to look. As warmups continued,
things only got worse, incompetence giving way to outright par-
ody. Harry Davis fell headfirst into a watering trough obscured
by weeds in foul territory and the crowd roared. Aaron Row-
and dove into fresh cowshit and Matthew Stairs stepped into the
bloated corpse of a farm cat, both incidents requiring a lengthy
break while the victim changed clothing. At a particularly ignominious point the ball went mysteriously missing, a search party
combing the grass, until they'd been forced to concede its loss,
sending Nate Chase, owner of the Leather Emporium, running
grudgingly to his bag in the bleachers for another.

From his place far out in centerfield, far from the expectations of triumph and glory he'd been harboring all week, Nat was
ashamed to be participating in this idiotic farce, ashamed at the
secret fantasies that had grown so unabatedly hot late at night
sitting in his office. *And how will I contribute to this humiliating idi-
ocy,* he wondered, *when the turn comes to me?* Nat's lips went numb,
ears keening, palms sweating. His mind spun through potential
excuses: injury, emergency at the prison, fainting spell…

Just as Eldon pointed the head of the bat to Nat, tossing the
ball into the air, the piercing sound of a train whistle and clattering wheels enveloped the field. Everyone turned to watch the
big black engine pulling ornate first-class passenger cars, so that
nobody saw Nat drift beneath the soaring ball, raise his glove,
step his left foot solidly upon the toes of his right, and fall sideways to a knee as the ball struck him in the thigh.

The crowd whispered behind their hands, breathlessly, as the conductor dropped down, running to throw open the doors of the five cars. From each car emerged a boy or a man or an old man carrying one or more canvas bags, bag carriers who the onlookers immediately disregarded as nobody. Then, after a pregnant pause, after the smoke had cleared, out came Mordecai Goldman's Travelling Hebrew All-Stars. Nine men with long pointed black beards to their belts, clad in pristine vertically striped red and gray uniforms with gray wool caps, strode from the train and swarmed over the field like an organism sending forth pseudopods in a perfectly synchronized infestation, pushing the Community Leaders into the periphery.

One man, older and heavier than the rest, bearing the sun-cracked face and faded eyes of a farmer, stepped to home plate. Facing his comrades, he tossed an ivory white ball into the air, striking it with a bat one-handed and driving a vicious one-hopper to the third baseman, who plucked it clean and in a fluid skip unleashed a bullet to the first baseman, who snapped the wicked rocket from the air, flipping the ball from his glove back towards the fat man, who rifled a line drive at the shortstop, the balletic whipcracking round continuing. Women in the crowd covered their hearts and shook their heads at the spectacle. Men slid their fingers into their mouths and whistled. Children pointed and shook one another by the shoulders. With growing ire Nat observed his teammates foolishly cheering the enemy's antics, shouting and stamping as if participating in a hoedown. When the warm-up concluded, the elder burly man relinquished the fungo bat and, grabbing a teammate, trotted down the left field line to loosen his pitching arm.

There was something, Nat thought vaguely, disconcerting about the lazy fluidity of the rotund man's movements. Whereas his teammates, lithe cervine fresh-faced boys, launched the ball with every ounce of their athletic bodies, an incredible spectacle of complete effort and utter commitment, this man scarcely exerted himself for the same result; he was a master craftsman slowing down the lesson for a dimwitted pupil. If the boys were playing like demons, then he was the devil, capable of destroying the world with a pinch of his fingers.

A portentous wind shifted inside of Nat. He smelled the bottom of the ocean. He heard the voice of his mother from the distance, repeating one flat indecipherable syllable over and over with the possessed insistence of a seizure.

Eldon came sidling alongside, shattering Nat's reverie. "You know that's Mordecai Goldman?"

"And what's this to me?" The question felt petulant leaving Nat's puckered lips.

"I can't claim to know what it is, or is not, to you Nat, but to them," he nodded at the opposition, "the insignia flying outside their private train cars reads 'The Mordecai Goldman's Traveling Hebrew All-Stars.'"

"And he's the proprietor?" Into the corner of Nat's eye, pitch after pitch went rifling like gunshots.

"He probably is. But more importantly, he's the Mordecai Goldman who pitched ten seasons for the Pittsburgh Pirates." Watching Nat for recognition, receiving none, the boy continued happily. "In the National League. That man made his living for a decade as a professional baseball player."

Nat shrugged. "Appears to have let himself go to seed."

"Maybe...Although it doesn't seem to be hampering him much. The corn looks about the same."

Side by side they watched Goldman vary the path of the ball from rising blur to corkscrew to floating bubble. The children shrieked with delight as he shook his large rump like a playful squirrel, crossing his eyes, cocking his cap, uncorking a pitch sailing twenty feet above the catcher's head, into the bleachers…

And then the disaster.

Hundreds of eyes swelled with horror and throats constricted as Goldman's errant pitch tore a paper cup of beer from Ikey Xavier's gargantuan hand, spraying suds across the giant lap of Ike's huge ugly wife. As Ikey rose, the entire town ceased to breathe. Every man in attendance had at one time or another witnessed Ike breaking a jaw or tossing a stripped spruce pole one-handed, and anyone who hadn't personally been in The Green Owl the night Ike had popped that mouthy New Englander's arm right out of the socket had at least heard the legend.

One cyclopean cork boot descended, shaking the bleachers and the ground beneath.

And Mordecai Goldman, in direct opposition to anything that had ever happened anywhere in the history of the world, smiled, cupping his hands to his mouth, shouting good-naturedly, "You shan't have one too many barley pops today, Tubby, I'll see to that! This is no husking bee!"

All the oxygen suddenly leaked from the universe. Men reached for their pistols, but went no further. Debra Elkin, foreseeing a bloody premature end to her special event, dispatched her eunuchs, but too late. Ike would rip off his arms, tear his jaw from his face, crush his skull like a music box. The giant clattered down off the bleachers, hands clawed, lips drawn back like a gargoyle…

But right at the verge of the kill he inexplicably stopped, titling his head, scenting the air like an animal, and did the one thing that no one could possibly have predicted.

Ike smiled, too.

He laughed and pointed at his red-faced wife. He re-enacted the incident, pouring an imaginary cup of beer on her soiled lap, spinning around in mock confusion and outrage. Into the ensuing atmosphere of happiness and relief, the umpire, shipped in from Portland on the Morning Star, threw his hand up into the humid air speared through with brash gaseous silver sun, shouting "Play ball!" The crowd roared. Every bird in the world exploded from the pine trees like tumbling cacophonous angels. And so it came to be that all through the game and for years beyond, everyone would tell the legendary story of how Goldman's unmitigated jolliness, his infectious laugh and naive assumption of universal good humor had extinguished the cruel giant Ike's tendency to rampage.

But Nat had seen something else as well.

Though indeed Goldman had laughed like a clown, holding his flabby sides, his eyes had concurrently communicated a much different message: a message that Nat, Nat the killer, Nat who spent his workaday life amongst killers, had read very clearly. And it had struck his blood cold.

As Goldman laughed, those jolly eyes had swung completely free of his mouth's pleasant chuckling curve into an entirely different hemisphere, a hemisphere of broken bones and sorrow. *I will do you this one favor,* Goldman's suddenly stone hard eyes had said to the pig eyes of the faux-murderous oaf tramping down the grandstand. *The favor, my friend, of this warning: at the end of this path you are about to pursue lies great suffering. Everything you have done unto others is about to be returned upon you a thousandfold.* And Ike, reading those eyes, turned around. He'd recognized the escape hatch of good humor and pounced upon it, forcing the laughter from his fat trembling lips. In the aftermath of the narrowly averted tragedy, everyone felt as if they had just been granted their own personal first day of spring, an extra year of youth.

Goddamn, it was time to play ball.

Stromwell, the accountant for Holding's Mines, squinted at the line-up card. "Hamelin," he said, "you're batting leadoff." To Nat's blank stare he added "That means first."

Someone stuffed a bat into his hand and with a rain of pats upon the back amidst raucous shouting Nat found himself propelled towards home plate. He felt the cool, smooth lacquered wood, and for reasons he could not understand in that hectic moment it threw him into a panic. As he aimed one foot before the other in a daze, with numb cheeks and dead feet, feverishly wishing for the sky to open in a deluge, the flood bell to clang, a contingent of enemy soldiers to storm the beach, it did occur to him that this must be how the inmates felt approaching the Tall House. He stepped into the batter's box, hoisting the wood upon his shoulder. He'd constructed a stance, practicing in front of the mirror in his office, emulating photographs of Zach Wheat and Tris Speaker, and despite the clattering disaster of his heart he retained the wherewithal to arrange his body parts into the correct order. After positioning himself Nat waited, watching the pitcher and the ball in the pitcher's hand with rapt dread. He began to nervously suspect that too much time had passed.

Goldman's ruddy, rubicund visage smirked. "Is that how you'd like to stand?"

"Throw the goddamn ball."

Goldman covered his heart in mock horror, then smiled again, kind and avuncular. "Here," he said, "I will demonstrate." He moved to the third baseman, sliding up behind him, resting his head on the younger man's shoulders while gripping his wrists, manipulating him through a slow delicate swing as if assisting a pretty lady. Retaking the mound, Goldman rocked back into his smooth flowing windup and pitched...

With the hissing of a serpent's tongue, the spitting of angry fire, the buzzing of a poisonous swarm, the ball came ripping onward (although this Nat could only confirm from the complementary facts of the white sphere rolling off the pitcher's fingers and the seemingly simultaneous explosive crack of the catcher's mitt). This, Nat realized in that instant, coughing as the dust rose from the catcher's pulverized glove, could never be. *If I should live to be a million years old, I could never do* this.

Before Nat could successfully smooth away the shock twisting his face the big pitcher smiled broadly. "Sorry sport," he said, projecting his voice into the stands, "always seem to let that first one slip. Old habits. I forget we're not exactly kicking up the dirt of the Polo Grounds, now are we? Ha ha ha. Here, Buck, let me reign it in for you." Nat grimaced the same sick-faced defiance with which he had approached the stacks of formaldehyde-soaked railroad ties as a six-year-old. "Give me what you have. I'll do the same."

Goldman's beaming smile broadened, consuming his face. He nodded. "Oh yes. That's the right flavor of ghost. Now we're getting after it, Bucky." He leaned back and gingerly tossed. This time the ball drifted softly forth, and Nat locked it into his sights, gliding forward, guiding the barrel of the bat to meet the slowly rotating sphere...

Lunging, Nat observed the puff of dust where the ball had inexplicably fallen as if dropped off a table, snatched on the hop by the catcher, who popped up and threw back to Goldman. The pitcher shook his head smiling as if Nat were a dull child who had inadvertently uttered something endearing. "Stuck on a hangnail," said Goldman, ogling an extended finger as the crowd howled. Nat felt his face turgid with blood and his teeth creaking as they clenched.

"Sir," said the pitcher, holding up a placating palm, projecting his voice to the rafters, "sir, I give you my word, upon my honor and my virtue" (a stage-whispered aside, glove pressed alongside his mouth, "though ladies, please do not trouble yourselves asking around too strenuously regarding the strength or consistency of the aforementioned virtue..." to which the aforementioned ladies blushed and giggled) "that you will successfully strike the next pitch. All I require is that you hazard to swing that pike perched so handsomely upon your shoulder."

Nat, realizing he was far too deep to avoid further disaster, went ahead and sneered.

Goldman put his fingers to his bottom lip, gasping in mock offense, smiling with his great shark's teeth, and threw. Nat swung viciously...

A hair's breadth from striking the barrel squarely and rocketing skyward, an exact replication of Nat's daily fantasy, the ball jumped in onto the handle detonating the bat into fluttering shards. A dull dead shockwave plowed up Nat's forearms rattling his teeth. The ball dribbled onto the grass, a pathetic aftershock of the spectacular explosion, where Goldman delicately plucked it up like a gentle white blossom, easing it underhand to the big snickering first baseman. Bowing to the crowd, the pitcher boomed "And you will observe, I am once again a man of my word!"

As Nat made his way back to the bench, every thread of his body and soul vibrating with impotence, the first baseman, built like a strongman on a beach, stepped into his path, smiling. "The game...it's a gag, Bucky, a lark. Imbibe. Frolic. Stop kicking. The Phillies shan't be out ascouting. You've drawn the man's ire because you're taking yourself too seriously. You can only come out at the little end of the horn."

"Get the hell away from me."

After Woody Love struck out on three soft imminently hittable pitches, swinging one-handed so as not to allow his tankard to break contact with his lips, Blayne Milford the stone mason, who had played pro ball in Louisiana, flew out to deepest left field, prompting Goldman to clap his approval, shouting "And each to his abilities! I salute the heavy-handed hitter, and the obese drunkard!" He dropped a bow to each of them.

The Community Leaders straggled onto the field. From his position in center, Nat watched the Hebrew All-Stars' lead-off man beat out a bunt. Then a walk to Goldman, after a protracted battle of foul balls and a knockdown pitch that sent the big man sprawling into the dust, springing up to tip his cap at Eldon Trole crying "And yes! Precisely what the situation warranted!" The next man grounded to Pop Valentine the tall skinny postmaster, who picked the ball clean but spoiled the play by inexplicably throwing to Blayne Milford at home, the only base to which no runner approached. Blayne, understandably nonplussed, allowed the ball to sail over his shoulder, skittering into the arid rows of the fallow melon field. In giving chase, Kal Benson the steel-welding shortstop arrived at precisely the same moment as Milford, the two clacking skulls as they simultaneously bent to grab the ball, knocking each other into the dirt. By the time Eldon, realizing the carnage, broke from the pitcher's mark, all three All-Stars had scored.

All of this Nat watched helplessly, a stooge by implication. Scarcely had the clownish pandemonium subsided, the crowd still shaking their heads chuckling, when the next hitter lofted a high infield pop fly that Woody Love tried to catch in his tankard of beer, the ball clanking off the rim, skipping under the bleachers for a house-rules double. The crowd's delighted laughter trembled in the bright early spring air like drifting dew.

Looking back, if only Nat could have anticipated the outburst, felt it welling up, he could have bitten his tongue, swallowed his pride, done something, *anything*, to avoid what happened next. The problem, he would realize later, reliving the incident in his mind, was that he had never in his life before that moment experienced shame. Pain, yes, and fear…but this was different. He couldn't fight, he couldn't run. Nat felt the words flowing from his mouth, but was somehow powerless to stop them.

"God*damn* it!" he shouted. "What the hell are you doing? Why are you out here? At least *try* to do your job! That, or get your slovenly load off the goddamn field, and make way for someone who will!"

Silence. Then a horsey guffaw from Goldman.

In the aftermath, Nat stood twice as stiff and shocked as any member of the crowd. Debra Elkins rose from her padded private box in the bleachers to frown at him. Mothers covered the ears of their children. Woody flushed red and his multitudinous offspring trembled at the verge of tears and the Community Leaders shook their heads in censure. "I…apologize, I simply…" Nat cleared his throat, pounded the leather of his mitt. "Let's get some outs fellows…"

Hands on his knees, crouching, through the haze of shame, through the enervating aftermath of the violent outburst and shock, Nat knew the universe well enough to foresee with perfect clarity the thing that would happen, the only thing that could possibly happen, next.

With the next pitch, the ball rose from the hitter, arcing out towards him, seeking him out, and he lifted the glove as the ball descended growing larger. Just as it dropped to gently slip into his mitt, someone threw a fistful of stars, sharp and combustible, into his eyes. Nat found himself sitting on the grass, involuntarily shouting with pain, blind. The hitter circled the bases and the crowd leapt into a laughing, bouncing riot. The ball, he would later learn, a thousand times over, had hit him in the eye and bounced over the fence for a homerun.

The All-Stars trooped back to their positions though no outs had been recorded, conceding their turn like the grown-ups in the kids' game. An atmosphere of hilarity pervaded. Everyone clapped Nat on the back and jostled his cap. He had been redeemed by his outrageous boner.

The remainder of the afternoon maintained the established theme. By the time Nat's turn at bat came up again, his eye had swollen black and shut. After delivering two quick strikes Goldman paused at the apex of his windup, balanced upon one leg, to shout "I am Nobody, Polyphemus!" before flinging the third fastball whistling past the flinching manikin of Nat.

Afield, Nat flubbed a half-dozen fly balls, the relentless procession of them arcing towards him with the warped syrupy feel of a nightmare. Twice, after pulling the ball from the grass Nat threw it bounding out into the pasture, and once, scrambling frantically but unable to locate the sphere, he slipped upon the ball as if it were a banana peel, legs scissors-kicking up above his head as he fell.

When the game was finally called due to darkness, the Travelling All-Stars, despite their best efforts at mercy, had bested the Community Leaders eighty-seven to two, the only hometown runs coming via a pair of homers lifted over the fence by Eldon and Kal Benson, both of whom Mordecai Goldman had saluted with fist thrust into the sky and the mighty yawp of a proud father. Amongst the day's happiest results were the growth of the city coffer, through the sales of tickets and concessions, by nearly two thousand dollars, and the plethora of newspapers as far away as Portland, Seattle, and Sacramento running laudatory pieces on the game, much to Mayor Elkin's satisfaction. Everyone, it seemed, went home happily sunburned and drunk.

Everyone except Nat.

Throughout the solitary train ride home, Nat sat grimly vapor-locked in chagrin; every time his name was spoken from now until eternity it would invoke only images of him floundering in the grass, striking out, shouting red-faced impotently clenching his fists as all of humanity gamboled and frolicked around him. Nat had fought and lost before, but never had he been used as a prop, a tool. The warden returned to his dungeon on the storm-thrashed coast with shame hot in his face and a pack of cackling pointing phantoms at his back.

Best arrived the very next day.

CHAPTER SEVEN

*T*he sound twisted through the wall of Nat's skull into his sleeping brain like a rapacious worm thrashing and biting, tearing out a mouthful of memory; he was up on the hill, staggering in a warp of fumes, hands turgid with infection, throat torn and burning. He flinched at the sharp reports of the railroad ties stacking, again and again, then realized it was not the ties he heard but the crisp rhythmic crack of the bat on the ball, echoing up from the boys in white beneath the hill on the lush grass...

Nat sat up out of sleep with a face like gray clay packed around bubbles of hot tar. Touching his throbbing head, working the fetid air with his cotton mouth, he realized that waking had not cleared the crisp pinch of the objectionable sound from his mind. He went to the window. Out in the yard beneath him one of the new boys from Idaho was hitting baseballs. From Nat's angle, there were two dark figures against the backdrop of the silver and aquamarine riot of the ocean; the kid, feet spread far apart, knees bent, bat bobbing against his shoulder, and further up the beach on her sandy perch, the vengeful angel. Ball after ball, whether lobbed into the dirt or over his head (the elderly inmate pitching was not a very skilled hurler), the kid drove high up into the fence enclosing the yard. A crowd had gathered, prisoners tracking the ball in mesmerized silence, heads whipping back and forth in unison.

Nat remembered consenting to the storing of the kid's baseball equipment, a bat and glove and some balls, but clearly *this*... this relentless reminder of his two most dismal memories, the deprivation of his childhood and his public humiliation during the baseball game in Tillamook...this would not do. He would send an order to confiscate the gear and burn it. But before he could turn from the window, something caught his attention.

The kid's swing. Watching him launch ball after ball, Nat felt something click in the pit of his gut and spark in the black part of his brain. This, he thought, was a force capable of tearing asunder the netting, the prison walls, the mountainside. Destroying them and melding them into a new and better thing.

Gobsmacked, he crossed to the filing cabinet, trying to remember the kid's name.

⌐━━⌐

If the kid felt any circumspection or even curiosity about his summons to the warden's office, he hid it well. Nat watched him.

"Andy Best."

The boy nodded. He wore his dirty blond hair cropped short, with a little flare poking up in front. His face was deeply tanned with a prominent white spot the size of a penny on his left cheek.

"I've called you here to talk about something. A couple of things, in fact."

"Yes, sir."

"First of all, having reviewed your file, I must say I'm not convinced that you had any hand in killing that old woman." Nat let that sink in. "Bad luck maybe. At worst, bad taste in friends."

Andy cleared his throat. When he spoke at length, Nat was shocked by the rich smooth baritone of his voice. "Well...certainly no disrespect to your opinion, sir, and I do thank you for saying that. But unless the rest of this talk is your plan for taking up my cause and getting me out of here, I can't say that your sympathy is going to do me much benefit, one way or the other. But again, I appreciate you saying it."

Nat raised an eyebrow, conceding the point. Seeing beyond the gelid eyes and imposing stature, Nat realized the kid looked scared, weary, worn out. "Well, at the end of the day I guess it's not really for either of us to decide, is it? But since you're here..." He paused, several beats, watching the kid's face, waiting. "I'm wondering if you might like to play some baseball."

"I'm not entirely sure what you're asking me, sir."

"I've been considering setting up a baseball team, here in the prison, to go around and play some of the local town teams, the semi-pro teams. If this were to happen...would you be interested in joining?"

"I would, sir. And for your information, I've done that sort of thing before."

"Okay then. Now, as far as putting together a team, have you happened to notice any of the other men who might be able to play?"

"The prisoners?"

Nat nodded.

"Henry can play."

"Henry...your partner?"

"That's right. He can play."

"Anybody else?"

Andy shook his head grimly.

"Although, it's not as if you've staged some sort of formal tryout. Perhaps if we were to—"

"I've been here a month, which is more than long enough. If anybody could play, I'd know." The boy cleared his throat, conscious of interrupting. "Sir."

Somehow Nat knew that this stranger, this child, spoke the unilateral truth. "How many more would we need?"

"Seven more."

"Seven more?"

"At least seven. And that's without anybody throwing out his arm or taking one off the jaw. And those things are bound to happen."

"Eight then? Nine?"

Andy shrugged. "We've got two. Finding seven more and going with nine would be better than not going. I've played with eight. But the more you've got, the less likely you are to be forfeiting a game shorthanded, sir."

Escorting the boy from his office, Nat told him "I'll look into this. I can say it's definitely something I'm interested in."

The shadow of a smile played over the boy's face. "I'm guessing you'll have an easier time finding ballplayers in prison than you would a lot of other occupations."

And with that, Nat set himself the task of finding seven killers for his baseball team.

CHAPTER EIGHT

After briefly entertaining a number of elaborate schemes, Nat decided to keep it simple. He dispatched a telegram to the warden of the largest prison in each state excluding Oregon, reading:

> *Will pay up to $50 for transfer of prisoner (plus prisoner's upkeep en perpetua) with considerable baseball experience for project.*

Within a week the telegrams had begun pouring in, punctuated by the occasional horse-borne messenger, breathless and chafed, sputtering out an emergency missive regarding some All-Universe ballplayer who just happened to have killed someone. Most were quickly revealed as attempts to dump an undesirable inmate. With a cursory glance at a file Nat ruled out any number of hermit necrophiliacs and cannibals, Russian anarchists and cross-dressing killers of Johns.

For the rare referral that survived this initial screening, Nat would put Andy, bookended by a couple of guards, on a train to conduct a tryout. All fall and through the winter Andy returned from these trips shaking his head over some washed up knock-kneed former ballplayer pocked with booze and laudanum exercising the last wispy glint of a mediocre talent. Then, on the first day of spring, amidst a riot of birdsong and erumpent wet shoots pushing up through the black soil, The Kid came back from Keokuk, Iowa with a murderer who could play.

Deacon Mnusch, pronounced *Man-oosh,* had always lived amongst more death than life. His crib had often shared a room with corpses, and he had never, save for nights spent in town with various girlfriends, slept without a cadaver beneath the same roof. Since earliest childhood he'd washed and shaved the bodies, rouged their cheeks, stripped and dressed them. Just as the farmboy knows the smells of hay and cowshit as the smell of the world, Deacon was most naturally at ease amongst the cloying scent of death and the chemicals used to stave off its ultimately implacable corruption.

Up on Drake Mountain, Deacon dug the graves and prepared the bodies. He carved the headstones and maintained the miles of ornate iron fence. He shot the dogs and raccoons and wolves that tried to dig up the bodies, the errant farm cats perched atop the stones with their eviscerated rodent prey, and over the years a half-dozen grave robbers. When a flock of Canada geese took up residence honking and shitting he killed a thousand of them over the course of three nights, moving like double-fisted Death through the darkness, like a lanky black demon with star-colored eyes, snapping their necks and burning heaps of their bodies in the crematorium.

Since the arrival of the first Mnusch from Holland, which according to mountain lore had coincided with either an eclipse or an infestation of bats, the family had tended to remain on top of the mountain, a clan of recluses descending into town only to collect the dead. Deacon, however, created the exception to this rule. He wanted everything. Dropping from the mountain like a spokesman for the plague he swooped down to sample all of the good things life had to offer. In the swankiest of waterfront restaurants and the lowest of broken-toothed, one-eyed dives he filled the ladies with a titillating fear of death and accompanying lust for life and lust. He sailed with his cosmopolitan friends in the lake at the center of town, and he captained Keokuk's professional baseball team, The Harvesters, descending like an avenging angel, like a great skeletal bat, to vanquish all opposition.

Sitting across the desk from Deacon's hollow cheeks, the long glowingly sallow face, long black hair and deepset eyes the color of scarred metal, Nat mused over the fact that, surprisingly, there was also something warm and pleasant to the former undertaker's first impression.

"So…" Nat picked up the file and tapped it against the desk. "What happened? Why did you kill your father?"

Although Nat was indeed interested to hear what the boy had to say, the question was largely rhetorical. Despite the court clerk's attempts to present certain facts as isolated or mysterious, everything within the file clearly coalesced into a tight simple narrative. Deacon killed his father in the family's sitting room with a pewter lamp taken from an end table that had been crushed to splinters, many of them lodging deep into the boy's back. Deacon's neck was bruised and his windpipe nearly collapsed. The first time he'd read the file, Nat had been shocked at the court's stupidity in missing such an obvious case of accidental murder in self-defense, until he'd read the roll of jurors. "Oh, I see," whispered Nat, pursing his lips sardonically as he came upon the list of names: De Jong, Jansen, De Vries, Van der Berg, Van Dijk, Bakker, Smit, and Meyer. Presided over by the Honourable Judge Gregorious.

Nat could only imagine that Darrin Mnusch had been a man of considerable standing within Keokuk. Fifth generation full Dutch, wealthy, a necessary business contact for all but those who never intended to die. While executing his paternal responsibility of correcting the wayward son, the man is brutally murdered. At the hands of, in an ironic twist worthy of Greek myth or Shakespeare, that very same ungrateful son. Clearly, sayeth the judge and jury, staid God-fearing Dutchmen all, an example must be made. In response to Nat's question, Deacon tilted his head in a you-know-how-it-is gesture. "I guess it was his time."

"Says who?"

Stooping forward like some carnivorous insect, nodding profoundly, Deacon waggled a finger in appreciation. "Well said, friend. *Exactly.*"

Nat frowned. "Exactly what?"

"Exactly as you put it. Who decides when it's our time to leave this world? Who, or what, makes those decisions? Is it even a *decision*, or..." The tall cadaverous man shook his head, eyes wide, raising his long dangling hands cosmically.

Nat looked back at the guard stationed by the door, who shrugged. "Son...what the hell are you talking about?"

The muscles in Deacon's face dropped and he brushed the dark hair back from his face and Nat suddenly realized he was in the presence of an extremely intelligent human being. "I can't explain it. I don't think it's something we can articulate. I hope, and I suspect, based on his actions, that ultimately my father made his own decision. Although obviously we didn't always see eye to eye, I sincerely hope he was at peace with it. Maybe he feared something worse was going to happen, should he remain. I don't know what. Why are you assembling a baseball team in your prison?"

Nat sighed through his nose, pressing his lips together. "I don't think I can really explain it."

Deacon raised his brows, smiling again. "So you know."

After a moment's hesitation, Nat nodded. "Why do you want to play?"

"Are you kidding me? I wouldn't miss it. This is one of the strangest things I've ever heard of. I cannot wait to see where this ends up."

Out in a light steady drizzle Deacon took up the longest of Andy's three bats and dug his heels into the sandy dirt. Henry stood sixty feet away with a tin pail of balls at his feet. Andy nodded, turned his cap backwards, and crouched. Deacon hunched, six eight, stoop-shouldered, black hair whipping wildly in the suddenly electric wind as it must have, eyes crackling and teeth barred, the night he'd killed his father.

Henry started true and easy, but after a dozen balls went slicing the length of the yard he bore down, throwing harder. The undertaker did the same, slamming the ball higher and further, rowing Henry up the Salt River until the big pitcher was grunting red-faced, yellow teeth grinding as Deacon continued swinging lightly, the ball hissing up into the net in rockets, far beyond the reach of Nat, standing out in some approximation of centerfield with a glove dangling from his hand gawking up into the net. Andy stood, pulling off the cap, wiping his brow with a forearm. "Alright Henry." He excused the pitcher, who walked away shaking his head and muttering, lighting a cigarette.

"What do you think?" the catcher yelled out to Nat.

Nat nodded. Lightning struck the ocean, turning it to some undulating, phosphorescent creature, shimmying as if to pounce.

Nat received a letter from the warden of San Quentin, describing a prisoner who they were eager to export due to problems his appearance was causing amongst the fellow inmates. "However," the letter went on to say, "if you're looking for a baseball player, we have a reasonably competitive intramural league going here, and I can attest that this fellow, Ralph Ellison, ought to be worth your money and the effort of looking after him. Don't pay me anything now. I'll send him over, if you want, and if he isn't what you're looking for, send him on back. I'll buy the ticket."

A week after replying in the affirmative, Nat called the ballplayers over from the corner they had staked out between the Tall House and the ocean. "We've got a fourth man coming in today. Ralph Ellison, from San Quentin."

"Sounds like a banker."

"Well apparently he doesn't look like a banker. In fact, I'm here to forewarn you boys; it sounds like he can play ball, but the reason they're shipping him out of San Quentin is because the other inmates have been taking exception to his appearance."

Henry's fat lips bowed. "Like what?"

"Well..." As if in answer to the question, the medieval door leading from the prison's back wall into the exercise yard grated open and a man emerged, hands cuffed behind his back, a guard at each elbow. The general population sneered, spitting in his direction, catcalling. The ballplayers assessed him carefully: average height, medium build, baggy hooded cotton sweatshirt.

"Looks like a monk."

Peering apprehensively into the shadow beneath the hood, Henry said "That's it? That's what those whipcrackers in San Quentin couldn't handle? That the man is black?" Hearing this, Ralph Ellison shook the hood from his head, turning to present the melted honeycomb of his left profile, a bloodshot eye within the smeared lidless hole in a waxy recast face. "Get my good side." Even Nat, who'd been warned, blinked.

"Goddamn," said Henry, "I didn't know being ugly was a crime. But I can see why they would of made an exception."

Ralph smiled, a see-through grimace. "It wasn't the honky-tonks giving me trouble. It was the Diguenos. Turns out I look a helluva lot like one of their demons." A guard undid the cuffs, and after introductions, Nat put a ball into his left hand, a disaster of whorled bubbling discolored flesh, the ring and middle fingers fused together.

"Here, Andy," Nat nodded, sliding a bat from the canvas bag. The players raised their eyebrows and looked at one another. This was like teaching the baby to swim in the shark pool. Andy would brutalize this poor deformed bastard. Henry, an edge to his voice, said "I could use a few hacks, Nat. Andy's already the biggest goddamn toad in this little puddle. He don't need no practice."

"I know you're there if I need you, Henry. Ralph, take the hill. Andy, get in there."

Andy nodded, digging in, crouching. They backed away to watch. Ralph rocked into his awkward, limping windup, uncorking a fat, slow pitch that hung in the strike zone knee high, waiting to be murdered. Andy strode and uncoiled, a beautifully violent thing, but a hair's width from his bat the ball bit suddenly into the dirt as if slapped by some celestial hand. In a rare moment of indignity Andy lunged twisting himself into a corkscrew, jamming the bat into the dirt like a cane to avoid falling over. "What in the hell…"

Ralph Ellison laughed, all teeth. Andy smiled at him, nodding. "Let me see that again."

"All day long." Ralph paused to admire the ropy rubbery spectacle of his own melted recast arm. "Like a bunch of rubber bands wound up together. Never gets worn out."

Andy watched the next two pitches dive identically, then scooted up to the foremost edge of the batter's box, standing straight up, and managed to put the head of the bat on the ball as it began its descent, pushing it harmlessly back to the pitcher with a hollow pock. The Incendiary Ralph Ellison held up his mutilated claw. "I'd played some at Wilberforce, but nothing to write home about. When they got a little team going inside Quentin, I figured I'd pass some time, so I went out there, wedged a ball into my flipper, and goddamn if it didn't fall right out of the air like that. I call it the Fireball." He grinned, the burnt and fibrously recast flesh stretching up off his teeth in a pattern like raindrops striking mud, like spiderwebs, like a reptile's foot, black gums, black irregular teeth jutting wildly.

That evening, Ralph sat across the burnished oak desk up in the warden's office. The topic was fire. He remembered, in the way that some people remember the darkness and hissing of the womb, being congenitally drawn to it, the crackling glittering tails and streams wavering above the pit, the voices babbling within as if revealing all the answers to the world's secrets at once. The warmth and the glow. "I grew up in railroad camps. Goddamn nasty places. Every night the men would get a fire going, dirty fire, tin cans and moldy blankets and dried turds.

But that was the one good thing in my life, the one thing I knew I loved. I didn't have no reason for it; I just knew I did, and that I should. Every night I'd fall asleep next to the fire and wake up next to the embers, just marking time until night so somebody'd come around and light it again. All day I'd sit there sick and terrified that nobody was gonna come to light it, that I'd never get the fire again. Until...I must have been six years old, the morning I figured out I could take control of it myself..."

Waking in an utterly deserted camp with his cheek to the pulsing heart of the embers where the fire of corn husks and stolen coal had stood the night before, mesmerized by a single flame twitching, no larger than a shard of glass, the child had stooped, extending a single errant husk popping into life, fire, beauty. With quavering hands and swollen eyes, with his stomach knotting up into his heart and his heart stuffed up into his throat he had walked over into the dead weeds at the periphery of the camp, extending the flaming husk, holding it steady though it singed the tips of his fingers..."It's like, imagine if somebody told you that water was bad. You weren't to swim, or go out in the rain, or bathe, or drink it. You're gonna get thirsty, and you're gonna get sick a being filthy, and you're gonna start to question whether this person knows what the hell they're talking about."

Nat tapped the file on his desk. His voice was gentle and polite. "So your father died in the fire at the railroad camp when you were small..."

Ralph nodded.

When the soldiers had burst into the clearing to rescue the boy, miraculously unscathed at the center of miles of scorched earth, amongst the dozens of casualties lay the boy's father who, in some infernal coincidence had fallen, charred and twisted, mere feet from the son. They had asked the boy whether or not he knew the whereabouts of his father, and the boy had said no, although in fact he was lying, and did remember quite clearly flinching as his father had come racing from the blazing, dripping husk of the woods, hair burning and skin sloughing, shrieking, falling at his feet…"And there you go with another thing. I lit that fire, and just like that," he pushed his fists together, flicking his fingers to indicate an explosion, "my life got a hundred percent better. *Thousand* percent. Somebody's gonna tell me not to do that. Shit, I was just a child. That one ain't my fault. You don't want me getting into things? Show me something else to do. Nobody looked after me in the camp. I ate garbage, and as often as not, somebody'd come around to kick my ass and take *that* away. Then I lit that fire…"

"I lit that fire, and two weeks later, I'm living in a house, eating at a table, going to school. I lit that fire, and woke up in a whole new life. *Reborn.* Fucking phoenix. It ain't hard to see why I would of stuck with that truth for the rest of my goddamn life."

Like a faithful devotee, every day Ralph had stepped out behind the familial home to burn something: a handful of shredded paper and lint, a coffee can full of wood chips doused in gasoline siphoned from an iron mule. As he watched the flames an inner peace twisted around his spine like a newborn snake. But ultimately the release granted by such insignificant flames equaled nothing but a pinprick in the pressure cooker, and periodically the boy would succumb to the need to project his truth out into the world in greater quantities, lest the container burst. So he'd light a barn, watching as the flames licked slapping against the sides, rising, the base of the structure aging to desiccated dust as if he had seized control of the passage of time and thrown it forward. Or a church, or a homestead in the woods. And if the occasional cow or horse, man woman or child came running and thrashing from the structure, beating at its burning clothing or fur, hair and flesh…well that was never his intention.

"Things were good. I had come a *long* way from those God-forsaken Kansas railroad camps. Had my college degree and a wife, four children, moved out to California where a Negro could get work keeping the books for a gold mining outfit. Then, of all the places in the goddamn world, they had to put in those petroleum works on the hill right above my backyard. If that ain't fate…" He shook his melted head. "Good fucking gravy, I might just as well of been staring into the face of God puckering up for a kiss." Ralph's eyes fogged over, recalling the first time he'd seen it there atop the hill, fifty feet tall, looming up to trivialize the night sky, a monolith. "I can't even claim to have tried and resist. Wouldn't have done no good. My plan was to knock a hole in a canister, let the gas run down the hill, and light it up. I figured even if it blew the top of that hill right off, there was nobody up there. I cut through the fence, poked a hole without throwing a spark, and was following the trail of gas when that poor old security guard came running. Why I hadn't thought of that possibility, I cannot say."

"I panicked. Believe it or not, in that moment a time, no other possibility came into my head. All I could see was that I was gonna have to make it happen right then, or I was never gonna get another chance." Ralph struck the wooden match on the zipper of his pants and dropped it into the stream of gasoline.

With a sound like the rushing of the ocean in his ears he watched the slender running blue flame twitch and swerve towards the tank, leaping up into the hole, a brief puff of smoke before the billowing explosion of orange flame rushed out to immerse him like blood in the water, like an exploding planet.

He threw back his head and arched his back stretching wide his arms like an angel. The police were photographing his smoldering dead body when Ralph sucked in a great lungful of oxygen and sat up blinking, two very bright eyes amongst the raw meat ruin of his face.

Nat nodded thoughtfully. He looked back over the file. "Though you had no intention of killing that watchman."

"I certainly did not. Though that ain't to say it wasn't my fault. That I didn't fuck up, letting something get ahold of me like that." Ralph's voice got quieter. "But I'm gonna tell you something. I believe I made a mistake, but that ain't to say I was wrong. I think sometimes, when a man sees the truth…he's gotta go after that truth. And keep at it. Regardless of what the rest a the world might say. Do you know what I mean?"

"I know exactly what you mean."

Melvin set the document on Nat's desk.

"They must have sent it to me assuming it was simply a matter of forgotten paperwork. I brought it to you the moment I realized what they're asking for."

Nat read the communique with a growing sense of unease. A missive from the Department of Corrections, requesting the documentation, immediately, for the two inmates who had been executed to make room for the two new admissions, Deacon Mnusch and Ralph Ellison. Between the fog of his recent malaise and the consuming focus of his new project, Nat had failed to anticipate this problem. With the arrival of Best and Hester, Rockaway Prison had reached capacity. In the old days, they might have had more leeway, but with the governor's well-publicized prison reform agenda establishing a firm cap on each institution's population, the books had to remain balanced. Iron-ically, Nat was required to kill lest his prison be classified inhu-mane. For every addition, he had to subtract.

The letter, sent from the central office in Portland, explained that they had received paperwork regarding the two new admis-sions, and assumed that a commensurate pair of executions had been carried out. The letter concluded with a reminder that the usual post-mortem procedure involved shipping the body in an iced car to Portland for identification and disposal, but that if perhaps some contingency had necessitated an alternative method of local disposal, that would be acceptable...this one time. Going forward, Nat would be expected to reinstitute the established protocol, lest Portland be forced to send in agents to assist. Placing the letter gently on his desk, sucking a single slow deep breath, Nat immediately realized that any type of cover-up would be impossible. Documentation of a new prisoner came not only from Rockaway, but the transferring facility as well. There was not, as far as he could tell, a non-lethal solution.

"Okay. Thank you, then." Removing a key from his belt, he opened the iron box of files tucked beneath his desk.

There were ten inmates who had exhausted all appeals, irrevoca-bly approaching a date with the hangman. Nat shuffled the files, pulling two at random.

Joe Billy had gone nuts, living down in the swampy flats near Nesquim, murdering all four of his neighbor's children with a heavy tractor chain. Nat flipped past detailed descriptions of small bones poking through torn flesh, jaws snapped clean in two, skulls folded leaking brains. Teddy Bland had ambushed a pair of young women at a company picnic, attacking them carnally before executing both with a pistol. Nat studied the inmates' photos, the dead eyes and unwholesome complexions, recognizing nothing of what ought to constitute a man. Alone in the shadowed office, with the sound of the ocean like death-watches skittering in the wall and a look as if he'd been fed spoiled meat, Nat sighed. He glanced about the room as if hoping for some secret exit. As much as he was repulsed by these two killers, he had no personal desire to end their lives. The image of Li Jun flickered heavily against his mind. Lolling tongue. Bloody erection. Nat became aware of eyes upon him, glancing up to find Melvin in the shadowed doorway. He composed himself.

"May I come in?"

"Of course."

The assistant warden approached nervously. "More than anything, I'd hate to be presumptuous…But considering the amount of work for which you're currently responsible, just know that now, or in the future, I would be perfectly willing and capable of scheduling, and even presiding over the executions, at such times that you might be occupied…with other business. There's a provision in the prison's operational manifest stating that, if the warden is incapacitated or otherwise indisposed, the assistant warden is allowed to serve as principal witness at an execution."

Nod nodded slowly, searching the younger man's eyes. "That could make sense. For the time being…"

One guard loosened the noose while a pair held the body at arm's length propped like a drunk tenuously erect, apt to topple over at any moment. As the rope came off, they laid him down, careful to avoid the shit and blood and urine on the corpse and platform. As a guard grabbed the gurney, Melvin stopped him.

"You fellows take a break. Go down on the beach and have a smoke. We don't want to overtax your nerves." Melvin smiled, gesturing towards the body. "He'll still be here when you get back." The guards looked amongst themselves skeptically. One of them nodded, the others shrugged, and they left, casting glances over their shoulders. After a moment, Melvin threw the bolt behind them.

Breathing deeply through his nose, he climbed the platform.

Teddy Bland lay on his back, neck crooked with a swelling the size of a musketball. Gently, Melvin removed the hood. One eye lay half open, the other closed. He'd bitten through his tongue; blood welled in his open mouth, striping his cheeks. Melvin squatted, leaning his face right down onto the killer's.

Big man," he whispered. "Big man with those poor girls." Melvin pictured the crime. "Never afraid of anything. Well look at you now. Look at you now...You're nothing." Melvin's face contorted, shadows falling into the creases like a possessed man in the process of transformation. An erection pushed painfully against his trousers like a fist. He slapped the cadaver's face, lightly, then harder, panting through his grit teeth. "You...are... nothing..." He spit in the face of the corpse.

The door handle rattled, followed by a loud knock, a call of "Is anybody still in there?" Melvin straightened up, catching his breath. He yanked the handkerchief from his pocket, cleaning the face of the corpse. He dabbed the sweat from his forehead on his sleeve, whipped the scrimshaw comb from his pocket and slicked his thin translucent hair, walking briskly for the door.

This, he thought, admitting the guards who looked at him nervously and dropped their eyes, was going to do just fine.

CHAPTER NINE

*N*at stepped into the midst of practice to announce that before nightfall, they'd have a pair of new teammates. Andy drove his fist into the catcher's mitt. "And they're what we've been looking for?" Nat smiled. He liked the question. "Yes, they should be."

First to arrive through the gates that afternoon was a sturdy-looking old man with a crooked gait. Bull-of-the-Woods with facial scars beneath a full head of iron hair.

"*That* old bastard's gonna play ball?" asked Henry.

Nat laughed. "That old bastard's capable of quite a few things that might surprise you. That old bastard's savage as a meat axe. On the field and off. That old man..." Nat held the pause, "that's Grainface." Everybody waited for a punchline. After a moment, Nat simply nodded. "Yep. That's him."

"Bull fucking shit."

Each man, upon hearing the name of the mythical gangster, harkened back to his earliest memories of the nightmarish villain. For most it had begun with a lurid painting on the cover of a magazine, an impossibly long muscular figure brandishing a huge pistol, looming demonically above some crew of innocents, women and children, men ripped up dead on the ground, blood filling the air like streamers at a parade. In each memory, far more harrowing than the blood, the stacked corpses, was the monster's face. Or rather lack thereof.

The signature of Grainface, the indelible imprint carved brutally upon countless childhood psyches was the shapeless mask, sewn from swaths of burlap grain sacks with rough black thread, like the face of some abject unloved doll attacked with a razor. Like a scarecrow bursting up from the soil to collect the devil's due. Grainface. Working alone, crashing on his unnaturally huge, smoking ebony stallion into wagon trains and locomotives, slaughtering all witnesses, amassing a fortune for God only knows what purpose. The men, returning wide-eyed from their haunted childhood reveries, stared at the ambling old man. "Pfft. That ain't Grainface. Just some old fart cutting shines."

Nat nodded towards the newcomer. "Go ask him."

They watched the guards cautiously moving the old man into the building. After a moment, Henry returned to the mound. "Nah," he said to himself, shaking his head, "That ain't no Grainface."

That night at dinner the ballplayers sat watching the old man eating with gusto at a table by himself. Finally Deacon arose, leaving his teammates as they whispered *No no wait don't ask him,* sat down across from the old man, and asked. The old man smiled, his sun-baked face crackling into a billion tiny fissures. "Hell yes. That's me."

Deacon motioned to the other players who, after a brief confab, approached, huddling around the old man. "You're Grainface?"

"That's right. And that ain't but the half of it. Before I was Grainface, I used to be Slade Matheusen."

Andy nodded. "I knew I recognized you."

Henry looked back and forth amongst everybody. "Who the hell's Slade Matheusen?"

The old man spread his arms beneficently, launching into his story with the air of a carnival barker, a salesman of snake oil. "Boys," he said, "gather round and listen up. I'm gonna start at the beginning."

"The only thing I ever wanted to be was a ballplayer. God knows why. Not there's anything wrong with it, but where in the hell I would ever have gotten that idea, pitching hay in Wichita, I do not recall. Must have been born with it in my blood. We had a church league, playing on Saturday nights against the Protestants or Lutherans or Mormons, and by the time I was twelve they said 'Slade you can't play no more. You're ruining it. We can't have the preacher or the mayor or the war hero giving up four homeruns while striking out four times himself. You're done.' So I went across town and caught on with the semi-pro. I saw the world, or at least the part of it that touches Kansas, and the day after I turned sixteen I signed my first major league contract with the St. Louis Captains. And damned if that wasn't my life and my livelihood for the next thirty years, and damned if I didn't love every minute of it."

"But just like everything else, boys, there comes a day when you realize you're just another seven by nine, thrown out with the shucks. My day showed up right in the middle of an at-bat. There I was, bases loaded, top of the first inning in the dead heat of a September pennant race. That pitch came floating in like a wet dream, boys, like the last woman left at the bar, fat and ugly. I said a secret prayer of thanks, preparing to knock it into the pasture…and discovered right then, right there, that I had nothing left. Now I'd seen other men try to hold on too long, and I always swore that the second I saw the writing on the wall, I wouldn't linger. Well the writing was on the wall, big and bright. I popped that pitch weakly straight up into the air, set down my bat, blew a kiss to the four cardinal directions, and walked out the exit."

"The second my foot came off that field, boys, the paychecks stopped. I had no savings, seeing how most of my money I'd spent on loose women and liquor, and the rest I'd just wasted. I could of worked, but after thirty years of playing ball for a living…anything else sounded like slow death. For a few months I managed, drinking through the kindness of others, I still had my fans, but eventually all those springs of goodwill dried up, and I had to get serious about a plan."

"The first time I robbed somebody was on a whim. I had no idea this was to become my calling and vocation. For a few weeks I'd been noticing the three boys loading their rig up and down Main Street every couple of days, two of them waiting, pistols drawn, while the third came high-stepping with a big canvas sack to be delivered to the local Capitol Merchant bank."

"My original plan was to stick them up with the pistol I'd purloined from a lady friend the night before, but at the last moment it dawned on me that just waltzing up and telling them, with the handsome face you see before you right now, to hand over all the money wasn't going to do. Even if I pulled off the heist, the marshals would be all over me within an hour. I was still famous, at least in that part of the country. I needed a disguise."

"Without any good ideas I stepped into an alley behind a restaurant to get out of sight and have a smoke. I'd more or less given up and decided, God forbid, that I might have to get a job after all, when I flicked my cigarette and found, there at my feet, a small burlap sack of rice that must have fallen from the restaurant's delivery. A muddy burlap sack like a gift from heaven. In a moment of pure inspiration, I stuck that sack with my pocketknife, emptied it, tore eyeholes and pulled it over my head."

"Now, when I approached those boys, I did so with a Derringer whereas each of them held a pistol as long as my third leg. But the second they laid eyes on that godawful scarecrow's head, one of them threw his pistol down straightaway and the other made like he was going to shoot but it was all for form's sake. He just wanted to be able to say he'd tried. He led with his jaw and I obliged, bringing up my free hand and laying him down. When the kid came out toting the money I had both his cronies tied and stacked like kindling, one of them bleeding profusely, and he handed over the box without me even asking."

"As time went on I got myself a bigger gun, I garnished the mask with a stitched up mouth, red paint around the eyes. And as I'm guessing you know," the old man winked, "the targets grew a hell of a lot more audacious. Train robberies. Ship robberies. The kidnap and ransom of the governor's wife." Slade's eyes shone wistfully as he sat back, crossing his arms.

Ralph exhaled sourly. "You get all misty thinking about murdering those Delacroix kids? Innocent children, after their parents already paid the ransom?"

Slade shook his head, smiling. "That, Boss, like a whole lot of other things you may have read, just isn't true. That's how you sell newspapers, my friend. My cardinal rule, and I followed it as best I could, given the circumstances, was never to hurt anybody."

"Seems you've been hurting practically everybody. More than the rest of us in here combined."

Slade grinned, spit on the cafeteria floor. "That's called propaganda, son. That's what they *want* you to believe. Makes you more apt to deputize yourself, more apt to go out looking to shoot somebody if you think that man's been waylaying old ladies on their way to church and burying children in the forest. I never killed a soul, until this most recent and regrettable episode, which, for whatever it's worth, wasn't my fault. I had my standards, and I stuck to them." Slade shook his head. "I mean hell, anybody can be a murderer, and get away with it," he winked at the assembled company, "no offense, boys. But what I've been doing...that takes *finesse*."

That evening, in the midst of something resembling an actual baseball practice, Slade covering the space between first and second like a massive tree stump, knocking down the ball with his barrel chest, laying out like a falling tree to smother line drives and grounders kicking into the hole the gates again spread, admitting a slender figure in a woolen cap and gray pea coat at the center of four guards in a diamond formation. Nat went over, ordered the guards to unlock the handcuffs, and returned with the new recruit. Before anyone could speak, the cap came off, long auburn hair falling out.

Nat stared back at the dumbfounded faces of the assembled team. "Here's our newest team member. Dorothy Baker." They all looked at Dot and she sighed, shaking her head. She nodded disdainfully at the men as if addressing a crew of shit-shovelers asking for a ride into town in her brand-new automobile. "Rest assured I could wipe those stupid looks off your faces by playing some ball. But right now, for tonight, I'm going to have to say hell with that. I've been on trains for three days, then another day rattling through the forest with these assholes, all in hand-cuffs. When's the next proper practice?"

"Tomorrow morning."

"Well, then, y'all gapeseeds can just wait there catching flies until tomorrow morning."

She turned, waving at the guards to escort her into the prison. In her wake, a moment of silence ensued.

"Well now, what the hell is this?"

Slade stroked his chin. "I believe that's a woman, Henry."

"Thanks, asshole. I mean what is she doing here."

"She's here," Nat pointed to the ballfield dirt beneath their feet, "because apparently she can play ball like a rip-staver. She's *here*," Nat spread his arms to indicate the prison yard, "because she killed her husband."

"Killed her husband?"

"Killed him…" Nat paused, unable to keep the ghost of a smile from tracing his lips, "with a baseball bat."

~~~

That night, perusing Dot Baker's file, Nat found the circum-stances surrounding the young woman murdering her husband to be much as he'd imagined. After the killing, she'd fled with her ten-month-old son from Baltimore to Fort Griffin, Texas, an area where, unfortunately for her, there were nearly no women at all. After failing to bed her, the men of Fort Griffin in their spiteful frustration had attempted to intimidate her into leaving. Failing that, they'd sent a contingent of men to drag her and the baby from the house she'd bought. Three of those men were still in the Houston hospital. At that point, the men of Fort Griffin had called in the Texas Rangers.

It wasn't the first time that Nat had heard this story. In Portland, on the rare occasion that a woman was executed, they'd bring her over to the gallows at the men's prison. In the days leading up to these events—and they were events; unlike the killing of a man, which might warrant a death notice on the back page of the newspaper, these executions garnered a week of lurid front page descriptions of the crime, character studies of the murderess, florid panegyric for the victim—Nat would grow increasingly appalled at the behavior of his colleagues.

It was not the non-stop sexual fantasies of what a man might do before, during, and after the hanging that had bothered Nat most. What he'd found far more disturbing was the desire for revenge based on the perception that one of "ours" had been wronged, and that one of "them" must suffer greatly to balance the books, regardless of the circumstances surrounding the murder. He'd seen the same tribal mob mentality directed towards black murderers and cop-killers.

Looking through the young woman's file, Nat was reluctantly thrown back to images of his mother, knocked onto the dirt floor of their shack, sitting at the periphery of the encampment with her head in her hands weeping. He'd wanted to approach her, sit with her, hold her hand…but he'd never figured out how to go about it. Why hadn't she done something like this? It would have been better. Why hadn't he? Nat could have shot the old man in his sleep. In the workers' encampment, gunshots were as common as birdsong, dead bodies garnered little more than a second look, and the police would not enter. They could have made it. Wherever the two of them might have gone, whatever they might have done…it would have been better.

Nat fidgeted, a small sound coming up from his throat. He stretched his eyes and jaw, shook his head, and returned his attention to the thick file, stuffed with newspaper clippings.

So what about her life before the murder? What about the baseball? Where had all that come from?

It all began with Dorothy's father, the Reverend Jerry Baker, sitting beneath a gum tree on the outskirts of Sydney, brooding somewhat darkly, somewhat desperately, upon his own failure to convert more than a handful of souls despite investing half his life and the entire lives of his eight children in the enterprise. For twenty years the Bakers had been travelling the world to proselytize and convert, first as newlyweds just passing from the halls of Goshen University straight into the jungles of Thailand, then as young parents living in bamboo shacks on Cuban beaches, in Congolese jungles and Ethiopian deserts, accumulating children as they traipsed across and over and beneath the world.

Perhaps it was time to give up.

Maybe it was God's will for us to fail, thought Jerry, looking up into the trembling coruscating leaves above him. Maybe He made us shitty missionaries so that we might be forced to quit and become…God only knew. Melancholy and pensive beneath the hot sun, the Reverend worked it over, and over, in his mind, trying to figure out exactly what had gone wrong. What he came up with was a matter of innate difference: Differences of appearance, different language (Blanche actually spoke sixteen, but still…), different food, different taboos, different customs accompanying birth and death. Maybe if they were seeking souls in Massachusetts, or Utah, or Texas…

but here, or Bali, or Greenland, the people saw nothing in the Bakers that resembled any part of them. How could they be expected to believe in Jesus any more than he and Blanche felt compelled to join the Inuits in worshipping Agloolik beneath the ice?

Jerry plucked up a weed and chewed at the sweet stalk, sighing. If only they could have hit upon some glint of irrefutable common ground. Well, he thought, throwing down the weed, shaking his head, I've got no right to sit here wasting the day in such a funk when I've got so many blessings to count, literally right here in front of me.

In a dirt clearing in front of the ramshackle mission the Baker children, all eight, played baseball with a dozen of the aboriginal kids, everyone chattering, chasing one another through the dust and heat, tumbling, laughing. The kids were good. Jerry didn't know the game that well, but he could tell that his sons and daughter possessed talent and had worked at it. None of the aboriginal kids had even known this game existed until the missionaries' arrival the year before, but the Bakers had coached them, and they'd caught on quickly. Although the games were competitive, the general vibe remained one of joy and mutual appreciation, and whenever something exceptional happened, some slick double play or bomb of a homerun clacking through the trees, the players on both teams would stop, clapping, paying homage to the beauty of it.

The ball was struck and Zeke, playing second base, dove to his left, spearing it, flipping it backhanded up into the air where Dot plucked it with her right hand at the same instant the toes of her right foot drug over the bag and she fired to Girra, stretching at first. All of the children whistled and danced. Passersby stopped to cheer.

An odd look crept over the reverend's face like that of an explorer who had stepped into the bushes to take a leak and accidentally fallen into the fountain of youth or city of gold. He leapt up, banging his head on the tree branch, staggering out towards the field wincing and motioning at his children.

Within the month they'd become the Travelling Bakers and commenced the decade-long journey that would take them barnstorming several times around the world. Their modus operandi was to roll into an area and annihilate every local team, from the guerilla squads of Venezuela to the factory teams in West Virginia to the nascent professional leagues in Indochina, leveraging their status as champions of the diamond to deliver the Word of the Lord. The Baker kids, with either mother or father hiding out in right field to make up nine, played baseball in the jungle, baseball in the desert, on concrete terraces and beaches and in alleys dribbling sewage. When the opposing team arrived with milk cartons instead of mitts, they traded. When the spectators arrived unshod they shod them, gave them clothing and Bibles. During the game, whichever parent wasn't playing manned the grill constructed from three oil barrels welded together, feeding every mouth in the stands.

Here, as Jerry Baker had realized that day beneath the gum tree, was your common ground, your transcendent collective humanity. They culled the sick from the crowd, administering shots and salves, knocking the gunk from a sick baby's lungs, popping the spine of a stooped old man to walk anew, treating infections in the eyes of the blind and giving sight.

In short, before and after the game, they performed miracles.

And the quantity of souls the Bakers had converted during the previous two decades came to equal a good night's work as the Christers swept a double-header from the local pros, then hosted a barbeque-slash-hitting clinic with a group baptism in the river for those who took the spirit.

One February night in San Felipe, after God's Soldiers had soundly trounced a squad billed as the national champions of Mexico, a short man in a sport coat and hat smoking a thick cigar grabbed Jerry's right arm pressing a greasy manila envelope into his hand. Jerry, perplexed, opened the envelope to wads and wads of pink and purple currency. "Wait! Stop!" he shouted, chasing after the man's tan jacket through the thick festive post-game crowd. But suddenly an idea bloomed in his mind like ethereal fireworks and he stopped short, mouth opening, eyes turning to the sky. If they had been able to do the work of Christ so efficiently on a shoestring budget, just imagine the work they might do, the souls they might save, with discretionary funds beyond the meager trickle coming from church headquarters. A lot of people showed up for cube steak on the grill, but what if they threw on some marinated carne asada? Beer and lime instead of homemade sangria?

Perhaps, thought the reverend, counting the bills, this envelope full of cash is another directive sent by God.

Two months later, after saving every soul and taking every peso available to them from Tijuana to Merida, the Christian Warriors applied their winnings to the construction of a white church in the shape, if seen from the sky or outer space, of a cross, with a wide staircase leading down into the lapping ocean water for baptisms, and a kitchen stocked and staffed to feed practically the entire peninsula should that become necessary.

The moment the final nail had been driven home, off they went to Panama, Sao Paulo, Jean-Rabel, Anchorage...

And so it was that Dot matured amongst blood and dirt and leather, breaking up double plays with her metal cleats, turning a shoulder into ninety-mile-an-hour fastballs, smashing into and on occasion entirely through wooden walls. When it came time for the progeny to scatter, to pursue other lives, within a month all seven of the Baker brothers were playing in one or another of the established American pro leagues, and Dot had opened a world class sports academy for girls, importing some of the best coaches in the world.

And it was one of these coaches, Joachim Rilke, with whom she would eventually fall in love, and marry, and whose brains she would eventually beat from his skull with her favorite bat.

⌐————º

Impassive as a beautiful bust, Joachim moved his long sun-browned body back and forth across the court, driving the ball with impossible hidden power, as precise as a razor blade. He cooked with a gourmet's flair and he wept reading Emily Dickinson. He constructed a greenhouse where he cultivated twenty-nine different hues of roses. On their first anniversary, he swept her away for a midnight stampede on horses through the forest and a mountain climb to watch the sun rise over the Atlantic. He was the light of the moon and the deep black sea. After a weekend she'd spent in New York recruiting, she returned home to discover he had, armed with only a wrench and a pair of leather gloves, reconstructed the school's plumbing system in a way that would resist the danger of contamination, either natural or deliberate. One night she awoke to him smashing out the wall separating their kitchen from their living room in order to improve the flow of energy. He knitted caps and gloves for the school's custodial and grounds-keeping staff. He built small shrines in their backyard. By the time she realized that her husband was insane, she couldn't decide if it mattered much. He was a good father and husband, and an excellent coach.

Then he began to see signs of the approaching storm.

One night she awoke with a vague sense of foreboding and urgency to find him crouching on his knees looking out their bedroom window. He turned and his face was pale, veins standing against the skin like root systems. The muscles around his eyes twitched and he attempted to speak several times before saying "It's coming."

"What's coming?"

He shrugged. "The storm. The oceans will come," he pointed vaguely towards the ceiling. "Wind will blow, and the ground will blow from beneath our feet." He exhaled, shook his head with tired regret. "And all of us will behave differently." Up until that point he'd been speaking as if he were alone in the room, but now he looked at her very carefully. "In ways we've never imagined. Sides will be drawn up…Children will oppose their mothers and fathers, wives will murder their husbands…" After a long moment, he turned back to the window.

A week later, at the conclusion of an overwhelmingly pleasant day during which he'd surprised her with a picnic and a languorous summer stroll along the boardwalk, he began to construct the shelter in the backyard. Joachim excavated the soft earth with a shovel. He had a truckload of bricks delivered, and within the subterranean space he built a floor and walls. He constructed a roof with branches culled from the forest behind the house, gently spreading earth upon the canopy. For a week, Dot watched him work, occasionally stepping out into the yard to let little Pierre play in the grass.

She didn't know what to do. Which is not to say she felt trapped or helpless; quite the contrary. There were many things she might do. She simply hadn't yet decided which tack to pursue. This was the school's busiest season, a month during which three sports began, along with the brunt of the recruiting for next year's freshman class. And while Joachim's recent behavior had certainly been odd, it had never seemed to portend any glimmer of malice or violence. She resolved, for the time being, to tolerate Joachim's eccentricities, while continuing to operate her school and raise her child. Come fall, she'd either ship Joachim out or get him some help.

But then he forced her hand.

Returning from a tennis tournament in Worchester, Dorothy found a contingent of staff at the front gate, pale with clenched teeth, reluctant to tell her the inexplicable story of Mister Rilke apparently attacking the elderly groundskeeper Claude with a fire poker.

"My God. Where's Claude now?"

"Laid out taped and iced and drugged in the infirmary."

Dot frowned, waiting for an explanation. "For God's sake why did you leave him there, instead of taking him to the hospital?"

"Well...with the hospital obligated to call the police and all that..."

"I'll be calling the police. What are you talking about?"

"With Mister Rilke owning the place...we just weren't sure how the two of you are wanting to handle this."

Dot stared. The voice of the cook, an older woman, broke from the uncomfortable crowd "And with Pierre..."

A pinch of panic twisted Dot's voice. "Pierre?"

"Well. Mister Rilke already picked him up from Missus Jeffrey's, so...we just thought we'd better check and see how you wanted to handle this before we had the police rushing in here…" Dot ran to the house, banging through the front door to find her husband in the sitting room. The little boy sat propped against his feet, quietly stacking blocks. She approached carefully. Joachim, without looking up from the boy, said "How was the tournament?"

"It was fine." Neither of them took their eyes off the child. "I heard you had some trouble with Claude."

Joachim waved a hand dismissively. "Just something we all needed to get out in the open. Something I needed to make sure everyone understood before we leave."

A chill grabbed Dot, sinking its teeth into her face and its nails into her back. "Before we leave?"

Smiling at the child dotingly, he said "Pierre and I are going to Rue Cantrelle. *Starting* in Rue Cantrelle. And from there…" He waved his arms expansively. "Well, it's a very big world. And we need to make the best of what little time we may have left." He looked at Dot in a pointed way that she was unable to interpret.

"When do we leave?"

"Oh, *mon cheri*, not this time. Perhaps next. But this trip… there are things, a lifetime of things, that a boy can only learn from his father."

She crossed the room in a flash, a leap, reaching for the child, but Joachim was just as quick and kicked her in the jaw. In a lifetime filled with flash floods, death squads and decapitations, snake handling, head shrinking, blood drinking, charging elephants and writhing alligators, fire running over savannah like ocean waves, earth cracked asunder like fired clay, hailstones the size of vengeful fists, this was the singular most shocking moment of her life. Dot had utterly misjudged. She'd missed everything. There was a ringing in Dot's ears and her head felt as if it had turned to plaster. She rose on wobbly pins as Joachim collected the boy.

"We leave tomorrow," he said. "Come see us off."

Dot picked the bedroom lock with a nail. Joachim had rigged a stack of pans to the door by a rope but she crossed the room so quickly that while he did manage to snatch the gun from the bedside table still she brought down the lacquered black bat, bat with the pocks of two thousand triumphs, bat that had carried her dreams, upon that handsome face, smashing the teeth and the cheekbones so that he sat up trying to shriek through a formless spasming hole with a throat full of shattered bone, throwing up his hands as the black bat snapped back both thumbs like an ax removing snags, black wood continuing through the ruined digits to crack an eye socket, the eye sagging into the sinkhole of the smashed face, rolling forward showing only white. Joachim rose from the bed, wobbling, head dipped so that now Dot could bring a natural motion to it, striding, unleashing the same smooth cut that had served her so well for so many years and her husband's forehead blew open in a spray of blood and gray sludge and he fell straight back, arms thrown wide like a man dropping into an incredibly agreeable slumber, pulling it down with him...Nat cursorily leafed through the transcripts from the trial. On the final page, he found a passage circled in lurid red ink, and a note in the margin reading "THIS IS WHAT YOUR DEALING WITH"

Within the crimson circle, the following transcription:

JUDGE ZUNINO: Do you regret what you did?

DOROTHY BAKER: I regret it horribly. My actions were inexcusable, and if there was anything I could do to take them back, I would. I must have been temporarily insane. I regret it every day. All that love and history…I'd collected over two thousand professional base hits with that bat, and now it's gone forever, nothing but splinters sticking out of Joachim's skull. And there's nothing I can do to bring it back.

Nat closed the file, took a sip of his water.

And that, my friends, is how it's done.

On the gravel of the foggy prison yard, the sun not yet risen above the trees, she walked a distance, turned, cracked her neck and elbows, and dropped into a stance. As Andy hit she lunged left, digging three steps, plucking the ball from her shoetops, unleashing a bolt that would have broken Andy's cheekbone had he not dumped himself backwards into the dirt. She pointed at him, "I would think you'd be wearing a glove." Andy nodded, saying something quietly to himself, and fetched a glove. For fifteen minutes the girl ate bad hops and ran down pop flies through the ankle-breaking minefield of the prison yard. They nodded to her. She nodded back, pulling off the glove, wiping her brow.

Now they had six.

CHAPTER TEN

*M*elvin had learned early on that he could not count upon his arms and legs to do the things the other boys did. When he was eight, exploring the stone quarry with his younger brother, a strange boy hit him with a rock. As Melvin plucked up a rock, attempting to retaliate, his thin femur broke with the motion of throwing. He lay amongst the stones shrieking impotent rage and fury as the boy laughed over him and his little brother ran for help.

The next time conflict arrived, a schoolyard bully singling Melvin out for a fistfight, having learned from his earlier injurious humiliation, he employed a different tack than he'd taken in the quarry, spinning on his heel to flee. But his feet tangled and he fell, writhing in the dirt with the wind knocked out of him until the bully arrived to hoist him up and beat him.

So Melvin discovered he could not fight, and he could not run. Nor could he gracefully accept this difference between himself and the blue-collar Brooklyn world navigated so naturally by his father and brothers, and seemingly every other male in existence. He watched them running on the beach, talking to women, wrestling, returning from their jobs covered in honest grime to sit on the front stoop with a well-earned ice-cold beer. He watched their tempers flare, their maudlin backslapping reconciliations. He surreptitiously watched their contemplative moments as they looked out over the neighborhood like masters of time and existence.

But no matter how closely Melvin watched, nowhere amongst these men could he detect any part of himself. He could not speak the language, present the shibboleths, and any time he tried it came off as awkward and foreign, serving only to cleave the division deeper. Though he compensated, earning an academic scholarship to Columbia, obtaining work at a prominent law firm, these accomplishments, instead of establishing his reputation, seemed only to set him further apart from his family, his roots. He was strange. And in his deepest heart, despite the silk suit, the penthouse overlooking Central Park, he would always be inferior, living in constant panic that someone stronger would arrive and simply take it all away.

That, he feared, would be the story of his life. Rising through the ranks of the law firm, he was forever watching for the square-jawed broad-shouldered new hire, who would simply clap the backs of the partners, regale them with stories of boxing and womanizing at Yale, and be awarded Melvin's office. Should he obtain a wife, he could not abide her leaving his side for fear of being cuckolded. Beginning with the pain and shame in the stone quarry, compounded by every memory of being shouldered aside, cut in line, belittled by some lout of half his intelligence, excluded from the conversation, spoken to as if he belonged amongst the children, the pressure built inside of him and festered.

Melvin began to fantasize.

To catch one of those swaggering ignoramuses in an alley, shoot him in the back of the knee, drag him out of sight for a slow, emasculating death. To tie him up, cut him, beat him, force him to apologize for everyone, for everything. Then once the victim had apologized, weeping, after doing everything Melvin had told him to do, to kill him anyway.

That, thought Melvin, would square the ledger.

He could do it. What he couldn't do was get away with it. Within this mysterious world of baritone voices, of coded threats and clenched fists, he'd be too conspicuous negotiating the dark, anonymous places where a suitable victim might be groomed and obtained. Of course, he could easily cull some rickety wino from the almshouse, but that wouldn't prove anything. That wouldn't suture the gaping wound. He needed a strong man to dominate.

So Melvin ground his teeth, surrounded by the bastards all day, in the streets, in the office, in the building where he lived. He swallowed down his resentment and he felt it festering, struggling to come back up in some poisonous, self-destructive explosion, but felt powerless to stop it. All of his problems stemmed from the fact that he'd been born out of time. He was more highly evolved than the half-apes he saw grunting and swaying through the streets of Brooklyn and the halls of the law firm. Melvin represented practically an entirely different species. He'd been born with gifts that the others were not even equipped to recognize.

When he received the letter from Columbia's alumni association, sent out to all recent graduates, announcing that several entities out west were seeking educated upwardly mobile young men for posts in business management and governmental apparatuses, Melvin immediately understood that therein lie his only chance at salvation. Finishing the final word of this invitation, his eyes whipped straight up into the ceiling, as if looking for the cold marble hand of Fate that had delivered it.

So then I will plunge out into the darkness, he thought. Deep into the No-Land. In the absence of any firmly established power structure favoring an outdated, primitive mentality, he would parlay his intellect into a position at the top of the food chain. While everyone else floundered in the nascent society's anarchistic primordial ooze, he would crawl from the stew first.

He would emerge fully erect, head high, discovering fire and inventing the bronze spear tip, so to speak.

As Nat felt a presence behind him and turned from the window to find Melvin in the doorway, bearing the black leather clipboard with the execution schedule, he smothered a twinge of repugnance for the boy. *Or is it guilt, since he's only doing what he does at my behest...?*

"Sir."

"Melvin."

He glanced at the clipboard. "Two more in?"

"That's right."

"Do you know how many more of the requested transfers we'll be admitting?"

Nat thought about this. "I don't."

Melvin nodded. "Okay. We received a telegram today from Portland telling us to prepare for an influx of new inmates over the next several months. The more state money allocated to police, the more murderers arrested...With this in mind, I'd like to know if you'd prefer to administer the scheduling, and simply pass along the names and dates," he extended the leather clipboard towards Nat, "or would you rather I manage that, and simply keep you appraised?"

"For the time being, let's maintain our current system."

Melvin tucked the clipboard beneath his arm. "Of course. Now, in assigning an order of execution…It's frequently difficult to determine, in the records accompanying the men from in particular many of the smaller prisons, precise tenure. Often times the date of the trial, or even the date of the crime or in some especially bungled files the man's date of birth is listed, but not the date the sentence commenced. This has resulted in a number of "ties," so to speak. In those instances, of which there are, as I said, a great many, would you prefer to set the criteria for order of execution?"

"I trust your judgement."

"With the impending influx, how do you feel about getting out ahead of the curve, carrying out the sentences of those with no hope of reprieve with enough regularity that we're operating below capacity? It could be in our best interest to begin processing the condemned outside the "one in, one out" eleventh-hour schedule we've been—"

"That sounds fine."

"Okay, then. I'll be periodically dropping off paperwork for your signature."

"That's fine."

As Melvin turned away, Nat stopped him in the doorway, calling his name.

"How's the book?"

"It's beginning to shape up."

"I'd love to see what you've got so far. When it's ready."

"You'll be the first to see what I've done."

On the first day of autumn, the world blazing bright orange with the scent of rotting apples and smoke, word travelled through the yard that due to overcrowding up on Neahkanie an Indian was about to be admitted. The men paused their various diversions, poker and baseball, tossing stones at squirrels, to watch the familiar battered red wagon jolting along the washboard road running parallel to the beach. The rig pulled up to the gate, guards dropping down, beckoning the prisoner to exit, each taking hold of an arm, hands handcuffed behind his back...

"*That's* a Indian?" scoffed Henry, pointing at the parted hair, the stiff white collar.

"Is it ever," mumbled Nat.

"Doesn't look like one."

"I don't know what to tell you, Henry."

"Looks like a actor. Looks like a fake Indian in a photo."

Andy, joining the crowd, took a look at their new roommate and began nodding. "I know that man."

"Moon Fox?"

"I don't remember his name, but I remember playing against him. He's Kootenai, right? Off the rez up above Coeur d' Alene?"

"That's right."

"You're going to want to get him down here with a bat in his hand." Andy looked back at his teammates. "We've got a centerfielder."

Nat smiled, shaking his head. "Well son of a goddamn bitch. An unexpected bonus. Manna. Isn't that something..."

Nat thought the dapper man seated across the desk matched the atmosphere of his office perfectly.

Moon Fox had acquired his refined sumptuary habits at Christ's Beneficence Indian School in Athol, Idaho, to which he'd been kidnapped by missionaries at the age of five. Upon his graduation as a sixteen-year-old, he had returned to the reservation, where, after a brief period of darkness following the revelation that his family, in the midst of some obscure conflict with the U.S. Army, had been murdered, he'd taken a job teaching Salishan languages and history in the one room Coeur d' Alene Indian schoolhouse. Quickly, his responsibilities had begun to multiply and expand, until he'd become principal, custodian, coach, and sole teacher. With utter control of the curriculum, Moon Fox created a revolutionary admixture of the Salish and the English, melding deep tradition with hard pragmatics.

While he sought to preserve the truth, he also believed that only a fool, marking the direction of the wind, would attempt to alter or deny it. He prepared his students for life in the modern world, while inculcating the importance of preserving the life of the people. He taught his students that each of us simultaneously occupies two worlds, and in order to avoid being torn apart we must trust the compasses of our hearts. We must prepare for the moment, unimaginable until it happens, when we are called upon for swift and irrevocable action.

One evening Moon Fox and his wife Aiyana went into Coeur d' Alene for their anniversary dinner. As they dined, a stranger, a gemstone purchaser from Hanover, walking to the lavatory from the bar, called out "Look at em," chuckling back to a group of colleagues gesturing their approval from the bar, "all dressed up for their big night on the town. Eatin with silverware, and everything." Moon Fox rose, quietly announcing that he would like to pay and leave. The man reached as if to grope Aiyana, and she pushed his hand away. The man spit in her face. A crowd gathered around them. Amongst the onlookers was the sheriff, who met Moon Fox's gaze, and smiled.

And within that smile, within the gradually constricting circle of men, Moon Fox saw that something very ugly was about to happen.

His time had arrived for epic and irrevocable action.

Snatching a wine glass from the table he jabbed it into the jeweler's face, base shattering, stem sliding through the man's blue eye. Fox grabbed the sheriff by the hair, slamming his head onto the table, yanking it up with shards of a shattered plate and a steak knife dangling from the flesh of his face. Both the injured men davened and staggered and shrieked until the one smashed through a plate glass window toppling into the lake and the other bashed his brains in on the concrete corner of a fire place. A fist extended from the crowd smashing Moon Fox's nose and he grabbed the arm and snapped it over his leg like kindling, then reeled the man in by the flopping arm and slashed his throat with the steak knife. At that point even the men in the crowd with guns backed away.

Fox shook his head at Nat. "Before all that, I'd never so much as been in a fistfight. No question who the spirits were with that night. I'm not happy those men had to die…But apparently they had to die."

Riding a horse like mad into the night Moon Fox and Aiyana returned to the reservation, accumulating warriors from the Palouse, Kalispell, and Nez Perce. When the white warriors arrived, as inevitable as a deadly January blizzard, the clash began without a word, interlopers twisting from their horses skewered with arrows, notches hacked into their skulls with tomahawks, braves tumbling into the dust with arms or legs blown off. After several minutes of this, the whites turned on their brown horses and rode away.

For the next week it seemed that perhaps the dual world had shorn in two, that things had simply started over, two separate worlds, one for each, until a single rider appeared, gangly red-haired kid with fear trembling in his eyes like gelatin, fear thick and hot in his sweat. "They…" his voice broke, facing the vanguard of warriors standing sentry at the border. He looked back over his shoulder to the forest. "We grabbed a couple of them Indian kids from their place over on Hayden Lake. It's going to be them going to the hangman, unless that killer—" The boy yanked the reins so that the horse stood and twisted and bolted. But the point had been understood. Moon Fox checked with the mother of the two supposedly abducted boys. They had, indeed, gone to stay at a fishing cabin on the lake the day before, and hadn't returned.

He rode into town, presenting himself to the brand-new sheriff.

With seven they coalesced, moving and breathing in relation to one another like the composite parts of some perpetual motion machine fueled by the crackling blurred circuit of the ball. While individually they'd each been privy to horrible things, sadness and blood, the moment that the players formed the fluid constellation dictated by the ball, each one of them shrugged off the cloak of darkness, the stain that clung to his or her heart. The ugliness, no longer poisonous or heavy, diffused harmlessly into the atmosphere. The players sensed it, felt the first flickering connections, the ghostly outline of the path that might lead to the renunciation of their unsavory pasts. With the life of the grass dyeing their shoes and the sun's gasses soaking their skin, the ballplayers formed a pattern around the spherical stitched center of the universe, and each one of them felt that he or she had after all been brought here for a purpose. And each one of them felt in his or her secret heart that perhaps I am not that bad.

That perhaps my shattered path has led me here to be repaired.

That perhaps my place within this circuit on the field, my crucial place, can become my place within the world.

⌐══⌐

One evening, lingering within some gold-washed memory of his brothers, Andy frowned, snapping his mitt around the frozen rope Dot unleashed after chasing a popup into left field, stuffing the ball into his back pocket. Something had been bothering him, and he'd just realized what.

"Goddamn," he said, stretching his arms, rocking foot to foot. "These Union suits have got to go." The rest of the ballplayers afield shook their heads sadly. That evening Andy requested an audience with Nat.

"Nat sir," he said, settling into the proffered chair across the mahogany desk, scratching his chin, sucking up the lacquered air of the warden's office, "these outfits are a sin to Crockett, and they're hindering our ability." Training his polar eyes on the warden he swung his arms awkwardly, twisting his hips with a thick rustling of fabric to demonstrate. "It's hard to get a gauge of what we can do, when we can't do it owing to these goddamn gunny sacks." In the boy's sour countenance and the greasy bunched cloth Nat flashed back to the coveralls, stiff as armor with blood and tar and turpentine, he'd worn in the railyard. He thought about those coveralls, and the white uniforms at the bottom of the hill…

"Once the team is formed, I'll make sure we're properly outfitted. But I imagine something can be done in the meantime."

"I really do think it would be in everyone's best interest."

The next morning, when the ballplayers opened the door of the metal equipment shed, they found jammed amongst the bats and balls and gloves a steel bin of old clothing, long johns and wool caps, wool dungarees, tank tops and soft denim jeans, all sizes. The men and Dot set upon the garments, selecting and discarding. As they rummaged Slade called out the elephant in the room, asking, "Where you think all this clothing came from?"

"I'm sure we all know where these came from," said Fox.

"There but for the grace of God." They stood thinking, garments dangling limply from their fists.

Henry broke the moment, shrugging. "Well shit…let's do em justice. Get dressed, shut pan, and let's play." So they dressed themselves in the surrendered clothing of the recently dead, leaving the stiff greasy prison-issue coveralls slouching from the shed's rafters like molted skins, like bodies in an abattoir, and every individual, though he or she might have resisted ownership of the thought, felt free-moving and refreshed, much better chasing down the ball in those new clothes.

CHAPTER ELEVEN

*N*at turned from the window shaking his head, rubbing his chin, teeth barred. "Shit…" Something was happening down there. The configuration was getting tighter, the movement faster, more synchronized. The game was moving at a pace Nat could hardly follow but the seven remained in perfect stasis. They were becoming something far greater than their individual parts.

And this is just the beginning. Barely a glimpse of it.

The raw force and delicate symmetry he'd seen in The Kid's swing had come to embody the entire group. Nat knew he could not in any conscience let this elemental perfection flare and die trapped within the prison yard. Reluctantly, with the air of a man unearthing some shameful secret from his past, returning to a perverse and vitiating vice after a long period of abstinence, Nat slowly unlocked the desk drawer, extracting the manila envelope as if it contained a diagnosis he'd been dreading. Therein lie the very first response he'd received to his request for ball-playing inmates, months earlier. Nat removed an article clipped from *The New York Times*, fifteen typed pages of testimony, and a note from the Superintendent of New York State Prisons reading simply:

To ensure you knew exactly who or what you would be receiving.

-Sage Garfield

The article, bearing the headline "Hardball Hero's Estate Becomes Unimaginable House of Horror" described the incomprehensible tragedy transpiring in Ithaca when, on a frigid gray December morning, Beaneaters star left fielder Josh Martin returned to his palatial home after splitting a cord of wood to cleave the skulls of his wife and three sleeping children. Nate reread the article and pushed it aside grimacing, turning to the typed sheets of interviews with Martin's former teammates. For two years Martin had distinguished himself as a fine ballplayer, and nothing else. Then came the incident at the Ansonia Hotel. In the words of former teammate Vic Bergen "We was eating breakfast in the hotel, talking about...hell I don't even remember, but nothing much. Nothing more controversial than the weather or who was likely to be pitching that day, when Martin, he was sitting across from me, not saying much, but he never really did. Quiet kid. But polite, friendly enough...Anyhow, Josh jumps up, out of nowhere, and throws a mug of hot coffee right in my face. For a second I think I'm blinded, but when the coffee clears I see Josh lunging across the table taking a butter knife right at my eyes...And the look on his face, good Christ. I don't even want to imagine what he was hoping to do to me, if it wasn't for the rest of the boys dragging him down. Took damn near the whole team, and they had to keep him pinned for a good half hour, thrashing and spitting and biting, until he ran out of juice. But the damnedest thing, the next day, there he is sitting across from me, buttering his toast, talking about the unfortunate likelihood of a rain delay like nothing happened. (Manager Harlan) Pillar came and talked to me about it, said the kid couldn't give any type of reason, and couldn't really understand why they were wanting to make such a fuss about it. Same as if they were questioning him about losing his jersey or waking up late for practice...no big deal. He asked me what I wanted to do about it and I said I guess nothing. But from then on, I was eating breakfast with a sap palmed, just in case."

Over the next four years, Martin grew increasingly prone to disappearing, failing to materialize for days or a week, then trotting out to left field moments before game time as if nothing had happened. A less talented player, management would have cut ties with a dozen times over, but every time Martin resurfaced he'd make up for his lost time with a torrid hitting streak and a flurry of game-winning homeruns.

As time went on, things got worse. In Cincinnati umpires physically removed Martin after he'd gone into the stands chasing "the man with the red hand." He adopted the habit, on the field and off, of spinning a circle every six steps, in order to check for anyone sneaking up on him. The young man became increasingly isolated from teammates after several altercations based on his beliefs that they were trying to poison him, and that they were mocking the recent death of his small son, who had drowned in a canal. Several teammates corroborated the latter complaint, describing a cadre of older players notorious for their cruel hazing pasting flyers for swimming lessons to Martin's locker, and asking if he'd be bringing the boy to the park on Father's Day.

Nat pushed the papers aside. Christ. Harassing him over the death of his son. A pang of sympathy stiffened Nat's jaw.

If he were in Martin's position, to have suffered such a tragedy, and then be faced with that bullshit at work…Nat had no
idea what he might be capable of doing. No man could hon-
estly say, unless he'd personally been put in that unimaginable
position. Although, Nat realized, there *were* some possibilities
that he could definitively rule out, such as murdering his family with an ax.

Outside, he heard the ball cracking from wood to leather.
It seemed the country's supply of incarcerated able ballplayers
had been exhausted. If he intended to provide for Andy and the
others a chance to see what they could become, he would have
to do things he might normally oppose.

Such as bringing in a man like Josh Martin.

"Would you play with him? I mean if he can still play."

"How's that?"

Nat tapped the article. "I'm not sure after putting down that
ax, you're able to pick up a bat again. I'm not sure those two
minds are compatible."

Half Andy's face smiled. "Well…I played winter ball in Mexico with Josh for a few months, and he's a weird son of a bitch."

"So you don't want him on the team?"

Andy shook his head. "No, my point is that I wouldn't be
surprised to find him just the same as he was before any of the
murdering. I don't know that Josh is too prone to be thinking
about things the same way you or I might, sir. As far as having him on the team…We've got seven players. I think we've
done about as much as we can, playing amongst ourselves out in
the yard." The Kid dug his right pinky into his left ear, smiling.
"It does occur to me that if I'd have held that standard, only

playing with a man whose character I endorsed…I might not have played a whole lot of baseball.."

"Alright." Nat nodded. "Unless the situation out in New York has somehow changed, I'll get him out here within the month."

⌒〜⌐

In retrospect, Nat was deeply chagrined not to have anticipated the problem.

Those seven prisoners walking the halls in a pack dressed differently than the rest, granted extended recreation time and access to special equipment…Crossing the mess hall to the ballplayers' table, the barroom murderer from Corvallis slid a guard's purloined black nightstick up from the neck of his jump-suit smashing Andy's head, like a man beating an animal to death. Andy went down, sending his tray of food flipping up into the air, hands reaching up, opening and closing uselessly as he fell, the back of his head striking the bench as the attacker leapt on top, raising the club, bringing it down…

Henry knocked the club askew with his left hand, swing-ing with his right the buck knife he'd bought from a guard, catching the huge man in the gut with a thick membranous popping and a grunt. As the attacker bent, the bloody knife came up laying open half his throat, and the dying giant lurched back, slipping in food and blood, staggering from the cafeteria. While Andy's teammates pulled him up like an unmoored scarecrow, with the guards' footsteps clattering in the corridor, Henry stepped over to the table from whence the big man had come and drove the knife into a sitting man's back, dragging him to the ground, twisting the knife and pull-ing it out trailing a ribbon of blood.

They heard the guards encounter the bleeding, staggering ogre in the hall, grunting and beating and getting beat.

***

Nat shook his head, sighed. "And the man you stabbed in the back?"

"That's what he gets for throwing in with that other piece of shit."

"How do you know they had anything to do with each other? Maybe he was just sitting near him."

Henry thought for a moment. "Well then he should have knocked him down. He was right there. Arm's length…" Henry held out his arm to demonstrate. "He's a…how do you call it? A accomplice."

Nat shook his head. "This might still turn into a much larger problem. As it is…Nothing like this can happen again."

Henry stared back noncommittedly. "It's your house."

Nat sighed. "Go on. I expect we'll be dealing with this again shortly, one way or another." Henry shrugged. As he left, Melvin entered, holding the clipboard with the schedule of executions.

Fuck. Now this guy. Pile on the misery.

Melvin seemed to read the warden's mind, cocking his head, thin lips trembling into a smile. "My apologies for impinging upon your time. But as I was waiting out in the hall, I couldn't help but overhear…Interesting thing, here, with the schedule."

***

"How do you feel?"

Andy nodded his head, misshapen like a cloth sack full of chestnuts. As if to confirm this he twisted his feet to grip the earth and crouched, exploding into Ralph's heavy sinker, lifting it up, following through like a man ripping open the sky with a sword, turning to watch the ball rising into the mist, a speck.

Nat nodded in approval. "Hasn't affected your hitting any. From here forward, we'll be moving you seven to the southeast hall," Nat pointed to the deadend rear wing of the prison, jutting between the Tall House and the dropoff to the ocean. "There's a door there, opens right out onto the diamond..." Nat saw no reason to mention he'd rearranged their meal schedule, ostensibly to accommodate the three daily practices, so that the ballplayers would have the cafeteria to themselves. Or that he'd given orders to the guards in charge of the yard to establish a border surrounding the practice field, beyond which no common prisoner was allowed to cross, under penalty of revoked outdoor privileges. To summarize, from this point forward the ball-playing prisoners would have absolutely no contact with any other inmates.

Andy launched another ball into the ether.

Walking away, Nat turned. "As a point of information, both the men involved in the incident had been scheduled for execution tomorrow evening. So that's done."

"Coincidence."

"Coincidence."

"Funny thing."

"Funny thing."

⟋⟍

Straightening his tie, slicking back his hair, Melvin threw the bolt on the Tall House door and opened it. The two guards sat on a wooden bench at a slight distance, smoking. He walked past them. "Both bodies are ready to be transported."

He thought one of them may have muttered something, the other chuckling, as he passed…But what of it? He'd heard the guards whispering about how one of the bosses fucked the dead bodies and the other was scared to come within a half-mile of them. He didn't mind. He relished his status as the Beast. They were terrified of him.

Let the soaplocks whisper out of their dirty faces. They were too far beneath him to lay a finger on his heels. For a month, ever since Nat had issued him carte blanche over the executions, Melvin had been killing men at will, setting the order according to his personal whims. He would canvass the halls, the cafeteria and yard, sometimes dropping in on a prisoner in his cell. The names of those who meekly thanked him for stopping by, referring to him as "Sir" were moved to the bottom of the list. Those who sneered and snarled and lunged to be restrained by the guards found themselves unceremoniously, without notice, no last meal, no last words or final letter home, roused at four A.M., bludgeoned into submission but not unconsciousness, and dragged out to fly on hempen wings.

Some of the bodies Melvin sent to Portland in the ice wagon, and some he simply had a pair of guards, in exchange for a pair of twenty-dollar bills pulled from the prison's Operations coffer, row out past the arches of the Twin Rocks and slide into the ocean. He liked to stand on the beach at night, looking at the rocks, imaging a dozen previously hearty bodies, the bodies of men who had spent their lives snarling, pounding, spraying saliva and semen, wedged against the base of the rocks swaying nakedly like plucked chickens, undulating in the surf, entangled ignominiously amongst the limbs of other men, straining and howling silently to get up the beach, get to Melvin, do the things to him they had done to everyone else…but to no avail. They couldn't. They were nothing anymore. They would never be, or do, anything ever again. He had won. Melvin listened to the ocean. The crashing tide reminded him of a thousand dead men trying to scream through clenched teeth, through the lockjaw of rigor mortis.

As he walked up the beach, through the dunes, he looked at the light burning in Nat's office window, and he began to think about the sword of Damocles, and the tender top of the warden's skull. If the powers-that-be were to request, which they might for any number of reasons, an accurate accounting of the ongoing flurry of executions, the ensuing cover-up would demand that leadership immediately be fired and banished. If a stay of execution were to come in for a man that Melvin had already killed, the charge would be murder.

In either scenario, the chain-of-command began, and ended, with Nat, as evidenced by the signatures Melvin had been so assiduously obtaining. So far, it seemed as if the beefy, florid heads of state in Portland were as feeble-minded as everyone else, and might remain too incompetent or lazy to detect and address the pogrom Melvin had been conducting on the coast. If the men responsible for monitoring this activity were too dim to uncover the scandal, Melvin might have to send them an anonymous tip. It was time for the warden to go. Melvin didn't mind doing him the occasional favor, such as moving the two men who had fought with Nat's pet prisoners to the top of the list, but any long-term working relationship was out of the question.

For a brief time after his arrival to Rockaway, he had thought perhaps he might partner with Nat. But at the end of the day, the warden was just like the rest of them: fatuous and posturing, trying to overcompensate for his own inadequacies with, of all ridiculous things, the formation of a baseball team. Not only had Nat revealed himself as an unfit horse upon which to hitch his wagon, it turned out there was simply no conceivable need. Melvin had become his own team of Clydesdales. What use the nag? *And just what do I intend?* he mused, looking over the gray water, out to the Twin Rocks looming like brutal primitive headstones.

Taking over the prison, for starters. And after that… the extermination of the rest of the scum. He would see that through, at least. And from there…

It's a big world. I'll keep my eyes open.

Suddenly, Melvin felt himself capable of absolutely anything.

CHAPTER TWELVE

"We've got ourselves a game lined up." Nat clapped once and rubbed his palms together. "Just as soon as our eighth man arrives…"

"Hell, yeah." The players smiled, nodding at one another. "Against who?"

A brief hesitation. "Oak Knoll. The head doctor up there formerly worked with me in Portland. She said they've got a good squad…"

Ralph's eyes twinkled within the mask of wrecked gore. "The nuthouse up Long Beach?" Nat nodded.

"Bunch of batshit lunatics?" Dot smiled. It was ambiguous whether the prospect repulsed or impressed her.

Nat nodded. "We've got a game. Everything has to start somewhere."

Henry nodded, laughing. "Hell yeah then. Let's do it. The killers against…probably also the killers. Just crazier."

⌐━━━⌐

The eighth man arrived on a morning marked by a strangely placid ocean, a field of undulating swells reflecting the dead white light of the sun. He came into the yard led by four guards, wrists and ankles shackled together. Henry nodded approvingly.

"Finally, not a old man or a girl. Not a burned up damn body. This man looks like a ballplayer."

Deacon smiled. He smelled it. "The kind of man you'd want as your neighbor, huh?"

Henry frowned. "I guess…"

There was little differentiation between Josh Martin's long thick neck and his weak-chinned long narrow head, all of it covered in short curly brown hair, from the hollow of his throat to the top of his head, giving the impression of a tubular nubby appendage growing up from his torso. His blue eyes were washed out, tired. His mouth sat slightly ajar. As Nat, who had seen the arrival from his window and come down to meet him, drew near, looking into Martin's face, the hair rose on the back of his neck.

Even the most vicious killers with the most heinous crimes lurking in their files, upon speaking with them for a moment, Nat could imagine the thoughts and circumstances that had led them to this place. Even when he did not condone, he could acknowledge. He could imagine the impulses, even when they were impulses he did not possess. Sometimes he would try to imagine what it must be like to be some other type of murderer, prolific or sadistic or deranged, and invariably he would discover that he could. He could imagine feeling that anger, or desire. He could imagine the feeling of relief, of an odious obligation discharged, an icy sense of peace, of blessed calm descending upon a previously fevered mind. After reviewing a file and conducting the intake interview, Nat could explain: *This is a man prone to anger, with limited intelligence and no education who learned that the only time he felt equal to other men was when he was badly hurting them. This is a man who viewed women as non-human objects because his father had taught him to do so. This is a man who was so horribly afraid of failing in the eyes of his family that the best solution for everyone after his firing was to get rid of them.*

But looking into Josh Martin's eyes, Nat could find nothing recognizable. *This is a…*He did not know what this was. He had an odd fantasy, standing within the unfocused gaze of those faded eyes. Nat was struck with the sense that just beyond those eyes was a dense block of black soil crawling with beetles and worms, or else an empty cavity housing a smaller head, wet and pinkish, with rolling bulbous eyes, crooked yellow teeth, howling…

Stepping closer to Martin, Nat spoke flatly. "I know you've been informed as to why you're here. We've got a game in three days, so we'll get you out of those chains, see what you can do on—"

Martin's eyes pulled away in slow motion, and he began shuffling towards the prison, still shackled.

Nat looked down from his window. Seven players. Three days since Martin's arrival, and he'd yet to appear on the baseball field. In the back hall, every cell vacant except Martin's, Nat leaned to the slat in the closed door. The new recruit sat on his cot talking inaudibly, gesturing with his hands.

Nat cleared his throat. "Josh."

Slowly, the eyes turned up to his.

"We need you out at practice. First game tomorrow—"

Martin turned inward, resuming the conversation Nat had interrupted.

Nat's voice rose. "You've been brought here, from New York, for a specific purpose. Needless to say, if you're unwilling to try and carry out that job…"

Martin was all alone in another universe. Nat turned away. If Martin won't play ball…*We'll have to get rid of him. What a fucking waste of time and effort. And still no closer to a ball club…*

Though Nat, of course, would not be handling the execution. Even the idea of signing the order tightened his stomach and clogged his throat. He sneered at an image of Martin extending that long head, biting into Nat's throat, and bearing him down to hell.

⌁

"Can you play with seven?"

Andy thought about it. "Not really."

Nat squeezed his upper lip between thumb and knuckle. "Shit. I feel like if this is going to happen…it needs to happen now."

"You'll play."

"…What?"

"Yeah. You can play, at least out at Oak Knoll. Right field. Fox can cover most of your ground. You'll bat last, hope for a walk. We'll still need another player, but for one game, it'll be fine." Nat opened his mouth, wavering, but Andy leaned into him, locking him up with those lupine eyes. "Let's do it. We'll figure something else out from there. But you're right… We're dead in the water, here. We need to get this going. Playing with you out there would be something. And that's better than nothing."

The game at the bottom of the hill drifted behind Nat's eyes like ocean mist. All of those boys are most likely dead, he thought…

⌁

As they came jolting up the cobblestone road on a peach farmer's flatbed trailer drug slowly by four horses the players whistled and pointed at the ornate fountains and marble sculptures, the crystalline swimming pools and steaming hot pools, the stately oaks and towering wooden cottages at the top of hundred-foot-tall ladders that Nat explained were viewpoints (when Dot asked "Don't the crazies jump off there and kill themselves?" Nat shrugged and answered "I guess they must not."), the bocce and tennis courts, the outdoor theatre and bandshell, the huge white buildings with Doric columns.

"Shit," said Slade, gawking at the opulence, "I think I do feel a touch of the crazies coming on. Check me in, warden..."

"You got a thousand dollars a month?"

"You got a shovel?" The two older men looked at one another and laughed. The field sat nestled at the zenith of the grounds, lush grass mowed into a checkerboard pattern, rich brown dirt with thick cottony foul lines and a freshly painted dark green wooden fence ten feet tall. The opposition came trotting from their dug-out, fresh pressed alabaster cotton uniforms, long-limbed and lithe, whipping the ball around and smiling with their white teeth, thin angular deeply tanned features. "Fucking Christ..." mumbled Henry as the Oak Knoll shortstop took a flip from the second baseman, plucking it barehanded ripping it on a line to first, "*these* are the lunatics?" He puckered his fat lips in disappointment.

"Don't look like they're hearing a whole lot of voices to me."

"Nor weaving too many baskets."

"Goddamn F.F.V., every one of them."

"Look at those uniforms..." The players looked from the crisp spotless adornment of their adversaries to the baggy wool trousers and long-sleeved beige shirts Nat had borrowed from Debra Elkins' surplus of emergency militia gear.

"I told you they had a team. Now if you boys are finished crying out all the reasons you're going to lose..." Nat shook his head pursing his lips, nailing a lineup to the dugout wall.

1. Dorothy SS
2. Deacon 1B
3. Andy C
4. Moon Fox LF-CF
5. Henry P
6. Slade 2B
7. Ralph 3B
8. Nat RF

Henry cocked his head skeptically. "Something I just thought of, Warden. No offense to Ralph…but can this crippled up son of a bitch handle the bat? Now that I'm thinking, I don't recall ever seeing him do it in practice. I'm asking because otherwise, we're only talking about half a player here, no good when I'm pitching, and we're going to have to keep looking for another man." He looked at Ralph. "Like I said, though, no offense."

"None taken."

Nat looked to Ralph. The Incendiary mimed swinging a bat. "I've learned to work quite well around the limitations the good lord gave me."

Deacon smiled, eyeing Ralph's garbled visage. "Good lord…? Hmm."

As the umpire called Rockaway for warm-ups, Nat, with a stone in his throat and a serpent in his gut, like a shell-shocked soldier cast back upon the blood-soaked earth, commenced the march across the outfield. He thought of his humiliation in Tillamook, and the boys at the bottom of the hill. *This time, it could be different. Eventually, it has to come out different. Right? Keep throwing the dice…*

A hand took Nat's shoulder, turning him around. Josh Martin.

"Hey Skip. Talked a couple of the screws into bringing me on the next train. Shall I take your spot?"

Nat nodded. Martin trotted out to left field, pushing Fox into right-center.

The guards who'd been escorting Martin parted, revealing Melvin. "I went in to see if I could explain the urgency of the situation. He seemed…for lack of a more accurate descriptor, a little better, today. I asked if he wanted to come play in the game. If that's not what you want, say the word, and I'll take him right back."

Nat shook his head. "No, I appreciate it. Stay for the game."

"I've got to get back." *Just wanted to see for myself, should I eventually be called to testify.*

In the top of the first, the Oak Knoll pitcher moved the ball around with the ease of an imaginary line, cutting it left, spinning it in right, pointing it into the dirt, so that Dot and Deacon struck out looking helpless and Andy torched a ball up the middle that the lanky shortstop ("And why the hell," asked Ralph, shaking his prunish head, gesturing out towards the field with his upturned webbed palms, "do all these sons of bitches look just like one another? Does being crazy make you tall and blonde and good-looking?") ducked into, scooping on a hop, pegging to first catching Andy by a quarter step.

In their half of the inning, the Oaks rattled Henry, drawing a couple of walks, bunting, slapping the ball around the diamond for three runs. The superior Oaks, benefiting from better genes, training, nutrition, and discipline, scratched out three more in the bottom of the second. Nat watched, pacing the dugout, scratching his jaw, tapping his teeth together.

On the train ride home that night, Slade would describe their comeback with the analogy of a big ugly drunk who's been sitting in a bar for the better part of thirty years getting into a fight with a fresh-faced college kid. The kid might start out smacking him a few in the jaw, but eventually that drunk is just going to keep coming and coming through the abuse, oblivious to the pain and shame, and bury him. In the same fashion, the Rockaways grimly ground out one at-bat after another, fouling off everything close, until the kid on the mound, big league arm but Faberge nerves, panicked, laying a fat one dead down the middle to be butchered.

As ball after ball came screaming and twisting off the convicts' bats, the fragile hearts and twitchy minds of the Oak Knoll boys, besieged by such relentless pressure, began to resist the work. Cracks appeared and spread. The Rockaway hitters showed bunt, pulling their bats back into the catcher's eyes so that he took pitches off the mask that rattled the fillings in his molars and pitches in the chest and gut that made it hard to breathe. Each player reaching base clapped and talked and paced back and forth until the pitcher, sweat rolling down his red face, lips trembling, threw the ball into the first base bleachers, the third base bleachers, out into center field. Every close play involved a kicked shin, a stomped Achilles, an infielder on hands and knees questioning why he'd come out here to be abused on such a beautiful sunny day.

Such were the tricks, Nat thought, shielding a smile, one learns living at a disadvantage.

By the fifth inning those Oak Knoll boys, for whom life had generally been accommodating and generous if frequently nerve-wracking, moved within a black cloud of dread, worms in their hearts, watching the wolf's eyes of their opponents as if Fate's throw of the bones, the fate of their very souls, could be portentously read there. When Henry skulked out for the bottom of the ninth and finished like a murderer slamming shut the cellar door on the scrabbling fingers of his trapped shrieking victims, the boys were not surprised to be victims and without resistance laid down as if they'd been expecting it all along.

With one exception.

"Now *that's* what I had been hoping for," said Deacon, pointing a long crooked finger to the right fielder. Amongst the slender blue bloods, amongst the greyhounds, this boy looked like a mongrel hoisted by his scruff up out of the gutter. When Deacon pulled a hooking line drive foul, a ball that every other player on the field instantly disregarded, the ratty wiry kid broke sprinting for it, a hopeless counterproductive gesture, until at the last second, *Jesus he might*, he dove headfirst into the fence, with a bang like a broken neck, knocking half a dozen boards slantindicular, popping up with the ball in his bare hand and blood pouring from his nose and mouth and the wide black gash beneath his left eye. His teammates stood frozen in horror as he shouted for them to cover second base, blood pulsing down his chin, until in exasperation he sprinted in from right field stomping both feet on the bag, doubling up Moon Fox who, wandering towards third with the foul ball aloft had been so nonplussed by the kid's suicidal antics he'd simply stopped and stared with his hands on his hips. When Nat ran out to argue that the kid had clearly trapped the ball, the umpire motioned at the bloody mess, declaring, "Perhaps. But let me tell you, if that weird bastard wants it that bad, I'm going to give it to him."

After several acts of similar insanity—leaning into a beanball with his chin, flipping headfirst over the right field fence chasing a Josh Martin home run that cleared by fifty feet, catching a line drive in his bare hands after fumbling his glove—the mongrel concluded his day on the diamond by running into Andy at the plate with such abandon that both boys ended up semi-conscious on their backs twenty feet from one another. As the two temporary corpses began to stir, it dawned on both simultaneously that the tag had not been applied, nor had the runner touched the dish. The kid propelled his half-broken body toward the plate as The Kid dove at him, another gland-rattling collision, the umpire leaping to straddle the carnage shouting and gesturing, "Safe!"

"And at that point," recalled Deacon that evening on the train, emitting the blue smoke of a clove cigarette from his clenched teeth, "a ten-run game. The kid rebreaks his nose for nothing. Skeery he is not."

"Nor too goddamn smart."

"Yes…" Andy grimaced, shifting on the wooden bench as the car plowed through a stretch of rough track, aggravating the kinks in his beleaguered skeleton, "still I'd rather have him on my team than the other. Give me nine of those…there's your championship squad. I don't care who or where you're playing."

CHAPTER THIRTEEN

*B*ack home in the death row prison, none of them acknowledged the accumulating frost on the ground or the leaves, sere then gone, the trees crooked and skeletal, Sagittarian grave markers along the horizon. The bat sent fire ants up their forearms into the nerves clustered within their elbows and the ball, struck soundly, fluttered a brief life and died, frozen to death. They practiced in silence. Injuries became a common occurrence as the players lost track of themselves, fading, watching the forest or ocean pensively until the jolt back to reality of a line drive upside the head or a teammate crashing into your knees.

This was the time of year to gather for the winter, to harvest, to slaughter, to caulk the cracks, to stock the armory and infirmary. Now, put in a position where they could only stand by, idly trusting that somebody else was taking care of everything, the ballplayers grew nervous and vague. Practicing in a mist like concrete dust, Ralph Ellison, squeaking heel to toe in the wet snow, tipped his chin out towards the accumulating snow on the field. "I thought it didn't get like this, on the coast."

Dot shook her head. "I don't think it does."

"But it is."

"But so it is."

Deacon laughed inside his closed mouth. "The dews grew quivering and chill…" Suddenly hinges creaked and screeched like the door to a tomb buried beneath the desert and they stopped, turning as one body, the ball still rolling. The metal door on the side of the tall rectangular building in deepest right field grated open, revealing a dim cinereal light, dark shapes of figures moving within it.

As the sun tore its way free of the clouds just above the dark rectangle, a pair of guards came forth into the orange smoky November light dragging a dead body dangling the severed noose from his neck. The players shielded their eyes, squinting into the sun. They drug him by his feet, with sour trudging countenances communicating their distaste for the man they'd just murdered. Nat strolled behind them, arms crossed, thoughtful, insouciant. Nobody breathed. This macabre quartet drew closer. As the figures emerged from the blinding sun, all at once the players realized they drug not a corpse but a tarp, a tarp from which jutted the long wooden handles of tools and a thumping metal bucket.

Nat spun his finger, signaling for the players to abandon practice, to come closer. "This ball club has just been converted into a work crew. We've got something washed up onto the beach, and we need to get rid of it before it starts to rot and stink." He led the team over to the fence to look at the thing heaped on the sand. Henry wrinkled his nose and swallowed. "Jesus. And what in the hell *is* that?" Nat shrugged. "Well, it's big, as you can see. But it's not a whale. Not exactly a whale." Nat unlocked the gate leading down to the beach and they went through, warden and prisoners, then the two guards dragging the tools and two more who had just appeared carrying rifles. The group moved around the creature washed up onto the sand, each man silent or talking softly to himself.

The size of a train car, the thing had degraded and spread, slumped, as if dropped from a great height. The color was no color, grayish pale. A dark brown stain fouled the sand all around it. The beast presented the impression of a slug, a creature of the mud, an amorphous thing that undulated in the permanent dark, with what appeared to be tattered fins, like a gnawed duck's foot, at one end, and at the other…The group clustered around the end that appeared to be the head and stared silently, tilting their own heads, staring…Big as a redwood stump, there was something very vaguely and disturbingly humanoid about the head, with an extended wet clump that might have been a nose, snout, and above that a pair of widespread indentations that might have represented sockets previously housing skyblue eyes, or blind rudimentary eyes. Each of the observers had the absurd thought that there was something inherently unhappy about the monstrous features, something not only ugly and bestial, but somehow trapped and yearning. The thing looked like the deformed ghost of a whale and the mutilated ghost of a man.

"What the fuck?" Slade chuckled, admiring the beast. "The ocean spits up some weird shit."

"Alright, then," said Nat, pointing the prisoners toward the whaling implements laid out on the greasy tarp at the base of the massive corpse. They approached hesitantly. Lying parallel were a dozen wooden poles, each as tall as a man, from which extended a curved steel blade as long as a man's arm. There were poles with long rusted hooks, and scimitars, and serrated knives.

Deacon nodded admiringly, hands on his hips. "That's the hardware with which you're going to outfit a bunch of deathrow killers?" Nat smiled meaningfully. "I trust you." He looked to the guards and everyone looked at Josh Martin.

Nat nodded at Moon Fox. "You know how to flense a whale?"

Fox shook his head. "I know how to gut a salmon."

"Just as well. I suppose we're not burning the oil nor carving the bones...out of *this*...This has not been brought to us to use. Hack and saw the goddamn thing into serviceable pieces. We've got a couple of flatboats coming from Tillamook. We'll drag the segments of this thing out to sea. See if the sharks won't eat it."

"*We'll* drag it out to sea?"

Nat nodded. "*You'll* drag it out to sea."

Moon Fox looked at the beast. "If the ocean will take it back."

"Yep. If it's all washed back up here tomorrow and we can't get rid of it..." Nat shrugged, "at that point we'll get going on a plan B."

The players took up the wood and steel of the trade and they hesitated. Any number of things seemed suddenly conceivable, achievable, imminently possible. Any man might lop off the warden's head. A sign could pass amongst their eyes and suddenly the guards are run through, helplessly vomiting blood, prisoners scattering into the forest.

But at that moment, the beach clear and bright, the water shimmering, fragrant breeze pushing the stench of the monolithic corpse out to sea, it seemed that first and foremost, this thing on the beach had to be disposed of. For its own sake. For the sake of the beach, the sea, the men...

Only once that was done could a person start considering what to do, where to go next. The prisoners descended upon the aberration en masse with their blades and hooks. "Careful, boys," said Nat. He held up his hands. "Mind your hands. You have no trade without your hands. And mind the hands of the man next to you. Don't cut off his fingers slashing at the fat."

As they began to cut, hesitantly at first, then with growing violence, a dark miasma of putrescence like the worst secret encased within the center of the earth gagged them and they returned frequently to stuff their noses from the sack of crushed lavender Nat had called over from the funeral home, all but Deacon whose closest childhood chum had been Death and Dot who had mopped the brows of leper colonies and dug the victims from earthquake rubble. When the brownish liquid from the adipose tissue splashed onto their bare skin it burned as if they'd become entangled in jellyfish. As they cut, the creature disassociated further, the nacreous hide slumping to an empty husk, seeping gelatin. As they hacked, teeth barred and squinting, the scene tilted dropping back to an earlier time, their bodies dark with dark fat, hacking, the smell of smoke and rotten flesh, of meat and primitive blood and sweat. They drug the strips and translucent clumps to the boats, which three times they filled, three times they transported the odious load out into the bucking ocean and slid the offal into the water as a thick black storm feinted and twitched on the horizon but drew no closer. And with each load they felt lighter, cleaner though in fact they were dirtier, coated with the stinking fat and blood, besieged by insects. They felt more energetic though the work was tougher than anything most had done for a long time.

After the last clump had been drug out, the unclean sand turned over with shovels, they turned from the ocean, crossing the beach in a gray gloaming, back to the prison, while out to sea the charnel sunk, tissue like cottony down, iridescent swatches of flesh sinking through the increasingly black water. A dark whirlpool gained momentum, building force through the stirring of some unseen hand or the unhinging of some gaping maw down in the sunless murk.

Heading to the showers, where each of them would feel more purely exhausted than at any point since childhood, if anyone heard Fox say softly, as the group broke up in the hallway, "Existence gives back. We won't be forgotten," they'd forgotten by the time they fell onto their cots.

That night Andy flailed from his cot into the echoes of a roiling, shredding field of thunderous noise. Lightning had struck the prison.

Pulling himself up to the window, he watched a mass of black cloud scudding over the barbed surface of the ocean, turgid with lightning, swelling, bursting open in a spray of mist and electricity, ripping gashes in the sea, scorching black patches onto the snowy beach, rolling onward, the night stuttering beneath strobe lights. Andy saw, directly above him, the dark eyes like twin gun bores open in the belly of the cloud. And then he saw Nat.

The warden stood on the rocky outcropping beside the statue, his fingers draped upon the sword, twin dark figures against the field of silver, standing at land's edge, watching the ripped furrows and black bowls of the ocean.

Andy thought Nat looked like a man poised to preside over a period of great change. Whether this change would be defined by festering decay or explosive growth, Andy could not determine.

The angel with the bloody sword or the angel with the panacea; who would win?

The next morning, with its immaculate sun and melted snow, Andy was uncertain whether he'd seen the warden, or even awoken within the storm, until Nat approached him during batting practice. "Remember that wild skinny bastard from the lunatics' asylum? The right fielder?"

"I do."

"Well, there you go. You said you'd rather have him on your team. He suddenly became available."

"Really?"

"Yep. He'll be here tomorrow. And that's not all. I think we're entering into a stretch of luck. With nine, I was able to get us a few games up the road. As soon as you get the kid up to speed, we'll head out."

CHAPTER FOURTEEN

*T*he night Israel Meyer Junior stabbed his best friend and constant travelling companion Charlie Whitewall to death at the Chelsea Hotel, the front desk had received a complaint about "shouting and strange noises" from the room registered to the young men, but had elected, for reasons unknown, to relocate the complaining party instead of investigating. That next morning, Israel came staggering through the lobby, bloody hands and face, shouting that he had found a dead baby in their room. When the police arrived, they found no baby, but did discover Charlie Whitewall, stabbed in the chest a single time, curled in a pool of blood on the bathroom floor. Less than twenty-four hours later, Israel sat on a train heading across the country to the asylum at Oak Knoll.

Nat frowned over the file by low lantern light. How had the boy avoided spending a single night in jail? How had he flown without, apparently, any prospect of ever being tried for a brutal murder for which he was the only suspect? Furthermore, Nat wondered, shuffling through the file, why was there not a single newspaper clipping? As if somehow, a bizarre killing at a five-star hotel had eluded notice by the media…

Oh, thought Nat, the furrows in his brow smoothing as he read the medical report, signed by Marshall Stubbs, Chief Neurologist at Bellevue Hospital and Israel Meyer Senior, Attorney at Law. The boy, asserted Doctor Stubbs, had suffered a temporary psychotic rift/fugue state, brought on by some as-yet-undiscovered triggering event. Clearly unfit to stand trial until said triggering event could be identified, a possibility for which time was of the essence, the boy must posthaste, with the psychic residue still fresh enough to be dredged for examination, be rushed to the doctor's colleagues, the top men in the field, at Oak Knoll.

Jesus. Nat could scarcely calculate the array of tracks that must have been heavily greased to facilitate such a maneuver. Both boys, the dead one and the murderer, had simply vanished into thin air. Coming to the final page in the file, Nat uncovered ten one-hundred-dollar notes paperclipped to a page reading:

To Warden Nat Hamelin,

It is imperative, and legally binding, that no mention of Israel Meyer Junior's tenure, or execution, at the Rockaway Beach Oregon State Prison pass beyond the physical walls of the structure, in any form, be it written, verbalized, or other. The administrative offices in Portland have been consulted in this decision, and concur.

In addition, the court shall require that any documentation of Israel Meyer Junior's admission, tenure, or execution, or any other document referring to Israel Meyer Junior, be sent directly to the offices of Meyer, Sheldon, & Shipley.

Israel Meyer, Attorney at Law, Esq.

Nat unclipped the bills, holding them pinched at each end, thoughtfully, for a moment before folding them and sliding the wad into his pocket. And why the transfer from Oak Knoll? Nat had been told only that Israel had been cured, clearing the way for his incarceration and death sentence to be carried out. No mention of extradition to New York, or a trial. Nothing in the file revealed anything further.

"You want to know why the boy, after seeming untouchable, whisked off cross-country with no trial, is now just as easily being passed on to you, to kill."

"You read my mind."

Doctor Zivin wore her hair swept back, tucked behind her ears, shoulder length, framing a long face, sharp nose, and eyes the color of a rainy winter ocean. During Nat's tenure in Portland, she had served as the city's chief coroner. Their acquaintance had been glancing and mundane at first; since most deaths in the prison tended to occur at night, inmates dying in their sleep, Eva would often come in to determine the cause of death first thing in the morning, with Nat working the front desk. For three years, she had simply presented her credentials, and Nat had led her to the infirmary (though she would eventually tell him she'd liked him even then, as the only employee within the prison who had understood and accepted the concept of a female doctor without some half-witted interrogation and a telegram to the office she oversaw). Then one day Nat asked her a question. "Can somebody really die of fright?"

"Yes. The heart can fail, in a reaction to extreme fear or anger. Why do you ask?"

"There's a young man in here, a kid, really, scheduled for execution, accused of strangling an old man. The boy maintains he didn't do it, and that he'd just intended to intimidate the old man, who'd been trying to lure his wife away with money, but that the old guy had gone and dropped dead. The prosecutor said that's a myth, which is apparently what the jury believed."

"And why are you interested?"

Nat thought about this. After a moment, he shrugged. "I guess I couldn't precisely say. It's not as if anyone's come asking after my opinion, or would care if I gave it to them." He thought further. "Although, I suppose it seems like a useful thing for me to know, as one of the people looking after him."

The doctor had nodded, watching him a moment longer. The "looking after him" stuck with her. From then on, whenever she was called to the prison, she found herself hoping he'd be working the desk. And more often than not, when he was, he would have a question for her.

How long can a man live in frigid water? Can a single bullet move in two opposing directions? Does a man ever live after a bullet's hit him in the head? Do the dead ever move? Can they talk? Can a dead woman give birth to a live baby?

Whenever Eva inquired as to why Nat wanted to know, his response invariably involved determining the likelihood of an inmate's self-professed innocence. Each time, she would leave the prison thinking about him, and his question.

For Nat's part, he'd been in love with her for nearly twenty years. He'd constructed elaborate fantasies, returned to in the moments before sleep, on his walks along first the boardwalk and now the beach, wherein they were married, discussing books over coffee, looking out over some pastoral tableau from a fantasy third-floor deck, making flushed intertwined love tangled in silk sheets.

Thus far, the situation simply hadn't presented itself.

Someday…he thought, a thought he'd had five hundred thousand times, each time with utter certainty, then refocused on what she was telling him. "The boy was sent out here, as I'm sure you surmised, due to the influence and wealth of his father."

Nat nodded. "The lawyer father wants to get the son as far from the murder as quickly as possible, to buy some time to figure out how to beat it."

The doctor smiled wanly, shaking her head almost imperceptibly. "That, in my opinion, would be far preferable to the truth. A desire to protect the boy, I would say unfortunately, had nothing to do with it. I would wager that the senator had been waiting for an excuse to ship the boy off for a long time."

"Senator?"

"Among other things. Former senator, shipping magnate, lawyer, owner of a distillery and a rubber factory…None of which were interests that Israel Junior was fit, in the eyes of the father, to inherit."

"No?"

"No. In fact, the boy had always been a potential liability. More so as he'd gotten older. I've wondered if perhaps the father hadn't ultimately gotten fed up or nervous, and sent someone to kill Charlie Whitewall, framing the son.

"The assumption that Junior committed the murder relies heavily on the fact that they were ingesting high doses of morphine and opium. But these were not Joe College experimental hijinks. The two boys had been heavy drug users, and accustomed to looking out for one another, since they were twelve years old. The premise that Israel would suddenly lose his mind simply because he'd taken drugs…None of what putatively transpired in that hotel room seems particularly plausible."

"So you think the kid's innocent?"

The doctor shrugged. "It's certainly nothing I can verify, or intend to pursue, but based on the circumstantial evidence, it wouldn't shock me. The father had the means, the motivation, and the constitution for it. Whereas Junior…If you get to know him at all, you'll see what I mean."

"The non-violent type?"

"He's a bit of a brat, and likes to put on a show, but he's got an exceptionally gentle soul. I don't think he could harm someone he despised, much less the one person who had ever reciprocated his love. I don't care what those boys had in their systems."

"So…"

"So they were lovers, Junior and Charlie. Had been, to one degree or another, since they were boys. Charlie's father was Israel Senior's longtime business partner. They'd been more or less raised together, though not, of course, by their own families. Israel's mother died and Charlie's left when the boys were both quite young. After that they were raised by nannies, and tutors, rarely leaving the shared compound. It's a sad story, quite frankly, and one that's very common amongst our clientele. When the boys became old enough, they began accompanying their fathers on business trips in order to learn the tricks of the trade. It sounds like it became apparent, quite early, that neither was particularly well-suited, or perhaps even willing, to carry on the family empire."

"And why was that?"

She smiled wanly. "Well, unfortunately of course I can't speak regarding Charlie. But I've ended up making something of a case study of Israel, and the boy's got fire in his heart that would not be fed by business transactions, which he found insipid and purely hypothetical. After Israel had been here long enough for the cataclysmic drug withdrawals to pass, and his true personality burst forth, I can't imagine him trudging through the life of a plutocrat. He's far too unique."

"What did he want to do instead?"

"He sculpts."

"He sculpts?"

"He sculpts." She sighed, shaking her head. "Rather, he sculpted. Regrettably, shortly after his arrival we had to restrict his art supplies to soft clay and tongue depressors."

"Why?"

"He cuts himself." The doctor presented her right forearm, tapping it. "Not uncommon. The boy's forearms, from wrist to elbow, are completely covered in scars. The cuts are shallow. Outside the risk of infection, the habit usually presents no great health risk, especially in someone like Junior, who's been doing it for a decade, and has the artist's steady hand. But even so, clearly we couldn't allow a self-injurious patient access to scalpel and chisel."

Nat nodded. He was aware of the practice. In Portland, there had been men under his supervision who'd engaged the compulsion with smuggled tacks and sharpened spoons and their own toenails, scorched into sharp points with a candle. At first, when he noticed the cuts, Nat would try to find and confiscate the sharp implements, but after several adherents had explained to him that ultimately, this outlet kept them from doing far more destructive things, he began to look the other way.

"Where'd the baseball come from?"

She laughed. "He picks things up quickly. I'm not sure that he'd ever played before. I imagine it might have seemed like an opportunity to bond with the other boys."

Nat thought about everything she'd said. "If your theory—"

"Purely ungrounded idle speculation."

"If your speculation is valid, and he simply wanted to get rid of his son, why give Charlie the short straw?"

The doctor shrugged. "Maybe, at the end of the day, the father still couldn't bear the death of his own son. Or maybe, knowing that the incident would be known by at least the inner circle responsible for cleaning up the mess, it seemed less ignominious for your son to be the drug addicted homosexual who overpowers and murders his lover, as opposed to the victim. More manly."

"And so the boy is sent out here."

"Indefinitely. We received a document from the state of New York judiciary declaring the legality of the medical report, accompanied by bank notes covering Israel's stay for the next half-century, along with a vague assurance that we would be contacted at some point in the future to obtain our assessment of whether or not he might be fit to stand trial."

"But the situation changed."

She nodded, and her voice came flatly. "It did. After a lonely and anonymous year here...Junior began confessing to a series of murders.

"He says it had begun when he was a boy, living on the family's West Virginia cotton plantation, under the care of a nanny who would simply lock him out of the house every morning with a sack lunch and instructions that he would be readmitted at dinnertime.

"In the forest surrounding the estate, the children of the coal miners would cross back and forth between their shanty towns and the mines, fetching forgotten tools and delivering messages. At first, young Israel had tried to befriend them. But there was an incident; a group of children beat him up and robbed him.

"Just as one man's monster is another man's god, the boy realized he had different needs and prerogatives than the miners' children. His entire life, he'd known he was different. Now he realized what he needed to do.

"The first time he acted on this impulse, he murdered a lone child in the forest with a sharp stone. Watching the blood seep into the black loam, he knew he'd found his true calling. As he'd continued killing the children, other things happened that seemed to verify his sense of purpose. A legend developed. A legend about a monster roaming the forest. This became *the* story, from the front page to the schoolyard. Bands of armed miners and policemen patrolled the woods day and night. Recalcitrant children were warned by exasperated mothers, 'Do as I say or I'll call The Thing in the Forest!' This bane of the wilderness was alternately described as demon or primate, a subhuman aberration so hideous and ungodly that even attempting to describe it was an affront to God. And still, despite the vigilance of the community, every so often a child would disappear, a body would be discovered.

"When Israel left the plantation and began to travel with his father, he simply took his show on the road, so to speak, changing the location and methods of the harvest. He stalked the streets of Calcutta, the subterranean tunnels of London and Germany's Black Forest, taking whomever, man woman or child, had the misfortune to catch his eye. After a dozen years of anonymous murder, Junior committed his lone misstep, shitting where he eats, if you will, with the killing of Charlie Whitewall. Which brings us to the present situation, the transfer to Rockaway."

Nat nodded slowly. "Clearly you can't keep housing such a prolific patient here at Oak Knoll. And the father obviously can't have such a sensational story coming anywhere near his business interests."

"Precisely. A relatively clean, easy solution. Although there is of course the ethical problem inherent in the fact that the boy didn't commit any of these murders, any more than he killed his boyfriend."

Nat thought about this. "Why not just keep it at that, then? I would imagine you've got no shortage of false confessions reaching your ears on a daily basis. I've yet to hear of a facility where that's not the case."

"Well...The problem there, is that a great many of Junior's confessions *have* been verified, beginning with the serial infanticide in the West Virginia wilderness; that legend exists. The actual deaths upon which it's precipitated predated Junior's childhood, and have continued in his absence, but there were indeed children mysteriously disappearing and dying in the woods near his home during the same time period that he claims to have been killing them."

"As any child in the general vicinity would have been aware."

She nodded. "Of course. The supposed murders after Israel began to travel become a good deal more specific, although in no case was he providing any information beyond the scope of a remarkable eidetic memory, a knack for extrapolation, and a little bit of luck. Or lack thereof. What ultimately sent the boy down the tracks was that he described the location of two previously undiscovered bodies, one a middle-aged banker in London and the other a dancer in Paris."

"Neither of which, you're saying, came to that state by his hand."

The doctor shrugged. "As a homosexual drug addict with money abroad, I imagine he moved in some alternative circles. Maybe he was there. Maybe he knew someone, or heard something. Maybe he was simply naming places where bodies had been stashed, or supposedly stashed, in the past. He did also provide information, with the same specificity and confidence, on several other locations that did not yield any bodies.

"But, as it stands, all of this together was more than enough to force Israel's removal from the facility while further investigations were conducted. He'd been declared temporarily insane during the murder of Charlie Whitewall, but not during the preceding twelve years. No sooner had I filed the paperwork than I received, bearing all of the appropriate signatures and documentation, instructions to surrender the boy to the Oregon State penal system, and Portland referred him to you."

"Why would he have told these stories? The boy sounds intelligent, from your description. He must have known where all this might be headed."

"Well, the most disturbing possibility is that Israel has come to believe the confessions, himself. I think he identifies with the monster in the forest. After a decade of heavy substance abuse, and the traumatic stress of the past year, there might be some truth to the diagnosis of psychic rift that sent him here in the first place. The boy is lonely. As a child, he'd been alternately invisible and despised. The father, while I have every reason to consider him immoral, I don't think is stupid or unobservant. He sensed the difference in the boy, and he rejected him. And with such a sequestered, insular life, there was no one around to offer a second opinion. Except, of course, Charlie Whitewall. This relationship became, for Junior, the sum total of the universe. They had plans to abscond, when the time was right, to create an entirely new life elsewhere. And then that future, that universe, the only thing he'd ever anticipated with any semblance of peace or joy, was taken away. And he was suddenly returned to the same, ultimately untenable situation. But even worse now, because he himself had caused it. He'd destroyed the only thing that had ever possessed any meaning. He felt as if he had somehow found the key to life, and then in an incomprehensible fit of rage stuffed it down the drain.

"In here, he was again invisible. The perpetual tragic stray. These are not kindred souls. These are boys with nervous disorders, in need of a few years of respite before returning to their lives as financiers and parvenus. Israel saw this void, this invisibility, stretching out before him for the rest of his life, And he decided to get everyone's attention.

"He would embody the monster that he had been deemed as a child. He began telling these stories to his fellow patients, and he was very convincing. We nearly had a mass exodus. I was contacted by two dozen detective agencies and police departments who had been enlisted by the parents of our patients to investigate these claims."

Nat pressed his lips together, tilting his head. "Has he tried to take it back, after seeing where all of that storytelling was leading him?"

The doctor shook her head. "No. That is a conversation he and I had prior to contacting the authorities in New York. I told him what would happen, and that it was not too late to alter that course."

"He finally got everyone's attention."
"He finally got everyone's attention."

Nat nodded to the kid slouched in the shadows of right field smoking, shoulders turned in and head bowed, with greasy jaw-length black hair and a pimpled face, looking like a victim brought in to be sacrificed among the criminals. Shaking his hand when he'd arrived, Nat had noticed the exceptional rawness in his pale sunken eyes, the light feathery scars, like etchings of the wings of a bird or an angel, cast across both forearms.

The kid nodded back sullenly.

Now this…now he had a baseball team.

CHAPTER FIFTEEN

*W*ith the onset of spring, they stepped off the train as gentlemen, even Dorothy, who, in order to avoid any questions over the legality of a woman playing with the men, had cut her hair and pushed her body into the same cheap pinstriped suit as each of her teammates. They came out into the sunlight of the dusty deserted street blinking as if they'd just been assembled from sundry parts heaped in crates in a dusty attic, derricked up out of the refuse heap and polished, returned to utility. Explosives dried, reflinted. Blades sharpened.

Following Nat to the hotel, with its boards askew and flaking paint, hearing no sound but the hum of the heat in the air, sighting no other human being save a pinheaded child sitting on the steps shirtless, morosely or seriously or sagely rolling two dusty stones between his overly long fingers, they felt the façade, briefly constructed, crumble away and they ceased to resemble a battalion or machine and commenced resembling what they were, befuddled or deadly, all of them thrashing and twisting in the stream, looking for redemption or love or maybe another victim or something else. As they filed silently somberly past the child Slade touched its thin silky hair pressing a hundred-dollar bill into its mantislike hand.

An hour later they reemerged from their squalid mold-and-piss-stained rooms, semen-and-blood-stained rooms, in burgundy pinstripes proclaiming "Rockaway Angels," florid cursive script between a pair of feathery wings etched in maroon surrounded by forest green, with their caps in their back pockets and their hair slicked back. Now, unlike the mirage conjured as they had dropped from the train, the image these vestments conferred upon the players did not fade out as they emerged onto the street. Each man took care to lift his feet to avoid scuffing his socks and stirrups.

They took the walk along the dirt Main Street in silence, past two-story brick buildings with shattered windows bearing the dark lash marks of some historical fire, past saloons where one or two thin men slouched staring into shadow, to the weedy field contained within the crumbling brick walls of the former paper mill. The team that awaited them, Andy saw at once, was little more than a sundry crew of identikit doubles of the tattered loggers and silver miners with whom he'd made his bones on the rock hard diamonds of Priest River a half-dozen years before. Perhaps a little meaner looking, more narrow faced with more deeply set darker eyes, maybe more desperate...But certainly no more adept at playing ball.

Before two dozen drunken spectators the Rockaway Angels' professional debut commenced with all the anticipation and enthusiasm of a walk home from a bar in the rain. "Time to go see the elephant, boys," said Dot, striding to the plate. When the first ugly pitch came floating in like a shotput she smacked it, as if repelling something repugnant she didn't want near her, over the shortstop's head into left-center field for a double. Next Deacon dropped a perfectly placed bunt in front of a drawn in third baseman, a sacrificial gesture that ultimately proved meaningless as Andy crushed a screaming twisting homerun far beyond (and continuing further, as if such a thing mattered) the right field fence, bounding out into the tall weeds where a pack of dirty rickety-looking children fought over it.

Watching Andy's arcing swing, the big body flowing like ocean mist and the ball rising like a tardy star making haste to join its mates the men of the hometown squad grew instantly hateful, more hateful than they had ever felt throughout all of their violent, hate-filled lives, because here, here was the beautiful thing, the not-I, the never-felt, and after finally recording the inning's final out with Israel beating out a single but curling left instead of right crossing first, tagged out on a technicality, the men chewed at the hatred like molasses and tinfoil and punctured the flesh of their palms with their fingernails and projected their revenge. They would ravage these cocksuckers like savage beasts.

And then the unthinkable transpired. These men had, throughout their lives, whenever encountering unattainable beauty, evened the scales by simply disgracing it, defiling it, knocking it into the dirt and bloodying it up, which was exactly what they intended to do to the Rockaway Angels. But as soon as Henry Hester took the mound, reddish sweat and barred teeth on his ugly face, emitting noises like an animal hurt in the brush, rearing back unloading the hissing ball cracking the catcher's mitt, the men realized that here lies a forceful brute they could not contend with. When Andy threw the ball back Henry snapped it out of the air stomping to the back of the mound, bitching at the dirt and beating the leather before again unleashing the spitting spherical beast.

The batters, each one of them at least ten years Henry's elder, sensed that this boy was primarily a fraud, that he was far less of a man, less of an animal, less of a murderer even, than many amongst their own ranks, and yet...

And yet Henry was doing to them, again and again, what they were used to doing to others. And there was nothing they could do about it. Henry tickled their chins with the buzzsaw seams of a fastball, knocking them into the dirt, then turned their knees to water with a soft tumbling curve. As the sun set red in the west, with the Angels leading seventeen to zero, the home squad elected to forego their final at-bat, leaving the field, shuffling exfluncticated back to their shitty houses, their resentful wives and illiterate children. Henry remained on the mound, staring after them, turning the ball in his hand.

As Nat left the dugout to congratulate his players, he was intercepted by a man in a suit, frayed and too small with torn knees, bald on top with long gray hair settled into the skiffs of dandruff on his shoulders. Nat extended a hand to shake and the man put an envelope into it. With a small mouth full of small brown teeth, the man said stiffly, "You, sir, have sold me a bill of false goods. This is a team full of ringers you've assembled. I'll honor the wager just this one time, since I am an honest man. Consider the remainder of our scheduled matchups canceled, and I'll also be spreading word throughout the rest of the Can-Ida Professional League." Before Nat could speak, the man turned and walked away.

That evening, at dinner in the doggery in the basement of the decrepit hotel, Nat footing the bill, calling over dish after dish of stewed meat and potatoes and loaves of bread and bottle after bottle of sweet red wine, he turned to Andy, who had finished the game with three homeruns and a perfectly orchestrated performance behind the plate, and said, half-smiling "I would think you'd be pleased with our result."

Andy shook his head at his plate. "*That…*," vaguely flapping his hand back towards the field, "that's no gauge of anything."

"And where, son, are you imagining that all of this might be taking you?" The assembled company interpreted the question hanging in the greasy air as ominously rhetorical, but Nat truly wanted to know.

Andy twisted his lips noncommittedly. "I don't know. But I do know that this won't do for very long. That's just standing still. That isn't going to serve us at all."

⁌―――⁍

When they arrived to their next game, four hours up into the black woods of Canada, the field was vacant save for a thin old man with a long neck and jug ears in clothes that were too small, squatting on the pitcher's mound eating an apple, who either could not speak or could not understand English. After leaving the Angels to run through their warmups on the rocky field, honeycombed with potholes, under the supervision of a pair of armed guards, Nat walked back into town to find somebody.

Unlike their first stop, this Canadian town seemed prosperous and vibrant, wooden buildings painted in pastel colors with white shutters and hanging signs advertising the sale of chocolate and woolen garments, skis and saws. After an hour of asking around, Nat tracked down the Trappers' manager, a fat man in a flannel shirt with wild white hair, sitting on the front porch of the general store drinking black beer from a metal cup. He shook his head. "Can't do it. Jarrett Garner sent a telegram up after your last game, first and last I guess, so I know the score. By which I mean the actual score of the game, as well as the situation."

"What are we talking about?"

"Do you deny that the Bonners nine had very little business being on the same field as your squad?"

Nat sighed, rubbing the back of his neck, looking off in the direction of the diamond. "What about we play and just split the gate, regardless of score, fifty-fifty?"

The Canuck thought about it. He spit on the boards beneath his feet. Slowly, his head began to shake. "Can't do it."

"Jesus. Alright, you take seventy-five. At least we can pay for the trip coming up here."

"No."

"Why not?"

"During the four months of the baseball season, we're the only thing going up here. You're either at the game or drunk in Duggar's, and the beer is a hell of a lot cheaper at the game. The fact that we've won the Can-Ida championship five years in a row, that's the pride of the area. Most of the spectators here have never been further than Moose Creek, and have no idea what poor competition they're watching. As far as they know, we might as well be the New York Yankees. If those people come out and see us go down against you tonight, looking like a bunch of goddamned clowns, how is that going to make them feel? How likely might they be to come out and spend a nickel tomorrow night? No sir. No. It can't be done."

"Well, goddammit…" Nat flapped his hands in frustration, "we came all the way up here."

He shrugged. "Well, you shouldn't have tried to bring that team in here and embarrass the rest of the league."

"Believe it or not, my friend," Nat half-smiled wistfully, "I really had no idea what type of cards I was holding until I laid them on the table." He sighed, looking off into the woods. *And now that I've got them, I have no goddamn idea what to do with them.*

⌒⌒⌒⌒

Nat sat behind his desk, looking pointedly at Andy, who looked out the window of the grim shadowy office into the bright day beyond. "Well I imagine you must be somewhat happy, not having to demean yourself playing with the scrubbinis any longer."

"No...We've only got the narrow window of baseball weather. Every day we're not playing is a day wasted. I'm not happy about that, at all."

Nat looked over the pamphlets and leaflets and brochures spread across his desk. There were three dozen professional leagues within travelling distance, but none of the elite organizations would admit a team of murderers and deviants, and any of the lesser leagues that took all comers had either already been warned about the Angels or would undoubtedly figure it out after a couple of drubbings.

Nat looked at Andy with a prolonged intensity. "Perhaps if you could simply lay back a little, take care of business but allow the other squad their moments, just enough to—" Andy shook his head like a big, heavy, polished stone. Nat's voice came in a tersely measured staccato. "I'm trying to help you, here. You do understand what can happen if this project becomes no longer viable?"

"Do what you need to do, Nat. As will I."

Nat's voice came sharper than he had intended. "There are a few scenarios where it could be out of my hands." He sighed. Reaching out, he pulled one of the laminated flyers nearer.

Leaning back in his chair, rubbing the glossy paper between his fingers, the solution hit Nat's brain like a rushing river.

Here was a way to uncover the answer to everything.

CHAPTER SIXTEEN

*N*at looked at the players, seated around the largest dining table, rough plank wood, in the locked mess hall cleared of guards. He spoke softly. "I've come to an arrangement with the league president. We will begin the season as the newest franchise operating within the Western States Professional Baseball Association. There are some special stipulations for us and us alone, that we're not to discuss with anyone else…"

"We're not to talk about the circumstances that have brought us together, nor our shared domicile. I can't imagine people aren't going to know, but we're not to talk about it. All of us are from Rockaway Beach. We play baseball for a living."

"And why in the world," asked Slade, "would they be letting us in?"

"That's the second thing…" Nat placed a check on the table. The men leaned forward to read it. They sat back sharply, looking incredulously at the warden. Nat tapped the check.

"So here's the arrangement. Look at the date on there. That's the day after the championship game. Look at the amount. That's my best estimation of the entire budget for the state of Oregon's prisons and corrections. That's all the money in the bank. If we fail to win the championship, the whole goddamn thing, whether we come in second on a poor call in the bottom of the ninth inning in the final game or lose every game, if we do anything short of first place, the league president will cash this check."

Dot shook her head. "Wow. Son of a bitch. And what'll that mean for you?"

"Well...I'll either skin out or go to prison somewhere. Unless I think of something else between now and then. During the ensuing fiscal catastrophe, this place will be allowed to fall into the ocean. Some very serious prioritizing will occur."

Israel frowned vaguely. "And where would we..."

Nat smiled. "If we fail to win the championship, and this progression of events is put into motion, then I suspect that all of your sentences will be carried out immediately. The state will have no funds to continue to support you. And I don't imagine they'll be transporting everybody back up Neahkanie."

Josh Martin frowned, spreading his hands on the table. "This isn't much of a plan."

"That's the one we're going with. And let it be understood, if I catch wind that this information has left this room, be it in the form of a rumor, a question asked, a leak to some two-bit newspaper in Fresno, I will immediately forfeit the remainder of the season. And we've already established what's going to happen, for all of us, should that come to pass. And do keep in mind, should the shit hit the propeller, so to speak, I alone have the capacity to try and run from these consequences. While you do not."

"And what if we win?" asked Andy from the opposite end of the room, still seated, the sinewy trunks of his forearms crossed on the table. The room froze like a painting of a bar fight. Nat cleared his throat. "The winner of the league championship takes home a hundred and twenty-five thousand dollars. If that's the way it goes, I will take one hundred, and the remaining twenty-five we'll split evenly amongst each member of the team."

"Hell of a lot of good it's going to do us in here."

"The day after that championship victory, your sentences will be commuted. Arrangements will be made for your release."

Dot hissed sarcastically. "I don't believe you."

Nat thought about this. "Well, I can't really convince you. But what if I *am* lying? Is there something you're going to do differently, one way or the other? Are you going to quit the team?"

Staring at him, after a moment she began nodding. "No. I suppose not."

"I guess you'll just have to wait and see, then."

"I guess so."

"If you're not opposed to letting us out of here, then why don't you just let us out of here? Why all this other shit along the way?"

"Well...first of all, if you go, I've got to go, and a hundred thousand dollars in my pocket ought to get me well beyond the sphere of having to answer for unleashing a dozen murderers back into society. But beyond that...I'm not really sure whether I'm opposed, or not. I've got a suspicion that maybe this is something that ought to happen. But I also don't think I'm probably the one to decide."

"Who's going to decide?"

"I guess you are. To a certain extent. You...and whichever way that ball decides to bounce."

The players looked at one another. "And why," asked Henry Hester, "the hell would you be doing any of this?"

Slade smiled. "If it's just money..."

Nat shook his head. "It's not. I can only imagine I've got my reasons." *And I imagine I'll understand them eventually...*

There were things that Nat had withheld from their meeting. Such as the fact that, while he still possessed checks, he certainly no longer had access to the department of corrections bank account. Such as the fact that he might very well be removed, for any number of serious and even criminal violations of protocol, at literally any moment.

Considering the files of the players as a collective body, Nat believed that they did not really belong here as inmates, any more than he belonged here, as warden. Just as he had come to realize that his journey would not end here, on the beach, he'd begun to suspect the same of these nine. Eight. Josh Martin would not be leaving with the rest. Martin could do this one good thing, helping propel the others onward, to partially atone for his atrocities, but Nat would not allow him to leave with his teammates.

If it was meant to be, Nat would free them, encouraging them to disperse into the world and perform good works. While this was not his ultimate purpose, perhaps it was his purpose here. And they would have to selflessly become the thing he'd seen developing in the yard, the better thing. Their only crucible to freedom involved surrendering their sullied pasts, becoming whole.

The terms had been set.

It had begun.

CHAPTER SEVENTEEN

$\mathcal{W}$ ith a month to prepare before the season, first they went east, two day's train ride to Fort Collins, to catch the National Colored Baseball League's Mississippi Pelicans at the westernmost edge of their barnstorming tour.

The field was lush and verdant, set ten feet down into the ground, thick mounded white foul lines, moist loam in the base paths, all encased within deep burgundy fencing extending to a tall wooden grandstand. As they filed through the players' entrance, descending the concrete stairs to the outfield grass the Angels smiled and nodded and shook their heads, and something about their admiration for the facility irritated Nat and he said that they were acting like a bunch of smitten rubes, and that they'd come here to win a ballgame, not to fall in love. The players liked this and nodded at him in appreciation.

When the Angels took the field for warmups, the Pelicans came to the top step of their dugout. With both teams clad in thick crisp cotton uniforms, the stands full of people, the steam of popping corn in charred kettles and the yeasty wet fumes of beer, with the sun surrounding like a pleasant memory, all of the players felt themselves becoming part of something ageless, a thing that every man and woman amongst them was sure had been present at the incipience of the world and would blink on long past the world becomes fragmented slabs and slivers drifting in space, something far larger than all of their misdeeds and personal redemptions combined.

To solve *this,* thought Andy abstractly, squatting behind the dish, looking to his teammates crouching in their precise configuration, would be to solve your place in the universe. As the Pelicans swarmed the field, whipping the ball like a bolo, the Rockaways raised their brows, opened their mouths and scratched their cheeks. Slade's eyes narrowed, and he licked his lips. "And now, boys, it appears we have ourselves a game." Andy smiled. "Yeah, well. We look like that, too."

Nat watched intensely, repeatedly pulling the lineup card from his pocket to scowl at. "This is the one, then. This looks like a pretty good measure. This should be about what we're going to be dealing with from here on out." He straightened the slip of limp twisted paper against the wall and nailed it.

1. Andy C
2. Dot SS
3. Israel RF
4. Slade 2B
5. Deacon 1B
6. Josh Martin LF
7. Henry P
8. Fox CF
9. Ralph 3B

When the pitcher took the mound, Slade shook his head, mouth dangling open. "Goddamn. You've got to be kidding me…Will you look at that."

"What?"

He looked up and down his teammates, face frozen in disgust or amazement. "You boys, and Dot, you don't know who that is?"

"Some old prick."

"Some old…" Slade whistled, shutting his eyes, kneading the bridge of his nose. "If you don't know who that is, then I'm afraid to say you sons of bitches don't know anything. Except for *you* I'm guessing." He pointed at Andy. "I'm guessing you know who that is."

"I think I do."

"Who?"

"Silas Pace."

Slade nodded. "Silas 'Silent Death' Pace."

"So what?" asked Israel, spitting and stomping his cigarette with a sneer.

"I'll tell you so what. I'll tell you exactly so goddamn what." The players gathered in around him.

"When Silas was a kid, he made his living as a blues musician, down in Louisiana. Alligator country. Down there they got alligators like here we got mosquitoes. Now, the music didn't make him enough to support his wife and kids, but the trappers up north were always paying top dollar for alligator hides.

"And that's how Silas Pace learned to pitch; killing alligators with rocks.

"The trappers paid by the square foot, so the bigger the better. But the problem was that the biggest gators were also the oldest gators, and they hadn't stayed alive that long by being stupid enough to swim right up within shooting range, let alone rock throwing range.

"But see Silas, not only could he throw hard and heavy enough to knock their brains out from two hundred feet, but he'd figured out a way to bend his throw right, left, make it rise up or drop down like a sledgehammer. Those old gators could be hunkered down behind a mess of tangled logs, practically invisible, and he could still kill em four different ways without them ever knowing what hit em. That's the first reason you call him Silent Death. The second—"

Israel spat, shaking his head, scratching at his forearms. "What do you mean he could make the fucking rock bend?"

"Oh you'll see." Slade smiled. "I'm sure you're gonna see exactly what I'm talking about, baby boy. Now the second reason they call him Silent Death…

"It was Buck Ewing, down catfishing in the off-season, who ended up with Silas as his guide. They used to fish for those big old ugly sons of bitches in the swamp using puppies as bait. And of course while Silas was guiding he'd multi-task, whenever a gator worth towing and skinning happened by.

"That day, there must have been some sort of reptile migration going on, because every fifteen or twenty minutes, Silas was popping up to heave a rock into a thicket of tangled bushes a mile away, and you'd hear the cracking of a gator's skull. Old Buck saw that and forgot all about the fishing.

"He went running back into town, banging on doors house to house like a crazy man until he found a kid with a mitt to sell him.

"Ewing told Silas to hit the mitt as hard he could, and the ball snapped right through the webbing and broke his nose. After they got the blood cleaned up and the mitt stitched, Buck drug an ashbin between the two of them and told Silas to come on around the corner and hit that mitt like a gator's head.

"Two days later, Buck comes back with John Brush slogging out into the swamp to see the same display, and that's how Silas Pace became the first negro to play in the major leagues, for the Troy Trojans.

"He only got to pitch once before every other team threatened to boycott, and of course at that point Brush didn't really have a choice. You can't sell any tickets if you're not playing any games. The other clubs claimed it was on account of keeping the niggers out, but everybody knew that was just an excuse, drummed up after hearing that Silas could pitch every day, and the Trojans were planning on running a one-man rotation. The other clubs had seen a future where nobody else might ever win another game.

"So off he went to the Cuban Kings, where the second meaning of 'Silent Death' came on, as Silas put to final rest many a game, and for those hitters unfortunate enough to find the Kings on their schedule often, many a career.

"Then the nickname took on a third meaning since whenever the Kings came rolling in, a good many of the opposing hitters would suddenly come down with mysterious twenty-four hour ailments."

"A triple nickname...goddamn."

"You said it, Sunny Jim. And that's how it's gone for the past twenty years. Most people who follow the game agree he's racked up more wins than Cy Young, more strikeouts than Christy Mathewson. I'd heard the rumor he was Mississippi's pitching coach now, but I did not expect to see the man himself climbing up onto the hill."

"He's gonna hurt himself. Bastard's gotta be practically sixty years old..."

"That's debatable. He said he was forty-five when he came out of that swamp, but I've heard that his *sons* were already at least that age, and he lied because he didn't think they'd give much of a contract to an old man."

"So you're saying that son of a bitch might be eighty years old?"

Slade shrugged.

They watched the pitcher softly toss in a couple of warm-ups, nodding that he was ready, pinwheeling his arm.

Andy selected a bat from the rack. "We shall see..." he said softly.

Whereas Silas slid through the top halves of the innings like veins of oil on water, Henry grunted and slobbered through his frames, screaming at the ball in his fist, breaking the bats of the Pelicans, mowing them down like scarecrows. Having become accustomed to playing with two outfielders, now with three it seemed as if they had a dozen, the trio of Martin, Fox and Israel each feeling as if he were responsible for maintaining the space of an elevator shaft, and no ball touched a blade of outfield grass. The Pelicans threatened in the third inning, loading up the bases with two outs for their cleanup man who looked like a one-man railroad crew in a hillbilly legend, but Deacon, lurking behind the runner leading off first like a spectre of death, like every murder twisted into a single knotted fluttering mass rolling like caustic smoke, like crows twisted and smothering in a sheet of oil, like the vulture who drops in to twist the flesh from the cracking bone, twitched his sallow cheek, the signal for a pickoff throw, and laid the ball upon the diving runner's head, smiling down from above, to squelch the rally.

As Andy approached to lead off the ninth, Angels trailing 3-0, Silas bowed to him, then turned, pointing towards the half-dozen fellows loafing on a bench in the right field bullpen, saying softly but in a voice that carried clearly above the drunk and raucous crowd, "Bring in the kid. No better place to start."

The boy who emerged was seven feet tall and wore his dangling arms like the unbound straps of a straitjacket. Taking the mound, wild-eyed as a horse in a storm he began to warm up. At the end of his lunging windup, which seemed to cover half the distance between the mound and home plate, a windup like a rolling tidal wave, like a falling tree, the ball appeared in the catcher's mitt and an instant later a sound like a shotgun firing inside a narrow canyon went clapping around the field.

"Jesus Christ," said Slade. "But the thing is," he wagged his index finger, "the thing is, boys, you can time that. You can always hit a man throwing only fastballs, no matter…"

On cue, the boy broke off a vicious biting pitch that slashed across the plate like a lunatic's razor. Slade tossed his hands in the air, let them fall to his thighs. "Well shit, then. Never mind. We're right back to guessing."

The umpire bellowed and Andy dug in. As the first pitch arrived, a blistering fastball, Andy unloaded but fouled it straight back into the screen. The next, a slider, came twisting in for a called strike at the knees.

The Rockaways shifted on the bench, pulling faces, shaking their heads. Shit. But had they been watching closely, someone might have seen, right before the next pitch, The Kid's head suddenly tilt slightly, one eye narrowing…

He stepped out, staring at the pitcher who looked back. He stepped back in with his hands cocked higher than before, feet closer together, chin up…

The slider came biting and Andy took a different swing, no stride and all wrists, slapping it foul. And again. Again. The lanky

kid began to sweat and spiked a slider in the dirt. Then he laid
an egg that didn't bite, coasting in a foot outside. Then another
good one that Andy slapped foul. And another. And another.
And another. Then a dud, rolling in chin level. The kid snapped
at the throw back from the catcher, tugged at his cap, reared and
erupted into a fastball that Andy fucking murdered.

Uncoiling, he sent the ball, a sudden white dot in the hot blue
sky, out beyond the silenced right field seats. Turning, craning, a
drunk fell off the bleachers in the wake of the ball. Coming into
the nodding clapping phalanx of teammates, Andy pulled them
into a huddle. "Before every pitch, glance over. If it's the slider
coming, I'll touch some part of my head or my face. If it's the
fastball, I won't do anything."

His teammates nodded, requesting no further explanation.

As Dot batted, Andy, hunching forward on the bench, whispered "Slider," scratching his cheek. The ball caught the corner
for strike one. "Fastball." She rifled a foul that sent the dugout
diving. Before the next pitch, Andy picked at his teeth and Dorothy served a slider into shallow right for a single.

"How the hell are you—"

"Shh."

Now the kid on the hill was sweating profusely, looking back
into the dugout at Silas, who shrugged, pointing to Israel's scur-
rilous form crouching in the batter's box. Andy smoothed his
eyebrow for a foul tip, then scratched his chin for a foul screaming into the third base side box seats, then rubbed his eye and
on that third pitch Israel had the slider sufficiently dialed in to
lay a slicing liner out into left center that kicked all the way to
the fence, scoring Dot while Israel himself swooped into third.
Slade, glancing in at Andy with a satanic wink, rode a slider
straight out to center, deep enough to score Israel, who ran with

the devil on all fours biting at his heels though no throw came in. After Deacon popped out despite knowing what was coming, Josh Martin smashed a fastball out to the utter limits of physical possibility, giving Rockaway the lead, before Henry fouled out straight back to the catcher on a dead red fastball.

"Alright Henry, three to go. Finish the job."

The bunched grimace that had contorted Henry's huge red face since an hour before the game concentrated itself to nothing but a tight blood-colored rictus surrounding his bloodless lips. The fury that had been radiating and spraying from his body coalesced to a wavering white light around his right hand and he wound tightly and threw and the hitters had no chance.

The Rockaways sprinted off the field pumping their fists.

As the Angels packed their gear, Andy, still in shin guards, a band of grime circling his cheeks and chin where the mask had rested, limping slightly, crossed the field to where the tall pitcher sat slumped enough for all the dejection in the world. His older mates, giving him space, moved up as if to block Andy's path but Silas shoed them off, he and Andy sitting down on either side of the kid.

"You've got a—"

"He's Haitian. No Engleez."

"He's got a tell."

Silas nodded.

"You know?"

"No, but I figured it must be something. I'm more a less blind, so unless I got my hands," he held up his impossibly long, knobby hands like leaping banana spiders, "right on him as he's pitching, I'm bout as useful as a extra pecker, far as knowing what the problem is."

"When the ball's behind his back," Andy demonstrated, "his forearm twitches loading up the slider." As Silas translated, the boy put his hand like a crab over his face weeping.

Andy frowned. "No, he can fix it. Just set the grip in his glove, like—"

"He ain't upset. He's crying because he's grateful. Says you might of just saved the souls of the family he don't even have yet."

Looking back across the field as the Angels left, Andy saw Silas huddled with the kid, showing him how to nail the grip without twitching.

Late that night, Andy sat rocking slowly in a chair on the deck of the hotel when the long shape of the kid materialized out of the darkness.

Andy smiled, nodding, as the tall boy placed an inch-long bone, dangling from a leather strop, around his neck.

"Thank you."

The boy nodded solemnly, touching himself between the eyes, fading back into the night.

Two nights later on the Kalispell reservation, Angels leading 4-3 with two outs in the bottom of the ninth, an eschatological collision transpired as a throw from Moon Fox came in soft and bounding, so that every witness, a hundred men, women, and children, held their breath in horror and elation as the runner bore down, hair flying behind him, muscles sliding, earth jolting beneath his feet...

And still the ball delayed, bouncing, Andy waiting still as a statue, a statue of the world just prior to its destruction, ball and runner and man in armor converging in a sonic convulsion, the mass of bodies hurled against one another like planets, the air torn amidst thuds and groans of animal death, bodies thrown, ripping up the earth as they tumbled.

Followed by silence. The umpire leapt over the carnage, turning the mitt to see inside.

The hand of God jumped into the air, twisted into a fist.

Out.

Another game won.

After the game they had a party, with a sheep roasting on a spit, corn and pumpkins buried in a bed of coals, an earthenware bowl of some chunky green liquid that set the Rockaways to giggling and stumbling and sleeping on their feet. As the night grew dark they stacked the fire higher, and before the flame thrashing like a wendigo the warriors clustered around Andy showing him how to bury a bucket of pine chips beneath the fire to produce the black tar they smeared along the handles of their bats. A boy with teeth sharpened into a wolf trap showed Andy how to file his metal cleats into vicious spikes. They showed him how to take the handle of the bat, and a bone...

As one of the men began to hand him a bone, Andy showed him the bone on his necklace, and the warrior fell silent, looking at the others.

~~~~

The following evening, on the train ride home, Josh Martin, Israel, and Deacon stepped out onto the back deck to smoke and found Andy there, on a stool he'd drug out from the bar, hunched, hands furiously working in his lap.

They stopped. Andy saw them, and nodded, but did not cease the motion near his thighs.

Josh's lifeless eyes watched the motion for a minute, and then he asked, "What in the *hell* are you doing?"

"Boning the handle."

Israel snorted, whipping the hair away from the beautiful pale green eyes set somewhat disharmoniously in his angular pimpled face. "Well, what is it?"

"You take this piece of bone," Andy held up a length of flat very white bone between his thumb and middle finger, "and you rub down the handle until it's so thin you can feel it flex. Like a whip."

"Why?"

"Those Kalispell players showed me."

"And why?"

"You saw the way they hit."

"…They could definitely hit."

Josh Martin nodded. "Hell, they ought to be able to hit. They sure as hell got nothing else to be doing up there."

"Just like us."

"That's my point. Those men, they don't do anything but play ball. Awhile ago, they got to a place where the *players* couldn't possibly get any better, so the equipment had to. They had to invent a new tool. They must have tried a hundred different things, bats in other shapes, made of different materials… nothing works…They're thinking about it all the time. And then one of them has an idea nobody's thought of yet. You know what a pogamoggan is?"

"I do not."

"In English it means 'the killing thing.' The warriors put this little weight, a musket ball or a round stone, it doesn't take much, at the end of a sapling...So one of the ballplayers gets to thinking about the pogamoggan, how with such a skinny whip and a heavy weight, with just the flick of a wrist you can crush somebody's skull...Now apply that to taking a full swing with a bat..." Andy straightened up, stuffing the shard of bone into his pocket. He took a swing, and the bat whistled like a switch, wobbling slightly on the follow through. He looked at it. "God-damn." He flexed the wobbly bat in one hand.

Deacon nodded appreciatively. "Cow-skin that ball."

"Next time this train stops, let's jump off and you throw a few to me."

With less than a week before opening day, the players laid stiffly awake on their cots at night, looking at the moonlight split by bars on the floors of their cells with their stomachs fluttering like the stomachs of children on the eve of some greatly antici-pated adventure. Time crawled and yet it ran too quickly, speed-ing them along towards the crucible, which could, each of them knew in his or her secret heart, in the midnight parts of his or her brain, just as likely as anything end in disaster, humiliation.

Nat gathered them in the yard, unlocked a gate at the back of the property and led them up a wooded hill across a sputtering creek to the new baseball diamond. The players walked around inspecting the freshly painted fence, the grandstand, the white and red Angels flags cracking at the soaring tops of the foul poles. "Home team takes sixty percent of the gate, seventy-five if they win," Nat explained. "We had to get ourselves a home."

As the players milled around inspecting the new field, Ralph faded from the pack, transfixed. "This ain't the worst way to live. I mean, you take away that..." He motioned to the metal building beneath them in the yard, the rectangle tipped on its end, tall and narrow, speaking softly, either to himself of everyone. "Silver mining, that's worse. Logging's worse. Trapping's worse. Hell, if it weren't for that," he nodded again towards the death house, and his patter faltered, "...if it weren't for that son of a bitch, this is probably about the best thing a man could do..."

Ralph nodded, licking his black gums. "Yep. You take away that..."

CHAPTER EIGHTEEN

*T*he mountainous tribes had known the coastland Indians by their smell, just as the pioneers would come to know them. The smell of the ocean, of saturating mist.

Mothers would warn of that scent, reeking of the root cellar, of permanent shadow, telling the children that, should they catch it on the wind, they had to run, run before the forest develops eyes and rippling sinews, a thousand limbs and hatchets...

Just as the other teams would come to smell it upon the Angels' musty cotton uniforms.

"God*damn*. Sons of bitches smell moldier than the corpses they're going to be in a couple of months."

The men would spit, shaking their heads, but it was nothing but bravado intended to avoid acknowledging the things their deeper brains smelled clearly beneath the incipient mildew and dank cloth. Such as the shapes the water might take, the skyscraping walls erasing the very earth upon which you stand. Such as the first slimy quiver of life working from the mud, and the unhinged jaw and flopping limbs of life's last gasp.

The opposing players smelled it on these denizens of the beach and some old part of themselves said these others were in league with all of that, having sold their souls, having been born with something else in place of souls.

Their amygdalas caught the scent and told them that this thing, with all the vastness of all the universes, might, might, periodically come back to take its wayward babies home.

Opening night in Oakland. Beneath a cold silver sun bleeding into a water-colored sky, the air was cold and wet as a death at sea. They'd been instructed to pretend they weren't murderers, and after donning their uniforms, boarding the coaches sent to take them from the hotel to the field, many had forgotten he was a murderer, and perhaps, with the obsidian stone of it temporarily purged from his heart, he was not.

Breathing the misty air of the diamond each player returned to a summer evening in childhood, sweat dried on lithe limbs, inhaling the absorbed heat of the day, listening to the trilling rhythmic life of the world like the limitless potential of a child's future.

Not one of these imagined futures involved a single murder, a single night spent in a cold stone cell.

Even the veterans felt like yannigans, walking slowly over the field, testing the lush grass beneath their feet, looking over the lacquered fence and the grandstands (nearly empty, the home-town fans having written off the game as a dull and certain rout, with the defending-champion Superbas functioning as a frontier farm team for the Cubs), as bright eyed as if a gash had appeared in the earth and they'd fallen in and discovered the earth was full of good things.

Then, so sayeth the umpire, it was time to play ball.

A minor furor rippled through the three dozen fans in attendance, a wave of confusion, as Dot strode to the plate with her long auburn hair bouncing on her shoulders, breasts untaped and hips ungirdled.

"Ah shit," muttered Nat, hopping up out of the dugout, trotting to intercept her.

"Need I point out this could cause a problem?"

Dot sneered. "Please. You think we're fooling anybody? With any of this?" She pointed at her teammates and shook her head. "If they were going to kick us out for what any one of us sons of bitches are, they wouldn't have let us in in the first place."

Nat thought about this. He looked at Dot, the woman. "It could make you a target."

She inclined her head and raised her brows, waiting for Nat to realize the stupidity of what he'd just said, which he did, flapping his hands, shaking his head. "Alright, then. We'll see what happens." He turned trotting back to the dugout.

Israel, picking at his scarred forearm, hissing smoke, said "She's got a point. I mean this son of a bitch," tilting his head towards Ralph, "...hillbilly state constitution says it's illegal for him to even be here."

"Although," said Deacon, leaning towards the melted pitcher, "I'm not sure you'd properly call him black, at this point. Just as much pink, yellow...more of an Everyman. If I *had* to choose a color..." Deacon grimaced at the daunting hypothetical task.

Ralph nodded. "It's all very complicated."

After the umpire, flipping through a rule book, shrugged and called "Batter!" Dot struck out against a perfectly average pitcher, as did Israel, both of them grinding their teeth swinging practically out of their shoes with the nerves of it.

Then Andy dug into the box, tapped the dish, and drove the ball kicking to the fence in left center. An easy double. But instead of pulling up at second, he rounded the bag, dropping his head, digging for third even though the shortstop had already received the ball in shallow left.

From his position coaching third Nat shouted "Stop!" then snapped his mouth shut, trusting Andy's judgement above his own despite any preponderance of evidence to the contrary. The third baseman received the ball, waiting in a crouch as Andy dove in headfirst...

Out by thirty feet.

But in diving, he had knocked out his left front tooth on the third baseman's toe. Blood ran from the socket as Andy stood looking fixedly into the dugout at each of his teammates.

The sacrifice did not go unheeded. No more bullshit said the grey eyes above the running blood.

It's time to play ball.

Jesus, said a few of the spectators, looking at the wolf-eyed kid with the bloody mouth. So striking was the spectacle of the shattered tooth, the defiant lupine glare, that several of the previously disinterested spectators were still watching as Henry took the mound, dispatching of the hitters as if he were throwing knives, shrieking and spitting like a sodomized soul in hell.

Jesus, look at this son of a bitch, said several fans, slipping away to fetch a friend from town. Another mini-exodus, followed by a multitudinous repopulation would occur later in inning after Israel put his head through the right field fence stealing a triple. And again in the fifth, after Henry drove a homerun knocking a post from the left field grandstand, so that a dozen drunks fell pinwheeling and splashing beer into the hot dust. Again as Deacon buggy-whipped a low pitch up into the twilight sky, where it dangled like a hypnotist's watch until dropping to bang off the centerfield fence, at which point Dot broke from first and Slade from second, the throw bounding in right as Dot, having caught the old man rounding third, shoved him staggering over the dish and toe-tapped it herself. Again as Josh Martin hit a ball that landed in left field in the form of a cube.

With all that running back and forth, the stands were full when Henry's delivery loosened up a little, some of the bolts in the machine shuddering loose. Nat watched from the dugout's top step with his jaw working and his fingers twitching by his sides like a gunfighter as the big red-headed pitcher walked a man and beaned another. Andy glanced over, nodded through the mask, and Nat motioned for Ralph to take the mound. The capacity crowd gasped at the infernal spectacle of the burned pitcher.

Taking the ball for warmups, Ralph held up both hands, calling to the umpire. "This one sprung a dozen stitches on the fence. Trade me out." He stepped to throw and the ump twisted away, covering up as if beset by bees, gasping "No no wait now—"

"What's the matter?"

"I shan't be touching that ball." He shook his head. "No sir."

Ralph thought about this. "That's leprosy you're thinking of. Or do you mean something else?" The umpire, a tall fat utterly hairless man named Seal Lochlin, stretched his neck frowning as if offended. "Of course not. I'm simply referring to the…" He pointed back and forth across his own face.

Ralph shook his head. "I'm just burned. In a fire."

After a skeptical moment, the umpire nodded, producing a ball from the pouch at his hip. "Alright, then."

After two hours of Henry shredding the air, threatening their safety, the men were wound so tightly they had no chance at taking a deep breath and keeping their hands back long enough to hit Ralph's wobbling tumbling Fireball. As the final out was recorded, a sky high popup that Israel snatched from the air with a slashing flourish, tracing his index finger across his throat, Nat exhaled through his teeth and shook his fist.

Well I'll be goddamned, said the town of Oakland, *if these fucked up bastards can't play some baseball!*

⌐━━━⌐

They rode through the night, giving up on sleep to have a smoke and a drink and a look out the window. It was shortly after dawn, a burning red gas fire over the scrublands, when Slade, checking the locked door to Nat's private room and the pair of guards nodding in the next car, leaned forward calling his teammates into a huddle.

"So…I still have some people…" Everyone listed to the creaking of the train and listened to the driving of the pistons. "And there have been some conversations.

"To be perfectly blunt, I have associates capable of laying the bossman," he nodded in Nat's direction, "low, and we make a run for it.

"Seeing as how, with anything of that nature, there's a tendency for bullets to start flying in directions you don't anticipate, I thought I'd take the temperature of the group before making any decisions."

"Your buddies kill him on a train and we…what? Jump off and run into the forest?"

Slade shrugged. "Pretty much. We'd have horses, a few days of supplies, outfitted for everybody." He winked. "You all could just pay me back when you get the chance."

Fox squinted one eye, bobbing his head side to side. "Something that bothers me about it. I get the sense that none of *this,*" he motioned at the assembled company, "is really his fault."

"Well…" Slade rubbed his chin, "I don't suppose that's really the point. Not really the point of much of anything, actually." He smirked, pleased at his observation. "For us to go, he's gonna have to go. Just like he said. And until that happens, no matter who's at fault, we're always gonna have that silver rectangle waiting on the horizon."

Swaying in the angry sunrise, they thought about it. Each of the players pictured thundering into the forest, the raw thrilling hope of the cold night air, trees whistling past, plunging through boughs, running until this place was just a distant odd memory. Their resolutions filled the smoky air of the train car: *I'll make an anonymous life, quiet and solitary, working on a railroad crew. / Tending bar in a small isolated town where nobody asks any questions. / I'll steer clear of the places they'll be looking, near my wife, my brothers, my home. / And the next time my husband strikes me, my father beats me, my wife is accosted, I'll do better, I'll…* As the thread of the fantasy dissipated, their minds drifted back to the night just past in Oakland. Andy spoke. "I vote stay. For now. Let's play a little more ball."

Several moments passed in the fiery dawn with no one speaking. Israel languidly waved his cigarette, indicating acquiescence, and the rest nodded.

Slade conceded with a half-smile and a shrug.

"Okay then. Of course, do know that should such a time come as my turn to take the long walk…The man is going down. I might not have much advance to give you.

"So I'd say get ready to run, boys. Assume it's gonna happen tomorrow. Assume that every time we get up on this train. Get set to hit those woods and scatter."

The Kid became Sideshow, dubbed thusly by the Sacramento Sun because he batted from both sides of the plate, scraped his bat with a chunk of bone dangling from a leather strop around his neck, coated his arms and hands in ship tar, and reputedly, according to the San Francisco Star, had been observed soaking his hands in a coffee can full of piss, a technique he'd learned from The Cuban Giants to reduce calluses (this same reporter had it from a good source that the young catcher also drank the blood of a chicken as part of his pre-game routine, but was not quite willing to publish such a detail without observing it himself).

Andy quickly distinguished himself as the best player in the league, and the other teams came after him, throwing at his head, hitting him in the face with a bat on the follow through, lodging their metal cleats in his tibia, slashing at his eyes with their fingernails as he slid. For a while the Angels dealt with it in the regular way, drilling and cleating commensurately, but it was impossible to square the ledger, with Andy's talent outweighing many other teams' entire rosters. Nat ultimately solved the problem in Boise, after Andy had been kneed in the skull for the second time in as many games, sending the Angels not afield to fight the opposition but in the opposite direction, out the gates, up Main Street smashing windows, knocking over produce stands, tipping lamp posts. The next morning the ownership consortium, the members of which also constituted the Chamber of Commerce and owned most of the city's businesses, issued an edict to the Boise Braves' manager to lay off The Kid. Word apparently spread, because it wouldn't occur again the rest of the season.

Bearing down like Cherokees in a wave of dust and fire and blood they tore through the league as men and a woman amongst boys. In their wake lay the hanging heads of shell-shocked pitchers and the scattered bodies of infielders knocked asunder in the basepaths.

⌇

Truckee. Less than ten miles from where the notorious anthropophagites had committed their appallingly unnatural or utterly natural deeds. Though the ballpark was new and bordered the forest, those past atrocities seemed to hang like a swampish miasma, painting the picturesque scenery gothic, hollowing the cheeks in the stands, glossing the eyes and chapping the long bony hands.

This moribund atmosphere infected the hometown baseball club as well, transforming a squad of formerly capable players into a crew of hapless, perennially cellar-dwelling sad sacks. No matter who the Truckee Infants brought in, within a month the new man would have succumbed to the enervating atmosphere just like the rest, developing a cough and a rash, waking late in a fog of malaise, dreading his previously wondrous occupation as a ballplayer.

The crowd, comprised mostly of prospectors and miners and loggers and drifters and fugitives, had a reputation for falling out of the bleachers, for fights spilling onto the field, for breaking glass, gunfire, and other assorted cacophonous calamities, so that the reaction time of the players came slower than it might have elsewhere when a portion of the left-center field wall collapsed in a splintering of boards and the Angels afield stood up out of their crouches to incredulously behold the unbelievable massive presence of the blond grizzly racing through the outfield grass.

Turning its boulder-sized head the beast seized Josh Martin around the waist as he shrieked and beat at its head. Hoisting

Martin's thrashing body the bear sprinted back through the splintered fence into the forest as a rain of gunshots from the grandstand tore chunks from the fence and the trees.

Everybody stood frozen in time. A tree cracked and toppled deep in the woods.

Josh Martin, weltering in adrenalin, felt no pain despite the clearly observable fact of the bear's massive fangs buried deep into his guts.

For miles he simply held on, remaining as still as possible. Coming into a dank shadowed clearing, the bear dropped him, backing away, watching with its blue eyes. He knew he was still alive, could feel the cold wet black dirt on his face, the blood slicking his body from the hollow of his neck to his knees, could smell the clammy fecundity of the soil and the metallic wetness of the blood, could hear birds and squirrels prattling in the trees, but he couldn't move. He tried to shout and heard a wispy leaking of air deep at the back of his throat.

Then the pain hit.

It started with a tremor, a twinge, a pinch deep in his gut, and then ice. The sensation of ice melting deep down into the center of his body. This was not the type of pain he would have expected with a ravaged torso. The feeling was vivid and not unpleasant; accompanying the pain was a sensation of peace, the first peace he had experienced in years. His heart swelled with gratitude and relief…

Then the forest tilted, trees flipping horizontal, the sky bleeding down like water, and slithering from a shadow between trees, as if crawling through an aperture, came his wife, Aleah.

He saw her winsome form in the light nightgown worming from the shadow, perching on the horizontal trunk of the tree. At that moment the pain, the real pain, arrived. A hot red fist took hold of his spine and yanked, vertebrae cracking, stomach muscles tearing.

He fought to keep his face held up to her, and tried to speak, but he couldn't understand his own words, and could no longer recall what he'd been trying to say. Aleah's face was darkly shaded, with shifting pockets of transparency, revealing the woods behind her.

As the next wave of pain hit, Aleah leaned closer, her neck elongating, the hole of her mouth expanding with the flesh of her face bunching up at the diminishing edges of its boundaries, until her head consisted of a circular void with folds and knobs of flesh twisted and stuffed at its perimeter, hovering just above his upturned face.

Though Josh could no longer hear, he understood in the legion of whispers echoing from the void of her mouth that he was about to begin suffering. That he may have thought that he'd suffered in his life, but that he had been wrong, and now he was about to begin suffering.

She said that she would bring the children to watch only right at the end.

Then the interior of his body burst as if all this time it had been precious fragile material and his skin some wet sack, the inside of him pushing from his mouth and ears and eyes and nose, the twisted peel of his body sloughing away to leave a mound of ruined black guts.

He became aware of the smaller bodies of the children, extending their long pale hands, moving toward him.

Perhaps, thought Nat, drinking his glass of tonic water in the smoky bar, *that* had been the ultimate point of everything preceding it. He'd survived his childhood, weathered the cross-country trek, become warden, and been inspired to form this baseball team all as a means to accomplish his ultimate destiny of bringing the murderer Josh Martin out here to Truckee to experience the true justice of being eaten by a bear. Because... because...

He shook his head. That was as far as he could take that train of reasoning. Because it was fucking stupid. He sighed. He didn't know what he was going to do. While Nat had never intended for Martin himself to be redeemed and emancipated, he *had* been counting on the outfielder's homeruns and circus catches to help facilitate the healing expiation of the others.

But perhaps Martin, as the lone smudge that could not be expunged, had been preventing the others from becoming cleansed. Perhaps Nat had been wrong to think they might benefit from this partnership with the devil, so to speak, wrong to think they could exploit Lucifer and then cut Him loose...

Nat became aware of a man standing beside his table and cleared his throat, blinking, sitting up straight, embarrassed to realize he may have been talking to himself. "Hello," said the man, short but physically imposing, dark with short black hair, a nappy goatee and the darkest brown eyes. He extended a hand to shake. "I'm Yuriel Gonzalez. Warden over at San Quentin. I sent Ralph Ellison..."

Nat composed himself. "Oh, of course. Thank you. Please sit down. You were certainly right about Ralph. He's won us a number of games."

"Good, good." He looked around the bar. "Listen..." he leaned in, shaking his head. The rigidly handsome face he'd worn slumped into exasperation. "I just got Heck Jasmine sent from back East last month, a decision made by the higher ups that, believe me, I would definitely not have conceded to if I had been given any choice. It was supposed be top secret but people are finding out. Half the inmates want his autograph and the other half want to make their reputation by killing him, I've got a dozen reporters trying to get in posing as prisoners every day... And let me tell you, with all the extra attention and security, the whole thing's about driving me up the goddamn wall."

Gonzalez leaned in closer. "What I'm wondering...You want him?"

Nat laughed a single time, like a bark, shaking his head at the ceiling. *Are you fucking kidding me?*

Even he had heard of Heck Jasmine.

CHAPTER NINETEEN

*I*f it weren't for the bombings, Heck Jasmine would never have put on a big-league uniform.

The first bomb, homemade and a hundred times stronger than necessary, had been placed inside a briefcase, identical to the briefcase Gordon Gayle, the Governor of Idaho, had been carrying between his home and office every day for the previous twenty years. But, for all that similarity, a different briefcase.

After a particularly contentious day of meetings with the owners of the silver mines up north and the leaders of the newly formed miners' unions Governor Gayle settled into the leather chair in his den next to a crackling fire and hoisted the briefcase up onto his lap, intending to take a few draws from the emergency flask of whiskey stored therein, when the bomb blew off both his arms and his face, so that the last image his family, racing in after the blast, would possess of their father and husband was a skull-faced torso spewing gore like an oil well. Within hours, the FBI had raided the homes of the union leaders, the brothels and bucket shops they frequented. No leads had been established that next morning when Jay Creely, lead investigator, rose from his bed at the Idanha Hotel, crossed the room, still half-asleep and groggy from the long train ride and the drinks he'd had at the hotel bar the night before, opened the door to the bathroom, and had his own head blown off, still clinging to the back of his neck by a flap of skin like a small high backpack when his colleagues came rushing in. The bomb had been dangling (quite ingenuously, the forensic investigators would concede amongst themselves) from a belt slung over the coat hook on the other side of the bathroom door.

At that point hundreds of reporters from all over the United States, Canada, and Mexico descended upon Idaho to witness and describe all hell breaking loose. But suddenly, unfortunately, right as they arrived, everything shuddered to a screeching halt. With the mines ordered temporarily shuttered, the scabs and the striking miners had nothing to fight over. For a couple of days, newspapers covered the mine owners bitching about the shut down, but a couple of days was plenty. Editors ordered their reporters to stay one more week, hoping for an arrest or, if they struck exceptionally lucky, another bomb.

On the Fourth of July with nothing to do, the bored pressmen descended upon a semi-pro baseball game with exceptionally heavy bricks in their hats. They drank from flasks and bottles stashed in their jackets, mocking the locals' rustic clothing and speech, bitching about the uncomfortable bleachers and yeasty beer and the smell of cowshit wafting on the breeze, making sport of the patchy field and peeling fence and the big stoop-shouldered kid pitching for the Weiser Onion Planters with the unnaturally long arms.

They laughed and snorted as the jug-headed big-nosed onion farmer, dirt in the creases of his long neck and thick knuckles, threw his hands up over his head, slack-jawed, falling back into his lumbering wind-up. At the apex, balanced on one foot, wavering like a Fata Morgana in the warbly lenses of their drunken eyes the bumbling hayseed transformed into a panther, a killer whale, bunching up in his leg kick like rolling flexing mercury, exploding forward, the ball hissing out of his left hand a white blur tearing the sound barrier. "Excuse me," said every reporter at once, trotting through the exit. Within an hour, the sports editor at every major newspaper in the country had received an urgent missive, which he then flung with utmost rapidity to the scouting director of the nearest big league ball-club. Over the next two days, a battalion of scouts descended upon Weiser so prodigious they made the legion of reporters look like a Ray Wollbrinck tapdancing show.

It was the middle of September, with both the National and American Leagues in the thick of torrid multi-team pennant races, setting off a bidding war like nothing the world of sport had ever seen. After a week of intrigue and disruption, with the Cleveland Spiders purchasing the only hotel in Weiser and evicting all enemy scouts, with phone lines cut, roads to the ballpark blocked by logs like ominous beaver dams and a half-dozen fires set to homes where rival scouts were supposedly housed, a militia formed to inform the baseball people they had until sundown to conclude negotiations and clear the hell out of goddamn town. Or else.

With this ultimatum, each team just went ahead and cut right to their final offer, and it was the Red Sox who returned home with the prize. The discovery of this unlikely gem in the rough, plus the bidding war and resultant astronomical contract, plus Heck's phenomenal splash of an entrance into the big leagues, practically single-handedly propelling the Red Sox into the World Series, logging six wins in his first six big league starts while allowing less than two runs per game, striking out a hundred and eight men in fifty-four innings, catalyzed such a prolonged media supernova that it was scarcely national news, an inch-tall blurb stuffed into the corner of the second page, when another bomb went off, blowing a hole through the torso of the recently promoted Lieutenant Governor's cousin, visiting from Oklahoma, as he flipped up the lid of the woodbox out back of the Governor's mansion.

After that, concessions were made to the labor unions, the bombings stopped, and Heck Jasmine continued his rise to become one of the biggest celebrities in America. The flashpoint of talent evidenced during his rookie year burned throughout the following season, as Heck won twenty-five games against only three losses, striking out three hundred and seventeen men. Nobody could remember a left-handed pitcher so dominant. Heck posed for magazine covers and billboards smoking cigarettes, sitting in automobiles, drinking Johnny Walker whiskey. There was vast speculation and very little confirmation regarding his personal life. Grainy photos and rampant rumors indicated he may have been associating with Harry Houdini, Tom Turpin, Upton Sinclair…When he married the actress Hollie Sawyer, the result was a perfect storm of gossip, an unceasing scrambling flood of paparazzi.

Hollie Sawyer had come from nowhere, a farm girl from Cotton, Arkansas, gone West dreaming generic Hollywood dreams, discovered standing on line to audition for a walk-by non-speaking part in a film about a bank robbery. Ten months later she'd starred in the year's top-grossing movie. Just as Hollie's fame reached the point where magazines and Sunday supplements came calling, the strange developments began. With so many fans hungry for information about her life, several publications requested a tour of her childhood home, interviews with family and friends, all of which were met with a vague and unprecedented refusal. Her parents were private people, she said, and as shy as she'd been growing up, she couldn't recall a single friend. I prefer to live entirely in the here and now, she said. The media, not needing her permission to descend upon Cotton, Arkansas, did so and, unable to locate any Sawyers (lots of actors change their names) circulated farm to farm with photos of the beautiful woman, without a single positive identification (although she'd been just a gawky farm girl back then), at which point they guessed that Ms. Sawyer (not her name) did not, in fact, hail from Cotton, Arkansas. They begged, pleaded, threatened to ruin her career, but Hollie Sawyer could not be coerced into giving out any personal information. And then a very odd rumor began to circulate.

Ten years earlier, the entire country had been briefly captivated by the tragic saga of Madilyn Acres, the young girl whose parents and two older brothers had been murdered in the service of her kidnapping from her bucolic Wichita farmhouse. Young Maddy's abductor, Alex Cole, had waylaid and murdered innocent travelers all the way from Kansas to Ciudad de Juarez before the authorities, following the trail of bodies, caught up, a trio of officers going down with him in the gunfight out in the desert.

The nation rejoiced over the miracle of Maddy's rescue, taken unscathed from her hiding place beneath the back seat of Cole's custom-painted gold Model-T. She was immediately placed in the foster care of the O' Haras, an oil family in Galveston whose matriarch, following the case with unabated bated breath, had publicly pledged to adopt the girl. The case then left the public eye, exiting on a happy note (minus of course the dead original family and myriad victims), with photos of the girl riding horses through the countryside, dining at a long table with a multitude of blue-blooded cousins, fishing in the estate's private pond...only to resurface darkly a few months later, as a number of odd details surrounding the Maddy Acres case began to bubble up like methane bubbles from a drowning victim.

First came the testimony, dredged from a neglected police file, of the elderly neighbor who, taking her morning constitutional along the dirt road running behind the Acres farm had reported gunshots, then a good looking young man walking calmly from the house, sliding into a futuristic golden car, honking the horn. At which point the girl, Madilyn, had emerged from the house a moment later holding a purse and a jewelry box.

Then came the (admittedly garbled disjunctive) testimony of the sole survivor of Alex Cole's rampage who, in what had previously been disregarded as a simple juxtaposition of pronouns, a small indiscretion amongst the myriad verbal glitches caused by cerebral hemorrhaging during the assault, repeatedly described, in recounting the harrowing incident, how among the attackers "she" had advocated for murder, and that "he" had talked "her" out of it, at which point "she" had gone berserk, attacking with a bat. While either of these events might have been easily discounted on its own, presented together, they raised questions. When the O' Haras suddenly unadopted the girl, citing the deleterious effect all the suspicious media attention was having on the biological O' Hara progeny, once again the water got muddier, and a different story surfaced.

Information began to leak from the house via a disgruntled housekeeper, then a former beau of one of the daughters, suggesting there may have been some improprieties between Maddy and the eldest brother, or by some especially salacious accounts the patriarch, whereupon the girl had been admitted, perhaps forcibly, into an institution called, vaguely, the Elysium Spa. At which point the nation had finally forgotten about Madilyn. Again.

Until…

Until a former Elysium orderly sold photographic proof to a Hollywood gossip magazine revealing that Madilyn O' Hara nee Acres had, upon her release from the Spa, become Holly Sawyer. The evidence, such as it was, consisted of a photograph depicting a group of young men and women on a picnic. The girl at the center of the grainy daguerreotype bore a near perfect resemblance, if that's what you were looking for, or little to none if you were skeptical. The girl on the picnic was thin and dirty blond, wan, with dark eyes and a mean face. Hollie Sawyer was red-headed, voluptuous, with burning Spanish eyes and a shadowed angular face so prepossessingly beautiful that otherwise staid respectable grown men kept secret copies of her head shot to simply stare at behind closed doors. Elysium Spa would neither confirm nor disconfirm Ms. O' Hara's release, nor anything else. An undercover reporter from the Hollywood Private Eye magazine obtained a job as an orderly at Elysium and worked there for six months, emerging to report there was no file on Madilyn O' Hara extant, no further revelatory photos pinned to bulletin boards, and that the staff steadfastly adhered to the admonition against discussing the clients, past or present. At which point, the story twitched and finally died, not to be reanimated again.

Heck struck everyone out, and his beautiful wife made increasingly odd esoteric movies in foreign countries. The couple smiled drinking champagne out of high-heeled boots on the pitcher's mound after the Red Sox won another World Series. They reportedly purchased a small island in the Caribbean where, according to various publications, they were reputed variously to be fishing, growing opium, establishing a commune. Then, on a humid September evening in St. Louis, Heck bounced an errant fastball off the side of Chink Bailey's head, knocking the little shortstop unconscious. An hour later, when the report from the hospital came back to the stadium, declaring the promising rookie dead, Heck set his glove onto the pitching rubber and walked away forever. That same winter, in the dead shallows of February, Heck slashed Holly's throat in the third-floor bathroom of their mansion in northern Vermont, in the bathtub to, as he purportedly said, avoid making a mess on the freshly polished floor. The police found Ms. Sawyer lying peacefully in bed, dressed in her white wedding gown, a white satin choker covering her injury, hands folded over her stomach.

Speculation, obviously, ran rampant. Had she been discovered in an affair? Had he? Had Chink's death drove him mad with guilt? They'd been photographed entering a party hosted by Alistair Crowley; were they Satanists? Was this a half-finished murder-suicide pact?

Nat raised his head from the file. He looked at the guttering candle. Hours had passed as he dug through the newspaper clippings and photos.

"Shit," he said, rubbing his eyes, massaging his cheeks. "Now that's a life…"

~~~

Henry let his mitt drop from his sweaty hand into the dirt and lit a cigarette. "Jesus buddy, not to pry, but why, why would you possibly murder a wife like that?"

"I didn't."

"No?"

"No. She did that herself."

"She killed herself?"

"Yep."

"Then why'd you confess?"

"I didn't." He spat on the ground, plucked a weed and slid it into his mouth like a man surveying his sprawling onion farm. "That was all bullshit. I didn't say a word, yea or nay, to the cops or anybody else. I just..." Heck glanced beyond the outfield fence to the ocean. "They showed up, I agreed with them that she was dead, told them no one had been there at the house but she and I, and that I wouldn't have anything else to say about it."

"Well why didn't you tell them what had happened?"

"It's nobody's goddamn business. She wouldn't have wanted the whole world to know. They would have been running that shit in the papers for a year. Her family didn't need to be reading that. Besides, if those imbeciles couldn't understand without being told, telling wasn't going to help anything."

Nat, listening from the other side of the fence, nodded, smiling. He'd been spying. One thing Gonzalez had neglected to mention was that Heck, upon staving in the head of Chink Bailey, had sworn he would never, come hell or high water, throw another pitch. With a sinking suspicion that he may have just invited a big load of dead weight, Nat had come to see if Heck could do anything else. And the happy answer, immediately observed from out beyond the fence, was *Jesus hell yes!* The huge jug-headed onion farmer galloped through the outfield like a panther, arm flashing to snatch the ball from the air like a chameleon's tongue. At bat, Heck ripped ball after ball sticking into the muddy hillside above the right field fence. Satisfied, Nat returned to the prison. Not only could the farmer play like a rip-staver, he, like every other member of the team, did not belong in prison, as evidenced by his profession of innocence. The fungus of Josh Martin, the disease, had been excised. The problem had fixed itself. Everything appeared to be coming together.

After a moment, flipping his cigarette, exhaling smoke through his nose, Henry began to shake his frowning head. "But now you're killing yourself, locked up in here, over spoiling her reputation. That seems pretty damn stupid."

"I didn't choose to come here. On the other hand, I will say I wasn't born in the woods just to be scared by a goddamn owl."

"But you don't belong here."

"I wouldn't go that far."

They all looked at him.

"I mean, I planted those union bombs."

"No shit?"

"No shit. All my cousins are union men. They're also a bunch of shit-for-brains who would without a doubt have blown themselves up, and probably half the town while they were at it. So I took over. I don't really have a dog in the fight one way or the other, but I couldn't just stand by while they killed themselves. I wouldn't have helped if it was just shooting somebody, but seems like if a man's upset enough over something to build a bomb, that bomb probably deserves to go off."

"Well I'll be damned," said Henry.

CHAPTER TWENTY

*H*enry took the machine of himself out to the mound and sent the ball hissing past their swings, through their splintering bats, cracking back and forth between him and Andy, the swinging of a pendulum, perpetual motion, a thing that would continue happening just like that forever, regardless of what any other person might or might not do.

Then in the top of the fifth inning, two outs, Henry paused at the apex of his windup. The eyes of the boy he'd been, sad and insecure, surfaced like the cube in a magic eight ball up through the dark liquid of the killing machine, the pitching and killing machine, squirming with a twinge of panic. The muscles in the rocklike florid face twitched, and as he threw his fingers fanned out, releasing the ball floating forth like a melon lobbed by a whip, seeming to wait patiently while the hitter gathered his wits and threw his hands into the strike zone and whacked it on a line out beyond the right center field fence. Andy stood. Henry glared in, snapping the ball from the air, biting his bottom lip. He wound and threw his body forward twice as hard, shouting like a beast dying in triumph…And incongruously, inconceivably, the ball drifted forth, high and soft, for the hitter to slam off the left field foul pole. Andy stood again and looked at Henry and

Henry chewed on his teeth. Andy walked slowly over to Nat, on the top step of the dugout. "His arm's dead."

"What's that mean?"

"Something tore, or wore out. Those last two pitches? That's what he'll have, the rest of the day."

"And then?"

"And then we'll see. Some come back, some do not."

"Shit." Nat looked around as if some magical choice might present itself.

In the dim light across the desk, only his face clearly visible, Andy spread open his long hands. "He can throw, with velocity, one, maybe two innings, every couple of days."

"That's not going to do it. Ralph can't pick up all that slack."

"Nope."

"So what are we going to do?...Christ." Nat looked out the window to the moon jiggling on the ocean, the white corpus of the statue leaning with her chin as if leading a charge of the land out into the sea.

"It would have to be Heck."

"Will Heck pitch?"

"No."

"You just said he would."

"I just said he'll have to. Not that he will."

"Shit. Send him up when you go down."

"Alright, then."

"Send Henry, too. Might as well take care of all of this at the same time."

Heck stared at him for several beats, chin pinched between huge thumb and forefinger.

"You know I can't pitch. And you know why."

"The situation has changed. The needs of the many."

"I won't."

"You'll go back to Quentin. You can't play if you don't pitch."

"I don't believe you. If you ship me off, you've got no team."

"If you don't pitch, we've got no team. At least in terms of us making a true run at the championship. And, I'm not sure how much the others have told you about our unique circumstance, but this is a rare case where I would much rather quit than lose. At least that would give me some time to figure out my next move."

Heck shook his head, looking to the ceiling. "Well fuck."

"Even with everything, you'd still rather play than not, wouldn't you?"

Heck snuffed. "You just described my whole goddamn life."

"I understand your dilemma. Although I have an idea. At the risk of sounding crass...Just don't throw hard enough to kill anybody. Or do. Maybe that would be better. Overcoming instead of avoiding. Facing your demons."

"See that's bullshit. It's everybody else that will be facing the demons, not me. It's my goddamn demons ran up and killed that poor kid in St. Louis. *You're* the one telling me to unleash those demons. Now what do you think that makes you?"

Nat chuckled. Henry leaned forward, stubbing his cigarette on the corner of Nat's desk. "And why am I in here listening to all this?"

"Because it's your slack, owing to the blown out arm, he's picking up. And to get yourself back in there in some diminished capacity, take some of the pressure back off Heck, you're going to have to learn how to pitch."

"Learn to pitch! Are you fucking blind? Have you somehow missed all the—"

"That's throwing. Pitch. Pitch. Use your goddamn head. Watch what the other man's doing. Guess what he's guessing, and do something else. Throw it here, throw it over there." Nat leaned back, steepling his fingers. "Both of you have been doing things a certain way. Now you're going to have to learn to start doing it a different way.

"This will be very good for you two boys."

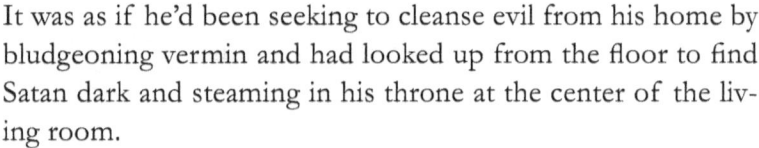

It was as if he'd been seeking to cleanse evil from his home by bludgeoning vermin and had looked up from the floor to find Satan dark and steaming in his throne at the center of the living room.

A foggy morning, crossing the yard to the Tall House, with his eyes and mind fully absorbed in the list of names he held; it was time to again request the warden's presence, and Melvin was selecting carefully. He'd just settled upon Orin Sullinger, a killer shipped over from Utah who'd murdered over the course of ten years two dozen secret slave holders, mostly cattle ranchers keeping sometimes whole extended families of Indo-Chinese immigrants locked in cellars, brought out to mend fence and shovel shit and clean house, and other duties, Melvin assumed, that the booking officer had left unmentioned out of propriety. The execution promised to be grotesque, as Orin weighed over four hundred pounds, and would most likely require multiple attempts, and extraordinary measures. The rope might break. The giant man might get lodged in the trap door. Melvin imagined they would most likely end up just strangling the fat son of a bitch, twisting a tourniquet around his neck, or two men pulling at the end of the noose as if attempting to lead a recalcitrant bull. The protracted, brutal nature of the execution, combined with the exaggerated spectacle a body that immense was sure to create as it died, combined with the morally ambiguous nature of the entire operation, due to the fact that Orin had been exterminating absolute scum involved in the most egregiously unredeemable abuses of utter innocents...Well, now. Melvin's lips twitched in the fog. This would be the perfect event for that spineless stuffed shirt to attend.

He had just snapped the leather folder crisply and decisively shut when the sun burned through, fog dissolving in whorling wisps. The ocean fell still and silent. The wind ceased. All of the sun's energy condensed into a single dense pillar, trained down upon Andy Best at the far side of the yard. The Kid's knees bent slightly, the wooden pike bobbed against his shoulder, big hands, coated in tar, twisting back and forth upon the handle. The gray eyes narrowed and flared, and what had previously appeared to be a man twisted like a thrashing star, like an axle at the center of the earth. The ocean roared back to life and the trees lashed in the wind as if history itself had paused, and now broke into thunderous applause as the ball cracked against the bat with a sound like an ax carving the first man and that white sphere leapt into space to celebrate with the other miracles...

Melvin's narrow mouth dropped open and the folder slid from his long thin fingers into the sand. Oh. My. A convulsion of anticipation ripped through his slender body. Here, in this one, I am beholding The Source. He pictured an endless procession of swaggering Alpha brutes, falling beneath his increasingly tired hands, and him gradually forced to admit it hadn't worked, he hadn't been vindicated, the flow of ignorance and violence hadn't been staunched, not even slowed, his life had been utterly squandered…or he could kill this one. This boy was the Alpha, and the Omega. Kingdom Come. Absolute perfection. Everything. With this, he could destroy Everything. He could accomplish what killing a million lesser men would not have accomplished. Best gently lifted another ball into the firmament, and Melvin's heart swelled to the point he could scarcely breathe.

And here behold the fountainhead. The God of Everything I Loathe. I will destroy him, he thought, like a paper tiger.

CHAPTER TWENTY-ONE

*I*srael, now playing under the pseudonym Ezra Baylor, lest his father somehow happen upon the son's name in some obscure press release, strode to the plate leading off a Sunday morning game in Lewiston, Idaho, the seats filled with sober families in pastels and whites. Easing a toe into the batter's box as if testing bath water, Israel dropped his bat. Stooping to retrieve it he stumbled, falling to hands and knees puking, biting through his lip, giggling with puke and blood dripping from his face and hair. "Good Christ!" shouted the umpire, sneering down at the kid, looking to the dugout for assistance. "You're out, and you're out of the game! Get him out of here!" Nat motioned for Henry to collect the boy but Andy beat him out of the dugout, shaking his head, waving his hands at the umpire. "That isn't the right ruling, Silk."

"No? This," he pointed to Israel, who Henry hoisted by the collar and belt, "is acceptable to you?"

"Of course not, and he has to be taken out of the game, but that isn't an out. It's somebody else coming up to hit. He's sick. It doesn't matter why he's sick, as far as the rule's concerned."

"No," the umpire shook his head vehemently. "No. Send your second man to the plate, one out. And I'll begin adding outs for every word spoken from this point forward." Andy nodded and returned to the dugout. Nat asked Henry "Where'd you put him?"

"Back there in the woods. He ain't going nowhere."

Nat sighed through his nose, surveying the field. He took off his hat and scratched his head. "Any indication as to what the problem is?"

Henry frowned as if watching an imbecile. "Yes. He's fucking shit-faced."

"I know that, Henry. I mean why. Why now? It hasn't been a problem before."

Henry shook his head. "I couldn't hardly understand him. He was ranting something about the date."

"Day of the year or an appointment?"

"Fuck if I know."

Nat nodded. "Okay. We'll play with eight. We've done it before." From the slightly delayed first pitch to the last the Angels treated the Millhands as no competition at all, and when the dust cleared Lewiston had been catawaptiously chewed up sixteen to zero. When Nat crossed the field to collect the winner's check from the official scorer, the thin young man shook his head, raising his eyebrows apologetically. "Bennett's boy came with a note from Bennett a half hour ago and took the check. I told him this was gonna cause a situation, but...Nothing I can do about it."

"What did the note say?"

"Just that I was supposed to give the check to Bennett's boy. Signed by Bennett."

Nat nodded slowly. Back in the dugout, he told Andy to take the team to the hotel, and that he'd meet them there shortly.

The dimly lit office of Mitchell Bennett, owner of both the Potlatch paper mill and the baseball playing Lewiston Millhands, consisted of lustrous dark wood, smelling of gun oil and lacquer. Mounted on the walls were a pair of long rifles, a comically uselessly outsized pistol, and the severed heads of large and dangerous animals: snarling grizzly, wicked cougar, wooly bison. As Nat stood waiting after being admitted by Bennett's secretary, a black-haired young woman with big red lips and big breasts and wide hips in a purple dress who nodded to Nat apologetically as she left him, Bennett continued writing on the papers spread across his desk.

"Mitchell."

He looked up slowly, inquiring in a cold tone "What can I do for you, Nat?"

Nat recognized the voice, the office, the posture, and knew exactly what would happen next. "You relieved the scorer of my check."

Bennett blinked, frowning. He spoke the words as if he'd been rehearsing. "Why, Nat, I would have thought this was understood, without any explanation. That wasn't an official game. Your own players were talking about it. Silk made a mistake. Your player who drinks and takes drugs, the boy who vomited on the field? What's his name? No matter...He shouldn't have been called out. Anything that happened following that was not official. The game, therefore, ended in a stalemate, zero to zero. Which means, of course, that the home team retains the sum total of the funds until we get a chance to replay the contest. We'll be happy to reschedule a makeup at some point in the future." He looked back down to his papers. "I'll be in touch."

Nat stepped to the desk, laying both palms splayed across the paperwork. "Think quickly and clearly, Mitchell. You know how our team is put together. In just a second I'm leaving. This is your last opportunity to pass over that check while it's still just you and I talking in your office."

Bennet's head jerked up and he began to speak and Nat, hearing nothing that changed anything, turned and stepped back outside.

The crooked figure came limping from the weeds, approaching the hotel. Henry stepped out of the shadow where he had been instructed to stand sentry, grimacing at the sudden overwhelming smell of gasoline.

"Jesus." Henry spit. "Ralph?"

"Yeah, Henry." Ralph stumbled by him, dreamy and wrung out, reeking like gas, climbing the stairs to his room. Henry faded back into the shadow and lit a cigarette. Nat had said that most likely Ralph would come first, and then...

And then another man came swiftly up the street to the hotel, stooping to the window of Nat's room, leaning in with some sort of tool, prying at the pane...At which point Henry did precisely as he'd been instructed, stepping from the darkness to smash the side of this phantom's head with his big freckled fist, dropping the stranger to the ground. Henry kicked the interloper under the chin, and stomped on his head, hoisting up the floppy body and throwing it out into the middle of the weedy field contiguous to the rear of the scraped brick hotel. Then he returned to his shadow and lit a cigarette. Nat emerged from the doorway of his room.

"Nice job Henry. Watch a little longer. A third man might be coming. He'll have a check. You can slide it under the door of my room, or give it to me in the morning."

No third man came.

In the morning, Nat led the team on a detour en route to the train station. As they drew within a half mile of Lewiston's Meriwether Field, Ralph stretched his nose into the wind inhaling pensively like an old land-locked sailor scenting the distant sea, an elderly pensioner catching the perfume of his first love, lost a half century before. Turning a corner to the field's entrance, the players stopped, gawking. "Holy fucking shit..." The outfield fence had burned, collapsing into a meandering heap of sodden black char, still hissing and crackling in black pools of the water used to put it out. The flame had jumped off the fence, incinerating the outfield grass to black crisp all the way to the infield dirt, collapsing the roof of the visitors' dugout. Near second base, speaking lowly and gravely, a man with a bandolier of carpenter's tools and a tablet motioned at the remnants of the fence while Mitchell Bennett shook his head, pinching the bridge of his nose. Nat broke from the players, approaching the two men.

"Good morning, Mitchell." Nat scanned the damaged facilities. "In light of whatever accident transpired here in the night, it looks as if we won't be able to reschedule that game after all. I'll expect our check to arrive in the mail within the week, however..." He looked pointedly at the damage. "And I'll expect it's in the full amount, despite the financial trouble you may be in, getting this diamond back up to standard. It would be very counterproductive if I had to send any of my employees back down here to settle up." Nat tipped his hat, walking away.

Bennett shook his fist, shouting at Nat's back. "You better make that check last, you son of a bitch. By the time you get back home, you'll be out." Blood flushed his face purple and he ground his teeth. "You're out, you bastard. I know what you are." Nat stopped, turning to face him with the shadow of a smile, bemused. "Mitchell, the way you're talking to me…I get the impression you have absolutely no idea what I am."

Nat looked up from the letter announcing their expulsion, signed by each of the league's owners, to a pair of figures jockeying for space in the doorway. Nat's eyes passed back and forth between Melvin and his least favorite guard, a short fat boy with thick jowls and a face covered in moles the size of rabbit turds. "Yes?" he finally demanded, flapping his fanned fingers in exasperation. Melvin stepped forward, saying "We'll need a moment," shutting the door in the guard's ugly face as he sputtered to speak.

Melvin approached, holding the leather clipboard in front of him with both hands. A dead frog stuffed itself into Nat's throat, twisting down to his stomach. "We've been working through the executions rather quickly. I thought you might need to take a look at the next few on the horizon." Nat accepted the leather clipboard as if it were made of hair and teeth. As he began to examine the list, he felt the heat of his assistant's eyes and anticipation. Bill Shaw, Jimmy Able…Andy Best…

Failing to check himself, Nat blurted out "Best practically just arrived…this can't be…"

"Everyone else is tied up in appeal; once that paperwork gets started, everyone's accounted for, and Portland's involved, so there's certainly no way around that. Knowing that this prisoner is…special to you, I've been holding Best out, moving him down the list as far as I'm able. But at this point, it's caught up with us. There's no one else eligible to move up the list, and no possible way to justify keeping Best alive any longer. We're okay for a week or two, but there's a batch of intakes gathering in Portland, bound for us within a month, at the outside. I can probably hold him out until then, but…" Melvin shrugged helplessly. Behind Nat's placid eyes, plans began to spin. Execute another inmate under Best's name, send Andy out in a laundry cart, crush the assistant's thin skull with a paperweight and throw Best on the next cargo ship to Hawaii…

Nat's frantic reverie was broken by the question of *Do I even care about this, now that our baseball season has been unceremoniously terminated?* And the answer was *Yes. Very much I do.* He wasn't sure why. Maybe he simply wasn't about to let this milquetoast pissant declare himself lord of all time and space. Maybe the project wasn't finished, despite all appearances to the contrary.

Before Nat could do, or decide, anything, the door opened and the guard stepped in, flushed and sputtering, with a mixture of irritation and anxiety, "Israel Meyer hasn't come down to practice. You want me to go see why?" Nat sensed that the guard had already seen something. "No. Thank you. I'll go take a look." To Melvin, he nodded ominously. "This situation requires my attention. I'll call for you later, and we'll discuss this matter further."

Melvin half-bowed with exaggerated obsequiousness, and took his leave.

Crossing to the back wing of the prison, Nat brooded darkly over the expulsion. This couldn't possibly be the way things were supposed to end up. Look at everything that had happened to bring them this far. The discovery of nine death row inmates who could play top-caliber baseball *and* had been wrongly, or at least unnecessarily, incarcerated. Like locating nine perfectly misshapen needles in four million square miles of haystack. The way they'd coalesced like the long-lost fragmented pieces of some forgotten, never-before-seen perfect thing. Clearly, some power, some purpose had been behind this.

Furthermore, regardless of fate or destiny, I want to win that fucking championship. I want to roll in with this raggedy crew of cast offs and shove it right up the asses of those smug bastards in their silk suits…

And most importantly, whispered the shadowy voice from the back corner of his mind, we need proof that this club I have, used to have, is superior to the boys in white at the bottom of the hill, superior to the Mordecai Hebrews. *I've got to figure something out.*

These thoughts shifted ceaselessly through his cycling mind like blocks in oil, bumping jarringly, fracturing into useless shards, as he unlocked and slid open the door to the boy's back, hunched over holding his elbows bobbing on the cot. Stepping into the cell, Nat stumbled, kicking something. Sliding over the wooden floor, spinning, was a sculpture. As it came to rest, he beheld the perfectly rendered spread feathered wings and luminous eyes of the angel, brandishing her vengeful sword, twelve inches tall, carved apparently from a chunk of wood hacked from the wall. "Junior!" The boy turned, standing to face the warden, face drained and sweaty.

Oh God, thought Nat, seeing the blood, *this little son of a bitch wasn't lying after all. Who, who did he…*but then he realized that the blood, the blood soaking the boy's prison dungarees, the blood on his cheeks and his teeth, in his hair, had come from no one but the boy himself. Israel extended his right arm, tilting back his fist to fully open the bloody aperture on his wrist, and dropped clattering to the wooden floor a twisted shard of rusted metal. He fell into himself like melting ice, puddling to the floor.

Dropping to his knees Nat seized the boy, cradling him like a son, running for the infirmary shouting for help.

"Were you trying to kill yourself?"

He shook his head, rubbing at the sparse growth on his chin. "I don't know...No. What do you care? You just don't want me to cheat you out of the pleasure?"

"Well..."

They sat in silence. Just as Nat rose to leave, Israel brought his striking eyes up from his stringy hair. "I don't know what to do," he said accusatorily. Softening, "I don't know what to do..." The eyes weltered, trembling. His hands flapped and fell back to his thighs. The tight mouth spread in a quivering smear. "What am I going to do? What is there..."

With no forethought, utterly shocked the instant he'd done it, Nat came from behind the desk, took a knee, and embraced the boy. Israel jerked back, chair scooting, every muscle in his tensile body seizing in horror, and Nat leaned away, beginning to apologize. But before Nat could speak the boy reached out for him, falling forward, breaking down. "It's okay," Nat whispered. "It's okay. We can..."

He sobbed a garbled litany. "I miss him. I don't know what happened. I miss him. I want him back! I want him...I'm sorry Charlie..." His thin frame lurched, wrung out as Nat held him, feeling the warm breath, wet mouth on his shoulder...After several minutes, gradually falling quiet, he slowly removed himself from the embrace, swallowing, wiping his eyes, slumping lower in the seat. "I'm sorry...It was the...anniversary, if you want to call it that, that day in Lewiston..." Israel had always seemed so tightly wound he appeared to be vibrating, about to come apart, but now, thought Nat, he resembled a thin child, tired and loose, ready for sleep. "I could smell it in the air, feel it...Just the same as the day...I had to get that out of my head. But it didn't work.

Not forever. So…" He looked to his bandaged arm, shaking his head. "I was just trying to cut myself. But I got angry. I'm sorry."

"Don't be. It's not your fault." Nat sighed. He was tired too. "I don't think any of this is your fault." They sat like this for awhile.

"Can you throw?"

❧

Slade watched the kid trot sheepishly out to right field, heavily bandaged right forearm tucked against his side as if no one was going to notice. The old man looked to Nat's window and sighed: *Sending the kid back out here, probably with a goddamn pep talk, even though the team's kaput, and the warden himself…who knows where that son of a bitch will end up when the bottom falls out of this boat. But he probably knew this is all that weird weaselly bastard has going. Take this away, he's goin for the other wrist, deeper, the second nobody's around.*

And this, Slade realized, much to his chagrin, was far from the only example of the warden's protectiveness. Kindness, even. Hell, they walked the halls with practically a retinue of body guards. And didn't he give them every chance, with the unsupervised practices and minimum-security train rides, to make a run for it, if a man really needed to? All of this was true. But so was the list that Slade had seen, brought to his cell by a guard who Slade had retained since his arrival, writing the boy a check each month for twice what the prison paid. Best would go first, of course, as the top dog, el jefe, the maestro of the crew. But certainly not only Best. Then Henry, then Deacon, Ralph…and Slade.

The old man sighed, shook his head. He really wished he could trust that the warden would take care of things. He knew Nat wanted to. But the man himself seemed to be fading, lately, losing his grip on things. And with their getting kicked out of the league, how much incentive would the warden have to be risking his neck trying to save a bunch of former ballplayers who were now, at the end of the day, just death row prisoners? Slade understood. Just like he figured Nat would understand that he had to make the call. He'd tried to convince them just to get the warden out of the way for awhile, long enough for Slade to get beyond the walls, and the woods, maybe down into Mexico. But these were not half-measure men. They did things a particular way, or not at all.

He sighed, and shrugged. "Sorry Boss," he said towards Nat's window. But at the end of the day, when a man draws his paycheck by keeping you locked in a cage, and then dead...

Well you're just gonna have irreconcilably different ways of seeing the world.

Nat sat in the dark mahogany office, hearing the surf like the circling roar of a beast, feeling the chill of the night mist in his bones.

He had assembled a team of superhumans. They had, in a thousand different ways, sworn and proven their fealty to the common purpose. They'd exceeded expectations far wilder than any fantasy he was capable of concocting. They needed only six more wins, six more wins in ten games, to clinch an appearance in the league championship. A feat this team could have accomplished in their sleep, on one leg, blindfolded...And now, all for naught.

Four weeks from today, Melvin would begin executing the ballplayers. Even if Nat had wanted to simply bail out, springing the prisoners, he no longer thought they could make it. Melvin was everywhere, asking vague questions, watching...Nat had noticed the guards huddling out of earshot, confabulating. Nor could he simply resume the heartless business of warden, even if he suddenly grew the stomach for it. Procedures had been severely violated. There would eventually come a reckoning. He could either make an anonymous, dead of night run for it, or go down with the team...A guard stuck his head through the doorway. "You got a boy down in the main office, boss, asking about setting up a exhibition game..."

Nat waved his hand. "That's fine. Why not? One last huzzah. Have Best handle it."

The following afternoon, Heck threw a game against the Fort Collins Frogs, a barnstorming team passing through en route to the Second Annual Showcase of Professional Baseball in San Diego. Watching the tall lefty doom and banish hitter after hitter like some god pulling black fire and earth-rending thunder from the sky, Nat nearly wept. To have caught or crafted this type of lightning in a bottle with no one to unleash it upon but the likes of the Frogs, and to no benefit but sixty percent of the paltry gate...

It was time to go. Fuck it. He could walk through the gates, take a horse from the stable, ride up over the mountain...He'd done fine with far less any number of times. The players would be left to fend for themselves. He'd go Monday morning, while Melvin would be away with a contingent of guards picking up the week's supplies in Tillamook. The pathetic irony of escaping from his own prison was not lost on Nat. Watching Heck slam home yet another coffin nail, Nat knew that, once he'd safely cleared the reach of Rockaway, he would head down a path of introspection that could very well erase everything he'd ever known. He'd step down a rabbit hole that might render him nothing but a dark spot in the darkness.

Then, like an angel sent from God, like an ugly pock-marked angel sent from some excessively idle and meddling God, came Al Marin.

CHAPTER TWENTY-TWO

*T*wenty years earlier Al Marin had been the second reporter to break the story of the Brooklyn Superbas game-fixing scandal, which was the same as being the one hundredth, or not writing the story at all.

After stumbling upon the rampant corruption infecting the nascent national pastime, Al spent three years consorting with gamblers and murderers and pimps, interviewing hundreds of witnesses and participants, documenting the bribes, the fixed games, and the violence unleashed on anyone who failed to comply. He then spent another six months writing the article. Al's Pulitzer-winning expose had been slated to run on the front page of the Saturday edition of the Washington Post, until a colleague who'd caught wind of Al's story, after bribing an assistant to steal his notes, broke his own version in the Chicago Times on the preceding Thursday. Though this story was nothing but a hastily pasted-together rendition of the unsubstantiated rumors that had been swirling for years, buoyed by a sloppy rendering of Al's purloined notes, its appearance suddenly relegated Al's life's work to yesterday's news. He'd been demoted from flag-bearer to water-carrier.

At that point Al sunk hard. He returned to his undercover haunts, though no longer as a documentarian, but a full-fledged participant. He paid fighters to take dives and ran guns over frozen lakes and served jail terms for beating or stabbing someone behind a blind tiger and every so often surfaced from the swamp to publish an article, the writing still crisp and incisive despite bubbling up from the pickled brain of a full-time bummer, this alchemy producing a voice such as the world had never seen. And through all of this, while certainly a far cry from his anticipated Pulitzer, in spite of himself Al unwittingly recruited an ever-expanding, ferociously loyal fan base.

After vanishing for weeks or months Al would resurface in the form of an article, published in some shitty-looking poorly rendered weekly out of Poughkeepsie or Astoria or somewhere else nobody had ever been or had any interest in going, with prose that muttered and shrieked, sometimes incoherently and at other times through the gossamer strands of a harp. The fact that Al might publish his next piece tomorrow or in ten years, on the front page of the Washington Post or a supermarket circular, created a hyper-vigilant, cult-like fan following.

With his inimitable eye for the bizarre and untouchable, it was unavoidable that eventually Al Marin's dark wanderings would bring him shuffling into the ballpark at Rockaway Beach to watch the team of murderers.

CHAPTER TWENTY-THREE

*F*rom his high window, Nat looked down to the team huddled around a newspaper held by Slade like a grandfather presenting the Sunday comics to his brood. "Hey," shouted Slade, waving up at the warden, "get your ass down here and look at this."

As Slade passed him the Oregonian, Nat was aware of all the players watching his face, raptly anticipating. Just as he opened his mouth to ask what he was supposed to be looking for, he saw it. The annual post-season Major League Honorary All-Stars Team, as voted on by sports writers, was about to be named, and here reproduced in the newspaper was a ballot submitted by an accredited writer named Al Marin:

C Andy Best

1B Deacon Mnusch

2B Slade Mathuesen

3B See P

SS Dorothy Jones

LF See P

CF Moon Fox?!

RF Ezra Baylor

P Heck Jasmine/Henry Hester/Ralph Ellison

The accompanying note Marin included declared that "This rogue independent Rockaway Angels squad has more talent lying in the ground, dispatched by everything from grizzly bears to electric chairs, than you will find propping up the stiff cotton uniforms of most big-league crews. Quite simply, this team is it. The end. No one else need attempt to play the game of baseball ever again. The spirit of the enterprise has been made manifest. It has been perfected. There is only one relevant thing to say regarding the Rockaway Angels. One thing that renders any mention of murder, or morality, or society, seem trivial. And this one thing can be laid out quite quickly. Anything beyond a brief note would be redundant.

Because the Rockaway Angels are quite simply, without a doubt, the best baseball team ever assembled."

Nat's eyes swung to the players with no less shock than if he'd just been handed his own obituary. "How does he know?"

Slade laughed. "Shit, Boss, this is reprinted from the New York Times, three thousand miles away. I think it's safe to say that as of now, everybody knows."

Both Nat and Slade turned away from the group silently rejoicing over a life that had just been saved. Or at least extended.

Like mirror images of one another, the two older men slid paper from their breast pockets; Slade a small tablet, Nat a wad of bills. Both passed something surreptitiously into the hand of a guard; Slade a note reading simply "NO," Nat a dollar for two more copies of that New York Times.

Guess I better roll the dice after all, thought Slade.

Nat would give one copy to his assistant, while sending one to Portland. No one would be killing any of the ballplayers until this whole thing got sorted out.

After this, the flood gates broke entirely open. Within the day Nat had received challenges from every team west of the Rockies, from the Pendleton Cattle-Ropers to the acclaimed Chief Seattle's Clippers.

First in to play, the very next weekend, were the Ocean City Terrapins, perennial champions of the prestigious Redwoods League. Nat marveled at the bleachers full of men with notebooks, at the crew setting up a camera on a tripod, the dandified young men and grizzled alcoholic old men with unfamiliar accents and well-dressed women whispering in pairs, all of them flocked from elsewhere to witness the perverse miracle, the idiosyncratic beauty of the dark renaissance men, the ball-playing psychotics. During this game Andy hit two homeruns and Dot recorded four base hits, each time stealing second base, knocking some hapless mid-infielder into the outfield with her rapier cleats, scoring from second on a bunt, scoring from second on a passed ball. Deacon hit a ball that rose into the hot sun and never came down. In his two innings of work Henry grunted like a bull and sweated bullets and threw so hard it sounded as if Andy had packed his mitt with gun powder. Then Ralph took the hill, working the ball like a snake charmer, allowing sufficient traffic for Dot and Slade to turn six pirouetting virtuosic double plays behind him. The game was a spectacle and a bizarrerie, as unique and inimitable in shape as an individual lightning bolt. The crowd filed out, comparing in their New England or hillbilly Arkansas or moneyed Michigan accents individual Angels to their big-league counterparts, comparing the game to a jazz show, a Jack Johnson fight, a knifing one young woman had witnessed in an alley.

That evening Nat ordered the nearby mountainside dynamited, the concavity leveled, fitted for bleachers constructed of ship planks leftover from building the prison. That's where the people from town could sit. Double the price for seats next to the field and sell them to the tourists.

~⁓⁓

And so it came to be that, thanks to Al Marin's article, Heck Jasmine's historical feat became known to everybody, when it just as easily could have become known to nobody.

The exhibition double-header with the Phoenix Desert Stars had been billed as Murderers versus Mashers, the Stars tending to batter their opponents by double-digits, with a lineup full of burly homerun hitters poached from the major leagues with better pay and free housing. Mingling before the game, quite a few Mashers, after expressing surprise at seeing so many of their former colleagues on the opposite side of the thin blue line, confessed to a combination of relief and disappointment regarding the team they now faced; they'd been led, it seemed, to expect, and take precautions against, a pack of sub-human degenerates only released from their cages to play ball. Both teams warmed up crisply, and with the massive crowd pressing up against the barriers separating them from the field, a very promising day of baseball began.

The Mashers pitcher was a mountain of man and red hair named Donny "Red" Dillinger, who had pitched with some success for a half-dozen years with the Detroit Tigers. He threw hard, a shushing rising fastball which he would distract from, every so often, with a biting twelve-to-six curve, so that the hitters could never get their timing locked in. After the Angels managed to scratch out a run in the third inning, Deacon lobbing a single just beyond the second baseman's outstretched mitt and Andy, who had smacked a ground-rule double, digging home from second, it remained uncertain whether or not either side would have another.

Heck was making the hitters look feckless, stumbling as they struck out, shattering their sticks, but that's what he tended to do and no one had recognized that anything out of the ordinary might be transpiring until former American League batting champion Shorty Haffner, after watching strike one come sizzling by, dropped his bat into the dirt shouting "Hell I might as well save my pine the sun exposure! I have no use for it up here anyway!"

When the Rockaways came in to hit, Ralph, frowning like some hellish bulldog, looking up and down the ranks of his teammates on the bench, asked "Christ. Has a single man even put the ball in play?" Henry winced as if he'd been stung on the cheek by a bee. He shook his head in utter blinking, mouth dangling, hand flapping disbelief. "Goddamn it," he hissed, eyes darting to see if anyone else had heard, "you stupid son of a bitch! You're not supposed to say anything…"

Ralph's riven features puckered. "I'm just wondering if anybody's hit the goddamn ball. And I know no walks have been issued…" At that point Andy, sitting in full catcher's gear, staring stolidly into some space beyond the field, turned to look at Ralph and slowly shook his head, bringing a finger to his lips.

Ralph, still frowning, slowly pressed his lips together and sat back with a look of puzzlement.

Throughout the game Andy crouched low, feet splayed out like a mazurka dancer, with the dish-shape of his mitt inches from the dirt calling for the slider, and he stood nodding for the high fastball, and he used every inch of the space in between like a sculptor freeing, nick by nick, the swan from the formerly meaningless block of clay. Like a painter stippling individually incomprehensible dots that eventually sprung into collective life as a masterpiece. As the third Masher of the eighth inning, former Cleveland Spiders third baseman Alexander Upton, struck out, he shot a look back to Andy, shaking his head. "Jesus. This son of a bitch could have used *you* in Beantown. He'd have run the fucking table. And I'll bet you wouldn't have let him kill his wife, either."

With two outs in the ninth, Hog Harrison, hero of the 1905 World Series, stooped to the dish, wiggling his slab of lumber like a particularly ugly and bellicose caveman. He unloaded on the first pitch, dead red fastball, fouling it straight back. A wisp of smoke curled up from the bat. Hog pointed out to the mound with a stogie of a finger dyed black with a lifetime of pine tar and tobacco juice. "Bring that shit in here again, Meathead, and let's see where it ends up." Heck rocked and fired, but the Neanderthal had unloaded early, guessing location, and he crushed it, lifting it into the wispy clouds in the hot sun and everyone held their breath several beats until the ball finally touched down explosively in a muddy creek. A carpenter in the stands leapt up with his tape measure, eventually shouting back a measurement of five hundred feet from home plate.

The umpire, pushing his way past Andy and Hog, watched the flight of the ball leaning, squinting, leaning, and after a moment's consideration, screamed "Foul ball!"

Into the stunned reverberating aftermath of the tectonic blast, Andy called for the change of pace. When Heck shook him off, the catcher ran out to the mound. He pulled off the mask, wiping grime from his face with the heel of his palm. "Pull the string back on this one. Screw that lummox into the ground."

Heck shook his head. "No." Andy looked at the sun sitting amongst the clouds, pink and orange beyond the centerfield fence, then back to Heck. "Why not?"

"You're not wrong. But I've been saving one. I'd rather do it like that."

Andy nodded. "Alright, then." He trotted back into his crouch. "Here it comes, big man."

"Shut the fuck up," hissed Hog.

That pitch, Heck's eighty-eighth of the day, came cracking and hissing, leaping forward like an optical illusion, snapping like a sonic fissure. Hog nearly came out of his shoes swinging and missing, and just as soon as the impossible feat had been accomplished, the deal sealed, the character Hog had been portraying, the villainous oaf, fell away split by a broad Faustian smile and he shouted "Goddamn, yes, yes! Well done! In all my born days! This caps the climax!" simply pleased to have played his part.

Twenty-seven up, twenty-seven down. A perfect game.

Andy ran out and shook Heck's hand as the team swarmed in.

⌒⌒

After eschewing their batting practice and infield warm up for an extra hour's rest in the shade of the woods beyond the outfield fence, the Angels made their dirt-and-blood-streaked way back to the diamond for the second leg of the double-header.

Nat had just nailed the lineup card onto the dugout wall, turning to trot out to the mound and deliver the game ball to Henry, when Heck blocked his path. "Shit, Skip, I don't think you can justify yanking me out of the game until at least one man's made it to first base." Nat thought about this. When Heck reached for the ball, Nat let him take it.

The crowd, still buzzing from the first game, flew into a screaming fever at the sight of Heck strolling slowly to the mound, left arm dangling with the white ball at the end of it. On the first pitch of the game, the Mashers' leadoff hitter swung and the bat exploded into a thousand fluttering splinters, the ball returning to Heck's glove as if tossed by a child. Harbinger. The second hitter approached the plate shaking his head.

For the next hour and forty-eight minutes Heck popped Andy's mitt and smashed bats and sent the hitters walking back to the dugout laughing at the cosmic hopelessness of it all. And again it was Hog, two outs, bottom of the ninth. As if it had already been written. "I think I'm about to make some kind of history," he said to Andy, smiling and digging in, pointing the head of his bat out to left center.

Heck directed the first two pitches from his fingertips like a necromancer stopping or reanimating hearts, and by the time Andy snatched the third strike from the air, Hog flipping the bat straight up like a bride's bouquet or a graduate's mortarboard, it was long since a foregone conclusion. Back-to-back perfect games. The crowd inhaled, blinking as if a star had just exploded. The players, locked into their positions on the field, sucked in the air of that moment, realizing that this, one of the more remarkable happenings in history, could only possibly have transpired in this air, beneath this sun, amongst this precise configuration of human beings.

And I am here, inside of it, each of them thought.

The next day the sports sections of every major newspaper in the country ran the story of Heck Jasmine's unthinkable, nearly unspeakable feat, striking out thirty-seven hitters while retiring fifty-four in order. This had never happened, anywhere; not in stickball games, nor sandlot games of boys, not in silly exhibitions featuring squads of chorus girls and elderly Civil War vets.

Al Marin's declaration had thus become empirical fact, no more subjective than gravity or death. By the end of the week every sportswriter from Seattle to Tallahassee had raised the call to insert the Angles into the American or National Leagues. Why should the public be deprived of a national treasure? The fans hadn't killed anybody; why should they bear the punishment? Any sins of these men (and Dot), could be exculpated by the contribution they would make not only to the lives of the average American, in terms of entertainment, pride, and diversion, but to the national identity. Furthermore, what could be more quintessentially American than a team made up of rough and tumble, up from under outlaw types? And besides all that, whispered some of the fringier publications, who hasn't dreamt about a murder?

Perhaps these are simply the ones who dared.

A few days after the story broke, they arrived. Later than Nat had expected.

You'll set the affairs of the prison in order, and retire, they said. The head of corrections smelled drunk. The governor kept looking behind him out the window.

I'll let the prison devolve into anarchy, Nat said. You have no one else to run the place. I'll go unlock the cells right now. The inmates will tear the town to shards and throw the shards into the ocean. They will set fire to the forest, drink blood, march east…The men looked at one another. You'll disband the team, they said. You'll disband the team and when the time comes walk away with a shred of dignity and a forlorn hope of some type of future life, or this thing will take you down in its inky icy arms…

It's taken you nearly a year to recognize what's been going on, said Nat. How are things going to go for you after I announce to any reporter who'll listen, and I think you'll agree that they're all listening, that you've been in on all of this? That you've been accepting the money the team earns. That you secretly authorized the illegal executions to protect the players. And that I have all of this documented.

The men stared like small, frightened, exceptionally stupid children. *What in God's name have we done?*

Nat stood, said Gentlemen, two weeks from right now, I'll do everything you're requesting. The team will no longer exist. I'll leave as if I had never been here. Melvin's already been shouldering a great many of my responsibilities.

Because it turned out there was one thing, Nat had realized, one thing exactly and only, that he needed. He did not need to join the American League, and he did not need to retire with a pension, or acquire the love and respect of the world, or fall in love, or save a man's soul, or find his path, or climb the mountain.

Nat needed to win the goddamn championship.

The bureaucrats looked at him as if he'd ascended into the air on golden wings or slumped into a dark putrescent puddle.

The governor shook his head. "Why, in God's name, would you have gotten involved in *any* of this?"

Nat shrugged. Gentlemen, he said, please excuse me. And do take heart in the fact that, one way or the other, this will all be over quite soon.

CHAPTER TWENTY-FOUR

*W*hen the invitation came, it came as a forgone conclusion, neither grudging nor conciliatory, without resentment or apology. And just as the letter contained no claim of a misunderstanding or change of heart, no rhetorical flattery, Nat's response was neither coy nor accusatory. They wanted the Angels back, for reasons of prestige and profit, and Nat wanted the Angels to return, for reasons he had no reason to explain.

So back they came.

It had not occurred to Nat or anyone else (or if it had, they'd kept it to themselves) to guard against the type of thing that happened after Lynn Baker slipped anonymously into Sacramento's Early Granderson Field.

Lynn, unlike the warden, had anticipated all manner of contingencies so meticulously that he'd spent the last two weeks following the team at a slight distance waiting for inclement weather, for the mist and drizzling rain that, while not sufficiently torrential to cancel the game, rendered the stands, as seen from the field, a smeared canvas of faceless heads. Leaning forward watchfully, hands clasped in his lap, the father did not have to wait long. To the second batter of the inning big Henry Hester threw four consecutive pitches biting into the dirt, *Hillbilly bastard still can't handle his own goddamn business,* bringing Nat trotting from the dugout. Lynn stood, sliding the long Colt Walker from beneath his jacket, drawing a bead on Nat's high forehead, gently squeezing the trigger in an explosion of pale fire.

Nat dropped to the ground in a horrendous spray of blood and caterwauling. Lynn's neighbors in the stands, ears ringing like whirling silver bores, parted like enchanted water, and Lynn, seeing Nat lying motionless in the grass with blood pouring from his head, calmly set the pistol on the bench next to him, held up his hands, and waited for what would happen next.

After a moment, with the crowd strangely calm, no stampeding for the exits, no shouting or sobbing, two policemen in brown uniforms, pistols extended, faces greenish white and trembling and sweating, began tentatively climbing the bleachers like lion tamers.

"Go on then," said Lynn, nodding at the huge pistol on the bench. "I'm finished with that barker. Grab it." And it was right as one of the policeman grabbed the pistol, the other gently applying handcuffs, that Nat reared up onto his hands and knees broadside like a big game animal stripped of all its survival instincts, bleeding from the head, looking around wildly. Disarmed, hands behind his back, Lynn the quadruple but suddenly no longer quintuple murderer, Lynn who had traveled a great distance to kill this man, could only watch as Nat, resurrected, somehow slowly stood, limping from the field.

"Son of a bitch," chuckled Slade from second base, "you just never know…"

The bullet Lynn had fired, Lynn the preternatural marksman, Lynn the circus-caliber sharpshooter, had, improbably, drifted left, passing through Nat's right ear. For years afterwards, those who knew the story would speculate that Lynn had simply been out of practice, or had neglected to properly adjust for the fog, or that Nat had caught a blink of sunlight off the pistol and lurched back just enough. But as only Lynn and Nat, two murderers who'd both fled West seeking their fates, would ever know, none of that was true.

The plan had been to blow off Nat's head and grab his boy, either killing, or more preferably backing down, the two policemen stationed at the edge of the field, walking into the forest where he'd hidden clothing, food and water, a couple of pistols, a telescope and a buffalo rifle, a train ticket to San Felipe and another to Chicago. Lynn would board the train for Chicago while Andy headed south. They would reconvene a year later in Utopia, Texas, where Lynn had surreptitiously relocated the family.

But at the last possible instant, the plan had changed.

Drawing a bead dead center on the warden's forehead, squeezing the trigger to splatter Nat's brains like the guts of a pumpkin, Lynn suddenly realized that to interrupt his boy in the middle of this would be the equivalent of someone intervening to pull the pistol out of his pocket as he'd headed into the mansion to confront his Uncle Conrad all those years before. As the flint ignited, Lynn flexed a muscle at the base of his wrist, causing the bullet to drift, aiming to vaporize the warden's ear, just enough to let the man know he could still be reached if the need arose, if Lynn changed his mind.

They locked eyes as Nat fell backwards, globules of blood dangling in the air. At the end of the day, Lynn said silently, that remains my boy. Not yours. Falling, Nat's dark eyes acknowledged.

He had needed the reminder.

He hadn't died in the railyard, nor at the hands of his psychotic alcoholic father. He hadn't died in the army, nor when the lieutenant's nephew had caught him in the bar. He hadn't died lost in the forest, nor leaping through the trees, nor having a gunfight with a cadre of disgruntled prison guards. He hadn't died when Andy Best's father shot him in the head.

Here I am, he thought, touching the bandaged lump of his former ear, looking through his high window to the field, freshly mowed and chalked for the championship game. But why...Is this...And then...

Here I am.

Back home, two nights and a day awaiting the game, the Angels caught themselves lingering by the windows, committing to memory the gray misty light, the smell of death swaying beneath the ocean. One way or another, all of this was about to be over.

And I may never pass this way again, each of them thought quietly.

CHAPTER TWENTY-FIVE

From where Melvin stood just outside the third base line, arms crossed, looking as if he were serving as extra security monitoring the sell-out crowd—which might not have been a bad idea; two freeloaders had hopped the gate for every seat sold, swarming over the guards Nat had posted, jockeying for position, a gleefully ominous mob as multitudinous as a new town sprung up along the coast gripped by insurrection—he vigilantly studied Nat's movements within the dugout. Melvin knew the warden was poised to run, and that Nat intended to give the ball-playing inmates a shot at it too.

Melvin had obtained this information by slipping into the warden's office late at night and discovering, tucked into a file on top of the desk, a collection of gubernatorial pardon paperwork, eight of them (Dot had never been officially admitted, for obvious reasons) each bearing the name of a player and the governor's undoubtedly forged signature. Beyond the fact that Nat would apparently be providing the ballplayers with a running start and a written excuse, Melvin had gathered no further specific details regarding how or when the absconding would take place. The fact that Nat had failed to protect such a preponderance of damning information in the first place led Melvin to believe the warden simply had no plan.

This made Melvin nervous. His stomach twitched and he fought the urge to piss. A man with no plan might do anything. He might do something extremely ill-advised. Something that might get him shot. Melvin had gone all the way to Portland to buy the gun. He'd told himself this was to avoid any chance of Nat sussing out what he intended, though in reality, in his deepest heart, Melvin had been ashamed over the probable reaction of his neighbors and co-workers if they'd caught word, smiling and tilting their heads, nodding bemused encouragement as if coming upon a small child or elegant lady purchasing a firearm.

The arms purveyor, black beard like moss, leaning his huge forearms covered in blue tattoos, anchors and mermaids, on the raw pine counter, had asked if he might suggest something else, his eyes turning towards the display of smaller guns with ivory handles, rose vines and stallions carved into the slender silver barrels. Melvin had cut him off, saying "That's the one I want," in a voice far more strident than he'd intended.

Melvin tapped the cool hard handle of the Kongsberg Colt. He'd have to watch very carefully. He was ready.

"Play ball!" shouted the umpire. The crowd roared back at the ocean like a rival ocean.

For eight innings, the game played like an exhibition of the best color and light the world had to offer, like a demonstration of glory. Both teams danced beautifully and fought like bears whose teeth and claws had broken off. A hundred spectacular plays left bodies sprawled in the dust. Neither team blinked nor twitched and neither team scored. Fucking glorious, whispered the crowd. Fucking glorious, whispered the players secretly to themselves.

Then with the first pitch in the top of the ninth, something happened that parted the lips and killed the voice of everyone in attendance.

The Oakland hitter, a ringer just arrived from Chicago after the Cubs' season had concluded, unaccustomed to playing in the ocean mist, lost control of the slick clammy handle of the bat, both hands sliding off right as the stick came off his shoulder. The bat, thrown back, shoved Andy's glove aside, tearing his mask off. Heck's fastball cracked him squarely on the chin, bouncing over the backstop. The field fell silent save for a collective inhalation that seemed to last forever...

While this gasp had been drawn in horror, by the time people began to breathe again, beholding the body of the catcher beginning to stir, the dread had turned to exhilaration. Now The Kid would have to do it like this. While carrying the residue of his recent slaughter.

Just when it had not seemed possible, the story had gotten even better.

﹏

Andy looked at Heck like a murderer. Like one murderer looking into the eyes of another. Heck nodded, swallowing. A worm began to twist in his stomach and his cheeks went numb. Never in his life had Heck personally concerned himself over the outcome of a game of baseball, or much else for that matter. He had not been anxious pitching in the World Series as a rookie, nor while building the bombs that would kill three men. All of that seemed like shenanigans compared to this. He looked to the faces of his teammates and the ocean. Lives, and seemingly the soul of the world, hung in the balance. This one, he would follow into the fire. Into the ocean.

This one, Heck would follow into the watery burning depths of every sort of hell.

~~~~~

As Heck threw, some microscopic fiber, some tiny thread within the mesh inside his arm sprung loose and the ball exploded into the world tearing the mask from Andy's face. "Ah Jesus—" said Heck, cutting the apology short beneath Andy's glacial stare as the catcher pointed a warning, ignoring the runner sliding into second. "That's the one. Every time. Don't take anything off of it. I'll figure it out."

Heck nodded. From that point forward, he gave his body and soul to every pitch, as if throwing clots of blood, as if tearing out his teeth or eyes and throwing them. He grunted and hissed through his teeth and the cords in his neck stood out. With every repetition he felt the tearing meat within his arm, a tiny attenuation of his life force, but he set his face in a terrifying way that no one had ever seen before, riding his live left arm like a whip, a strop, slashing the air all around those Oakland hitters like a man with a sword. After a sinker bounced off Andy's shin guard, allowing the runner to coast into third, they threw nothing but fastballs. Despite the ball hissing like God's scalpel, slamming in at a speed that no one had ever imagined anything moving, Andy knocked it down, holding the runner at third, snatching it up and tagging the batter on both third strikes. With two outs and a man on third, the Oakland manager Frog Hershey called in a pinch hitter, light hitting backup shortstop Shep Haniger, bringing a twitch to Heck's upper lip and throat. Andy sludged out to the mound. "What's the problem?"

"This little son of a bitch…" Heck puffed his cheeks, shook his head. "He was with the White Sox the whole time I was in Boston…And I could not get him out. He'd be hitting two twenty, I'd be the best pitcher in the world that day, and every goddamn time, he'd drag me into a ten pitch at bat, fouling off anything close, and then poke a bleeder into left field. I'd rather pitch to Ty Cobb than this little bastard…" Heck looked to Andy for an answer. Andy shook his head. "Just make it happen. Execute."

Heck nodded. He wound and threw, the ball flung forth like shrapnel, Haniger flicking his wrists to graze the ball so that it popped back, tearing off Andy's mask. The catcher worked his jaw, stretched his neck, and took a knee. Screaming like a berserker Heck lunged and threw, the ball ripping forth like a meteor. The little shortstop flicked at it and it spun back, ripping the mask from Andy's face. He staggered out to the mound.

A cold sweat popped from Heck's forehead.

Andy's voice rose through sludge. "This is all I've got."

Heck nodded.

"I mean this pitch. I can't take another one off the jaw. I think the lights are going out. Thirty seconds from now…That's it. Too late." Heck thought about this. "I don't think I can just get it past this son of a bitch. Not even today. I can wear him down, but that's apt to take awhile."

Andy nodded. "Throw the sinker into the dirt."

Heck's eyes involuntarily flashed to the runner at third.

"I know. I won't let it past." Andy motioned with his glove to the ground, and Heck nodded, returning to the mound.

Heck breathed deeply, brought glove to his chest, wound, and uncoiling like a lizard's tongue twisted the ball as hard as he could right at home plate as if trying to knock it into the center of the earth. As the hitter swung, his bat coasting harmlessly over the ball by two feet it struck the rubber dish bouncing up to crack Andy's chin knocking the mask into three pieces, kicking off towards the third base dugout, so that the hitter flipped the bat and tucked his head and broke like a sprinter from the blocks towards first right as Andy fell straight back.

Andy arose like a voodoo corpse beckoned up out of the ground, trailing blood like a dragon's beard, leaning to seize the ball in a claw, flinging it towards first as his momentum carried him back to the ground, reinterred, rattling his head like an aquarium dropped exploding on concrete ...Deacon stretched back up the line like Death, absorbing both runner and ball simultaneously into his billowing uniform and long arms like Death embracing a wayward or prodigal son.

As the umpire's fist shot up into the air, Andy's sighed, trotting off the field on wobbly pins.

Good god, the story just kept getting better.

Leading off the bottom of the ninth, Andy crouched in the batter's box like a famous statue.

But was it the statue of the hero or the martyr?

He twisted his cleats into the dirt, crouching, tilting his head. Two images of the pitcher faced back at him, circling around one another. He heard the rhythmic breath of the ocean like the blood swelling in his head, like the beating of some giant heart. Andy had experienced a vision, or maybe just a dream, lying unconscious on his back. Revealed across the dark, quiet canvas of his mind, Andy had seen a story. Just the merest corner of it, because the story was epic, timeless. There were many places in the story, the apocryphal corn field where he'd seen the shirtless soldiers play, the dirt yard behind the Methodists, Fenway Park, clearings in forests and jungles and the very dirt upon which his battered face lay. And many, many people. And with every exceptional event, the story spread. It became the language through which a parent expressed their love for a child, it became the light of hope and transformation. It became breath. Ultimately, it was a story that said things continue. No shadow resists the sun permanently. For every sere night of loss, there would be a new morning, with dew on the grass, freshly chalked lines. Some things were, and would continue to be. Andy had been granted a chance to create a part of the story that would spread prodigiously. He would be contained within that story, passed along, kept alive forever.

The pitchers rocked back into their mirror-image windups and the light in the world went haywire, flashing and trembling, warping, undulating in waves, all sound warbling as if the world were ending. Through the chaos and destruction he focused on the ball, stepping to it, throwing his hands...

CHAPTER TWENTY-SIX

*I*t wasn't a bad pitch, diving low on the outside corner. Andy extended his vine-choked oaks of arms, head down, driving the ball up and out, so that the pitcher just threw down his glove and began walking off the field without even turning to watch as it left the park, game over, championship won one to zero in the bottom of the ninth, beyond the weedy dunes, the crowd arising to shake their fists and scream like marauders as the ball continued on towards the ocean...

But down on the beach, something had been happening.

On any other day, somebody, some carpenter on a roof or solitary child digging in the sand would have noticed the unprecedented development.

Fifteen minutes earlier, the pattern of the waves, repeated trillions upon trillions of times, suddenly stopped. The frothing tide began to recede...and never returned. It ran, out beyond the scope of the eye, out beyond sand of a dark hue never exposed to the sun, further, so that dark wet sand stretched beyond the horizon as if the ocean had simply left. With no waves, the world fell unnaturally silent save for the sound, also unnatural, of fish suddenly exposed and thrashing in the muck.

But everyone was at the game, and no one bore witness. No one raised the alarm.

The first object that the water consumed, upon its stunning monolithic return, flying in upon the land like a towering trembling wall of glass, was the ball, the championship-winning homerun, still in flight. The ball struck the smooth vitreous face of the tidal wave in a sparkle of droplets.

And on it came.

Climbing the beach, surrounding the dunes, plucking scrubby trees from the sand the water came charging up the hill to push down the outfield fence, foaming and whorling over the diamond, ripping the concrete dugouts from the ground, smashing the bleachers, flipping and throwing and spinning bodies like leaping salmon.

Melvin drew and fired his gun, one two three fo— before the water hit him, washing the guttural shout from his mouth, driving his head straight into the ground pushing his brains through the back of his skull with the final mortal thought *I shot my gun!*

Those watching from the base of the mountain stood motionless until fear, blunt survival, as persistent and mindless as a shrieking white vortex inside their eyes overpowered the mesmerizing unreality, their minds finally declaring *Even though this isn't happening this is happening* and they began to run, attacking the forested slope like some clownish army, thrashing through knee and then waist deep water, pitching forward in the climbing water, struck down by slabs of wood and the heavy bodies of their neighbors, climbing trees that were themselves torn down, impaled on shattered branches, screaming pointlessly for loved ones though the entire world was clearly coming apart, the boundaries and definitions shattered.

The Angels' dugout cut through it all like a bullet, uprooting trees, smashing through the houses of the guards behind the prison, crushing skulls and pulverizing spines until striking the large boulder overlooking the statue of the angel whereupon it too exploded, throwing bodies to the wind.

That night in the darkness, despite the preponderance of water, an alternative world of water, veins of red fire crept across the hillside, thick black smoke running over the land like a dark jellyfish pushing away the sky. Shadows splashed furtively, patting down the dead, turning out the pockets of the dead and cutting things from their persons. No body interfered with any other. No one saw or committed anything to memory. Briefly, the guards shot the prisoners and the prisoners drug down the guards to be drowned or strangled but quickly that ran its course and everyone began to go their separate ways, groping in the water and darkness and fire. People screamed.

As the wave plucked Nat from the dugout, bearing him up to the sky, spinning, he saw all around him blinding white patches of color, like the uniforms at the bottom of the hill, floating in the amniotic fluid, until with a great sigh of relief he inhaled the sea and blacked out.

He was surprised to awake sitting on top of the boulder. He leaned forward, looking for the statue that the rock had formerly overlooked but, like so many things, she was gone. He looked out over the vast reflexive gray plateau of water beneath him. An entirely new world. Where the prison had been, a dark underwater smear of wooden beams. No hint that the field had ever existed. The ocean, in an instant, either arbitrarily or with implacable intent, had reached out and claimed the town, leaving floating boards and cloth, the slowly spinning or bobbing corpses of pigs, cows, chickens, a woman in a hoop dress and a thin teenage boy. A hand bobbed in the water far beneath him, angled as if waiting to be kissed. Nat could not ascertain whether an accompanying body existed beneath the surface, or if the hand had been severed.

A dark laugh bubbled up clogging his throat. He'd spent his entire life running from the ocean, only to come up against another ocean. For a moment Nat considered stepping from the stone, a short fall, letting the ocean do with him whatever it chose. In the midst of this fantasy, a glint in the periphery drew his attention. Nat slowly turned to his left...

And there was the angel, raising her sword, ripped from her base and wedged between two trees so that her bare feet hovered ten feet off the ground. Nat smiled, expelling a sharp breath from his nose.

So...this hadn't been it, after all.

Or on second thought, maybe it had. Maybe it *really* had.

The story of everything continued. He would think of something.

Deacon was spotted pulling himself up into the dark woods, dragging a broken leg like a club.

When somebody asked "Where are you going?" he turned back over his shoulder, pale face and black hair, red eyes. "I'm going to walk for awhile."

"And then?"

"And then." He turned and bled into the darkness and the dark foliage.

Moon Fox crouched walking over clumps of high ground, dislodged logs, shattered bleachers, protruding dunes, perhaps the backs of a few dead bodies. Upside down wedged across what had formerly served as the entrance to the field, a canoe. Fox tipped out the water, righted it, ripped a slat from the fence and began to paddle.

He followed the moonbeam across the unnaturally placid sea like a boulevard.

Years later an itinerant showman-preacher performing Feats of Strength for Christ would enjoy a run of popularity throughout the logging villages and trading outposts of southwestern Canada. With his freckled arms as big as hogs and cinderblock of a head beneath a turf of red hair, Hank Hogart hoisted tractor axles, smashed boulders atop one another and cleaved ice blocks with his head, all the while shouting and pounding his chest over his love of Jesus. And it was after one such performance that the strongman, packing the accoutrements of his trade into the mule-drawn wagon, was approached by an old man brandishing a soiled tablet and stub of a pencil, who introduced himself as Al Marin, asking "Didn't you used to be…"

The post-diluvial whereabouts of the rest remains a mystery.

ADDENDUM

*T*hey called him Ace. Briefly he resisted the name, but eventually resigned himself. Nyln "Ace" Angel. He declined to give interviews, but the Cleveland press wrote about him so incessantly he might as well have carried around a recording device in his hip pocket. The Cleveland sports writers could only describe so many mortar-launched homeruns, so many bullet throws from behind the plate, and so they began to invent interviews from whole cloth. Some depicted Angel as a humble genius, others as a bumpkin, or a bragging horse's ass, so that with all these putative personas the ballplayer came off as absolutely schizophrenic.

In reality, throughout the entirety of the season Nyln was rarely seen in public, beyond a couple of trusted restaurants and the car ride between hotel and ballpark, and in the offseason he disappeared altogether, whereabouts utterly unknown.

The league had never seen a player like this. Maybe Ty Cobb in 1911, Cy Seymour in 1905. But an argument could be made that even those seasons did not measure up to either of Nyln Angel's first two campaigns. And this third season, halfway through, did not appear to be shaping up any differently.

The July East Coast sun beat down on an overflowing crowd, sold out and another few thousand who'd hopped the gates, packing in until security had just gone ahead and said screw it, fine, come in. The crowd, it was understood, had not necessarily come to see the fifth place Naps play. In the top of the first inning, one man on and two outs, "Ace" Angel dug into the batter's box, tapping his front toe lightly, calm in a way that made even the drunken jostling spectators sit still and take notice.

He was a menagerie of eccentricities, his skinny handled bat spackled with black gunk, white powder coating his huge hands and forearms, what looked for all the world like the bone of a man's finger dangling from a leather strop around his neck, soot smeared from beneath his eyes down his cheeks like war paint. He was a tome drug up from some subterranean vault of apocryphal origin, etched in blood, bound in human flesh and hair, carrying the history and gravitas of carvings on the wall of a cave, of bones dug up and reconstructed in an order that nobody was entirely sure of. And as such, he merited close examination.

The first pitch came in high and tight, knocking him down, though he shifted so quickly and calmly back to his feet, resuming an identical, toe-tapping crouch that many amongst the crowd, conversing or glancing down, had to ask a neighbor what they'd missed. After two more wasted balls the pitcher, with a fatalistic sigh and glare, threw a hittable pitch that came back up the middle so sharp and low that he himself hit the deck, watching from his knees and elbows as the ball continued burning through the grass all the way to the fence, so that Nyln stood on third, waiting hands on hips, as the centerfielder's throw came bounding in. The crowd cheered and booed raucously.

Angel walked into a big lead as the pitcher, already half beat, shaking his head, face bloodless and lips red, took a big backwards step into his windup. Ace broke for the plate, kicking up dirt in a black spray behind him, cords in his neck standing, hissing rhythmically through his clenched teeth, massive body improbably accelerating, exploding, so that the ball had scarcely left the pitcher's fingertips before he barreled into batter, catcher, umpire, clearing the deck, slapping the plate with his hand as the crowd damn near lost their minds.

And so on. In the third inning he smashed through a thigh-high section of the wooden backstop, spearing a foul ball in a tricky wind with his bare hand, coming up spitting blood, wiping his mouth with his forearm. In the sixth he dropped down a bunt with the knob of his bat, and he recorded the final out of the game holding onto a weak late throw from left field as Hippo Hellhake, two hundred and seventy pounds of him, knocked Nyln fifteen feet off the dish. Cleveland won. A relatively rare occurrence, even with the havoc their young catcher had been inflicting upon the rest of the league on a daily basis.

If Nyln, leaving the stadium that evening from a discrete service door, was surprised to see the man framed against the orange sunset waiting for him on the sidewalk, it didn't show. The older man smiled, they shook hands. "I think your game bears an eerie resemblance to that of a killer I used to house in my prison."

They talked for awhile, parting ways as the sun set blood and gold in the west, each implacably approaching an ocean.

www.ingramcontent.com/pod-product-compliance
Lightning Source LLC
Chambersburg PA
CBHW031100260626
47172CB00001B/151